THE BELOVED RETURNS
LOTTE IN WEIMAR

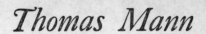

Thomas Mann

THE BELOVED
RETURNS

LOTTE IN WEIMAR

Translated from the German by

H. T. LOWE-PORTER

VINTAGE BOOKS
A DIVISION OF RANDOM HOUSE
NEW YORK

First Vintage Books Edition, October 1983
Copyright 1940 by Alfred A. Knopf, Inc.
Copyright renewed 1968 by Alfred A. Knopf, Inc.
All rights reserved under International and Pan-American
Copyright Conventions. Published in the United States
by Random House, Inc., New York, and simultaneously
in Canada by Random House of Canada Limited, Toronto.
Published in the United States by Alfred A. Knopf, Inc.
in 1940. Originally published as *Lotte in Weimer*,
copyright 1939 by Bermann-Fischer Verlag A.B.,
Stockholm.

Library of Congress Cataloging in Publication Data
Mann, Thomas, 1857-1955.
The beloved returns.
Translation of: Lotte in Weimar.
Reprint. Originally published: New York:
A.A. Knopf, 1940.
1. Kestner, Charlotte Buff, 1753-1828—Fiction.
2. Goethe, Johann Wolfgang von, 1749-1832,
in fiction, drama, poetry, etc.
I. Title.
PT2625.A44L62 1983   833′.912   83-5819
ISBN 0-394-71745-7 (pbk.)

Manufactured in the United States of America

PREFACE

THERE cannot be in all literary history another figure so
well documented as that of Johann Wolfgang von
Goethe. He was a genius of the most universal and
copious order, with immense intellectual and emotional
energy, exceedingly interested in the phenomenon
which was himself; the documentation proceeds in the
first instance and overwhelmingly from his own pen.
Now, as Thomas Mann has somewhere said, a great
genius must be at once representative and unrepresenta-
tive of his time; and in both these respects our world
today has, so to speak, lost track of Goethe. The charms
of the present volume may well incite us to make good
our lacks. As we now are, most of us want the documentation needed for the present novel; which is, in effect,
not only an accounting of all Goethe meant in his time
and place, but also (the recurring theme of the author)
an allegory of all that genius is and means in all times and
places. So, then, to a summary account of the facts that
form the warp of our allegory.

In the spring of 1772, being then twenty-three years
old, young Goethe went to Wetzlar, a town in central
Germany, to get practice in jurisprudence at the Imperial Court of Justice there. He had left his native city

of Frankfurt at sixteen, and passed through two periods
as law student, in Leipsic and Strassburg, with an interval of illness at home. In the Leipsic period falls the early
episode with Käthchen Schönkopf, in the Strassburg time
the love-affair with Friederike Brion, "Friederike of
Sesenheim," ending in the flight of the lover and the
slow fading of the beloved. This was presumably the
earliest instance establishing the Goethean pattern of loving, leaving, and remorse. Goethe arrived in Wetzlar
with his portfolio full of verses, plays, sketches and
drafts; his head of ideas, ambitions, and fantasy; his heart
of genuine warmth, rebellion, and youthful melancholy.
He had just finished his first play, *Götz von Berlichingen*.

At the Imperial Court Goethe met a fellow student
named Kestner, and through him the latter's betrothed,
Charlotte Buff, housekeeper to her father and a flock
of brothers and sisters in the House of the Teutonic
Order. The scene of the meeting, as portrayed in
Werther, was pertly parodied by Thackeray:

> Werther had a love for Charlotte,
> Such as words could never utter;
> Would you know how first he met her?
> She was cutting bread and butter.

In real life, the meeting took place at a country ball, and
Lotte, a young "spindle-shanks" of seventeen, wore a
white frock trimmed with pink ribbon bows. One of
these, or the absence of it, plays a coquettish rôle in the
present novel. Goethe, Kestner, and Lotte spent an idyllic summer, Goethe falling in love first with the mutual
love of his friends, then with Lotte herself, lastly and

most of all with his own emotions as poet and lover. In the autumn, after mild admonishment from the pair, he again and suddenly absented himself from felicity. Kestner and Lotte married. But the affair was big with consequence. A little after this there was tragedy in Wetzlar: a fellow student, Jerusalem, shot himself for unrequited love and weltschmerz. The effect of the crass event on Goethe combined with his own recent emotions to produce a novel, *The Sorrows of Young Werther*, the stuff of which was none too implicitly the Wetzlar romance. It embalmed the malady of a continent. Goethe became famous.

Forty-four years passed. Goethe lived in Weimar, adorning the little provincial court of the post-Waterloo period. Thackeray, again, has parodied it for us, in *Vanity Fair*. But Goethe's cosmopolitan figure is vastly out of drawing in such a picture. He was too big. He was poet, playwright, novelist, statesman, scientist, lover, administrator of affairs, grand gentilhomme — nothing human was foreign to him — save the field of politics. He had contempt for the people — " when the masses fight, they are respectable; but their opinions are not delectable " — and boasted that he had never had the misfortune to be in the opposition. — His stature ranked with Napoleon's and Beethoven's; his house was the shrine of pilgrims from all over the globe. He was, and is, Germany's great man; though scarcely, in the Germany of today, so viable a manifestation as Frederick the Great. Yet Goethe, the good European, in his time sympathized with Napoleon's spacious designs, and many pages of the novel are pregnant for us today. His productivity was vast. The collected edition of his works, published by Cotta, runs to forty volumes: plays, novels, poetry, treatises, critiques — almost every kind there is of literary expression. He wrote some of the most beautiful lyrics in all literature. He wrote *Wilhelm Meister, Hermann and Dorothea, Elective Affinities*, the *West-Eastern Divan*. And he wrote, almost throughout his lifetime, *Faust*. Yet even so, he felt that what he *was* had not got itself fully expressed in what he wrote. His life, he thought, and its setting in time and place, fretted the freedom of his art. He had come to Weimar when he was twenty-six, at the invitation of the reigning prince, Karl August, Duke of Saxe-Weimar. The two, partners at first in high-spirited excesses, formed a life-long friendship which put Goethe in command of the administration of the Duchy. And he, conservative and lover of the *status quo*, governed it with a brilliantly practical common sense which displays not the least remarkable side of this many-sided genius. Another side still is shown in his scientific activities: Dr. Mann gives us a lively picture of his mania for scientific theorizing, his collections, and the famous controversy over the theory of colour: Goethe, in brief, felt himself so much the child of Nature that she would reveal to him, sooner than to the pedants, her hidden secrets.

Any account of Goethe's life would omit almost no great name of his time: Schiller, Lessing, Jean Paul, Herder, Wieland, Byron, Heine, Schopenhauer; Winckelmann, the archæologist, who imbued the poet, and all Germany besides, with a passion for Italy and classical culture — the list is too long, its implications too many.

But Weimar, the Athens of Germany, had drawn some of these great men to herself: Herder, poet and preacher, lived there until his death in 1805; Jean Paul; " Uncle " Wieland the poet; Meyer the art historian; above all the beloved Friedrich Schiller, author of *Wilhelm Tell, Don Carlos, Wallenstein, Maria Stuart, The Robbers,* almost peer with Goethe in German hearts. His statue, clasping hands with Goethe's, stands in front of the Theatre in Weimar, and the group symbolizes the long, close literary association of which the present novel gives so moving an account. Schiller, too, to his friend's great loss, had died in 1805, leaving Goethe bereft of his advice. The circle is full of lesser figures, almost every one historic, some of them permitted to air their anguish at the too close proximity of genius: Dr. Riemer, the peevish scholar-assistant, John the unappetising copyist; Ottilie, bride of Goethe's son August, and Adele Schopenhauer her chronicler, sister to Arthur the philosopher, at this time a young man interested in Goethe's colour theory. Adele and Ottilie are captivatingly depicted, though we see the latter only at second hand; Ottilie and August actually did marry, and their union was as disastrous as Adele's most anxious fears presaged. Frau von Stein appears not at all, however large a part she played in the poet's life. Christiane, " the Vulpius," supposed to be the heroine of the *Roman Elegies*, mother of August and finally Goethe's wife, had died in 1815. Among the host of the poet's loves, we have glimpses, afar off, of a few: Friederike Brion, Maxe Brentano, Lilli Schönemann, Minna Herzlieb, Marianne Willemer (the Zuleika of the *Divan*), Bettina Brentano von Arnim, daughter of

Maxe, and so on — Dr. Riemer in the novel compares
them to the loves of Jove, and Charlotte feelingly remarks: "It is a sort of dance that I have joined." In the
poet's mind, by 1816, they were all recurrent phases of
the beloved, nourishers of his creative force; in the figure
of Helena, in the second part of *Faust*, he worshipped
their ideal, unfadable form. Thus it is for its figurative
quite as much as its literal sense that the title of the English version has been chosen.

And Lotte? Her life had been as private as Goethe's
was public. She had borne eleven children to her good
man; some had died, the rest had prospered. She had
lived in honourable widowhood now many years. When
she was sixty she too made her little pilgrimage to the
shrine. It is historic: the letter is extant — the novel
quotes it — that she wrote, after meeting the great man,
to one of her sons. Her expectations, even to herself,
were not quite clear. She had felt warmly and generously, in the long-ago — so far as honour and decorum
allowed — and she still thought that she and her good
man had been used. That rankled. She may have known
Byron's famous line, but she would have considered
"butchered" a grossly tasteless figure. She was aware
that genius is worth its price; but she wanted to understand, to heal the years-old fester. And so the beloved
returned — this novel, with its crowded allusiveness, tells
the tale of her three weeks' sojourn in Weimar in the
autumn of 1816, and its singular — even uncanny — satisfactions. But above all, it tells, with devastating psychological acuity, how genius thinks and feels, and those
who live and breathe in its air.

                                        H. T. L.–P.

THE BELOVED RETURNS

LOTTE IN WEIMAR

Durch allen Schall und Klang

Der Transoxanen

Erkühnt sich unser Sang

Auf deine Bahnen!

Uns ist für gar nichts bang,

In dir lebendig;

Dein Leben daure lang,

Dein Reich beständig!

WEST-ÖSTLICHER DIVAN

CHAPTER ONE

In September of the year 1816, and late in the month, though the weather was still almost summery, a singular experience befell the head waiter at the inn Zum Elefanten in Weimar. His name was Mager — a man not without some pretensions to culture. Thrilling, even bewildering the experience had been; though there was nothing supernatural about it, Mager could scarce persuade himself that he was not in a dream.

On that morning, shortly after eight o'clock, by the regular diligence from Gotha, three women were set down at the famous hostelry on the market square. At first glance — or even at the second — there was nothing remarkable about them. They were mother, daughter, and maid; so much was easy to see. Mager, bowing in the entry, looked on as the steps were let down and the ostler helped the first two to alight upon the pavement. Klärchen, meanwhile, the abigail, took leave of the jehu; she had sat beside him on the drive, and quite evidently enjoyed herself. Now, holding up her skirts, with coquettish, unnecessary twists and turns she got herself down from the lofty seat, the man watching her with a side-

wise, retrospective grin, probably at thought of the outlandish dialect the travellers had spoken. Then he pulled
at the cord of the horn slung on his back and began to
blow with great unction, to the joy of some watching
urchins and a few early passers-by.

The ladies still paused, with their backs to the house,
while their modest luggage was fetched down from the
top of the coach; and Mager stood awaiting the moment
when, their concern for their property being satisfied,
they would turn their faces in his direction. Then, quite
the diplomat, he advanced upon the pavement to meet
them, with a smile at once cordial and deprecating on his
rather sallow face, framed in side-whiskers of a reddish
auburn. He wore a buttoned-up tail-coat, an expansive
collar, and a much washed neck-cloth; his trousers ta-
pered down to a pair of enormous feet.

" Good day, my friend," said the more maternal of the
two ladies then. A matron she was, at least; no longer
young, certainly at the end of her fifties, and plump.
She wore a white frock, a black shawl, and worsted
mitts. Beneath a tall capote her hair peeped out; it had
once been blond but was now an ashen grey. " We re-
quire accommodation for three: a double room for myself and my child " — said " child " being nearer thirty
than twenty, with brown corkscrew curls and a little
frill round her neck; the mother's small, finely arched
nose had in the daughter's face turned out rather sharp
and severe — " and an attic, not too far away, for my
woman. Could you give us that? "

The lady's fine if tired blue eyes were directed past the
waiter's head upon the façade of the inn. Her mouth

was small and the movement of the lips as she spoke uncommonly pleasant, embedded though these were in the
plumpness of her aged cheeks. She must in her youth
have been prettier than her daughter was now. The most
striking thing about her was a trembling and nodding of
the head; it looked, however, only in part like weakness,
suggesting as it did a lively and decided temperament and
a challenge to the agreement of the person addressed.

" Quite easily," responded the waiter, as he attended
mother and daughter inside the entry, followed by the
abigail dangling a bandbox. " Our hotel is, as usual, well
occupied, and we might at any moment have to decline
the advances of even persons of station; but we will spare
no pains to satisfy the ladies' needs."

"That is most gratifying," replied the stranger, exchanging a glance of amusement with her daughter, for
the waiter's words, though well turned, had a strongly
local, Saxon-Thuringian flavour.

" May I beg you to be kind enough to step this way? "
said Mager, ushering them into the lobby. " The reception-room is on the right. Frau Elmenreich, the proprietress, will be pleased to see you — pray come in."

Frau Elmenreich had an arrow stuck in her hair, and
her high-corseted bust was enveloped in a knitted jacket
against the draught from the outer door. She sat among
her pens and sand-shaker, enthroned at a calculating-
machine behind a sort of counter shutting off from the
rest of the lobby the recess which formed her bureau.
There was likewise an assistant, who had left his standing
desk and stood on one side talking in English with a man
in a coachman's cape, the owner, presumably, of the boxes

piled by the door. The proprietress viewed the new clients with phlegmatic eye, acknowledging the elder's greeting and the younger's slight curtsy by a dignified bow, though her gaze went past instead of resting upon them. She lent an ear to the request for rooms, communicated by the head waiter; and taking up the house-plan, a fanlike arrangement on a stick, she moved her pencil-point to and fro upon it.

"Twenty-seven," said she at length, turning towards the green-aproned boots who stood waiting with the ladies' effects. "But I cannot oblige with a single room. The mamsell will have to share with the maid of the Countess of Larisch from Erfurt. We have at the moment many guests attended by their own domestics."

The abigail pulled a face behind her mistress's back; but the latter raised no obstacle. The two would soon get on quite well together, she declared, and, turning away, requested to have the room shown her and the luggage sent up at once.

"At once, madame," said the waiter. "There is but one formality, a small one. In heaven's name pray write us a few lines. Not on our account, we are not so pedantic; it is the ' holy Hermandad.' It can never forget anything. It seems as though laws and rules kept on propagating themselves like a disease. Would the lady be so gracious? "

The lady laughed, casting another side-glance at her daughter, while her shaking head seemed to express her amused surprise.

"Yes, of course," said she. "I forgot. I will do whatever is proper. And I am pleased to note, my man, that

you are well read and know your literary allusions."
She used the third-person form of address; probably it
had been the custom when she was young. "Here, give
it to me!" And turning back to the desk, she took in the
slender fingers of her bemitted hand the crayon the proprietress handed her; it hung there on a string beside the
register, whereon were already a few names.

As she bent and slowly wrote, her laughter died away,
subsiding into faint little gasps like an expiring echo of
her mirth. The nodding and shaking of her head showed
plainer than before, probably because of her awkward
posture.

They watched her as she wrote. The daughter looked
over one shoulder; the pretty, evenly arching brows
which she had from her mother were lifted high, and a
wry, almost mocking expression sat on the firmly closed
lips. Over the other shoulder peeped head waiter
Mager, partly to see if the lady was correctly filling in
the rubrics, partly from small-town curiosity and the
malicious satisfaction one gets when somebody has to
abandon the grateful rôle of incognito and admit his
name and status. For some reason or other the clerk and
the British traveller had also left off speaking to observe
the lady where she stood bobbing her head and forming
her letters with well-nigh childish pains.

Mager blinked as he read: "Frau Councillor Charlotte
Kestner, widow, née Buff. From Hannover. Last address
Goslar. Born Wetzlar January 11, 1753. Accompanied
by daughter and maid."

"Will that do?" queried Frau Councillor. As nobody answered, she was fain to do so herself, and said:

"It must." She laid aside the crayon, forgetful that it was fastened, with such energy that she pulled down the metal stand whereon it hung.

"Stupid!" she admonished herself, flushing, with another swift glance in her daughter's direction, who, however, kept her eyes cast down and her mouth disdainfully shut. "No matter, it is soon mended — and now do let us get up to our room!" She turned abruptly.

Daughter, maid, and waiter followed her across the yard to the stairs, behind them the bald-headed boots with bandboxes and bags. Mager had not ceased to blink. He blinked as he went; first winking two or three times in quick succession and then staring straight ahead with his inflamed eyes. His mouth gaped open — but it was not a stupid, rather a delicate, well-regulated gape. On the first landing he brought the party to a stand.

"I beg pardon," said he. "I most humbly beg pardon, if my question — it is not actuated by unseemly curiosity — but — have we the honour to be entertaining Frau Councillor Kestner, Madame Charlotte Kestner, formerly Buff, of Wetzlar — ?"

"The same," the lady confirmed, with a smile.

"But I mean — of course it cannot — I mean — it cannot be the same Charlotte — or Lotte for short — Kestner, whose maiden name was Buff, from the house of the Teutonic Order at Wetzlar, the former — "

"The very same, my good man. But I am not 'former' at all, I am present in the flesh, and would wish to be shown at once to the room — "

"This very instant!" cried Mager, and took a running start, with his head down. But then he stuck again, as though rooted to the spot, and wreathed his hands together.

"Good gracious me!" said he, with great feeling. "Goodness — gracious — me, Frau Councillor! Frau Councillor will pardon me if my ideas — if I cannot all at once adjust my thoughts — the revelation of your identity, and the prospect — it has come upon me, as they say, out of a blue sky. Then our house has the inestimable honour and distinction of entertaining beneath its roof the actual original — if I may so express myself — in short, it is vouchsafed me to behold Werther's Lotte in the —"

"That is indeed the case, my friend," replied the Frau Councillor with quiet dignity, reproving the tittering maid with a glance. "And I should be glad if that were a reason the more for showing us tired travellers to our room without further delay."

"This instant!" the flunkey cried again, setting himself in motion afresh. "But the room — number twenty-seven is up two pair of stairs. Ours are easy stairs, as the Frau Councillor sees. But if we had dreamed —! We could probably, despite our crowded — however, the room is a good one, on the square, Madame cannot fail to be pleased. Only a little time since it was occupied by Herr and Frau Major von Egloffstein, from Halle, when they were visiting their aunt, the First Lady of the Bed-chamber, of the same name. And last October the adjutant general of His Imperial Highness the Grand Duke Constantine — a historic date, one might say. But, my God, why do I talk of history when, for a man of senti-ment, it cannot compare with . . . Just a few steps far-ther, Frau Councillor! Down this corridor, no distance at all from the stairs. We have had to renovate very thoroughly, since the visit of the Don Cossacks, at the end of 1813: stairs, chambers, passages, salons, and all. Maybe the renovation was long overdue; anyhow, it was forced upon us by the violent, world-shaking course of events. They taught us, perhaps, that it is precisely violence that is needed to produce all memorable and historic moments. Yet I should not give the Cossacks all the credit for our improvements. We had Prussian and Hungarian hussars in the house as well — to say nothing of the French who came before them! Ah, here we are — may I invite the Frau Councillor to walk in? "

He bowed and opened the door wide with a flourish as he ushered her within. The ladies with swift appraising glance took in the starched mull curtains at the two windows, the gilt-framed console mirror, rather dull and tarnished, between them; the two white-covered beds, sharing a little canopy, and the remaining conveniences of the bedchamber. The wall was adorned with a copper-plate engraving, a landscape with an antique temple. The well-waxed floor shone with cleanliness.

" Very nice," the Frau Councillor said.

" We shall be overjoyed if the ladies think they can do with it. Whatever they need — here is the bell-pull, close at hand. I will see after hot water myself, of course. We shall rejoice if we can serve the Frau Councillor to her satisfaction — "

" But surely, my good man. We are unspoilt people, with simple tastes. I thank you," said she to the boots, as he deposited his burdens on the floor and the luggage trestle and took his leave. " And thanks to you, too,"

with a nod of dismissal to the waiter. "We are well provided, all we need now is a little rest — "

But Mager stood fixed, his fingers interlaced, his red-
eyed gaze devouring the old lady's features.

"Ah, my God, Frau Councillor, what an event! An
event to be set down in memory's tables! Perhaps the
Frau Councillor cannot quite enter into the emotions of
a man of feeling at a happening so unhoped for, so unexpected, so pregnant with thrilling possibilities! Frau
Councillor is used to her situation, and her identity with
a being so sacred to us all — it is an everyday matter to
her, she takes it lightly. She cannot guess at the emotions
that must animate the soul of a man, literary from youth
up, to whom now, all undreamt of — to whom is
vouchsafed acquaintance with — if I may say so, I humbly beg pardon — is vouchsafed the sight of a being so
surrounded with the effulgence of poesy and, as it were,
borne up on fiery arms to the heaven of immortal
fame — "

"My dear, good friend!" said the lady with a deprecating smile. One might at the same time have interpreted as agreement the nodding of her head; at the
waiter's words it came on more than ever. Behind her the
abigail peered, greatly tickled, into the man's face —
actually, it was moved almost to tears. In the background
the daughter with ostentatious indifference busied herself about the luggage.

"My friend, I am just a simple old lady, with no pretensions, a human being like everybody else. You
have so unusual and high-flown a way of expressing
yourself — "

"My name is Mager," said the waiter, as though in explanation. He pronounced it Macher, with a soft, middle-German enunciation which made it sound propitiatory, even touching. "I hope I shall not seem to boast if I say that I am the factotum here, the proprietress's right hand, she having been widowed these ten years. Herr Elmenreich died *anno* six; falling victim to the violence of historical events under tragical circumstances which are at the moment neither here nor there. In my position, Frau Councillor, and even more in such times as our city has lived through, a man comes in touch with all sorts of people. Many a personage striking for birth or achievement passes before his eyes. So much so that he can grow callous to the claims of even the most resounding names and the most prominent actors on the stage of world history. So it goes. But whither now, Frau Councillor, has fled the indifference by rights belonging to my calling? Never in all my life, I confess it, has it been my privilege to perform a service so near to my heart as today's, so worthy to be set down and enshrined in the tables of my memory. I knew, indeed, without knowing, as a man will, that the admired female, the original of that immortally lovely creature, still dwelt amongst us — in the city of Hannover, to be precise. Ah, yes, I knew, but only now am I aware that I knew. For my knowledge had no reality heretofore; never would it have entered my head that I might one day stand in her sacred presence, face to face. Never could I have dreamt of such a thing. When this morning — but a few short hours since — I awoke, it was in the conviction that today was like a hundred others, to be filled with the

wonted activities of my calling: waiting at table, keeping
my eye over the house. My wife — for I am married, Frau
Councillor, my life-partner occupies a superior post in
the kitchens of the establishment — my wife would tell
you that I had no presentiment of anything out of the
ordinary. I thought nothing else than to lie down tonight
the same man as when I arose. And now! The unexpected always happens — how true the popular saying is!
I trust Frau Councillor will pardon my confusion and the
perhaps quite unwarranted way my tongue runs on. ' Of
what the heart is full, the mouth runs over,' as the saying
goes, and how true that is, however uncouth the form!
If Frau Councillor but knew the love and veneration
which from my birth up, so to speak, I have felt for our
prince of poets, the great Goethe; my pride as a citizen
of Weimar that we may call this eminent man our own;
if she realized what fervent echoes this very work, *The
Sorrows of Werther*, awoke in my heart. . . . But I say
no more. It is not for me to speak — though well I know
that a masterpiece of feeling like the work in question
belongs to high and low and to humanity as a whole,
animating it with the most fervid emotions; whereas
probably only the upper classes can aspire to such productions as *Iphigenie* or *The Natural Daughter*. When
I recall how oft Madame Mager and I have sat beside our
evening taper and our souls have melted as we bent together over those celestial pages . . . and now their famous and immortal heroine stands before me at this very
moment in the flesh, a human being like myself — good
gracious heavens! " he cried, and struck his brow with his
fist: " I run on and on, Frau Councillor, and all of a

sudden it comes over me in a burning flash that I have not even asked Frau Councillor if she has had coffee! "

" Thank you, my friend," responded the old lady, who had been listening to the good man's outpourings with a reserved air if a slightly twitching mouth. " We took it betimes. But my dear Herr Mager, you go too far, you greatly exaggerate, when you simply identify me, or even the young thing I once was, with the heroine of that much lauded book. You are not the first whom I have had to warn; I have been holding forth about it, indeed, for four-and-forty years! That character in the novel did become so real, so living, and so widely celebrated that actually a person could come to me and say that between us two she was the real and more substantial one — the which I was, of course, most seriously concerned to disclaim. But the character in the novel is quite different and distinct from my former self, to say nothing at all of my present one. For instance, anyone can see that my eyes are blue, whereas Werther's Lotte is well known to have black ones."

" Poetic licence! " Mager cried. " As though we did not know what that is! But no amount of it, Frau Councillor, could suffice to diminish by one jot the verity of the identification. What if the author did avail himself to some small extent of — what if he did play hide-and-seek a little to mystify us — "

" No," protested the Frau Councillor, with a shake of her head, " the black eyes are from another source."

" And even so! " retorted Mager, with some heat. " What if the likeness be a little blurred by such small variations — "

"There are much greater ones," interpolated the lady, weightily.

" — yet there remains unshakable, there remains wholly untouched, that other identification so interwoven with and inseparable from it: the identification, so to say, with itself — with that other personage of legend, of whom the great man has lately drawn for us so glowing a picture in his recollections. If Frau Councillor is not, down to the very last hair, the Lotte of Werther, she is, even so, in every particular the Lotte of Goe — "

"My worthy fellow," interrupted the lady, stemming the waiter's eloquence in full tide, "it was some little time before you had the kindness to show us our room. It obviously escapes you that till now you prevent us from occupying it."

"Frau Councillor!" implored the waiter of the Elephant, folding his hands as in prayer. "Forgive me! Extend your pardon to a man who — my conduct, I know, is unpardonable; yet none the less I beg for indulgence. By taking my leave at once I will . . . and indeed," he said, "quite aside from considerations of propriety and manners, I am urgently summoned, I am called away and should have been off long since. There is so much to do — and when I think that up to this very instant Frau Elmenreich has not the faintest idea, that in all likelihood she has not cast a glance at the register, and even so her simple mind . . . and Madame Mager, Frau Councillor! How I itch to be with her in the kitchen, to tell her of the great local and literary sensation of the hour! And yet I venture to implore leave and pardon for one single question more, to fill the cup of novelty to the brim: in these four-and-forty years — ah, four-and-forty years! — has the Frau Councillor never, even once, beheld the Herr Privy Councillor again? "

"So is it, my friend," answered she. "I know Dr. Goethe, the young lawyer of the Gewandsgasse in Wetzlar. The Minister of State for the Duchy of Weimar, the famous poet, I have never beheld with my mortal eyes."

"It is too much! " breathed Mager. "It is too much for a human being to support! And so the Frau Councillor has come to Weimar to — to — "

"I am come," the old lady interrupted him with slight hauteur, "to Weimar to visit my sister, the wife of Councillor Ridel, of the Board of Domains, whom I have not seen for many years; and to bring her my daughter Charlotte, who has come to me from Alsace, where she lives, and accompanies me on this journey. Counting my woman, there are three of us; we should overburden my sister if we lodged with her, she having a family herself. Will that content you? "

"To my heart's depths, Frau Councillor! And even though we thus lose the pleasure of the ladies' company at our table-d'hôte. Herr and Frau Councillor Ridel, Esplanade 6 — as well I know. So Frau Councillor Ridel was before her marriage a — of course, of course! I knew the circumstance, it but escaped me for the moment only. So then — ah, merciful God! — the Frau Councillor Ridel made one of that troop of children who thronged round Frau Councillor in the entry of the hunting-lodge when Werther for the first time entered it, stretching out their little hands for the bread and butter Frau Councillor — "

"My dear, good man," Charlotte broke in once more, "there was no Frau Councillor at that hunting-lodge. And our Klärchen is waiting to be shown to her room. But before you go, pray tell me, is it far from here to the Esplanade?"

"No distance at all, Frau Councillor. The merest step. In Weimar there are no distances. Our greatness is of the spirit alone. Most joyfully would I myself be at your service to show the ladies the way, unless they prefer a hired coach or post-chaise — the capital abounds in them. But one more, only one more little question, Frau Councillor, I implore: Frau Councillor is here, of course, to visit her sister. But surely she will take occasion to go to the Frauenplan — "

"We shall see, we shall see! But now, only make haste and bestow my maid in her quarters for I shall soon have need of her."

"Yes, and on the way," the young thing twittered, "you can tell me where the author lives that wrote *Rinaldo*. Oh, what a ravishing book! I have read it five times without stopping. Do you think we might chance to see him in the street?"

"Yes, yes," replied Mager distractedly, turning towards the door. But on the threshold he braked again, one leg in the air.

"Only one single word, Frau Councillor," he begged; "one single question, quickly answered; Frau Councillor must perceive, when one stands, all unexpected, before

the original, when it is vouchsafed one to inquire at the
very source, one cannot refrain: Frau Councillor, that
very last scene before Werther takes his leave; that heart-
rending scene between the three of you, where you
speak of the dear, departed mother and the final parting
and Werther grasps Lotte's hand and cries: 'We shall
meet again, in all the world we shall know each other's
forms again!' — that was real, was it not, it actually happened, the Herr Privy Councillor did not make it up?"

"Yes and no, my friend, yes and no," she good-
naturedly answered his importunities, her head shaking
more than ever. "But go now, go!"

And the waiter hastened off, his head in a whirl, with
the mamsell beside him.

Charlotte heaved a sigh and took off her hat. During
all the foregoing her daughter had been busy hanging
up her own and her mother's clothes in the wardrobe and
laying out the contents of their nécessaires on toilet-table
and wash-stand. She now looked up, with mocking eye.

"So now your crown of glory stands revealed," said
she. "The effect was not so bad."

"Ah, child," the mother replied, "what you call my
crown is in truth more like a cross! But cross or crown,
it remains a decoration visible whether I will or no. I
cannot obscure, I cannot hide it."

"Yet hidden it might have been a little longer, dear
Mama, if not for the whole duration of this rather fantastic journey, if we had chosen to stop with Aunt Amalie
instead of at a public inn."

"Lottchen, you know yourself it was not possible.
Your aunt, your uncle, and cousins have no room to

spare, despite the excellent quarter they live in — or perhaps on that very account. The three of us could not burst in upon them and discommode them, even for a few days. Your uncle Ridel has his living as an official, but he is not a rich man, he has had his troubles, and in 1806 he lost every penny. To live at his charges would not be right. Yet who could take it ill of me that I wished, after all these years, to embrace once more my youngest sister, our Malie, and rejoice in the fortune which is hers at the side of her honest and energetic helpmeet? Recollect that I may be useful to her: your uncle has pretensions to the post of director of the finances of the Duchy, and I may perhaps help her by being on the spot, with my old friends and connections. And the moment seems to me well chosen — when you, my child, are beside me, after ten years' separation. Shall I then hesitate to follow the dictates of my heart, simply because of that strange episode which once fell to my lot? "

" Certainly not, of course not, Mama."

" And how could we expect," the Frau Councillor went on, " that we should run into such a fanatic as this Ganymede in side-whiskers? Goethe in his memoirs complains that people pester him to find out who was the real Lotte, where she lived, and the like. He says that no incognito could protect him from their importunity — speaks of it, I believe, as a perfect penance, and declares that if he sinned in the writing of his little book, he has paid for it over and over again. But see how men — and poets too — think only of themselves! He never once reflects that we, too, have to endure the inquisition, on top of all the harm he did to us, your dear, departed father and me, with his wicked mixture of truth and make-believe."

"And blue and black eyes."

"The injured party may be sure he will be laughed at too — and certainly by Lottchen. But I had to prevent the crazy creature from calmly identifying me with Werther's Lotte."

"It was impertinent enough that he consoled you for the uncertainty by saying that you were Goethe's Lotte."

"But I stood out against that too, I did not mince matters. I know you too well, my child, not to be aware that your sterner nature would have kept the man in check from the beginning. But tell me how. By denying my identity? By showing him that I wished nothing to be known of myself or my connections? Have I the right to do as I like with these, which, after all, are public property? Our natures are so different — which, I hasten to add, does not in the slightest detract from my love for you. But you are not what one would call affable; and by the word I mean something very different from the spirit of willing self-sacrifice. Indeed, it has often seemed to me that a life of sacrifice and service develops a sort of routine, a — I might, in no spirit of censure, but rather the contrary, call it a hardness, which is little conducive to affability. My child, you can doubt of my respect as little as of my love. For ten years you have played in Alsace the part of good angel to your poor, dear brother Karl, when he suffered the double misfortune of losing his young wife and his leg as well. Misfortunes seldom come singly. My poor, afflicted lad — where would he be without you? You are his nurse, his aide, his house-

keeper, a mother to his orphaned children. Your whole
life has been a selfless labour of love; how then could
you have failed to evince those serious traits which are
opposed to idle sensibility whether in yourself or in
others? You set greater store by sterling worth than by
what is merely interesting, and how right you are! Relations with the great world, the world of beauty, intellect, and passion, such as have fallen to our share — "

"Our? I have no such relations."

"My child, whether we like it or not, they will remain ours and attach themselves to our name, unto the
third and fourth generation. And when on their account
people of sentiment importune us — out of enthusiasm or
even out of mere curiosity, for it is hard to distinguish
between the two — have we the right to be chary of ourselves and contemptuously repulse the interest we evoke?
Herein lies the difference between us. Life was serious
for me too, it did not lack in resignation. I was, I trust,
a good wife to your dear father of loving memory; I
bore him eleven children, and brought up nine of them
to man's estate, two being taken from me. But I have still
been affable — or good-natured, if you like to call it so.
The harshness of life has not made me harsh, and simply
to turn my back on Mager and tell him: ' Leave me alone,
you fool! ' — no, I could not bring myself to that."

"Dear Mama," replied Lotte the younger, " you speak
as though I had reproached you, or unfilially presumed
to set myself above you. I had not even opened my
mouth. It does vex me when people try your patience
and kindness to such lengths as happened just now, ex-
hausting you with their importunity — and would you be

vexed with my vexation? — This frock," she said, holding up one taken from her mother's box, white, garnished with pink ribbon bows, "should it not be pressed out a little before you put it on? It is badly crumpled."

The Frau Councillor blushed. It was an appealing, a becoming blush, it strangely brought back the charming girl of long ago, one could see what she had been like at twenty. For a few seconds that rosy glow evoked the tender gaze of the blue eyes beneath the evenly vaulted brows, the finely arched little nose, the small, charming mouth; one could see the warden's stout-hearted little daughter and mother to his brood of children. Even the fairy heroine of the Volpertshausen ball came surprisingly to view in the radiance of that elderly blush.

Madame Kestner had laid aside her black shawl. She stood there in a white frock much like the one her daughter was holding up, though simpler in style. She affected white frocks for summer wear, and the weather, as we have said, was still warm. But the one in her daughter's hand was trimmed with pink ribbons.

Both mother and daughter had averted their gaze, as it seemed involuntarily; the one from the frock, the other from her mother's blush, which affected her painfully with its sweet suggestion of reawakened youth.

"No," responded the mother to Charlotte's suggestion. "We need not trouble. That sort of crêpe shakes out quickly with hanging — besides, who knows whether I shall put the thing on my back?"

"Why should you not?" the daughter said. "Why ever else should you have brought it with you? Surely you will put it on, for this or that occasion. And that brings me back, dear Mama, to the question I ventured to ask before: might you not replace the breast- and sleeve-knots, which are rather too light, with a darker colour, perhaps a rich violet? "

"Oh, be quiet, Lottchen," said her mother, almost pettishly. "You have no mind for a joke. Why would you deprive me of my pretty and suggestive little allusion? Really, I know very few people with so small a sense of humour as you! "

"One should not," responded the daughter, "take a sense of humour for granted, with people one does not know, or no longer knows."

The elder Charlotte would have retorted; but the colloquy was interrupted by the return of Klärchen, bearing hot water. The puss reported blithely that the Countess Larisch's maid was not half bad, they would get on well together. And that droll Herr Mager had solemnly promised she should see the librarian Vulpius, author of that glorious work *Rinaldo*, and brother-in-law to Herr Goethe to boot. Mager would point him out as he passed to his office, and his little son too, named Rinaldo after the hero of the famous work, going by on his way to school.

"Very nice," said the Frau Councillor. "But now it is high time for you both to be off. You must go to the Esplanade, Lottchen, to announce our arrival, and Klärchen shall attend you. Aunt Amalie does not dream that we are here, she expects us at earliest by afternoon or evening, thinking that we broke our journey with the Liebenaus in Gotha instead of coming straight on. Go, my child. Have Klärchen inquire the way; kiss your

dear aunt for me, and make friends with the cousins. Being an old lady, I must lie down and rest for an hour or
so, when I will follow you."

She kissed her daughter, to make up for the late little
tiff; acknowledged the abigail's curtsy, and was presently
alone. On the console table were pen and ink. She sat
down, took a sheet of paper, dipped the pen and wrote,
her hand hurrying over the paper and her head nodding
above it, the words already composed in her mind:

> My honoured friend:
>
> With my daughter Charlotte, I am paying a visit to
> my sister and shall spend a few days in Weimar. It is
> my wish to present my daughter to you; and I myself
> should rejoice if I might look once more upon a face
> which, while each of us has been pursuing his appointed
> lot in life, has become so well known to all the world.
> Weimar, Hotel Elephant, October 6, '16.
>
> Charlotte Kestner, née Buff

She strewed sand upon the writing, let it run off, folded
the sheet of paper, dexterously slipping one end inside
the other, and wrote the address. Then she pulled the
bell.

CHAPTER TWO

CHARLOTTE for a long time did not find the repose which indeed it is likely she did not sincerely seek. True, she put off her outward garments, lay down on one of the beds beneath the little mull tester, and covered herself with a shawl. The windows had but their muslin curtains, so she shielded her eyes with a handkerchief against the light, and beneath the handkerchief kept them well closed. But she employed herself with her thoughts, which were of a sort to quicken her heart-beats, rather than with any sensible attempt to summon the much needed slumber. She did so the more in that she fancied her unwisdom, taking it as a sign that she was still young and unchanged despite the years, and with a covert smile rejoicing in the same. In a farewell letter Someone had written: "And I, dear Lotte, rejoice to read in your eyes that you believe I shall never change." There it is, the faith of our youth; we never, at bottom, relinquish it; never, however old we grow, do we tire of reconfirming its truth, of reassuring ourselves that we are still the same, that growing old is but a physical, outward phenomenon and naught can avail to alter that innermost, foolish self

of ours which we have carried about so long. And
herein lies the blithe and shamefaced secret of our dignified old age. This was an old woman, so called and
daily mocking herself as such, and journeying with a
daughter of nine-and-twenty, the ninth child she had
borne to her husband. Yet here she lay, and her heart
throbbed like that of a schoolgirl caught in some mad
prank. Charlotte could conceive of folk who would find
that charming.

Not so Lotte the younger. The mother had granted
her daughter a forgiving kiss. But now she lay and felt an
inward rankling at the humourless stricture the daughter
had made upon the frock and its trimmings; it was at
bottom a stricture upon their whole journey. Young
Lotte had dubbed it fantastic, this reasonable, well-
founded enterprise. It is not pleasant to travel abroad
with a companion who is too shrewd not to perceive that
she is a pretext. Such keen-sightedness is uncomfortable,
it is offensive, it is not keen-eyed but cross-eyed; among
all the involved motives for an act it sees only the subtle, unuttered ones, blind to the sound and obvious reasons or dubbing them pretence. Charlotte resented psychological penetration of that or perhaps of any kind,
she found it insulting. It was her resentment that spoke
when she reproached her daughter for a lack of affability.

These sharp-eyed people, she thought, have they, then,
nothing to fear themselves? Suppose one turned the
tables and exposed the ground for their sharp sight, which
probably lay deeper, even, than simple truth-lovingness?
Lottchen's repellent coldness — one might, if one were
ill-willed, look beneath it and find nothing very lovable.

Experiences such as had fallen to the mother's lot had never been vouchsafed to this admirable child of hers. Lottchen's nature made it improbable that they ever would be — experiences such as that famous three-cornered one, which in its inception had been all joy and peace, but thanks to the mad folly of one of the three had declined into confusion and tormenting pain, and a great temptation honourably overcome by a well-regulated heart. — And then one day, ah, then with what pride and horror to see it published to all the world, to have it become a reality above all realities, attain to a higher life and stir and distract mankind as once it had stirred and distracted a simple girlish heart! Yes, it had seized upon the world, that experience, had ravished it with emotions often rebuked as dangerous in the extreme.

Children, thought Charlotte, are hard; they cannot brook that their mother should have a life of her own. Their filial piety is inhibited by selfishness, their love can turn to its contrary — the more quickly, and more culpably, when there mingles in it a trace of ordinary female jealousy. Envy of a love-affair might then disguise itself as contempt for the notoriety involved. No, the austere Lottchen had never known anything so beautiful, so guiltily, deathly sweet as that evening when the bridegroom had ridden away on business and He had come, who had no right to be there again till Christmas. She had sent out to friends, in vain. She must be alone with him. He had read Ossian aloud, and the hero's sufferings had overwhelmed him with the black melancholy of his own. He had sunk down at her feet, the dear, desperate youth, and pressed her hands to his poor forehead and his

eyes. And she, stirred by profoundest pity, pressed his
hands too; unawares their burning cheeks had met and the
whole world been lost in the storm of kisses which his hot
lips had printed on her stammering, resisting ones.

But then she bethought her that neither had she had
that experience herself. It belonged to the larger reality,
and beneath the handkerchief she had confused it with
the smaller one, in which events had not moved so tu-
multuously. The mad youth had only snatched a kiss as
they were plucking raspberries in the sun. Or, if the
phrase were not adequate to either's feeling, he had kissed
her roundly, half whirlwind, half hypochondriac, ardent,
eager, tender, and desirous; and she had suffered him.
But afterwards she had borne herself as blamelessly in
the small reality as in the great. That was why she might
stand in the one immortalized, a suffering, noble figure;
because in the other she had behaved as must have satisfied the most filial-minded daughter. That kiss — it had
been in all truthfulness quite mad. It came out of a different world, it was a prince-and-vagabond kiss, she was
too good for it and not good enough. The poor prince
of Vagabondia had had tears in his eyes, forsooth, and so
had she. But she had comported herself with utmost
propriety, saying: " Fie, for shame! " If such a thing
happened again, they must part. She would not conceal
it, he should understand that. That very day she would
tell Kestner of it. And however much he had begged her
not to, she had honourably confessed to her good, upright bridegroom, who had to know; not so much that He
had kissed, but that she had suffered Him. Albert had
been most distressed. They had talked for long, and on

the ground of the inviolable bond between them, based on reason and good sense, had decided to be a little strict with their dear friend and make it clear to him where matters really stood.

Lying there with her eyes shut, she could see, as though it were yesterday, most vividly indeed the face he put on at his very cold reception on the day after the kiss and particularly on the ensuing day, when he had arrived bearing flowers, at ten o'clock in the evening as the pair were sitting in front of the house. She received his tribute so carelessly that he flung it away and harangued them in a string of veiled, fantastic metaphors. He could make a very long face indeed, in those days; his nose looked large and drooping beneath the powdered hair rolled over his ears, the faint shadow of a moustache just showed above the feminine mouth and weak-looking chin, and the brown eyes, small compared with the nose, but with the prettiest silky black brows above them, put on a beseeching, almost a tragic look.

He had been like that when on the third day after the kiss she told him, in the baldest words, what she and Kestner had resolved, that he might act accordingly: he could look for naught from her but simple friendship. But had he not known as much, that his face fell so and he grew so white, whilst the eyes and silky brows stood out darker than ever? Our traveller bit her lips under the handkerchief to repress a smile, recalling that childishly disappointed, woeful face. Afterwards she had told Kestner how he had looked, and they had felt so sorry that on his and Kestner's common birthday, the now immortal 28th of August, they had sent the absurd, beloved youth, together with the pocket Homer, that ribbon, a ribbon from her frock, that he too might have something to cherish!

Charlotte flushed beneath her handkerchief and her sixty-three-year-old schoolgirl heart beat faster still. Lotte the younger guessed not how far the mother had gone in her symbolic little jest: the new white frock, like Lotte's frock of yore, lacked that ribbon. It was missing because He had it, had received it as a consolation, with the bridegroom's consent, and had bestowed upon the warm-hearted souvenir a thousand rapturous kisses. Brother Karl's housekeeper would only draw down the corners of her mouth if she knew this particular of her mother's inventive fancy. Let her! For the whole had been devised in honour of Lottchen's own father, that good and loyal man, who in the long-ago had not alone consented to but even instigated the gift. Despite all his sufferings at the hands of the turbulent vagabond prince, he had mingled his tears with his Lotte's when He, who had so nearly robbed him of his love, had been up and away.

"He is gone," they said to one another, reading the notes which he had scribbled at night and in the morning: *I leave you happy, and would be cherished in your hearts. . . . Adieu, a thousand times adieu!* He is gone," they told each other in turn, and even the children went about the house as though seeking something and sadly saying: "He is gone." Tears had come in Lotte's eyes as she read, and she might weep unashamed, with no need of concealment, for her bridegroom's eyes were humid too and he could not speak the whole day save

of their friend: what an extraordinary man he was,
extravagant in many ways, in some not wholly pleasing,
but so full of genius and with somewhat about him so
strange and moving that he evocated all one's concern
and heart-felt admiration.

Thus the good man. And how she had felt drawn to
him in thankfulness, more nearly than ever before, at his
so speaking and finding it only natural that she wept for
him who was gone! She lay there, our traveller, under
her handkerchief, and her unruly heart renewed in all
its warmth that thankfulness. She stirred, as though to
nestle to a comfortable breast. Her lips reshaped the
words they then had uttered. She was glad, she murmured, that he was gone, that friend from abroad, for
she could not have granted him his desire. Her Albert
was glad indeed to hear that; for the departed one's
native brilliance and pre-eminence had fairly dazzled him
too, well-nigh to the shaking of his faith in their own
reasonable and purposeful love. One day he wrote her
a letter offering her back her troth, that she might be
free to choose between the dashing stranger and himself. She had chosen — and how had she chosen, and
whom, save him again, her simple equal in birth, her
destined and proper mate, her Hans Christian! Not
entirely because love and loyalty were stronger than
temptation, but also because deep within her she feared
the mystery of the other's nature, a something unreal, irresponsible therein, to which she could not have given
or dared to give a name. Later she did: she called him a
creature " inhuman, without purpose or poise." Yet how
strange! He could be, that inhuman human being, so

dear, so good, so sincere, that even the children missed him
and sadly mourned: " He is gone! "

A host of summery scenes flitted before her bandaged
lids, came to speaking, sunlit life, and faded away. Scenes
where all three of them figured, when Kestner was free of
his office and could be with them: walks along the mountain crest, with a view upon the river winding through
the meadows, the valley and the hills, the cheerful vil-
lages, the castle and tower, the ruined cloister and citadel.
And He, beside himself at thus relishing earth's lovely
richness in company with dear, familiar friends, would
launch upon high themes or play a thousand pranks and
parts, till the pair of them could no longer walk for laughing. Then there were the hours of reading, in the living-
room or out of doors in the grass, when He recited aloud
from his loved Homer or the Song of Fingal. Suddenly,
his eyes filled with tears, in a furor of exaltation he would
fling aside the book, beating on it with his fist — but then,
seeing their amaze, would burst out in a healthy, hearty
laugh. There were scenes à deux, when he helped her
in kitchen and kitchen garden, sliced the beans, or with
her gathered fruit in the orchard of the house of the
Teutonic Order. He was all the faithful friend and comrade, easily checked with a word or look when he tended
to turn lackadaisical. She saw and heard it all: herself,
him, their words and gestures, their play of feature; the
tales, the jests, the call and admonitions: " Lotte! Dear
little Lotte! " " Leave off the theatricals! Climb up and
toss me down the fruit into the basket! " The strange
thing was that these pictures and memories had their extreme vividity and brilliance, their fullness of detail, not,

as it were, at first hand. It was as though memory had not originally been so concerned to preserve them in all their detail, but had had to yield them up afterwards, bit by bit, word by word, out of its very depths. They had been searched out, refashioned, reproduced with all their attendant circumstance — given, so to say, a fresh coat of paint and hung in a strong light, for the sake of the significance which they had unanticipatedly taken on.

And so, mid the heart-throbs which they begot, a most natural adjunct to such a return to the scenes of her youth, the pictures melted and mingled together, became a tangled weave of dream and fantasy, and so passed at length into slumber. Tired out with early rising and the fatigues of travel, she slept, this sixty-three-year-old lady, a matter of two hours.

Whilst she slept, forgetful of her surroundings and the inn chamber where she lay, that prosaic station upon her journey back into the land of youth, the bell of Saint James' Church tolled for ten and half past. And still she slumbered. She awaked of herself, yet probably under a mysterious awareness of an outward summons. Her inward response would have been less immediate and strong had she not somehow been aware that the coming summons had to do not with her sister but with other and more exciting claims upon her attention.

She sat up and looked to the hour, with a little start at its lateness. Her mind was bent upon the need to set out for her sister's house without delay. But scarcely had she begun her toilet when there came a knocking.

"What is it?" she called, with some sharpness of annoyance in her tone. "You cannot come in."

"It is only the waiter, Frau Councillor," came a voice from without. "It is no one but Mager. I ask pardon for disturbing, Frau Councillor, but there is a lady — a Miss Cuzzle, from number nineteen, an English lady stopping in the house."

"Well?"

"I would not venture to disturb you," Mager went on, "but Miss Cuzzle is apprised of the Frau Councillor's presence in the city and in this hotel; and she urgently begs the favour of a call, if only of the briefest duration."

"Tell the lady," responded Charlotte at the crack, "that I am not dressed, that I must go out directly I am, and that I must regret."

But rather contrarily to her words she was pulling on a dressing-jacket as she spoke; entirely minded to repel the sudden invasion, yet not, even so, to feel herself taken unawares.

"I have no need to tell Miss Cuzzle," Mager answered from the passage. "She can hear herself, for she stands beside me. It is a matter — Miss Cuzzle has the most instant need to wait upon the Frau Councillor, if merely for the briefest moment."

"But I do not know the lady!" Charlotte cried, with some warmth.

"That is just it, Frau Councillor," the waiter gave back. "Miss Cuzzle sets the greatest store by making Frau Councillor's acquaintance at once, however fleetingly it must be. She wants just to have a look at you," he added, in English, in an affected voice, out of the corner of his mouth, as though speaking through it for Miss

Cuzzle. The person appeared to consider this a signal to take matters into her own hands — or mouth; for her high piping treble now sounded from without, like an excited child's. It seemed not to be able to leave off, a stream of much stressed "most interesting's" and "highly important's" ran on and on, until the victim inside was convinced that the speediest way of stemming the flow would be to show herself. She had no mind to make it easy for the female to waste her time in verbal parley. Still, she was German enough to declare her surrender by a half-jesting "Well, come in, please," in English, and then had to laugh at the "Thank you so very much," with which Mager made his habitual bowing entry into the room to let Miss Cuzzle pass.

"Oh dear, oh dear!" the little person said. She looked an original and pleasing type. "You have kept me waiting — but then, that is as it should be. It has often cost me much more pains than that to gain my end. I am Rose Cuzzle. So glad to see you." She spoke in a mixture of German and English and went on to explain that the chambermaid had told her of Mrs. Kestner's arrival in town and her sojourn in this hotel, in quarters but a few doors away from Miss Cuzzle's own. Without more ado she had taken steps to meet her. She well knew ("I *quite* realize") the important rôle which Mrs. Kestner played in German literature and philosophy. "*Sie sind eine berühmte Frau*, a celebrity; and celebrities are my hobby, you know, the reason why I travel." Would *dear* Mrs. Kestner b so *very* gracious as to permit a quick sketch of her charming face?

She bore her sketch-book under her arm — quarto, with a linen cover. Her hair was a thick mop of bright red curls, and her face too was red, with a freckled snub nose and thick but pleasantly rounding lips, between which glittered sound white teeth. Her eyes were blue-green and now and then she squinted agreeably. Her voluminous frock of light flowered material had the classic high waist; its extra fullness was drawn away from one leg to be gathered over her arm; while her bosom, freckled as her nose, seemed bursting for mere jollity out of the top of her frock. A sheer lawn was draped about her shoulders. Charlotte gauged her at about five-and-twenty.

" My dear child," said the elder lady, her middle-class conventions something shaken at all this blithe infor-mality, yet ready to meet it in a calm, cosmopolitan mind, " my dear child, I do appreciate the interest with which my simple personality inspires you. And let me add that I like very much your resolute spirit. But you can see how little prepared I am to receive calls, to say nothing of sitting for my portrait. I am about to go forth, my dear family await me. I am glad to have met you, even with the brevity you yourself have prescribed; upon it, I must, alas, insist. We have seen each other, more would be contrary to the bargain. You will permit me, then, to make my greeting coincide with my farewell."

It is a question whether Miss Rose so much as followed her words; she gave no sign of heeding them. She con-tinued to prattle on with her droll, thick lips, addressing Charlotte as " my dear," explaining with easy, whimsical *savoir-faire* the motive and the urgency of her visit, and speaking with great candour of her own indefatigable career, which was dedicated to a penchant for collecting lions.

She was, actually, an Irishwoman. She travelled and sketched, and it was hard to tell which was means and which end. Her talent, very likely, was not great enough to dispense with the sensational appeal of the subjects she chose, her vivacity and initiative at the same time too great for contentment with the simple practice of her art. Thus she was perpetually on the hunt after famous names and places; and wherever possible, the sketch of a celebrity in her book would have its authenticity confirmed by the original's own signature beneath it — often obtained under incredibly trying circumstances. Charlotte was amazed to hear and see where-all the girl had been. She had charcoal sketches of the bridge at Arcole, the Acropolis of Athens, and the birthplace of Kant in Königsberg. She had paid fifty pounds for the hire of a jolly-boat, and while it rocked up and down in the roadstead at Plymouth she had drawn the Emperor Napoleon, standing at the rail of the *Bellerophon* after dinner, taking snuff. It was not a good picture, she confessed as much. A frantic press of boats full of shouting and huzzaing men, women, and children, the roughness of the sea, and the brevity of the Emperor's stay on deck had disadvantaged her efforts. The great man, with his cocked hat, his ventripotent waistcoat and spreading coat-tails, looked absurdly foreshortened and distorted, like a figure in a conjuring-glass. All the same, she had contrived to get his signature, through an officer acquaintance on board the fateful ship — or at least a hasty scrawl which passed for such. The Duke of Wellington had given her his. From the Congress of Vienna she had reaped a splendid harvest. She worked so very fast, did Miss Rose, that even the busiest man could find a moment to accommodate her. Prince Metternich, Monsieur Talleyrand, Lord Castlereagh, Herr von Hardenberg, and many another honest European broker had done the same. Czar Alexander had set his signature beneath a side-whiskered likeness adorned with a highly caricatured nose — probably because the artist had cleverly given to the fringe of hair round his bald pate the semblance of a laurel wreath. Portraits of Frau Rachel von Varnhagen, Professor Schelling, and Prince Blücher von Wahlstatt showed that she had not wasted her time while in Berlin.

Everywhere she had rendered good account of it. The linen covers of her sketch-book enclosed many another trophy which she displayed to the astonished Charlotte with a lively running commentary. Now she was come to Weimar (" oh, this *dear* little place! "), drawn hither by its fame as centre of the world-renowned German culture; for her it was a happy hunting-ground of celebrities. She lamented that she had come too late. Old Wieland, Herder (whom she called a " great preacher "), and " the man who wrote *The Robbers* " had escaped her in death. But some yet survived, she was informed, local writers whom it would be well worth while to collect — she mentioned Falk and Schütze. Schiller's widow she had already captured, and Madame Schopenhauer, and two or three principal actresses from the Hoftheater, the ladies Engels and Lortzing. She had not penetrated to Frau von Heigendorf, or rather Jagemann, but was

pursuing her eagerly, the more because she hoped that
through the beautiful favourite she might achieve entry
into the court circle. That was in fact not unlikely, since
already she held certain threads which would lead her to
the Duchess and Hereditary Princess. As for Goethe —
she mispronounced his name and some of the others so
frightfully that Charlotte for some while did not know
whom she meant — she was on his trail, but had not yet
run him to earth. And now she had been electrified by
the news that the famous original of his youthful novel
was in the city, in her own hotel, almost in the next room.
Electrified not alone on Charlotte's account, but because,
as she frankly phrased it, she hoped to kill two birds
with one stone — or even three. Werther's Lotte would
smooth the way to the author of *Faust*, whom then it
would cost but a word to open the door of Frau Charlotte von Stein. In her note-book, under the rubric
" German Literature and Philosophy," she had divers
notes on this lady and her connection with the character
of Iphigenie — with the greatest naïveté she repeated
them to the other original with whom she was just now
conversing.

In brief, it fell out that Charlotte, all as she was, in her
white dressing-jacket, entertained Miss Rose Cuzzle not
the few minutes she had purposed but quite three quarters of an hour. Engaged and diverted by the little person's artless charm, her gaiety and dash and by the
names too of the great folk whom Miss Rose had tracked
down, as her book gave evidence, Charlotte was even
shaken in her tendency to condemn as silly this sort of
chase; and her goodwill was enforced by the flattering

experience of being herself numbered among the celebrities who gazed at her out of Miss Rose Cuzzle's pages. So she sat, a sacrifice to her own affability, in one of the two cretonne-covered arm-chairs the inn bedchamber boasted, and listened to the prattle of the peregrinating artist who sat in the other and sketched her.

Miss Cuzzle drew with a bold virtuosity in her strokes, which however seemed not always to hit the mark, for she often quite unaffectedly rubbed them out with a big rubber eraser. It was pleasant to meet the slightly squinting eyes, whose gaze was absent, as though elsewhere than on the subject of her talk. She looked so healthy, with that bouncing bosom and those full, childish lips that narrated tales of far lands and famous folks, displaying between them the while the bright enamel of her pretty teeth. The situation seemed as simple as it was agreeable — Charlotte could quite easily forget how late it was making her. Lotte the younger might have been vexed — but she could not have put forward as ground her concern for her mother's nerves. There was no need to worry about any indiscretion on this little Irishwoman's part, she would never go so far as that. So secure did Charlotte feel that the occasion truly charmed her. It was the artist who talked, she who blithely listened. She laughed heartily at one of the tales which Rose spouted as she worked: she had succeeded in adding to her gallery the captain of a robber band in the Abruzzi, named Bollarossa, a bandit terrible for intrepidness and savagery. He had been flattered by her attention, pleased as a child with the ferocious aspect of his portrait; and when they parted, his band had fired a salvo in Miss

Rose's honour from their funnel-shaped flint-lock muskets and given her safe conduct out of the region of his evil exploits.

Charlotte was hugely amused at the barbaric vanity of this partner of hers in the immortality of Miss Rose's sketch-book. Too shaken with laughter even to be aware of surprise, she stared at Mager, who suddenly appeared in the room, after his repeated knockings had failed to make themselves heard above the sounds of mirth.

"I crave your pardon," said he. "I regret to interrupt. But Herr Dr. Riemer would deem it a favour if he might present his respects to the Frau Councillor."

CHAPTER THREE

CHARLOTTE got hastily out of her arm-chair.

"Is it you, Mager?" she quavered, in a daze. "What is it? Herr Doctor Riemer? What Herr Doctor Riemer? Are you announcing another caller? What can you be thinking of? It is quite impossible. What o'clock is it? — surely very late! My dear child," she turned to Miss Rose, "we must break off this pleasant colloquy. How ever must I look! I must dress and go out. I am awaited. Adieu. And you, Mager — pray present my compliments to the gentleman and say that I am unable to receive him, I am already gone out —"

"Very good," responded the flunkey, while Miss Cuzzle still sketched tranquilly away. "Very good. Yet I would not wish to transmit your message without some assurance that Frau Councillor realizes the identity of the gentleman who has come —"

"Identity indeed!" cried Charlotte in dudgeon. "Pray leave me in peace with your identities! I have no time for more of them. Tell your Herr Doctor —"

"By all means," answered Mager obsequiously. "But I esteem it my duty to make clear to Frau Councillor that this Dr. Riemer, Friedrich Wilhelm Riemer, is secretary and companion to His Excellency the Privy Councillor.

It might not be out of the question that the Herr Doctor bears a message — "

Charlotte, taken aback, stared into Mager's face, her cheeks flushed, her head visibly trembling.

" Oh! " said she, quite daunted. " But even so, I cannot see this gentleman. I cannot see anyone — and really I should like to know, Mager, what you can be thinking of to suppose that I should receive the Herr Doctor! You talked me over into receiving Miss Cuzzle here — do you propose that I should entertain Dr. Riemer too, in my night-rail, as it were, and in the disorder of this inn bedchamber? "

" There is no need for that," Mager replied. " We have a parlour, a withdrawing-room in the first étage. If the Frau Councillor permits, I will invite the Herr Doctor to content himself there until the Frau Councillor has finished her toilet, and then ask the Frau Councillor's gracious permission to conduct her thither presently, for a few minutes."

" I hope," Charlotte said, " you do not mean minutes like those I have been devoting to our charming young friend here. My good child," she turned to Miss Cuzzle, " you sit there drawing, and you see the predicament I am in. I do sincerely thank you for this pleasant little interlude, but what your drawing still lacks you really must supply from memory — "

Her warning was unnecessary; Miss Rose declared, showing her teeth in a smile, that she was quite finished.

" I'm all ready," said she, holding her work at arm's length and squinting at it. " I think I did it pretty well. Should you like to see it? "

But it was Mager who leaned forward eagerly to peruse the sketch. "A most valuable piece of paper," said he with the air of a connoisseur. "And a document of permanent significance."

Charlotte, looking wistfully about for her garments, hardly had an eye for Miss Rose's performance.

"Yes, yes," said she, "very nice indeed. Am I like that? Well, yes, I suppose there is a likeness. . . . My signature? Here then, quick! "

She seized the charcoal and signed her name standing, with a result that left nothing to choose between it and Napoleon's for carelessness. With a hasty nod she acknowledged the Irish girl's adieux. Mager she instructed to beg Dr. Riemer to wait for a few minutes in the sitting-room.

When, dressed to go out — for she expressly made a street toilet, hat and mantle, parasol and reticule — she left her room, she found Mager awaiting her in the passage. He escorted her down the stairs and ushered her past his own person, with his usual gesture, into the first-floor sitting-room. At their entry the visitor rose from his chair, beside which he had set down his top hat.

Dr. Riemer was a man of middle height, at the beginning of his forties. His abundant crop of brown hair had but just begun to thin, and he wore it brushed down in locks over his temples. His eyes were set rather far apart, standing out prominently from shallow sockets. His nose was straight and thick, his mouth weak, with a rather peevish, sullen set. He wore a brown overcoat with a high, tight collar, over a piqué waistcoat and folded neckcloth. His white hand, the forefinger adorned by a seal ring, grasped the ivory knob of a walking-staff with a leather thong and tassel. His head drooped rather to one side.

"Your servant, Frau Councillor," said he, bowing, in a sonorous, throaty voice. "I have to reproach myself with a scarce pardonable lack of patience and consideration in forcing myself thus early upon you. And lack of self-control is least of all becoming in a pedagogue. But I have learned to resign myself to letting the pedagogue now and then be beguiled by the poet in me. The rumour of your presence, running like wildfire through the town, roused in me the irresistible desire to pay my own homage to you. I would bid welcome to these walls a lady whose name is so closely interwoven with the cultural history of our land — I might well say with the cultural history of all our hearts."

"Herr Doctor," answered Charlotte, returning his bow, not without ceremonial deliberation, "the attentions of a man of your merits could never, I think, fail to be agreeable to the recipient."

She felt, as she spoke, disturbed by the thought that she was in the dark as to the nature of these merits. True, she had learned that he was a pedagogue, and that he was also a writer; and she was glad to hear it. At the same time the information surprised and even annoyed her. The man's description of himself did violence to his sole notable quality in her eyes, that of services performed by him in a certain quarter. He seemed to lay stress on his own dignity and worth apart from those services — and surely that was fantastic. Surely he could see she could only be interested in him as the possible bearer of a message from that quarter. She resolved to confine the conversation to its single practical bearing, and felt glad of having dressed herself for the street so as to leave her position in no doubt. She went on:

"Pray accept my thanks for what you call your impatience. It is a chivalrous impulse, and for it I could feel nothing but respect. I am, indeed, surprised that such a private occurrence as my coming to Weimar had already reached your ears. I ask myself from whom you could have heard it; perhaps," she added, with a certain precipitancy, "from my sister, the Frau Chamberlain, to whom you see me on my way. I am very late, but she will pardon me more easily when I am able to tell her of your esteemed visit. And I have a further excuse: a visit from an earlier caller, not so important as yourself, yet in her own way most diverting. I refer to a travelling virtuoso of the pencil, who came determined to add to her gallery a sketch of a simple old woman. So far as I could judge, she succeeded only moderately in her task. But will you not be seated?"

Riemer bowed again, his hand on the back of his chair. "You seem to have had to do with one of those persons in whom desire outruns performance; they want, with too few strokes, to accomplish too much:

> 'Too true, 'tis but the outline
> Of what I see that I can grasp today,'"

he quoted, with a smile. "But I can see I was not first in the field, and thus my remorse for my impatience weighs a little lighter upon me; though at the same time I feel

constrained to make the more sparing use of the favour
I now enjoy. True, we human beings tend to value a
a thing in proportion as it is difficult to obtain — I confess,
Frau Councillor, I am loth to give up my present advantage, the more so in that it was not at all easy to get access
to you."

" Not easy? " she asked, surprised. " Our good Mager,
who seems to hold sway here, has not the air of a Cer-
berus."

" No," admitted Riemer, " that he has not. But if the
Frau Councillor would care to convince herself — " and
with the words he conducted her to the window; like that
in Charlotte's chamber, it looked down upon the market
square. He lifted the starched muslin curtain.

The square, when she first saw it, had lain in all the
emptiness of early morning. But now it was full of people standing in groups gazing up at the windows of the
Elephant; while at the entrance to the inn was a little mob
kept in check by two city beadles, who strove to keep a
passage free. Here were artisans, young shop-assistants
of both sexes, women with infants in their arms, even settled and dignified citizens; the throng was constantly
increased by the arrival of more and more children.

" In heaven's name! " Charlotte exclaimed, her head
shaking anew as she peered out. " Who are they looking
for? "

" For whom else than yourself? " the doctor answered.
" The report of your arrival flew like the wind about the
town. I can assure you, and indeed the Frau Councillor
can see for herself, the place is like an ant-hill stirred up
with a stick. Everybody is hoping to catch a glimpse of

your form. Those people at the entrance are waiting for
you to leave the house."

Charlotte was overcome by a desire to sit down.

" My God! " said she. " It is that wretched sentimen-
talist Mager who has served me like this, and nobody else.
He must have advertised my arrival to the sparrows on
the house-tops. And then this amateur artist and lion-
hunter had to hinder me from getting away while the
coast was clear! Tell me, Herr Riemer, have those people down there actually nothing better to do than to lay
siege to the lodgings of an old lady who does not know
how to play the lion and would like just to go about her
own affairs in peace? "

" Do not be vexed with them," Riemer said. " After
all, that crowd down there does bear witness to something higher than ordinary curiosity. It bespeaks the
bond our simple populace feels between itself and the nation's highest concerns. It gives evidence of a community
of spirit which is truly touching and commendable — even
though it may contain an element of economic self-
interest as well. Must we not rejoice," he went on, as he
returned with the still dazed Charlotte to the back of the
room, " when the common herd, contemptuous as it is
by nature of the things of the mind, is yet compelled to
venerate them in the only way it can understand, by seeing that they serve its interest? Our little city is become
a resort of pilgrims; it reaps no small tangible profit from
the national renown concentrated, in the eyes of the
world, within its walls — and even, of late, in the person
of one single great man. What wonder that the good
folk of Weimar find themselves converted to a respect

for something that otherwise seems to them sheer humbug? What wonder if they come to feel a proprietary interest in belles-lettres and the things of the mind — even though in themselves these things are as much a sealed book as ever to them, and their interest can only find vent in curiosity over the small detail, the personal and private side? "

" It seems to me," retorted Charlotte, " you take from these people with one hand what you give with the other. This curiosity of theirs, so burdensome to me, you first try to base upon loftier, more spiritual grounds, and then you admit its real foundation to be something quite common and materialistic. That cannot make it better for me; indeed, it just makes it worse and more offensive."

" Dear lady," said he, " how can one speak otherwise than equivocally of so equivocal a creature as man? To do so has never yet been regarded as an insult to humanity. Indeed, I find it a kindly and optimistic attitude, to get the good from human nature's manifestations without shutting one's eyes to the other side of the pattern, where all the knots and loose threads can be seen. I have good ground to take up the cudgels for those little people down there; it is only my rather higher station in society that separates me from them, and if I did not occupy this enviable position up here with you, I should be making work for the constable in that charming rabble below. I had the same impulse as theirs, if in a little more refined form, when my barber, as he lathered me, told me the gossip of the town an hour ago: that Charlotte Kestner had arrived by the early morning post-chaise and had been set down at the Elephant. Like him, like all

Weimar, I knew in my very soul what that name meant. I could not bear it within doors; I dressed earlier than is my wont and came in all haste to pay my homage — the homage of a stranger, yet of a man and brother, and partner as well in a common destiny. For in my masculine way I too am one whose life is interwoven with that great life, the wonder of the world. Mine is the fraternal greeting of a man whose name posterity must always cite, as that of a helper and friend, wherever people speak of the Herculean achievements of our great genius."

The doctor's words did not make too favourable an impression upon Charlotte. They sounded pretentious; moreover she thought to notice that as he uttered them the sullen expression round the man's mouth grew more pronounced. It was as though he misdoubted whether posterity would concede the peremptory and righteous demand he made upon it.

" Ah," said she, looking into the smooth-shaven scholar face. " So your barber is a gossip? Well, that is his traditional rôle. But only an hour ago? It seems to me I am making the acquaintance of a late riser, Herr Doctor! "

" I confess it," he responded, with a rather rueful smile.

They had sat down, on two hollow-backed chairs, at a little table by the wall. Above it hung a portrait of the Grand Duke as a youth, in jack-boots and the ribbon of his Order, leaning on an antique pedestal adorned with martial emblems. For further decoration the rather bare salon had a plaster cast of a Flora in flowing drapery; while the transoms were painted with pretty mythological scenes. As pendant to the goddess, in the other corner, stood a white tile pillar-stove, with a band of genii running round it.

"I confess," said Riemer, "my weakness for sleeping late. If one may say that one cherishes a weakness, I would express it in that way. Not to have to leave one's bed at early cock-crow is a sign of being a free man, in a favoured social position. I have always reserved this freedom for myself, even all the years I lived in the Frauenplan. The master of the house himself had to grant it to me, though he, with his meticulous, I might even say pedantic time-cult, began his day hours before I did mine. Human beings differ. One man gets satisfaction from being ahead of everybody else and setting to work while they still sleep. Another finds it sovereign to linger in the bosom of Morpheus while others must already toil and moil. The main thing is, there must be mutual tolerance — and in tolerance, I must admit, the master is great, even though his tolerance does sometimes make one uneasy."

"Uneasy?" she queried, taken aback.

"Did I say uneasy?" he asked. He had been gazing absently about the room, but now he fixed her, as though challenged, with his rather staring, far-set eyes. "One is even very easy in his company — how else could a sensitively organized man like myself have borne it to live with him almost constantly for the past nine years? Sometimes, in making a statement, one has first to put it in exaggerated form in order to make clear its limitations. The extreme carries with it its own contradiction. The claims of truth, dear lady, are not always satisfied by logic. To satisfy them, one must contradict oneself now and then. In saying this I speak but as the pupil of the master; in his utterances one often hears what seems like pure inconsistency — whether in the interest of truth or out of a sort of two-sidedness or love of paradox, I do not know; at least I could not swear it. I should like to assume the first, for he himself says that it is a harder and more honest thing to satisfy human beings than to confuse them. But I fear to divagate. As for myself, I am serving the truth when I declare that you enjoy in his company an extraordinary sense of well-being, while at the very same time you are conscious of the opposite, of an uneasiness that hardly lets you sit still in your chair, so tempted you are to run away. Dearest Frau Councillor, these are contradictions of nine years' standing, or even of thirteen; they are resolved in a love and admiration which, as the Scriptures have it, pass all understanding. . . ."

He gulped. Charlotte was silent. First because she wished him to go on; but also because her mind was busy, calling up memories of the distant past to set them beside his hesitant, at once distraught and distracting revelations.

" As for his tolerance," he began again, " or, better expressed, his *laissez-faire* attitude (you see I am quite collected, I have not lost my train of thought), it would be well here to distinguish between two kinds: one comes from gentleness, from a Christian — in the broadest sense Christian — sense of one's own fallibility and need for indulgence. It comes actually, I mean at bottom, from love. But then there is another tolerance, whose source is indifference and disdain. It is harsher, and its effect is harsher, than any severity or blame. It would be in-

tolerable and destructive, even if it came from God —
though in that case, according to all our belief, love could
not be wholly lacking. And probably it is not; it may in
fact be so that this tolerance is a mixture of love and
condescension, which gives it something of the divine,
and that is how it comes that one not only bears with it
but submits oneself in lifelong servitude. . . . What was
it I started to say? Could you tell me how I came on the
subject? I confess that for the moment I have lost my
train of thought, after all."

Charlotte looked at him as he sat, his scholar hands
folded over the knob of his stick, his troubled, ox-eyed
gaze lost in space. Suddenly, plain and clear, she knew that
he came not to her, not at all on her account. He was using her as an opportunity to speak of the master and so to
reach nearer the heart of a long-standing riddle which,
it might be, dominated his whole life. She found herself
all at once flung into the rôle of Lotte the younger, who
saw through all the foregrounds and pretexts and made a
wry face at pious self-deceptions. And she felt inclined
to beg Lottchen's pardon; after all, she said to herself, we
cannot help seeing through things, our perceptions come
uncalled and there is much that is unpleasant about them.
It was not very flattering thus to serve as a means to an
end; however, she felt she had no ground to reproach the
man, since she had as little received him for his own sake
as he had come for hers. She too had come hither urged
by unrest, by the lifelong discomfort of an unresolved past
grown unexpectedly to undreamt-of proportions. She
had felt an irresistible wish to revive that past and connect
it with the present, in a way that could only be called

"fantastic." They were, her visitor and she, in a sense
accomplices; they were drawn together by a hidden
bond, a third factor gratifying and tormenting at once,
and holding them both in painful tension. Their coming
together might help them both to solve the riddle and
lighten the burden. She smiled a rather forced smile and
said:

"Is it any wonder, my dear Herr Doctor, that you
lose the thread of your discourse, when you are beguiled
into weaving a web of fine-drawn moralizations about a
simple little human weakness like oversleeping? The
scholar in you has led you astray. But tell me this: you
could indulge yourself, in your former position, for nine
years long, in what you call your weakness — I simply call
it a habit, like another. But now, if I understand you
aright, you are a school-master in the city schools, a
docent, are you not? How does this foible of yours, on
which you seem to lay stress, fit into your present position?"

"Excellently," he replied, crossing one leg over the
other and holding his stick slantwise on his knee, "excellently, out of respect, that is, to the earlier one, which
continues almost in full force alongside the new and
is so well acknowledged that every deference is paid to
it. The Frau Councillor is quite right," he said, and assumed a more sedate posture. It was as though he found
the other untenable in the long run and had only yielded
to the temptation to relax out of the pleasure he took in
speaking of the consideration he received. "For four
years I have held a position in the Gymnasium here, and
have kept house for myself. The moment for a change

had come and could no longer be postponed. Life in the house of the great man afforded endless joys and most varied amenities; but it became a matter of manly honour; a man already thirty-nine years old had in one way or another at last to stand on his own legs. I say in one way or another. For my dreams and desires rose higher than the pedagogic middle class; what I should have liked was a university activity, after the pattern of my revered teacher, the famous classical philologian Wolf of Halle. It was not to be. Up till now it has not been. Strange, is it not? One might ask why my long years of such illustrious collaboration were not the best avenue of approach to my goal? Surely it should have been easy for so lofty and influential a friend and patron to procure for me the university position I yearned for. I seem to read these questions in your eyes. I have no answer to them. I can but say that the aid and patronage, the grateful little word from a high source, were not forthcoming. Contrary to all human expectation, they were not vouchsafed. What use to harbour bitterness about it? Oh, yes, one does so, of course, when one broods over the puzzle at odd hours of the day and night. But bitterness does not — and cannot — lead to anything at all. Great men have other things on their minds — they cannot dwell on the individual welfare of those who aid them, no matter how deservingly. Obviously they must think of themselves first; they must weigh our interests against their own, and if they decide that we are indispensable, the decision is in itself so flattering that we must gladly unite our will with theirs and submit to it, with a mingling of pride and joy in the midst of our bitterness.

So it is that when lately a call came from the University
of Rostock, after mature consideration I put it aside."

"You declined it? And why?"

"Because I wished to remain in Weimar."

"But, Herr Doctor, pardon me, then you have nothing
to complain of."

"Am I complaining?" he retorted as before, with some
surprise. "Such was not in the least my intention, you
cannot have heard me aright. I was only musing aloud in
the esteemed company of a woman of intellect, upon the
cross-purposes of life and of the heart. Part from Weimar? Oh, no. I love it, I lean upon it, for thirteen years I
have been part of its civic life. I came hither when I
was thirty, direct from Rome, where I had acted as tutor
to the children of our Ambassador von Humboldt. I owe
to him my introduction here. The drawbacks and limitations of the place — ah, well, Weimar has the lacks and
failings of humankind, and of provincial humankind in
particular. It is *borné*, it is a hive of court gossip, its
upper classes are arrogant and its lower stupid; an upright
man has a hard time here as elsewhere — perhaps harder;
the rascals and good-for-nothings are on top, as elsewhere
— perhaps more than elsewhere. But, for all that, it is
a stout, substantial little town; I would not know where
else I ever would or could live or have lived. Have you
seen its sights? The castle, the parade-ground? Our
Comédie? Our beautiful parks? You will see them, of
course. You will find most of our streets pretty crooked.
The stranger must always remember that our sights are
remarkable not in themselves but because they are Weimar sights. Considered as architecture, the castle is not

much and you imagine the theatre more imposing before you have seen it. The parade-ground is of itself simply dull. Take them as they are and you cannot see why a man like me should live all his life in just this particular stage setting, or why he should feel so bound up with it as to decline a call which seemed like the fulfilment of all his youthful wishes and dreams. I return to the subject of Rostock, Frau Councillor, because I felt you were somewhat a stranger to the position I took up. Well, I I took it under pressure — the pressure of circumstances. The acceptance of the call was forbidden to me — I purposely put it this way because there are things nobody need forbid one, because they do the forbidding themselves — though the prohibition may express itself in the form of a look or gesture from a person on whom one depends. Not everybody, dear lady, is born to go his own way, lead his own life, and be the architect of his own fortunes. Or, rather, many a man who thinks he may cherish his own plans and hopes has the unexpected experience of finding that his life and inmost happiness consist in giving them up; that they consist, paradoxically enough, in self-abnegation, in service to something other than himself and to a cause not his own. It is not and cannot be his, for it is so very personal as to be actually more a personality than a cause; and therefore his service to it must be largely of a subordinate and mechanical kind. Yet even that drawback is made up for by the extraordinarily high honour which is his and will be his to posterity, as a servant of the cause. By the immense honour. One might say that a man's honour consists in leading his own life and directing his own affairs, however humble. But fate has taught me that there are two kinds of honour, one bitter and one sweet. For the honour of my manhood I chose the bitter — in so far, that is, as a man chooses at all, instead of destiny choosing for him. No doubt it requires much skill in the business of life to adapt oneself to the dispensations of fate, to strike a bargain, as it were, with the terms of one's service and compromise between the bitter honour and the sweet while all the while one's desires and ambitions remain concentrated upon the latter. But the honour of a man is a sensitive thing; it was that which led to the unavoidable unpleasantnesses which finally terminated in my leaving the roof beneath which I had spent so many years. I decided to take the secondary teaching position which for so long had been distasteful to me. So there you have the compromise; it was even accepted as such by the authorities. The programme of the Greek and Latin curriculum was so arranged that when — as was the case this morning — I am not needed in the Frauenplan, I may exercise my prerogative of late sleeping. And I have still further confirmed and strengthened the compromise between sweet and bitter — in other words, my manly honour — by setting up a home of my own. Yes, two years ago I married. But even here, dear lady, we have striking evidence — in my case peculiarly striking — of the fact that all life is a compromise. The very step meant to strengthen my independence and self-respect, my emancipation from the house of the bitter honour, has only served to bind me more closely to it. One cannot speak of a step at all, in any real sense; for I did not actually detach myself. Caroline, my wife — Caroline Ulrich

was her maiden name — is a child of that house, a young
orphan received into it some years ago as a companion to
the deceased Frau Privy Councillor. It was quite clear
that I was looked upon as a desirable husband for the
young woman; and when I saw this to be the case, the fact
made a compromise with my need of independence,
since I really found the girl attractive and sympathetic. . . . But your kindness and patience, dear Frau
Councillor, betray me, I fear, into speaking too much,
far, far too much, about myself."

"Not at all, pray," responded Charlotte. "I am listening with the greatest interest."

But in truth she had felt a faint repugnance — or at least
a mixture of feelings. The man's sense of injury, the
claims he made, his vanity and impotence, his vain efforts
to be dignified — they irritated her; she felt a half-con-
temptuous pity, at first unfriendly, but by degrees turning into a sort of solidarity with her guest and as such
quite soothing. She perceived that his way of talking
made her free — no matter whether she condescended to
take advantage of it or not — to utter and relieve her own
feelings.

Despite all that, she shrank involuntarily from the turn
he presently — as though he had guessed her thoughts —
sought to give the conversation.

"No," said he, "I must not take advantage of this absurd blockade wherein we are the victims of popular
curiosity. The wars are not so far back that we have
forgotten how to adapt ourselves with dignity and even
humour. What I mean is: it would be an ill use to make
of the privilege of this favoured hour to take an exag-

gerated view of my duty to explain myself to you. In all
sincerity, what brought me hither was not the wish to
speak but rather to see and hear. I said this was a favoured
hour; I should have called it a priceless one. I stand here
face to face with a person who is the object of the most
ardent and reverent sympathy; whom high and low,
gentle and simple, crave to behold and know; the woman
with whose name the story of our genius begins or almost
begins, since the god of love himself interwove it im-
perishably into that story and therewith into the cultural history of the fatherland, the *imperium* of German
thought. . . . And I too am one to whom it has been
vouchsafed to play a part in that history; to stand as a
man at the hero's side and breathe, so to speak, his heroic
atmosphere. Must I not then see in you an elder sister, a
mother, if you will, in any case a kindred soul? To her,
so soon as I knew of her presence, I must come to pay
homage; to her, indeed, I could not help yearning to
speak, and far more still to listen to her words. . . . Tell
me — for the question has long been hovering on my
lips — tell me, dear madam, in return for my much less
important confessions, tell me. . . . We all know, and
it is humanly quite understandable, that you and your
good husband now resting in God have suffered for the
indiscretions of the genius and his making free with your
names and histories for his artistic ends, in a way
humanly hard to justify. He recklessly exposed you to
the gaze of all the world, mixing truth and fiction with
that dangerous art which can clothe the actual in poetic
garb and give to invention the hall-mark of reality, till
the boundary between the two is dissolved and done

away. You have suffered, in brief, from the ruthlessness, the offence against loyalty, he was guilty of when he went behind the backs of his friends to glorify, yet at the same time to desecrate, the tenderest relations that can subsist between three persons. I know it all, dear lady, and I feel for you. Tell me, then, for I would give my life to hear: how did you and your departed husband finally come to terms with the dismaying experience of being sacrificed against your will? I mean, how and to what extent have you been able to reconcile your pain and chagrin at having been thus made use of, and bring it into harmony with other, later feelings inevitably aroused in you as the life of that third person soared to greater and greater heights? If I might but hear something of all this . . ."

"No, no, Herr Doctor," Charlotte hastily replied. "Not now, perhaps later — or, rather, of course later, if you wish. Another time. For I must convince you that it is not a mere *façon de parler* when I say that I listen to you with the profoundest interest. It is right that I should, for your relations with the great man are certainly immeasurably more considerable and important."

"That is a question, dear lady."

"Let us not bandy compliments! Tell me, Herr Doctor, you come from North Germany, do you not? Something in your pronunciation — "

"I came from Silesia," Riemer said guardedly, after a short pause. He, too, felt divided in his mind. He did not like her changing the subject; on the other hand, it gave him the chance to go on talking about himself.

"My dear parents were not richly blest with this

world's goods," he went on. "No praise of mine can be too high for the way they made it their greatest concern to further my studies and develop the talents God had given me. My teacher, the much-loved Privy Councillor Wolf in Halle, thought highly of me. To live by his light was my heart's dearest wish. My ideal career was that of university teacher, honourable in itself and affording leisure for the cultivation of the muses, who have not wholly denied me their favour. Yet whence should I draw the means to support myself while I waited at the gate of the temple? Even that early I was at work upon my large Greek dictionary, which I brought out in 1804 at Jena — possibly you may have heard of it. Wolf had obtained for me the position of tutor to the children of Herr von Humboldt, just then leaving for Rome; and my duties left me free time for my own work — which, on the other hand, earned me no bread. Thus I spent several years in the Eternal City. Then my employer recommended me to his illustrious friend in Weimar. That was in the autumn of the year 1803, a year memorable for me, memorable too perhaps for the inner history of German culture. I came, I presented myself, I inspired confidence. The great man, at our very first interview, offered me a place in the domestic circle in the Frauenplan. How could I have refused? I had no choice. I had no better, no other prospect. Rightly or wrongly, I found a high-school position beneath my dignity, lower than my gifts. . . ."

"But, Herr Doctor, pray let me be sure that I understand. You must have been overjoyed with such a position, and with an activity far outshining all others, not only in the teaching profession but anywhere else! "

" My dear lady, I was. I was overjoyed. I was proud and happy. The daily contact, the daily intercourse with such a man! An incalculable genius, as I was poet enough to perceive. I had shown him some of my work; and even if I subtract something from his judgment on the score of his great kindliness and affability I must still say that it was not unfavourable. Happy? I was happy in the extreme. The connection raised me at once to a position of signal and enviable importance in the world of learning and culture. But let me be candid. One crumpled rose-leaf there was: I had no choice. May it not be, sometimes, that a sense of obligation will slightly diminish the gratitude we feel? It robs it, in a way, of joy. Let us be honest. We tend to be sensitive towards a person when we owe him so much; has he not taken advantage of our need? He may be quite innocent; fate is to blame, in its unequal bestowal of its gifts. But the advantage is his, and he is using it. . . . One needs to have felt all that. . . . But again, my dear friend, I am losing myself in moralizations. The great, the uplifting and gratifying thing was that our friend thought he could use me. Ostensibly, of course, my position was that of Greek and Latin tutor to August, the only surviving child of the Demoiselle Vulpius. But although matters were really in a bad way there, I soon saw that the lessons were fated to drop into the background and give way to the far more attractive and important task of service to the father and his work. That had doubtless been the idea from the beginning. Of course I know of the letter the master wrote to my teacher and patron in Halle. In it he connects my appointment with his great concern at the boy's lack of classical training, an evil he had not succeeded — as he put it — in overcoming. But that was nothing but courtesy towards the great philologian. For the master sets small store by any systematic scholastic regimen; he would leave it to youth itself to gratify in freedom the natural thirst for knowledge he attributes to it. There again you have his easy-going, live-and-let-live attitude. In it I do admit there is a sovereign breadth of view and a benevolent sympathy for the young as against mere pedantry and scholasticism. I do not deny it; yet it is coupled with something less admirable: something contemptuous, an underestimate of youth, a failure to realize that it has its rights and is not there simply and solely for the parents' sake, to grow up to them and gradually to take over their life."

" My good Herr Doctor," interpolated Charlotte, " in every time and place there have always been, even with great affection, much misunderstanding and many cross-purposes between parents and children; much youthful impatience of the parents' personal lives, much corresponding failure on the parents' part to realize the rights of youth."

" Undoubtedly," said her visitor. He spoke with a certain inattention, his face turned up towards the ceiling. " Often, in his study or while driving, we have discussed these pedagogic questions — scarcely arguing them, for, in all respect, I was more concerned and curious to hear his views than to air my own. What he means by education is a ripening process; and that, under favourable circumstances, may be left more or less to itself.

For his own son — at least with respect to himself, for the mother . . . well, with respect to himself he had a right to assume that the circumstances were of the most favourable. August is his son; and to the father's mind the boy's existence exhausted itself in that fact. Its meaning and significance were nothing else than to be his son, and in time to relieve him from the weight of his daily tasks. That would come about of itself, as the lad grew up. There was much less thought of the son's personality and of fitting it to serve its own ends. Why then force, or torture with systematic education? We must remember that the master's own youth was free from them. Let us give things their right names: he never had a proper schooling. As boy and youth he studied scarcely any subject with thoroughness. Few could detect the truth save by long and intimate intercourse, and then only if measured by another person's exceptionally solid scholarly equipment. His mind and perceptions are so quick, his memory so retentive, his intellect so lively, that he has mastered and assimilated over a very wide field; and thanks to his arts of eloquence, style, charm, and humour, he knows how to make his knowledge avail more than the greater fund of many another scholar."

"I follow you," said Charlotte, skilfully managing the visible trembling of her head to make it look like a rapidly nodded assent. "I follow you with a feeling of suspense I fail to account for even to myself. You speak so simply, yet what you say is thrilling; for thrilling it is to hear, for once, things about a great man uttered not with the usual extravagant enthusiasm, but quietly and objectively, with a realism springing from everyday experience. When I look back and summon up my memories — they may be very far back, but they concern this selfsame young man whose easy-going way of educating himself is your present theme — well, he has gone so far with it that he has some right to prefer it to harsher methods. This man, then, this youth of three-and-twenty, I knew him very well. I observed him for a long time, and can but confirm what you say: he worked scarcely at all, his industry and interest amounted to very little. Really he never did anything at Wetzlar; in that respect he was far behind most of his fellows, the candidates and practitioners of the 'Round Table': Kielmansegge, or the Legation secretary Gotter, who was a poet too, or Born, or others, even poor Jerusalem himself, not to mention Kestner, whose life was already very full and serious. I could not but compare the two and remark how easy it is to be a good fellow and shine among the ladies when a man has nothing on God's earth to do and is completely free; while another comes to his loved ones after a long hard day's work and cannot be to them all that he would wish. I could see the injustice of it, and I never laid it up against my Hans Christian. Besides, I doubt if most of these young folk, even with more leisure — and some leisure, after all, they did have — could have displayed the exuberant spirits and ardent, fiery intelligence of our friend. On the other hand, I schooled myself to attribute some part of his brilliance to his idleness and the fact that he could give free rein to his gift for friendship. Some part only, I would say. For there still remained unexhausted that lovely capacity of heart and mind, that — what shall I call it? — brilliance of life; so that even when he wore his long face and was at odds with the world, he was more interesting than any of the diligent on a feast-day. My memory is quite clear on that point. Often he made me think of a Damascus blade, though I have forgotten the precise connection; or of a Leyden jar, in the sense that he was charged, highly charged, for that was the impression he made. You felt that you might get a shock if you touched him with your finger — like an electric eel. No wonder that other, quite excellent people seemed dull in his presence — or even in his absence. He had, as I remember, a peculiarly open gaze; not that his eyes — they were brown, and rather close together — were particularly large. But they were wide open, and soulful, I mean almost literally full of soul, and they turned black when they sparkled, as they often did, with his warmth of feeling. Has he the same eyes today? "

"The eyes . . ." said Dr. Riemer, "the eyes are ofttimes irresistible." His own, protruding glassily, with a thought-worn groove between them, betrayed that he had only half heard, preoccupied as he was with his own reflections. He could scarcely take exception to the nodding of Charlotte's head; for when he lifted his large white hand from the top of his stick to put it to his face, delicately touching his nose with his ring-finger, as a man of refinement will to relieve a slight itching, it was plain that the hand was visibly trembling. Charlotte saw it and was so unpleasantly affected as to stop her own shaking at once — a result she was always able to bring about when she put her mind on it.

"It is a phenomenon," the doctor went on, pursuing

his own train of thought, "which one might ponder for hours, though the result might easily lead to
nothing and be entirely unfruitful, and one's inner reflections be better characterized by the word 'day-
dreaming.' I refer to the sign-manual of the divine, I
mean of loveliness and the charm of form; I like to conceive of it as being smilingly imprinted by nature upon
a chosen spirit, which then becomes what we call a
genius. It is a word we use — rather mechanically — to
describe a type appearing amongst us to rejoice the hearts
of men; yet, seen and observed however closely, it remains an inscrutable, disturbing, even a painful puzzle.
You spoke, if I mistake not, of injustice. Well, here too,
certainly, it comes in play: an injustice sanctioned by
nature and thus to be respected, revered — yet not without its sharp thorn for the side of him who is privileged
to see it and sit under it day in, day out. One sees
things change in value, they are undervalued, over-
valued — and one submits, or even pays tribute of involuntary applause. For else one would be a rebel against
God and nature. And yet in private, and in all modesty, you must, out of your sense of justice, disallow all
that. A man may be aware that he possesses a fund of
knowledge; that he has striven hard to possess it, and
displayed his mastery in repeated rigorous tests. And
then he experiences a bitter, a laughable, yet somehow a
splendid thing. For that other, that choice and chosen
and complacent spirit, can take a poor fragment of your
fund of knowledge that he has somehow got hold of — or
that you gave him yourself, for the office you perform is
to be the purveyor of knowledge — and by dint of charm

and art (but these are mere words), no, rather simply by the fact that it is he and no other who gives out what has been given, can double and treble its value. It is as though by addition of *himself*, by stamping his own image on what he has picked up, he can make the whole worth infinitely more than all the book knowledge in the world. Others may drudge and scrape, hoard and refine; it is the king who mints the ducats. This royal prerogative — what is it? We talk about personality. He himself likes to talk about it; we know he has called it the greatest gift of God to men. That is his verdict, and the world has unconditionally accepted it. It is not a definition, it is not even a description — for who can define what is a mystery? Obviously man cannot get on without mysteries. If he has lost his taste for the Christian ones he uplifts himself with the pagan, or the nature-mystery of personality. For the first kind our prince of the mind has not much use; poets and artists who take up with them must be prepared to be out of favour. But the other kind he holds in high esteem, for it is his own — the greatest gift. It cannot be anything else; otherwise how explain the fact that real scholars do not consider themselves defrauded but rather honoured when they gather about the genius and pay him court, purvey knowledge to him, act as living lexicons so that he need not be encumbered with academic baggage? To say nothing of a man like myself, who will do common scribal duty year in, year out, and beam with pleasure until he looks silly even to himself! "

Charlotte had not let a syllable escape her; now, quite aghast, she broke in: "Dear Herr Professor, permit me —

but surely they were not merely clerical services you gave for so long to the master? "

" No," Riemer answered, after a pause to collect himself. " That I will not say. If I did say so, I went too far. One must not put too fine a point on things. In the first place, all that one is privileged to do for a great and beloved master has no high or low, all service is the same. I am not speaking of that. And, indeed, to take from his dictation is no job for an ordinary quill-driver, it is much too good. To entrust it to some common secretary fellow would be casting pearls before swine; while a man of intellect and understanding would be bound to feel an envy such as did him credit. Only such a man, only a scholar like myself, can appraise at its real value the whole beauty, charm, and marvel of the situation, and so be worthy of it. That dramatic flow of words, poured out hour after hour without a pause save when it trips over itself for fullness! His hands behind his back, his gaze lost in distant visions, he invokes the word, he invokes the form, with sovereign and as it were spontaneous power and reigns in an intellectual kingdom of bold and untrammelled freedom — and you hurry after him with dripping pen, and so many abbreviations that you have your work cut out to make a clean copy afterwards. Dear and honoured lady, one need only know all this, and the amazement of it, to be jealous of the office and unwilling to give it up to any empty-headed clod. To be sure — and I console myself with the reflection — the actual dictation is not a matter of inspiration. It does not spring like Athena from the head of Zeus; it has been brooded over for years, even

for decades, and some of it has been prepared in detail
beforehand. It is useful to bear in mind that one is not
dealing with an improvising mind; rather with one
which hesitates, procrastinates, is very undecided and
circumstantial. Above all, it is very easily tired, works
fitfully, never sticks long at the same task, and often
when most active is most digressive, so that it will take
years to bring a particular work to completion. It is a
nature given to slow and secret growth and unfolding;
it must warm for years — perhaps since early youth — a
work in its bosom before it can issue in reality. Its industry is quite essentially patience; by which I mean that
even in all its need of variety it sticks stoutly and unre-
mittingly, through long periods of time, to its task of
spinning its web. Such is his nature — and believe me,
dear lady, I am an impassioned connoisseur of this heroic
life. People say — he himself says — that while something is shaping within him he keeps silent, he reveals
himself to nobody, lest the growth be marred. For no
one save himself can understand the charm it works upon
him who creates it. But the silence is not quite so inviolable as that. Our Herr Hofrat Meyer, the art-historian — they laugh at him in the town because of his
Zürich dialect, but the master thinks great things of him
— Herr Meyer plumes himself very much because the
master, while he was carrying *The Elective Affinities*
about with him, told Meyer the whole story. And it may
be true, for one day he told it to me, the whole plot in
the most enthralling detail; that was before he told it to
Meyer. What pleases me and does me good in such a
revelation, such communicative candour, is the human

need it betrays to confide in someone. It is so satisfying
and consoling, it makes one feel so glad to have a great
man show his human side, to come now and then on his
little feints and self-deceptions and perceive the hus-
bandry in an intellectual establishment so incomparably
greater than our own. Three weeks ago, on August 16th,
in conversation with me, he made a comment on the
Germans; rather biting, of course; we know that he
sometimes has no good to say of them: ' I know our dear
Germans very well,' said he. 'First they say nothing;
then they criticize, and reject; then they steal the idea
and drop the subject altogether.' Those were his exact
words, I wrote them down at once, because I found them
capital, and because they are such a good specimen of
his lively and highly articulate gift of language. The
different stages of typically German bad behaviour came
so crisply and pat from his lips. But Zelter — I mean the
choir-leader and musician from Berlin; he and Goethe
are on such terms that they say thou to each other, and
one has to bow to these elections, capricious though they
are, and one feels like quoting Gretchen and saying: ' I
know not what in him thou seest ' — well, no matter,
Zelter told me this very phrase, that I wrote down on the
16th, was in a letter from the master, from Tennstädt
Spa, dated the 9th. So that it was already worked out and
down in black and white when I had it served up to me
impromptu. A little manœuvre which one smiles at and
takes *ad notam*. All together, the world even of so
mighty a spirit, however spacious it is, is a closed world,
existing within limits. It is a unit, where the motifs repeat
themselves and the same presentation recurs at large in-

tervals of time. In the wonderful scene in the garden, in
Faust, Gretchen tells her lover about her poor little sister,
whom the mother cannot nurse, so she feeds it herself, ' on
milk and water.' How far back the picture must have lain
— to come up again when one day Ottilie nourishes the
beloved infant of Charlotte and Eduard ' on milk and
water '! On milk and water. The picture of thin blue
milk out of a bottle must have stuck for a lifetime in that
mighty brain. — Will you tell me how I come to be
speaking of milk and water, or any such idle and irrelevant details? "

"You were speaking, Herr Doctor, of the great dignity belonging to constant collaboration in the work of
that great friend of my youth, a collaboration one day to
become historic. And I hasten to deny that you have
uttered a single idle or irrelevant word! "

"Better not deny it, dear lady. We always speak idly
and irrelevantly when our interest in our theme is all too
burning. We talk feverishly around and about it and
never touch the heart of the matter, suspecting privately
all the while that what we are saying is being said precisely in order that we need not come to the point.
We are governed by God knows what sort of panic folly.
Or it may be a damming-up process: if you swing a bottle full of liquid quickly round, bottom uppermost, it
will not run out although the mouth is open. No, the
comparison is inept and irrelevant, I note the fact with
chagrin. And yet how often do not much greater, infinitely greater men than I indulge in such! Let me give
you an illustration of my ancillary activities — actually,
in truth, the main business of my life. For years now we

have been bringing out a new twenty-volume edition
of the collected works; it is published by Cotta in Stuttgart, and he is paying a goodly sum for it, sixteen thousand thaler. He is a bold man, with large ideas; and believe me, he is doing it at a sacrifice, for it cannot be
denied that much of the master's work the public will
not touch. For the purposes of this new edition the two
of us have gone through the whole of the *Apprenticeship*. We have read it aloud from A to Z, and there has
been much in the way of finer points of grammar, orthog-
raphy, and punctuation where I could be useful. And
how I enjoyed the good talk when we discussed his style
and I defined and interpreted it, to his no small entertainment! For he knows little about himself, and, at
least at the time when he wrote the *Apprenticeship*, on
his own admission went to work as though he were
walking in his sleep. He takes a childlike pleasure in
hearing himself elucidated with wit and understanding —
and that neither Meyer nor Zelter, but only a philologian
can do. Those were glorious hours that we spent reading a work which is the pride of the age and abounds in
occasions for rapture — though, oddly enough, the poetry of nature and the charm of landscape are notably
lacking in it. And, on the other hand — we spoke anon of
irrelevant comparisons — what long passages of very cold
comfort there are in the book! What a weaving together
of unimportant trains of thought! Very often, one must
confess, the charm and the merit lie in that something
long ago thought and said here receives its final happy
and refreshingly apt formulation. Added to that of
course there is always some novel and charming turn,

a boldness of vision, an audacity to take your breath
away — and this combination of amenity and daring, or
even recklessness, is just what gives rise to the amazed be-
witchment this unique author inspires in us. One day,
with all due reserve, I expressed this feeling. He laughed
and answered: 'My dear child, if sometimes heads get
hot from my brew, I cannot help it.' It may seem strange,
in and for itself, that he calls me 'my dear child'—a
man more than forty years old, and in some matters able
to instruct him. Yet my heart is both soft and proud at
the words, for they give evidence of intimate com-
munion wherein distinctions of noble and ignoble service
are abrogated quite. Ignoble service? Dear lady, the
words make me smile. Actually, for years I have carried
on his correspondence, not only to dictation but also quite
independently, or rather as though I were he, in his place
and in his name and spirit. You see, the independence
rises to such a height that it turns dialectically as it were
into its opposite, it is abrogated, the surrender is of such
a kind that I am not present at all, and he speaks out of
me. I do my spiriting in such quaint and curial phrases
that the letters which I compose myself may be more
Goethean than the ones which he dictates. As everybody
is aware of the nature of my activities, there is sometimes a vexatious doubt whether a letter is from him
or from me — quite unnecessarily, of course, since it
comes to the same thing in the end. Doubts, indeed, I
entertain myself: but they have to do with the problem of
human dignity, which remains the most difficult and per-
plexing in the world. In the task, for one's own masculine
ego, there may, speaking generally, be something to be

ashamed of — at least I now and then suspect it. Yet if one thus become Goethe and write his letters, a higher valuation is not unthinkable. On the other hand — who is he — in the last analysis, who is he, that it should be an overwhelming honour and nothing else to sink oneself in him and make sacrifice of one's living ego? Poems, glorious poems — God knows they are. I am a poet too — '*anch' io sono poeta*' — an incomparably lesser than he, I say it in all humility. To have written the 'Ganymede,' or 'My Heart Beat High,' or 'Knowest Thou the Land?' — only one of them, dear lady — what would one not give, supposing one had it to give? But the rhymes of which he is sometimes guilty I could not set down, in the first place because I am not a Frankfurter, a *g* and a *ch* do not sound alike to me, either spoken or written — and in the second place because I would not allow myself slovenly rhyme. But are these the only human frailties in his work? By no means, not at all; it is the work of a human being and not in the least a succession of master-pieces. He does not flatter himself it is. 'Who is there writes nothing but masterpieces?' He often says that, and quite rightly. A shrewd friend of his youth — but of course, you know him, it was Merck — called the *Clavigo* trash; and he himself seems to hold much the same opinion, for he said about it: 'Does everything always have to be in the superlative degree?' Is that modesty, or what is it? A dubious modesty, in any case. Yet at the bottom of his heart he is truly modest, modest as probably no one else in his place would be; I have even seen him cast down. When he finished the *Wahlver-wandtschaften* he was really disheartened, and only later

took heart to think as highly of the work as it doubtless
deserves. He is sensitive to praise and gladly lets himself
be persuaded that he has written a masterpiece, however
many doubts he may have entertained at first. Yet this
modesty of his is matched by a consciousness of himself approaching the prodigious. He is capable of speaking of his peculiarities, of weak or difficult elements in
his composition, and adding quite calmly: 'I look at that
sort of thing as the other side of my great advantages.'
One opens one's mouth, I do assure you; one almost shudders — even while admitting that it is just the admixture
of such naïveté with such extraordinary intellectual gifts
that captivates the whole world. But is there no more
to say than that? Does it entirely justify the sacrifice
of a man? Why *he* — and only he? That is what I often
ask when I read other poets: the spiritual Claudius, the
beloved Hölty, the noble Matthison, in them does not
nature ring as true, have they not inward fire and heart-
warming German melody as well as he? 'Once more
thou fillest grove and vale' — that is a gem, I would give
my doctor's degree to have written even two stanzas of
it. But Wandbecker's 'The moon is risen' is not so far
behind it. Need he blush to own Hölty's 'Night in
May': 'When the silver moon through the coppice
peers'? Not at all. On the contrary. One can but rejoice, when other voices besides his rise pure and fresh;
when, undaunted by his greatness, they challenge his
naïveté with their own and sing as though he were not!
Their song should be esteemed the more highly for that.
It cannot be wholly gauged by the single product, for
there is a moral valuation as well, depending on the con-

ditions under which it was written. Again I ask: why only he? What else comes in to make him a half-god and elevate him to the skies? A great character? But what about Eduard, Tasso, Clavigo, what about Wilhelm and Faust, even? When he portrays himself he makes problem characters, weaklings, unstable human beings. Indeed, dear lady, I have times when I think of Cassius' words in *Julius Cæsar:* ' Ye gods, it doth amaze me a man of such a feeble temper should so get the start of the majestic world and bear the palm alone.' "

A pause ensued. Riemer's large white hands, with the gold signet ring on the right forefinger, trembled visibly though they rested on the crook of his stick. The quick nodding of the old lady's head had its way again. Charlotte said:

" Almost, Herr Doctor, I could feel myself constrained to take up the cudgels for the friend of my own and my husband's youth, and for the author of *Werther.* You do not mention it at all, although it was the foundation of his fame and in my opinion remains the finest of all he has written. For I feel in you a certain — you will pardon me — a certain rebellion against his greatness. But I am less tempted, or called upon, to defend him when I recall that your solidarity with this greatness is no less than my own. You have been for thirteen years his helper and friend, and your criticism — or whatever I may call it, I did call it the objectivity of your attitude — presupposes a measure of genuine admiration, such as makes any defence of mine seem absurd and mistaken. I am a simple woman; but I well understand there are things one only says because one is more

profoundly convinced than anyone else could be that
the subject of them can easily sustain triumphantly the
worst that one could say. Thus enthusiasm seems to be
using the language of ill will, and carping becomes a form
of glorification. Have I hit the mark? "

"You are very kind," he answered, "to defend one
who needs defending and at the same time to turn my
remarks in the right way. But I must confess that I do
not know what I have been guilty of saying; I gather
from your words that I have been guilty of mis-speaking.
It sometimes happens in a small matter that we mispro-
nounce a word or two with comic effect, so that we are
obliged to join in the laughter of our listeners. But in a
large matter we mis-speak on a large scale, and a god
keeps turning the words round in our mouths, so that
we praise where we think to revile and curse when we
think to bless. I imagine that the halls of Olympus are
filled with Homeric laughter at such linguistic contre-
temps. But to be serious: there is something idle and inadequate in always saying of the great: 'Great, great!'
It is insipid to use petty phrases to describe the height
of charm. For that is what we are speaking of: the most
winning form that greatness can take on this earth, the
genius as poet; greatness at the loftiest height to which
charm can raise it. As such it dwells among us and
speaks with angelic tongue. With angelic tongue, dear
lady! Open his work where you will — take the Pro-
logue to *Faust* — I read it over this morning while I
was waiting for the barber; or take that blithe and
yet profound little trifle, the 'Parable on the Death
of a Fly':

'It sucks with greed the treacherous potion,
   Unceasingly, at the first draught betrayed;
   How pleasant 'tis — and yet the motion
   Is lamed in the fine limbs and powerless made . . .'

though it is the merest, most arbitrary chance that made
me choose just this and nothing else out of that rich,
that infinite store. Is it not all uttered with an angel's
tongue, and rounded by the perfect bow of godlike
lips? Whether we take play or song or story or German
apophthegm, is it not all stamped with the hall-mark of
the most individual charm — Egmont charm? I call it
so, and the play comes into my mind, because it possesses
a peculiarly happy unity and inward fitness, and the by
no means blameless charm of the hero corresponds with
the by no means blameless charm of the play in which
he moves. Or take his prose, the stories and novels — I
have, I vaguely think, spoken of them before and perhaps I spoke as I did not mean to. There is in all the
world no more golden seductiveness, nothing more gen-
ial, modest, and happy. No pompous, high-flown sentiment, no elevation in any exterior sense, though the
inner meaning is loftiness itself — and every other style,
most of all an elevated one, seems flat beside it. No for-
malism, no priestly attitudinizing, nothing bombastic or
exaggerated, no blaze of lightning nor blare of thunder;
it is in the still small voice, dear lady, that God speaks
here. One might almost call the style dry or even punctil-
ious; but no — for what he says always goes to extremes,
though always the key is sobriety and moderation itself. The boldness is courteous and discreet, the daring

masterly, the poetic tact unfailing. Of course it may be
that I am only expressing myself badly again; but I
swear to you — though the subject is hardly suited to
extravagant oaths — that in all my contradictions I am
taking the greatest pains to speak the truth. What I am
trying to say is that everything is uttered in the middle
register and volume; it is measured throughout, entirely
matter-of-fact. And yet this is the most marvellously
compelling matter-of-factness the world has ever seen.
A new-minted word smiles with entrancing meaning, it
wells into wit and gaiety, it is so happy, such pure gold,
it is utterly sublime. Agreeably sustained, most pleas-
ingly modulated, full of shrewd, innocent magic, presented with restraint and boldness at once."

"How well you express yourself, Herr Doctor! I
hearken and am compelled to gratitude by your reasoned
precision. You have a way of putting a case which speaks
of long and penetrating study. And yet I confess I suspect
that you are justified in your misgivings lest you say things
you do not quite mean in discussing this extraordinary
subject. I cannot deny that my pleasure and my praise
are far from meaning complete agreement and satisfaction. Your panegyric betrays — perhaps by its very ex-
actness — some disparagement. It has something cavilling
in its tone, which secretly disturbs me and challenges my
heart to refute it. I am inwardly tempted to call it de-
traction. Perhaps it is silly to be always crying: ' Great,
great! ' You may like better to go into detail, and believe me, I do not fail to recognize that such a method has
its roots in love. But — forgive me the question — can
such details arrive at the heart of the creative furor? "

"Furor," Riemer repeated. He nodded heavily several times, sitting crouched over his stick and the hands clasped upon it. Suddenly he stopped; then the movement turned to an emphatic shaking, right and left.

"You are wrong," said he, "it is not furor. It is something else, I know not what; something higher, perhaps, let us say. He is illumined. But inspired he is not. Can you imagine the Lord God being that? He is the object of our fervour; but to Him it is of course foreign. One ascribes to Him a peculiar coldness, a destructive equanimity. For what should He feel enthusiasm, on whose side should He stand? For He is the whole, He is His own side, He stands on His side, His attitude is one of all-embracing irony. I am no theologian, my good friend, and no philosopher. But my experience has often led me to speculate upon the relation between, yes, the unity of the All and the Nothing, nihil. And if it is allowable to derive from this sinister word a cult, a system, a mental attitude towards the world, then one may justly go on to equate the all-embracingness and the nihilism. It follows that it is wrong to conceive of God and the Devil as opposed principles; more correctly, the diabolic is only one side — the wrong side, if you like — of the divine. If God is All, then He is also the Devil; and one cannot approach to the godlike without at the same time approaching to the diabolic — so that, in a manner of speaking, heaven looks at you out of one eye, and the hell of the iciest negation and most destructive neutrality out of the other. But whether they lie close together or far apart, it is two eyes, my dear lady, that make up one gaze. So now I ask you: what sort of gaze is that wherein

the horrifying contradiction of the two eyes is united?
I will tell you, tell you and myself: it is the gaze of absolute art, which is at once absolute love and absolute
nihilism and indifference and implies that horrifying approach to the godlike-diabolic which we call genius.
There you have it. As I utter it, I seem to realize that it
was what I wanted to say to you from the first moment
the barber told me you were here. I knew that it would
interest you, and besides, it urged me hither for the sake
of relieving myself. You can understand that it is no
small thing, that it is no little *échauffant*, to live with this
experience, in the eye of this phenomenon day by day;
that it means a certain strain. But to tear oneself away, to
go to Rostock, where the like would certainly not occur,
is quite impossible. If I were to enlarge still more upon
my theme — and I think, from your expression, I may
take for granted your interest and your wish to hear
more — in short, if I may waste more words on our subject, I will say I am often reminded of the Bible story
of Jacob, at the end of Genesis, where, you may recall,
it says of Joseph that he was blessed by the Almighty
'with blessings of heaven above, blessings of the deep
that lieth under.' Pardon me the digression, it is only an
apparent one, and I am not in danger of losing the thread
of my discourse. For we were speaking of the union,
in one human being, of the greatest intellectual gifts
with the most amazing naïveté; and we said that this combination exerts the strongest fascination upon mankind.
But the blessing of nature and the spirit, that is the blessing of humanity as a whole — though very likely it is a
curse as well, and a cause of apprehension. Man belongs

fundamentally, with a large part of his being, to the world of nature; but with the other, one might say decisive part, to the world of spirit. We may say, employing a rather comic metaphor, which yet brings out quite well the apprehension I mean, that we stand with one leg in one world and the other in the other — a precarious position, as Christianity has taught us most vividly and profoundly to feel. To be a Christian is to understand this distressing and often shameful position, and to long for release out of the bonds of nature into a world of pure spirit. Christianity is yearning — I think I am right in this. I seem to be talking at random — but do not be alarmed, I forget nothing and hold all the threads in my hand. For here we have the phenomenon of greatness, of the great man, who is as much man as he is great, in that the blessing-curse, the horrifying human double situation, seems in him to be at once exaggerated and resolved, in the sense that one cannot connect him with yearning or craving to be filled. For the combined blessing, from heaven above and the deep that lieth under, has lost its curse and become the formula for a harmony — I will not call it proud, but at least unhumbled — a harmony absolutely noble, and an earthly bliss. In the great man the spirit reaches its height without derogation of the natural; for in him spirit confides in nature as in the element of creation itself, because it is in some way bound up with it and its familiar in creation — it is brother, so to speak, to nature, and to it she reveals her secrets. For the creative is the common brother-sister element, it binds together nature and spirit, and in it they are one. Such is the phenomenon of the great mind, the

darling and familiar of nature; a phenomenon of un-
christian harmony and human greatness. You can understand that it is one to keep a man enchained not nine
and not fourteen years, but a whole eternity; against it
his manhood's honour could never assert itself and survive, if the survival involved separation. I spoke of sweet
and bitter honour, I laid down the distinction between
them. But what honour could be sweeter than the service of love to such a one, the privilege of living at his
side, daily drinking in the sight of him — 'unceasingly,
at the first draught betrayed'? Did you ask me if one
is easy in his presence? I seem dimly to recall that we
spoke of the exceptional well-being one feels, accompanied withal by some distress, so that at times you cannot sit still in your chair, but would like to run away.
Ah, now I remember the connection: we were speaking
of his tolerance, his complaisance, his *laissez-faire* ways.
Well, you might call them that, but it would be misleading; for it makes one think of Christian gentleness
and that sort of thing, whereas complaisance is not an
independent phenomenon, it depends on the unity of the
All and the Nothing, God and Devil, allness and nihilism
— actually it is the issue of this unity, having nothing to
do with gentleness, and amounting to a most peculiar
coldness, a crushing indifference; to the neutrality of
absolute art, my dear lady, which always takes its own
side and says in the words of the old rhyme: 'I care for
nobody, no, not I.' It amounts, in other words, to an
all-embracing irony. While we were driving one day
he said to me: 'Irony is the grain of salt without which
nothing we eat would have any savour.' My mouth went

open, and not only that, a cold shiver went down my
back. For I am not like that man who had to learn how
to shiver and shake; I admit that I shiver easily, and here
was reason enough. Think what that means: nothing
has savour without irony. *Id est* nihilism, that is nihilism
itself, the destruction of all feeling save for absolute art —
if you can call that feeling. I have never forgotten those
words — though in general I have observed that one
easily forgets his words. Easily. That may partly be because one loves him and pays too much heed to his voice,
his look and expression, to have much left over for the
sense. Or perhaps if you take away the voice, look, and
gesture there is not enough left, they being so peculiarly
bound up with what he says that it is purely personal
to him and without him may not be true at all. That
may be, I would not deny it. And yet it is not quite
enough to explain the ease with which one forgets what
he says. There must be another cause, something in the
utterances themselves. What I have in mind here is the
contradiction which they often contain, a nameless ambiguity, that seems to be a characteristic of nature and of
absolute art and makes what he says less valid and less
easy to retain. Poor humanity can only retain and profit
by the moral. A man cannot keep by him what is not
moral but a-moral, neutral and puckishly misleading,
what is, in short, elemental. I said elemental, and let us
stick by the word. I mean it to express and characterize
something out of a devil-may-care world that has a destructive tolerance for everything, a world without end
or aim, where good and evil both have the same ironic
right. A human being cannot retain that, because he

cannot trust it, except, of course, with that unbounded trustfulness which he does feel towards it too, and which only proves that a man cannot help having an ambiguous attitude towards the ambiguous. For this boundless trustfulness, my dear friend, responds to the boundless good nature which is part of the elemental, dæmonic essence. Responds and yet opposes it too; for it resists and answers: 'What dost thou know of human needs?' Answers: 'And one clear word evokes the splendid deed. Only too sore man feels his human need, And gladly counsel he will heed.' So the natural-elemental and the all-embracing irony, out of sheer good nature, becomes moral. But to be perfectly frank, the enormous confidence which one gives to him is not at all moral — otherwise it would not be so enormous. It is in its turn elemental, natural, and all-embracing. It is the unmoral but humanly satisfying trust in a good nature which makes a man possessed of it a born father confessor and grand penitentiary, knowing all and seeing all, to whom one can and would say anything and everything, because one feels that he would gladly help mankind and set the world right for them and teach them to live; not exactly out of regard, but out of love, or let us say sympathy. I choose this word because it corresponds better to the sense of well-being one has, as I said, in his presence. I come back to that because I have not yet succeeded in expressing myself fully about it. Sympathy is a more correct, more revealing word than the other, and less emotional. For the well-being itself is not emotional; it is not spiritual, but rather — you see how I grope for words! — of an engaging, sensuous kind. But the contradiction

is present too; for there is extreme misgiving and apprehension as well. I spoke of the panic urge to flight, seiz-
ing on one till one cannot sit on one's chair; and that
must be part of the unspiritual, unemotional, unmoral
nature of the well-being one feels. Above all, however,
we must bear in mind that this extreme discomfort has
its source not primarily in oneself; it comes from the same
source as the sense of well-being — I mean from the
unity of the All and the Nothing, from the sphere of
absolute art and all-embracing irony. And that no joy
dwells therein — of that, dear lady, I have so uncanny an
intuition that I sometimes feel my heart will burst with
it. A Proteus, assuming all shapes, at home in each, who
is always Proteus but always someone else, who quite
simply 'cares for nobody' — let me ask you if you
would consider that a happy nature. It is to be a god, or
something like it; and we feel the godlike at once. The
ancients have told us that a sweet odour is bound up
with it, by which we know it. By this divine ozone we
breathe in his presence we realize the god and his godhead, and indescribably beneficent it is. But when we
say 'a god,' we also mean a being not Christian; and in
all that I have been describing there is nothing Christian,
you may be sure. No faith in anything good in the
world, no espousal of the good, no feeling or enthusiasm
for it. Our enthusiasm we keep for the ideal world —
for enthusiasm has to do with the world of the idea,
whereas the spirit become nature sets no store at all by
ideas. It is an unbelieving spirit, it has no heart, or rather
one which manifests itself only in the form of sympathy,
and in a kind of light and casual trifling. Its real essence

is an all-embracing scepticism, the scepticism of Proteus.
The wonderfully pleasant feeling that we have must not
mislead us to believe that joy dwells therein. For joy,
unless I am entirely wrong, dwells only in faith and enthusiasm, yes, in taking sides — never, never in mocking
irony and destructive indifference. Divine ozone — oh,
yes! One never tires of breathing it. But one does not
enjoy the bliss of this *fluidum* for nine years and then four
more without having certain experiences and coming
on certain manifestations. And of such I must say that
they make one recognize, with shuddering, the truth of
what I said about joy. There is a great deal of sullenness,
disgust, and helpless dumbness. These his company must
expect of him, when chance — or mischance — wills. Not
when he is host, no, that he does not permit himself; but
when he is a guest, and falls into moody silence and
moves from one corner to another with his mouth grimly
closed. You can picture the consternation. Everything
is hushed — for when he is dumb, who shall speak? And
if he goes home, everybody else creeps away too, quite
cast down, saying to themselves: 'He was *maussade*.'
He often is, a little. He shows a coldness and stiffness,
a defensive formality hiding secret embarrassment, a
strangely sudden fatigue and unwellness; then a turn of
his nature, a rigid routine: Weimar, Jena, Karlsbad, Jena,
Weimar; a growing desire for solitude; pedantry, aloofness, intolerance, crotchetiness, affectation — a sort of
possession. My dear, good lady, all that is not age alone.
Age need not be what I have seen here, what I have
learned to see. These are the uncanny signs of consummate scepticism, and all-embracing irony. What it has, in

the place of enthusiasm, is amazing activity, a time-cult
and a regimen dictated by another world than ours. It
has no faith in ideas — freedom, fatherland, and all that are
not the natural order, they are so much chaff. But, you
will ask, if it signifies absolute art, has it then no belief in
art? Not a bit of it, dear lady. He feels contempt, at
bottom. 'A poem,' I have heard him say, 'is nothing at
all. A poem, you see, is a kiss which one gives all the
world. But no children come of kisses.' Then he would
say no more. But you wished to speak, I think? "

The hand he stretched out, as though to give her the
word, shook intolerably, even alarmingly. But he seemed
not to notice the fact. Charlotte urgently wished he
would take it away; but he kept holding it out regardless in the air, with fingers shaking violently, or even
dangling. The man appeared wholly exhausted, and no
wonder. A person does not talk at such length, all in
one burst and with such eloquence and vehemence, on
such a theme — so burning to the speaker as this obviously
was — without expending himself utterly. He showed
signs which Charlotte noticed with apprehension — to
use a favourite word of her visitor. She even felt a certain distaste. He was pallid, beads of sweat stood on his
brow, his ox-eyed gaze was blind and staring, his mouth
was open, his breath came in audible gasps. The expression on his face was like a tragic mask.

Only slowly did the panting and quivering subside.
Charlotte — very bravely, for no sensitive female finds
it pleasant or proper to see a man gasping with emotion
before her, however good the cause, and her own excitement was almost as great, yes, wild — very bravely

Charlotte essayed to relieve the tension by laughing at
the joke about the kiss. In fact she had taken it as a cue
and reacted to it with a movement which the doctor
interpreted as a wish to speak. He had been quite right,
though it was not so clear what she wished to say. Yet
she began, somewhat at random:

"But what would you have, my dear Herr Doctor?
No harm or injustice is done to poetry, to liken it to a
kiss. On the contrary, it is a pretty simile, and renders
poetry to poetry, as is its due, setting it in proper and
worthy contrast to life and reality. . . . Would you
like to know," she asked abruptly, as though she had
thought of a way to calm the distracted man and put his
thoughts in a more tranquil train, "how many children
I have brought into the world? Eleven, if I count the
two whom God took again unto Himself. Forgive me
for boasting. I was passionately maternal, and I am one
of those who like to let their light shine and boast of their
blessings. A Christian woman need not fear to commit
fatal offence with such words, as did that pagan queen —
what was her name? — Niobe, whom such disaster befell. Children run in our family, the number is no personal merit. Our home in the house of the Teutonic
Order would have boasted sixteen but for the death of
five — the little troop to whom I played mother before
my time. The world knows of them; and I still recall the
joy of my brother Hans, who was especially friendly
with Goethe, when the *Werther* came and passed from
hand to hand in the house. There were two copies; we
separated them into quires and pages to enjoy them at
the same time; the young folk, especially our lively Hans,

outdid themselves in delight at seeing their very own
home and family so prettily pictured in a novel, however shocked and hurt we felt, my good man and I, at
this public exposure, and at so much truth tacked on
to so much untruth — "

Her visitor was beginning to recover himself. " It was
about just those feelings," he threw in, " I wanted to
ask."

Charlotte went on: " I don't know how I came to
mention the subject, and would rather not linger on it.
The wounds are healed over, scarcely even a scar remains. I used the expression ' tacked on ' because it
played a part in the correspondence we had at that time,
and our friend defended himself vigorously against it.
It seemed to touch him to the quick. ' Not tacked on,'
he wrote; ' interwoven with ' — you or anyone else to the
contrary! Very good, then; ' interwoven with.' That
did not make the thing better or worse for us. He tried
to appease Kestner too, by saying that he was not Albert,
not at all. But if other people thought he was? That I
was not Lotte he did not assert. But he sent me a ' warm
hand-clasp ' through my good man, and a message: my
name was on thousands of godly lips, uttered in all
honour and reverence; that, he thought, was enough to
offset all the female gossip. Perhaps he was right. From
the beginning, I was not so much concerned about myself as with the injury done my good man. Life repaid
him for his fine gifts with many solid satisfactions, and
I rejoiced with him from the bottom of my heart — in
particular that he was the father of my nine or eleven
children. In them the other, to do him justice, always

felt a warm interest. He would like, he once wrote to us, to hold each one in turn at the baptismal font, because they were as dear to him as we ourselves. Indeed, we made him godfather of the eldest, born in 1774, though we did not want to call him Wolfgang, as our friend had wished, and gave the child the name of George, behind his back. But in 1783 Kestner sent him silhouettes of all the children that had been born to us — and he was greatly pleased. Six years ago my son Theodor, the doctor, married a Frankfurt girl, named Leppert, and Goethe helped him to get his citizenship papers and the professorship at the Institute of Medicine and Surgery — yes, in this last case, my dear doctor, he did use his influence. Last year Theodor and his brother August, counsel to the Legation, waited upon him at Dr. Willemer's 'Tannery,' and he received them both most cordially. He asked after me, and even spoke of the silhouettes their dear departed father once sent to him, when they were still little urchins — so that he knew them already. I made Theodor and August tell me about every detail of the visit. He talked about silhouettes and regretted that it was no longer the fashion to send these sensible and practical remembrances, the veritable shadows of beloved friends. He must have been very affable; only rather restless during the conversation in the garden, where a small company was gathered. He walked up and down among the people, one hand in his pocket and the other stuck in the front of his waistcoat; when he stood still, he weaved on his feet, or even leaned against the wall."

"They would not recognize it," said Riemer; "he was *maussade*. And that about the silhouettes going out of fashion was quite meaningless and insincere, something just to make conversation. We will not put it in the record."

"And yet I do not know, Herr Doctor. He may have learned to enjoy the charm and utility of 'scissor pictures.' How else could he have any picture of my children? For despite his great attachment he never took or made any occasion to see them or even his old friend Kestner again. So the silhouettes proved themselves useful. You must know too that he had a silhouette of me, from the Wetzlar days (I wonder if he has it still), and displayed almost excessive delight when Kestner gave it to him. His fondness for them might well come from that time."

"Of a certainty. I cannot say whether the relic is still preserved among his pictures. It would not be unimportant to find out; I will willingly try to ask him, at some favourable moment."

"I should like to do that myself. In any case, there was a time when he practised a ritual with the poor shadow. 'A thousand, thousand kisses have I pressed on it, saluted it in my comings and goings a thousand times.' So he wrote. In *Werther* he bequeathed the picture to me, but, praise be to God, he did not shoot himself, and so he must still have it, unless it has perished in the course of years. He could not have willed it to me, for it was not I but Kestner who gave it to him. But, Herr Doctor, tell me: despite all his storm of feeling over the picture given him by my betrothed and thus by both of us, and in his great devotion to it, has he not shown extraordinary restraint and moderation?"

"It is the moderation of a poet," Riemer answered, "to whom something might be fullness whereas to others it was starvation diet."

Charlotte nodded. "Just as he was content with the shadow pictures of the children instead of living acquaintance with them. Though that would have been so easy to have, with all his many journeys to and fro. If Theodor and August had not boldly visited him at the 'Tannery,' on their own initiative, he would never have seen any of my family, for all his saying he would like to stand godfather to them each and all, for they were as dear to him as we ourselves. His 'dear old Kestner,' my good Hans Christian, who was taken from me sixteen years ago, never saw him again; and though he inquired most courteously for the health of my boys, he never throughout our long lives took any steps himself. And if I, now at the eleventh hour, am doing so — and perhaps I should hesitate, but I am indeed only paying my sister Ridel a visit, and anything else, of course, is purely an à propos. . . ."

"Dearest lady," and Riemer bent towards her; his voice sank, he did not look at her, his eyelids were drooped and his features were rigid with the purposefulness of what he meant to say; "dearest lady, I respect the à propos, I quite understand the hurt feeling and slight bitterness in your words. You feel a pained surprise at a lack of initiative injurious to our human feeling and perhaps not quite natural. Let me beg you not to be surprised. Or rather, try to reflect that always, where there is so much ground for admiration, there is also some for wonder too. He never came to see you — you who were once so near and dear, who inspired in him immortal feelings. That is strange indeed. But if it be true that the bond of blood relationship counts for more than even gratitude or strong attraction, then there is evidence of a kind still more striking; it may console you for your own chilling experience. I speak of a peculiar distaste, of inhibitions hard to characterize, manifested in extraordinary, even offensive ways. How has he always behaved to his own relatives? He has not behaved at all; according to all the ordinary standards of family loyalty he has culpably neglected them. Even when he was young, when his parents and sister were still alive, he found it hard to seek them out or write to them, from some sort of shyness we cannot venture to judge. He has never been in touch with the only surviving child of poor Cornelia. The same is true of the Frankfurt aunts and uncles and own cousins. Madame Melber, the aged sister of his deceased mother, lives in Frankfurt with her son, but there is no contact between them, unless one may speak of a small income he receives through them from his mother. And then his mother herself, the little mother from whom he got the joyous nature and love of spinning tales?" The speaker bent down over her, he dropped his voice yet more, his gaze sought the ground. "My dear friend, when eight years ago she departed this life, he had not seen her for eleven years. He had just returned to his freshly decorated house from a long, restorative sojourn in Karlsbad. Not for eleven years — I state the fact, one does not know what to say about it. He was upset, he was profoundly shaken. We saw that, we knew it, we were glad that Erfurt and the meeting with Napoleon helped him over the shock. But for eleven years it did not occur to him, or he did not manage, to return to his paternal home. Yes, there are excuses, there were obstacles: wars, illnesses, necessary sojourns at resorts. I speak of them to fill in the picture; but actually they make the matter worse, for precisely on these journeys he could so easily have gone to Frankfurt. He did not take the occasion — do not ask me why. When we were boys, our Bible teacher tried in vain to explain to us the Saviour's question to his mother: 'Woman, what have I to do with thee?' The words, he said, were not meant as they sounded; neither the apparently disrespectful mode of address nor the rest of it; the Son of God was simply setting His higher, world-redeeming mission above the ties which bind us all. — It was no use. Expound as he would, our teacher could not reconcile us to a speech which seemed to us so little exemplary that we could not have let it pass our lips. You will forgive me the reminiscence. It came to me in the present connection, as I tried to make plausible to you that strange and puzzling lack of initiative. When in the autumn of 1814 he went to stay in Frankfurt after his travels on the Rhine and Main, he had not seen his native city in seventeen years. Why? What fears, what shrinking embarrassment and retrospective sense of shame condition the relation of the genius to his origins, the place whence he came, the walls which looked down on his infancy and from which he issued into the world? Is he ashamed of it or is he ashamed before it? We can but inquire and speculate. Neither his native city nor his delightful mother took the least offence. The Frankfurt *Post Office*

Gazette devoted a whole article to his visit — I have it still. As for the mother, her indulgence with his greatness equalled at all times her boundless devotion and her pride in the marvel which she had given the world. True, he was far away. But he sent her one by one the volumes of his collected works, and these, with the poems, she kept always by her side. Until the July of her death she had received eight volumes, and had them bound in half-calf — "

"My dear Herr Doctor," Charlotte interrupted, "I take no shame, I promise you, either from the complaisance of his native city or from his mother's love. You press them upon me as examples — as though I needed that. I have made my little arrangements in all calmness — not without a sense of their strangeness, but without bitterness. You see, I am like the prophet who went to the mountain when the mountain would not come to him. If the prophet were sensitive he would not come. And let us not forget that he comes only incidentally. The point is that the prophet is not minded to avoid the mountain — it would only go to prove that he felt sensitive. Pray do not misunderstand me; I do not mean that the maternal forgiveness of our dear Frau Councillor now resting in God would be quite after my own heart. I also am a mother, I have borne a goodly troop of sons, and they have grown up to worthy, capable men. But if one of them were to treat me as her fine young gentleman son did the Frau Councillor, and not visit me for eleven years, travelling past me to watering-places and back — I would teach him his manners, believe me, doctor, I would show him what was what! "

Charlotte seemed possessed by a mood of lively scorn.
As she uttered her blustering words she gave a thrust with
her parasol; her forehead reddened under the ashen-grey
hair, her mouth went wry in a way that does not betoken
laughter, and the energy with which she spoke — or
something else — brought tears to her blue eyes; they glittered there as she went on:

"No, I confess that such maternal indulgence would
not be in my line. So much moderation I would not put
up with, even as the other side of such enormous advantages. You can believe me; for am I not come even now
to see the mountain — not because I have any claim on
him, God forbid, I am not his mother, he may be as
moderate as he likes so far as I am concerned. Yet I will
not deny that there is an old score between me and the
mountain and it may be that has brought me hither: that
old, never-settled tormenting score — "

Riemer looked searchingly at her. The word "tormenting" was the first she had used that corresponded
to her expression and the tears in her eyes. The clumsy
man wondered and admired. Women can do such things,
he thought. They can employ subterfuge for their feeling. She had sought and found a text which she could
use to interpret — and misinterpret — the wet eyes, the
drawn mouth, and the expression of a torment which had
obviously been a lifelong one. The torment had always
been there, but she had been able to attach it to the
half-jesting, half-angry speech she made, so that when
she uttered the word, nobody could fail to misunderstand
it. . . . "A subtle sex," Riemer thought. "Enormously
skilled in dissimulation, capable of blending it with

straightforwardness till you could not tell the difference; absolutely born for social and amorous intrigue. We are simply bears, unfit for polite society, we men, by comparison. I can see through it, of course; but that is only because I suffer from the same or a similar torment, because we are accomplices and fellow sufferers." He took care not to disturb her by interrupting; but kept his wide-eyed gaze expectantly on her wry lips as she went on:

" For forty-four years, since the time I was nineteen, these things have remained a riddle to me, a tormenting riddle — why should I conceal it? The being content with poetry and silhouettes, content with kisses, and from them, as he well says, no children come. No, they come from elsewhere: from Kestner's and my true and honourable love — eleven of them, if I count the two that died. Consider all that, else you cannot understand how it is that in all my life I have never got free of it. I do not know if you know the circumstances: Kestner came to us in Wetzlar in '68, with the delegation of the Imperial court from Hannover. He acted as secretary to Falk, who was the legate of the Duchy of Bremen. All that has a place in history, as we know, and anybody who lays claim to culture in the future will need to be cognizant of the facts. So then: Kestner came as secretary to the Bremen Legation; a quiet, genuine, solid young man. I was then a young thing of fifteen; and straightway I felt a confidence in him, when he began, as much as his important office allowed, to come to us in the house of the Teutonic Order and to mingle in our numerous household. Our dear, sweet, unforgettable mother had just died — the world knows of her through the *Werther*

novel — and our father, the warden, was desolate in the
midst of his children. I was the second eldest, myself
not much more than a child; and I had to try to fill the
place of our dear departed to the best of my powers, to
see that the young ones had what to eat, and wipe their
noses and the rest. Line, our eldest, had no mind or skill
for such things; she later married Hofrat Dietz, in 1776,
and bore him five fine sons; the eldest, Fritzchen, is now
Hofrat and archivist of the Imperial court at Wetzlar.
All this is public property and material for future literary research, everyone must know it; but besides I tell
you to show you that Line too, in her way, became a
splendid woman, and history must be just to her too.
But she was not splendid then; I was the splendid one, by
common consent. And yet at the time I was just a flaxen-
haired, blue-eyed spindle-shanks. My womanhood developed in the next four years — deliberately, as it were,
for Kestner's sake, as I can see now, and to give him
pleasure. For he had early cast an eye on my housewifely
and maternal splendours and fallen in love with me, not
to be too modest about it. He always knew his own mind,
and so he knew from the first day that he wanted me,
Lottchen, for his beloved wife and head of his household,
when he had got position and pay enough to be a suitor.
That was of course our good father's stipulation, that
Kestner must first have something to show, before he
gave his blessing to our union; he must first prove that
he could keep a family — to say nothing of my being
only a fifteen-year-old spindle-shanks at the time. But
we were definitely betrothed and vowed our mutual
heart-felt vows; he, good man, wanted me because I

was so splendid, while I, with all my heart, wanted him because he wanted me and because I trusted him so. In short, we were promised and vowed for life. And in the next four years I developed physically and took shape as a woman, quite a pretty shape — but that, of course, would have happened anyhow, and my time was come, poetically speaking, to turn into a blossom from a bud. Yet in my heart I felt that it was something else; that I unfolded from day to day as though by design, in response to the love of my loyal bridegroom who longed for me, and in his honour. For when he could present himself as a wooer, at that moment I must be ready to present myself as a bride and future mother of his children. Can you understand the emphasis I lay on this, that in my fancy I unfolded into a woman, and a pretty or at least a good-looking one, expressly for the good and loyal man who waited for me? "

"I think I understand," Riemer said, with his eyes cast down.

"Well, then, when things had reached this stage, there came in the third party, the friend, the man of leisure, and sharer of our joys — he came from outside, like a gay butterfly or bird of passsage, and alighted amongst our sober, settled circumstances. Pardon my calling him a butterfly, for certainly he was no light-headed idler — though light-headed he was indeed, a little mad, a little frivolous in his attire, a little fast too, and fond of posing and showing off his youthful prowess. He loved to be the most brilliant in his company, to play the prettiest game and attract the best dancer in the room. All that is true, although even so the high spirits and brilliant plumage did not always sit on him so well; he was too weighty, to full of moods and musings for that. But it was just the love of seriousness and the pride in his own deep thoughts that made the bridge between his frivolity and his gloom, his sombre moods and his self-complacency. All in all, he was most delightful, that I must confess; so dear and well-favoured, and so ready in the goodness of his heart to atone for any folly he might commit. We liked him at once, Kestner and I; all three of us felt drawn towards each other. For he, the outsider, was enchanted at the footing he found us on, and full of joy that he might stop amongst us and taste our happiness as third party and friend. And he had plenty of time, for he let the Imperial Court slide, for good or ill, and did little or nothing, whereas my good man slaved early and late, to get on as fast as he could for my sake. I am convinced to this day, and I contribute the fact to historical research, that our friend was enchanted also by this feature of the situation; I mean by Kestner's hard-working life. Not because it gave him more time with me alone — he was never disloyal, no one must say that he was. Indeed, he was not in love with me at first, you understand. He was in love with our being in love and with the happiness of our waiting time, and felt like a brother to my good man in his joy, with no thought of disloyalty. He could lay his arm about his shoulders and love him and me together, sharing in our well-knit bond — his arm around Kestner's shoulders, his eyes on me. But it would sometimes happen that he grew forgetful of the arm, it lay there unconscious, while the eyes forgot themselves in another way. Doc-

tor, pray put yourself in my place; for I have thought
about it so much, in all the years while I bore my children and brought them up, and since then, even to this
day! Good heavens, how well I knew, and could have
been no woman not to know, that there came in time a
conflict between his eyes and his good faith; that he
began to be in love, no longer with our love, but with me;
that is, with something belonging to my good man — unfolding in those four years for him and for his sake, who
wanted me to be his for life and would be the father
of my children. One day the other gave me something
to read; it betrayed, as it was meant to do, how matters
stood and what he felt for me, quite regardless of his arm
around Kestner's shoulders. It was something he had
had printed in a paper — for he was always writing and
composing, and had brought a manuscript with him to
Wetzlar, something like a play, about Götz von Berlichingen with the iron hand, which he read to his friends
at the Crown Prince, and they always called him 'honest
Götz' among themselves. He wrote reviews too, and
this was something of the like, which had appeared in
the Frankfurt *Literary Gazette*, about some poems by
a Polish Jew. But it was not only about the Jew and his
poems. It went on, as though irresistibly, to speak of a
youth, and of a maiden whom he discovered in the peaceful countryside. In that maiden, with whatever feelings
of shame and modesty, I was forced to recognize myself,
for the text was full of allusions to my surroundings and
person and our quiet, busy, affectionate family circle.
The maiden had grown in goodnesss and in charm as
second mother to her younger brothers and sisters; and

her loving soul resistlessly drew every heart to itself (I
am quoting his actual words). Poets and wise men came
gladly to sit at her feet and gaze with rapture upon so
much inborn well-being, virtue, and grace. In short,
there were such endless illusions that I must have been
stricken foolish not to understand. It was a situation
where shame and modesty strive to close one's eyes, but
in vain. The worst and most alarming thing about it —
it made me go hot all over — was that the youth offered
the maiden his heart, young and ardent like her own, so
he said, and made to yearn with her towards the far and
cloudy blisses of this world — those were his expressions.
Enfolded in his quickening society — again, how could
I have failed to understand? — she might mount and
hover in golden realms of eternal union and undying
love. I quote him literally."

"Permit me, dearest Frau Councillor!" Riemer cried.
"What is this you are bringing to light? You tell me
these things — yet you seem not quite to appreciate their
importance for literary research. Nothing is known of
this early review — I hear of it for the first time as I sit
here. The old man — the master — has absolutely concealed it from me. I assume that he has forgotten it."

"That," said Charlotte, "I do not believe. Such things
one does not forget. 'To yearn with me towards the far
and cloudy blisses of this world' — certainly he has forgotten that as little as I have myself."

"Obviously," said the doctor eagerly, "it is full of
references to Werther and the experiences which were
the basis of that book. My dear lady, this is a matter of
the greatest importance. Do you still possess the article?

It must be searched out and made accessible to the scholar."

"It should be an honour to me," responded Charlotte, "to be of service to scholarship with such a reference — though I might say to myself that I have already deserved well enough of it in the same way before now."

"Very true, very true!"

"I do not possess the review," she went on. "I am sorry to disappoint you. He only gave it me to read and insisted I should do so in his presence; I would have refused, be sure, if I had dreamed how I was to suffer, caught so between my comprehension and my modesty. When I gave him back the printed page I did not look at him and know not what sort of face he wore. 'Do you like it?' he asked me, in a suppressed voice. 'The Jew will not be much edified,' was my cool reply. 'But Lottchen herself,' he urged, 'is she edified?' 'I am quite untouched,' I told him. 'Oh, if I were!' he cried. As though the review itself were not enough and I needed such an outburst to teach me that his arm lay forgotten round Kestner's shoulders and all his soul was centred in his eyes, as he gazed on that which was Kestner's and had opened and bloomed for Kestner's sake alone and the warming, awakening power of his love. Yes, all I was and had — what I suppose I must call the sweetness of my nineteen years — belonged to my good man and was dedicated to the upright purposes of our life together. It had not ripened for 'far and cloudy blisses' or to hover in any 'golden realms of undying love.' Not at all. But you can understand, doctor, and the world, I hope, will understand too, that it is pleasant to a girl's heart when not only the one whom it concerns perceives her bridelike bloom, because he has evoked it, but others — third parties — have eyes for it too. For that strengthens our belief in it, ours and his to whom it belongs. So I was always glad when Kestner rejoiced in my success with others, and especially with the one particular, brilliant friend whom he admired, and trusted as he did myself. Yet not in the same way, and with not the same respect. For me he trusted because he was secure in my good sense and sure that I knew my own mind; but the other he trusted just because he simply did not know it at all, but loved without aim or sense, as a poet does. In short, you see that Kestner trusted me because he took me seriously, him because he did not, though admiring his brilliance and genius and pitying the pangs of his aimless poet love. Pity I felt too, for his sufferings on my account, and because he had fallen from good friendship into this pass. But sometimes too I was hurt on his account, because Kestner did not take him seriously; my conscience smote me to see the lack of respect in my good man's love for our friend. For was I not robbing my dear one of something, when I suffered for the other because of the quality of Kestner's trust in him? Yet that he did trust him was a calming influence; it made me shut my eyes and not look, when the other's friendship changed for the worse and he quite forgot his arm that lay on Kestner's shoulders. Can you understand, Herr Doctor? Is it clear to you that my sympathy for our friend's hurt feelings was a sign of my own forgetfulness of duty and good sense, and that Kestner's tranquil confidence in me made me a little light-headed? "

"I believe," answered Riemer, "that my high service has given me some schooling in the penetration of such subtleties as these. Neither do I minimize the hardships which lay in the situation for you, Frau Councillor."

"Thank you for that," Charlotte said. "And my gratitude for your sympathy is not lessened by the fact that it all happened so long ago. It does not often happen in life that time plays so small a rôle as here. I may almost say that throughout these forty-four years the situation has retained its full freshness and immediacy and its compelling power over my thoughts. Each and every year brought its own fullness of joy and sorrow; yet scarce a day passed that I did not anxiously think back on the past. Its consequences, and its effect on the literary world, make that easy to understand."

"Quite understandable."

"How good, Herr Doctor, that you say that! How encouraging and beneficent! It is good to talk with someone who is always ready to speak those words. It seems that the mark of what you call your high service has really, so to speak, 'come off on you' and given you some of the characteristics of the father confessor and grand penitentiary, to whom one will and can say everything, for it is all 'quite understandable.' You give me courage to confess still more of the oppression and bewilderment of those days. I am speaking of the rôle and character of the 'third party' who comes from abroad and lays his emotions like a cuckoo-egg in a nest already made. I beg you not to be offended by the comparison; remember that you lost the right to take offence when you used

some such yourself, whether we call them offensive or
merely bold. For instance, you used the word 'puckish'
— a not less doubtful word, to my mind, than 'cuckoo-
egg.' And 'cuckoo-egg' was the one that came to me,
after years of constant and intense brain-racking. Pray
understand, it came, it was not the result. That would
be neither fine nor dignified, I admit. Nay, such epithets
are in a measure just the strain itself, and nothing else. I
am saying, and would say, no more than this: a youth
of parts may devote to a certain girl his love and his
homage — woo her, in short, and make on her an impression, the greater, of course, the more brilliant, extraordinary, and socially gifted he is; and he may kindle some
natural response in her breast. But he, I think, must
actually make free election of her on his own account. He
must discover and choose her, realize her worth and draw
her out of the darkness of the unknown to give her his
love. Why should I not ask you the question I have
so often asked myself in these forty-four years: what sort
of youth is that, be he never so socially stimulating, who
fails in that independent seeking out and finding, and
comes, a third party, to love her whose bloom is destined
for another's joy? Who is infatuated with the love he
sees in others, settles himself on their preserve, and in-
dulges himself in feasting at another's board? This falling in love with a bride — that it is which has dumb-
founded me through all the years of my marriage and
widowhood — this, hand-in-hand with loyal love of the
bridegroom, and in all the love-making which is inseparable from love, noways minded to encroach on the
rights of the finder, at least not by more than a kiss or

so. Such a love would leave intact for the bridegroom all serious duties and rights, contenting itself in advance with being godfather of all the children and with acknowledging the receipt of their silhouettes! Can I possibly explain to you what all that means, and how it can become a years-long, heart-breaking riddle? It was that for me, because, try as I would, I could not put out of my mind a certain word: the word 'parasite.' . . ."

They were silent. The old lady's head shook. Riemer closed his eyes and compressed his lips. After some time he said, with deliberate calm:

"When you found courage to utter that word, you counted on my having courage to hear it. We were both shocked into silence by the sound. But you will agree that our alarm was only due to the adumbrations and echoes of the divine, which we heard ringing in it. Surely they did not escape you as it fell from your lips. Let me reassure you—I too have risen to that height. There is a parasitism which is of the god: a divinity alights and broods upon the human—we are familiar with the conception. The god swoops upon and partakes in earthly joys; there is a higher election of one already elected, and the prince of the gods feels passion for the wife of an earthly man. And that man is devout enough to feel no injury or humiliation, but rather an elevation and new honour. That tranquil confidence of his is due precisely to the 'vagrant' nature of the god; to the man's recognition—despite all his reverent admiration—that the passion is in a certain way without content or significance. You will see that this has reference to your words about 'not taking seriously.' And in very truth the godlike is not to be taken quite seriously, when, that is, it lodges temporarily in the human form. The earthly bridegroom is justified in saying to himself: 'No matter, that is only a god.' He may say that while yet being full of the sincerest reverence for the nature of the god-like."

"Just that it was, my friend. He was full, too full of it. For I could often see in my good Kestner many scruples and doubts. He questioned whether he was worthy of what he had, in view of the other's more ele-vated if not quite serious passion; he doubted whether he could make me as happy as that other could, whether, perhaps, he ought not to resign himself, though with the liveliest pangs, to giving me up. I confess that there were times when I was not quite inclined, not quite ready, to relieve these scruples. And that, doctor, al-though we both privately knew that the other's passion, no matter how much suffering it might bring in its train, was a sort of play; you could put no human dependence on it, for it was something like an emotional means to an end that was unreal and extra-human."

"My dear friend," said the famulus with emotion, yet with a didactic note and even lifting his ring-finger warningly, "poesy has nothing extra-human, aside from her divinity. For nine and four years I have been her apprentice and privy secretary, and in familiar inter-course have reaped some experience which I may share with you. Truly she is a mystery, the divine made hu-man; actually just as human as divine, a phenomenon which reminds one of the profoundest mysteries of our Christian doctrine — and of some charming pagan ones

too. It may be because she is double, being human and
divine, or perhaps because she is beauty itself; but she
reminds me of that enchanting old picture of the boy
who leans to gaze enraptured at his own charms. She
tends to mirror herself. Smiling she reflects herself, in
language, feeling, thought, and passion. This self-wor-
ship is not thought well of in bourgeois circles; but in the
higher ranges, my friend, it carries no offence. Why
should not poesy, why should not the beautiful, rejoice
in herself? She does, even when anguishing with passion; for she is human in her anguish, but godlike in her
pleasure. And she may gratify herself with strange forms
and kinds of love; for instance, with love for a bride, for
the pre-empted and forbidden thing. I have known her
to find bliss in entering into a human relationship,
adorned with all the beguiling marks of her other-
worldly origin and sphere; to share in it, intoxicated by
the sense of guilt she has herself invoked. She behaves,
let us say, like the grand seigneur — and he has much of
her in him — who spreads wide his cloak before the
dazzled and adoring eyes of some little girl of the people. How easily he cuts out the simple lover, by showing himself in all the splendour of his court dress! Of
such a kind as this is poesy's self-esteem."

"It seems to me," Charlotte said, "there is too much
moderation in it — I cannot quite justify your description. What still remains to puzzle me after all these
years, I confess, is the way in which this same godhead
humbles itself to the need for pity. An ugly word
escaped me, and you have interpreted it to give it a high-
sounding, majestic meaning. I am grateful. But must the

godlike guest be at the same time so poor that we simple
mortals feel ourselves enforced to pity him, who is in
every way much higher than ourselves? Why had he
to be the receiver of our alms? For what else were the
silhouettes, and my breast-knot that Kestner gave him?
Certainly they were more than that — they were an offering, an appeasement, as I, the bride, well understood
in consenting to the gift. And yet I have never ceased
to puzzle over the self-control of the godlike youth. Let
me tell you something which I have long — forty years
long — brooded over without getting to the bottom of it.
It was told me by Born, the advocate, who was in Wetzlar at the time, a son of the Burgomaster of Leipsic.
Born knew *him* from their student days, and liked him,
and us, especially Kestner. He was a fine, well-bred lad,
with upright feelings, and he felt distressed. In particular he did not like the other's attitude towards me; it
looked like a common flirtation, injurious to Kestner, as
though he meant to take me and cut Kestner out. And
so he spoke to *him*, and reproached him — Born told me
after everything was over and he had gone. 'It won't
do, my dear fellow,' he said; 'what will be the end of
it? The girl will be talked about, and by God, if I
were Kestner, I would object! Better come to your
senses!' And do you know what the other answered
him? 'I am fool enough,' he said, 'to take the girl for
something out of the ordinary. If she deceives me' (if *I*
deceive *him*, he said) 'and shows herself ordinary, using Kestner as solid ground on which to work her charms
the more easily — the moment I see that, the moment
which thus brought her closer to me would be the last of

our friendship. I would see her no more.' What do you think of that? "

" It was a fine and noble answer," Riemer said, looking down again. " It shows the confidence he had in you, and in your not misunderstanding his advances."

" Not misunderstanding. I am still trying not to misunderstand. But what is one to understand? No, he did not need to fear, I had no such idea, I was far too simple for that, or, as he has it, not ordinary enough. But what of him? Was not our betrothal the solid ground on which he could work his charms? Had not his passion to do with one already bound, to whom it was forbidden to come closer? Was it not he who deceived and tormented me with his godlike power of attraction? It could stretch my little soul to bursting, yet he could count on my not responding, since respond I would not and could not. That lanky Merck, his friend, came on a visit to Wetzlar too. I did not like him, he had a mocking eye and an ugly face, almost fierce, it always drew my insides together. But he was clever, and besides he really loved *him*, in his own way, though otherwise heartless. I could see it, and I always felt kindly towards him on that account. Well, later I heard what he too had had to say. We were at a dance and game of forfeits, with Annchen and Dorthelchen Brandt, the daughters of Procurator Brandt, who lived in the manor-house of the Order. So they were my neighbours and friends. Dorthel was tall and handsome, much handsomer than I, who was still rather a bread-and-butter miss despite my bridal bloom in Kestner's honour. She had eyes like black cherries, I often envied her for them, because I knew

that *he* preferred black eyes to sea-blue ones. It was
there that Merck took Goethe to task. 'Idiot!' he told
him. 'Why do you waste your time playing with children? There is that Junoesque creature, the black-eyed
Dorothea; why not take her? She would be nearer right
for you and she is free. But you are not happy when not
wasting your time!' Annchen, Dorthel's sister, heard
him, and told me afterwards. *He* had only laughed, she
reported, and given no heed to what Merck said about
wasting his time. It was the more flattering for me, if
you like, that he did not think he was wasting his time,
nor that Dorthelchen had greater advantages because she
was free and I was not. Perhaps he did not think her
freedom an advantage at all, or else one which he could
not use. Yet he gave Dorthel's black eyes to Lotte in
the book—if they are hers. For some people say they
come from Maxe La Roche, who married a Brentano.
He dined with them so much in Frankfurt, when she
was a bride and before he wrote *Werther*, that at last
the husband made a scene, and it cured the young man of
his fancy. Some say the black eyes are hers; some, even,
that Werther's Lotte is not more like me than like many
others. What do you think, doctor, and what is your
judgment as a man of letters? Is it not a bitter pill to
swallow, that just on account of a pair of black eyes I am
not to be Lotte after all? "

Riemer saw, in consternation, that she was weeping.
The old lady's face was turned away a little, the small
nose was red, the lips quivered, the slender fingers groped
in her reticule for a handkerchief, to forestall the tears
welling from the winking forget-me-not eyes. But, at

before, the doctor noted that their ostensible source was not the real one. With feminine guile she had improvised a false and rather foolish, if also more plausible explanation for the tears which had long threatened. For a while she held the handkerchief pressed to her eyes.

"My dear good madame," said Riemer, "is it possible? Can so offensive a suspicion move you or give you even a moment's distress? This present siege, whose patient and I hope resigned victims we are, must surely leave no doubt in your mind whose figure the nation has enshrined and immortalized! I say this as though there could be a moment's question after what the master himself has said in — pardon me — the third part of his confessions. Must I remind you? He says that an artist is allowed to compose a Venus from the study of various different beauties; so he took the liberty of using the appearances and qualities of several pretty girls for his Lotte, although the chief were taken from the one he loved best. The one he loved the best, dear lady! And, accordingly, whose home, whose origins, whose appearance and nature, whose cheerful activities does he describe, with the tenderest, most unerring care, in — let me see — the twelfth book? There may be idle dispute as to whether there was one model or several; but the heroine, dear lady, of one of the most lovely and appealing episodes in the life of our hero, the Lotte of the youthful Goethe, is beyond a doubt a one and only."

"I have heard that once before today" said she, her smiling and blushing face peeping from behind the handkerchief. "Mager, the head waiter here, permitted himself the observation."

"I have no objection," responded Riemer in a measured tone, "to sharing with the simple the credit for insight into truth."

She gave a gentle sigh and dabbed at her eyes. "At all events," said she, "it is not so burning a truth that I must keep it every minute before my eyes. A single heroine is enough for one episode — but there have been many episodes; people say there still are. It is a sort of dance I have joined — "

"An immortal dance," supplemented Riemer.

"In which fate has placed me," she corrected herself. "I will not complain. She has been kinder to me than to some of us. For she granted me a full and useful life beside my good man, with whom I kept faith. But amongst us are paler, sadder forms, who faded away in lonely grief and found peace in an early grave. And when *he* writes that he parted from me, not indeed without a pang, but with a clearer conscience than from Friederike, I must answer that his conscience should have smitten him in my case too; for he made no bones of laying siege to me on the basis of my betrothal and strained my poor young heart nigh to bursting. When he was gone and we read his letters, when we were alone, we simple folk, among ourselves, we were sad, of course, and could talk the whole day only of him. But we were lighter-hearted too; yes, we felt relieved; and I still recall how I consoled myself with the thought that now we were back again in our own natural, simple, peaceful, everyday life, for always. Yes, God help me, I actually thought so. But that was only the beginning. The book appeared, and I became the immortal beloved — not the only one, God forbid, there was a whole row of us — but the most famous and the most talked about. I became a literary and historic figure, an object of research and pilgrimage; a madonna, enshrined in the cathedral of humanity and visited by thronging hosts. Such was my lot. Only, with your permission, I ask myself why it came on me. Why did he need to grow so great, that youth who tempted and distracted me all summer long, that I must grow great with him and be held in lifelong bonds, in the same painful tension into which I was flung by his aimless adoration? What were my poor foolish words, that they had to be uttered for immortality? When we drove to the ball, in the carriage with my cousins, and talked about novels and the pleasure of dancing, I prattled on, never dreaming, God knows, that I was prattling for the centuries and my words were to stand for ever in cold print! I would have held my tongue or tried to say something more fit for immortality. I am ashamed, Herr Doctor, when I read it, ashamed to stand there with it in my shrine before all the people! The youth, being a poet, should have known how to make my words sound nobler and cleverer, more fitting for me as I stand there in my niche — it was his duty, since he dragged me into immortality against my will. . . ."

She wept afresh. When tears have once come, they flow the easier. Again and again, shaking her head in helpless dismay over her fate, she pressed the handkerchief to her eyes with her palm.

Riemer bent over her other hand, in its mitt, as it lay

in her lap, with her reticule and the knob of her parasol. Tenderly he laid his own upon it.

"Dearest, most honoured lady," said he, "the emotions stirred by your sweet words in the heart of that youth will for ever be shared by a feeling world. For that, as a poet, he has taken care; the words are no matter. Come in," he went on mechanically, in the same gently consoling tone, and without changing his position. Someone had knocked.

"Be humbly glad," he went on, "that your name will shine for all time among the feminine names which mark the several epochs of his creative genius — lovers of culture will have to learn them by heart, as they do those of the loves of Jove. Surrender yourself — but you have long since done so — to your destiny. For you, like myself, belong in the ranks of those men, women, and young maidens upon whom, through him, the light of history, legend, and immortality falls as it does upon those about Jesus the Christ — What is it?" he asked, sitting erect, in a voice even gentler than before.

Mager stood in the doorway. Hearing the name of the Lord Jesus, he stood with his hands in an attitude of prayer.

CHAPTER FOUR

CHARLOTTE hastily stuffed her handkerchief in her reticule. She blinked her eyes rapidly and gave several quick little sniffs of her small reddened nose. Thus she put a period to the situation interrupted by the waiter's appearance. To the new one now created belonged the face she made — a face of unconcealed annoyance.

"Mager! Again?" she asked sharply. "It seems to me I told you I had important matters to discuss with Herr Doctor Riemer and wished not to be disturbed."

Mager might have disputed it, but he respectfully refrained from attacking her false position.

"Frau Councillor!" was all he said, as he raised towards the old lady his hands, still clasped. "Frau Councillor may please be assured I have delayed disturbing her as long as possible and to the uttermost minute. I am inconsolable — but in the end it could not be helped. For three quarters of an hour another visitor has been waiting, a lady of Weimar society, in hope to be admitted. I could not longer delay the announcement and resolved to rely upon the doctor's good nature and your own; that, doubtless, has accustomed you, like other high and sought-after persons, to share your time and treasures in order to satisfy the claims of the many."

Charlotte got up.

"It is too much, Mager," said she. "For the past three hours, longer for aught I know, and on top of my over-sleeping myself, I have been about to go out to see my family, who are certainly by this time disquieted about me — and now you expect me to receive more visits! It is really too much! I was angry with you about Miss Cuzzle, and again about the Herr Doctor, though it turned out that his was a visit of extraordinary interest. But now you are proposing to me a further delay! I must really doubt the sincerity of your protests, when you expose me like this."

"Frau Councillor," said the waiter, red-eyed, "your reproach rends a heart already torn by conflicting sacred claims. For how shall I not recognize as sacred the ob-ligation to shield our illustrious guest from annoyance? But will Frau Councillor, before she condemns me, gra-ciously consider how sacred, how wholly comprehen-sible to a man like me, must be the feelings of persons of station when, hearing the rumour of your presence in our house, they are animated by a passionate desire to come before your face?"

"It would be well," Charlotte said, stern-eyed, "to raise the question by whom this news was put about."

"Who is the person inquiring?" Riemer asked. He too had risen. Mager replied:

"The Demoiselle Schopenhauer."

"H'm!" said the doctor. "My dear lady, the good man is not so far wrong in having taken on himself the responsibility of announcing her. If I may explain: she is Adele Schopenhauer, a young lady of breeding and the very best connections, the daughter of Madame Johanna Schopenhauer, a rich widow from Danzig, who has lived here for a decade. A devoted friend of the master, herself with some literary gift. She presides over an intellectual salon, where the master often spent an evening when he was more inclined than now to go out. You were kind enough to consider that our conversation was not without interest. But if it has not worn you out, and time should still permit, I would venture to recommend you to bestow some few minutes upon Fräulein Schopenhauer. Aside from the great joy you would confer upon an eager young heart, I can guarantee that it would be an opportunity for you to learn something of our circumstances and situation — better, certainly, than could be afforded by conversation with a lonely scholar. And as for him," he said with a smile, " he will now in any case void the field, for he has held it far too long."

"You are too modest, Herr Doctor," replied Charlotte. " I am grateful to you for this hour; it will for ever remain a valued possession in my memory."

" It was two, anyhow," Mager threw in as she put out her hand to Riemer and he bent over it with feeling. " It was two hours, if I may be allowed to note it in passing. And as the midday meal has been thus delayed, may I suggest to the Frau Councillor that she take a little light refreshment before I introduce Mademoiselle Schopenhauer — a cup of bouillon with biscuits or a refreshing glass of Hungarian wine? "

" I have no appetite," Charlotte said, " and moreover I am in full possession of my faculties. Farewell,

Herr Doctor! I hope to see you during these next days. And you, Mager, in God's name, ask the young woman to come in, but put it to her that I have only a few minutes left and even they are a scarcely excusable theft from the dear family who await me."

"Very good, Frau Councillor—but if I might just remind you, want of appetite is no sign one does not need food. If Frau Councillor would just permit me to come back to my suggestion about refreshment. . . . It would certainly do her good, so that she might then be inclined towards the proposal of my friend Ruhrig, the city beadle. He and a colleague are keeping order down below, before the house, and he just stepped inside with me. He thought the populace would be easier to move off and send about their business if they might just have a glimpse of the Frau Councillor; she would be conferring a favour upon the guardians of public order if she consented to show herself for a moment at the entrance or even at the open window."

"Certainly not, Mager. Under no circumstances whatever. It is a quite absurd, a ridiculous proposal. Perhaps they would like me to make a speech! No, I will not show myself! Under no circumstances. I am no potentate—"

"Frau Councillor is more than that, more and higher. At our present cultural level it is no longer the potentates the crowd collects to see, but rather the stars of the intellectual firmament."

"Nonsense, Mager. You think you can teach me about the mob, and the all too crass motives of their curiosity, which at bottom have pathetically little to do with

mind. That is all tomfoolery. I will go out without looking to right or left, when I have done with my callers.
Let there be no talk of my 'showing' myself."

"Frau Hofrätin must decide for herself. Only it is a
pity — one must confess that perhaps if she took a little
something she might see matters in a different light. I
am going. I will tell Mademoiselle Schopenhauer. . . ."

Charlotte employed the few minutes of solitude in
going to the window, where she held the muslin curtains
together with her hand and peered through them to convince herself that everything on the square was as before and the siege of the inn entrance had scarcely
lessened its force. Her head shook very much as she
peered and her cheeks had not lost the rosy flush en-
gendered in the long and exciting conversation with the
great man's famulus. Turning round, she put the backs
of both hands upon them to test the warmth, which was
also burning in her eyes. She had by no means spoken
falsely when she said she felt fresh and alert, though she
was probably more than half aware of the hectic nature of her condition. She seemed moved by an un-
bridled communicativeness, a feverish, unrestrained lo-
quacity, an impatient craving for yet more talk, and at
the same time an almost intolerable consciousness of her
own state. She looked with considerable curiosity at
the door which would presently open upon a fresh
visitor.

Mademoiselle Schopenhauer, when admitted by
Mager, sank down in a deep curtsy, and Charlotte
stretched out a cordial hand to raise her up. The young
lady — Charlotte guessed her to be at the beginning of

her twenties — was very plain, though intelligent-looking. Indeed, her nervous intelligence was betrayed by the very way she sought, from the first moment, with frequent winkings and with darting glances to and fro and up and down, to conceal the very apparent squinting of her greenish-yellow eyes. Her mouth, though large and thin-lipped, wore so shrewd a smile and was so obviously practised in eloquence as to make one overlook the drooping nose, long neck, and grievously outstanding ears, with the little *accroche-cœurs* coming down beside them on the cheeks, beneath the coquettish, rose-garlanded straw hat. The girl's figure was puny. Her white, undeveloped bosom was confined in a short-sleeved batiste bodice with a standing frill round the lean shoulders and throat. She wore white open-work mitts, displaying at one end her thin arms and at the other her red and wizened fingers, with their bleached nails. She was clutching not only the handle of her parasol but a rolled-up parcel and the paper wrappings of a bunch of flowers.

She began to speak at once, rapidly, flawlessly, with no pause between the sentences, and with the glibness already anticipated by Charlotte from the shape of the girl's mouth. It watered a little as she talked, the fluent, slightly Saxon accents rolled out as though oiled, and Charlotte had a private misgiving lest her own newly discovered volubility might be checked thereby.

"Frau Hofrätin," said Adele, "words fail me to convey my gratitude for your kindness in granting me the happiness of paying you my homage" — and without drawing breath — "I do so not only in my own modest person but also in the name, if not precisely by commission, for there was no time for that, of our Muses' Circle. I refer to our literary society, which has brilliantly confirmed its traditions and its fine solidarity on the thrilling occasion of your presence here. For it was, indeed, one of our members, my beloved friend the Countess Line Egloffstein, who brought me the news on swiftest wing the moment she learned it from her maid. My conscience whispers me that I should in return have warned Museline of my intention — pardon me, that is the name Line goes by in our club, we all have such names, you would laugh if I told you them — for very likely she would have come too. But in the first place I really only thought of it after she left me and secondly I had important reasons for wishing to greet you alone, to bid you welcome to Weimar and to speak with you. Permit me to offer you these few asters, larkspurs, and petunias, together with this modest specimen of our local art."

Adele's pronunciation of the word "petunia" made Charlotte smile, and she had no need to disguise her amusement, for she could attach it to the name Museline. "My dear child," she responded, "this is charming of you — what a delightful colour combination! We must get some water for these exquisite blossoms. Such fine petunias" — she overcame her desire to smile again — "I cannot remember to have seen."

"It is a good region for flowers," answered Adele. "Flora is propitious." And she gave a glance at the plaster goddess in its niche. "The Erfurt nurseries have been renowned for over a century."

"Charming," Charlotte repeated. "And this that you call a specimen of Weimar art—what may it be? I am an inquisitive old woman—"

"Oh, my description was euphemistic. A mere trifle, Frau Councillor, my own handiwork and a modest tribute indeed. May I help you to unwrap it? Like this—permit me. It is a silhouette, made of black glazed paper and carefully stuck on to white cardboard—a group picture, as you see. It is nothing else than our Muses' Circle, the portraits as good as I could make them. This is the Museline I spoke of, Line Egloffstein. She sings divinely and is the favourite court lady of our Hereditary Princess. That one is Julie, her pretty sister, the artist, called Julemuse. And here am I, named Adelmuse, quite unflattered, you will admit, and the one with her arm round me is Tillemuse — in other words, Ottilie von Pogwisch — a charming head, do you not think? "

"Very charming," said Charlotte, "and how incredibly lifelike it all is! I am amazed at your skill, my dear child. How wonderfully you have carried it out! These frills and buttons, the little chair- and table-legs, the curls, the little noses and eyelashes! In a word, it is quite out of the ordinary. I have always been fond of silhouettes and held the view that it was a loss of taste and feeling when they went out of fashion. So much the more do I admire the enthusiasm and industry you have devoted to develop an obviously unusual natural gift."

"In Weimar we all have to develop talents, and above all we have to possess some," the young lady replied. "Otherwise we are nobody in society and are not re-

garded. Here everybody pays tribute to the muses, it
is good *ton* — and that is a good *ton*, don't you think so?
I could imagine a worse. From childhood I have had a
capital pattern in my mama, who even in my father's
lifetime, before she settled in Weimar, had done some
painting, though she began seriously to cultivate her talent only after she came here. She was also my precursor
at the piano, and she took Italian lessons of Fernow, the
art-historian, who lived in Rome, before his death. She
has always watched over my little poetic efforts with
the greatest care, although it is not given her to write
poetry, at least not in German, for once she actually
wrote a Petrarchan sonnet, under Fernow's supervision.
A most accomplished woman. What an impression it
must have made upon my thirteen or fourteen years to
see how she contrived to get a footing here, and in a
hand's turn to make her salon the meeting-place of all
the finest spirits! If I achieve anything in silhouettes it
is thanks to her and her example, for she was and is a
mistress in the art of flower-cutting, and at our tea-
parties the Privy Councillor himself has shown the greatest pleasure in her skill."

"Goethe?"

"Yes, forsooth! And he was not content till Mama
agreed to decorate a fire-screen with cutout flowers, and
he industriously set to work helping to stick them on. I
can still see him — he would sit half an hour together
admiring the screen, when it was done."

"Of course. The great man's love of everything made,
every product of artistic industry, of whatever sort — in
a word, of all the works of the human hand — is truly

touching. You cannot know him if you have not seen this side of him."

"You are right," Charlotte said. "I do indeed know this side of him, and I see that he is still the old Goethe, I mean the young one. When we were young, in Wetzlar, he took pleasure in my little embroideries and coloured silks and faithfully helped me with my designs. I recall an unfinished temple of Amor, and a returning pilgrim standing on its steps, being welcomed by a friend. He had a great share in its composition."

"Heavenly!" cried her visitor. "What you tell me is delightful, fascinating, dear Frau Hofrätin! Pray go on!"

"But not before we sit down, my dear child," responded Charlotte. "That I could fail to ask you to be seated, after all your kind words and charming gifts, makes me even more remorseful for your long waiting."

"I had to be quite prepared," Adele answered, as she sat down beside the old lady on a canapé with footstools before it, "to be neither the first nor the only person to break through the cordon of your popularity in order to arrive before your face. You were certainly engaged in most interesting conversation. I met Uncle Riemer as he came away —"

"What, is he your uncle?"

"Oh, no, not really. I have called him that since I was a child, as I did all the other regular or frequent guests at Mama's Sunday and Thursday teas. The Meyers and Schützes and Baron von Einsiedel, the Terence translator, Major von Knebel and Bertuch, the counsellor to the Legation, who founded the *Literary News;* Grimm

and Prince Pückler and the Schlegel brothers and the
Savignys. I called them all uncle and aunt and still do —
I even said uncle to Wieland."

"And do you call Goethe uncle?"

"No, not him. But I called the Frau Privy Councillor
aunt."

"The Vulpius?"

"Yes, the lately deceased Frau von Goethe; he brought
her to us directly after the marriage. Only to Mama, for
elsewhere it was a bit difficult. One might say the great
man himself came to us almost exclusively; for though
the court and society generally winked at his free union
with the departed Frau Privy Councillor, the legal tie,
when it came, irked them very much."

"And the Baroness von Stein," asked Charlotte, her
cheek flushing a little, "she was probably irked too?"

"She most of all. At least, she behaved as though she
particularly resented the legal tie — as though the connection itself had not been for years the source of much
pain to her!"

"One can feel for her."

"Of course. But on the other hand it was a fine trait
in the master to make the poor creature his legal wife.
She stood bravely and loyally at his side in the frightful
French days in 1806, and he definitely felt that two
people who had lived through all that together belonged
to each other in the sight of God and man."

"Is it true that her conduct left something to be desired?"

"Yes, she was common," Adele said. "'De mortuis
nil nisi bene' — but common she was, in the extreme,

greedy and garrulous, with fearfully red cheeks; mad
about dancing, and loved the bottle more than she should;
always with theatre people and young men, though she
herself was no longer of the youngest; always at dances
and redoutes, skating parties and student balls; and the
Jena students thought they could play all sorts of vulgar
pranks with the Frau Privy Councillor."

"And Goethe tolerated such goings-on?"

"He shut his eyes, and probably he laughed at them.
Perhaps that was the wisest thing he could do. You might
even say to some extent he sanctioned them; on the
ground, I suspect, that they gave him a sort of right to
salvage his own emotional freedom. A poetic genius, it
seems to me, cannot draw his literary inspiration exclusively from his married life."

"You have very broad, very strong-minded views, my
dear."

"I am a true Weimarese," Adele said. "Amor is a
great god here, he is granted considerable privilege,
within the limits of the *convenable*. When Weimar society commented adversely on the Frau Privy Councillor's rather gross love of life, it is certain that the
grounds were rather æsthetic than moral. In justice one
must say that she made him a capital wife. She always
looked out for his physical well-being and understood
the conditions of his productivity, though of course she
had no smallest grasp of what it meant, the intellectual
being a sealed book to her. However, she always displayed the greatest reverence. Even after his marriage he
never weaned himself from his bachelor habits, and lived
for months at a time by himself, in Jena, Karlsbad, or

Töplitz. She died in one of her attacks, last June; died in the arms of a strange nurse, for he himself was ailing and in bed that day; in fact, he had been for a long time in indifferent health. Whereas she was a picture of health — even painfully so, by any æsthetic standards. — When she was dead, they say, he fell across her bed and cried out: 'No, no, thou canst not leave me!'"

Charlotte was silent, and the visitor, whose cultural tradition could brook no gap in the flow of speech, hastened on:

"At all events, it was very shrewd of Mama, alone in all Weimar society, to have received the woman and helped her, with the most delicate tact, over the worst of her embarrassments. For she thus attached the great man more closely to her growing salon — and he was, of course, its chief attraction. She made me call the Vulpius aunt. But I have never said uncle to Goethe. It would not have done. He probably liked me, he often joked with me. I was allowed to blow out the lantern he used when he walked over to our house; he let me show him my toys, and danced an *écossaise* with my favourite doll. But still, to call him uncle — he was too much of a personage for that. Not only for me, but for the grownups as well, and of course I saw it. Besides, when he came he was often a little silent, in a way embarrassed; he would sit quiet, by himself, at his table, and draw. Yet he dominated the room, simply because everybody took the key from him; he tyrannized over the company, not so much because he was a tyrant as because the others submitted to him and positively forced him into the rôle. So then he played the part: he ruled them, rapped on his table, ordered this and that; he read Scottish ballads aloud and made the ladies repeat the refrains in chorus with him — and woe to anyone who laughed! His eyes would flash, he would say: 'I won't read another word!' Mama would have great trouble patching things up and guaranteeing good conduct for the future. Or else he would amuse himself frightening some timid lady with ghost-stories and gruesome anecdotes till she almost fainted. Above all else he loved teasing. I still remember an evening when he made Uncle Wieland almost jump out of his skin, simply by persistently contradicting him. Not in earnest, but just making little quibbles. Uncle Wieland took them seriously and got very angry; then Goethe's henchmen, Meyer and Riemer, began patronizing him: 'Dear Wieland, you must not take it like that.' It was not very tactful of them. Even as a little girl I could feel that, and perhaps others did too, but not Goethe himself, strangely enough."

"Yes, that is strange."

"I have always noticed," Adele went on, "that society, especially our German society, actually takes pleasure in bowing down. It likes to spoil its favourites and superiors, and force on them an exaggerated pose of authority, until both sides suffer and nobody gets any pleasure from it. One whole evening long, Goethe once teased the company to the point of extreme ennui, trying to make them guess, by the method of question and answer, the subject of the new and unknown piece of which he had just held a rehearsal. It was impossible, there were too many unknown quantities. Nobody succeeded in guessing, faces got longer, yawns more and

more frequent, and still he persisted, until the game
became actual torture. One asked oneself: Why does
he not feel what a compulsion he is putting on them?
No, he did not feel it, society had got him used to not
feeling it. Even so, one can hardly believe that he was
not bored to death with his own callous insistence.
Tyranny is certainly a tedious business."

"You may be right there, my child."

"And in my view," Adele went on, "he was not born
to be a tyrant, but rather a friend to humanity. I have
always drawn that conclusion from the fact that he loved
to make people laugh—and knew so very well how to
do it. He showed it when he read aloud, and when he
told impromptu stories. Tyrants are not like that. Or
when he described funny scenes and people. We all
know that his reading aloud is not always happy. Of
course his voice is pleasant in itself and has a fine depth.
But in serious scenes he falls too much into the declama-
tory and heavy pathetic, he thunders too loud, it is not
always agreeable. The comic, on the other hand, he
produces with such natural and telling force, such priceless observation and unfailing fidelity, that everybody is
ravished. As, indeed, when he tells funny stories or loses
himself in a web of fantastic nonsense. At such times we
always laughed till we cried. It is remarkable what sobriety and moderation prevail in his written works.
They may now and then make you smile, but for laughter—not that I know of. Yet personally he likes nothing
better than to see people dissolve in laughter at what he
says. I have seen Uncle Wieland cover his head with his

napkin and beg for quarter, while everybody else at table was out of breath with laughing. He himself always preserved his gravity. Yet he had a strange way of looking at his expiring audience, with flashing eyes and a sort of eager delight. I have often wondered what it means, when such a marvellous man, who has lived through so much, borne so much, and achieved so much, takes so much pleasure in making people burst out in peals of laughter."

"The thing is," said Charlotte, "that in all his greatness he has remained young, and amid the seriousness of life has kept faith with laughter. That would not surprise me, and I should know how to esteem it. In our youth we laughed much and heartily, the two and the three of us. At the very moment when he wanted to degenerate into tragedy with me and lose himself in melancholy, he would take a grip on his feelings, face straight round, and turn everything to laughter with his tricks, just as he does at your mother's tea-table."

"Do go on talking, Frau Councillor," the young girl begged. "Go on telling me of those immortal days of your youth and about the two and the three of you. What must I be feeling, foolish young thing that I am! I knew to whom I was coming, to whom I was irresistibly drawn. Yet, sitting here, I almost forget who it is sits beside me on this sofa, until with terror I am driven back to a realization by your words. Oh, I implore you, tell me more!"

"Much rather," said Charlotte, "much rather would I listen to you, my dear young friend. You entertain me

so charmingly, I must continually reproach myself for
your long waiting, and thank you yet again for your
patience."

"Oh, as for my patience! I so burned with impatience
to see you, and perhaps to pour out my heart to you on a
certain subject, dear and honoured lady, that I deserve
no praise in that I practised patience for impatience's
sake. Good conduct is often only the product or the
medium of passion; art, for instance, we might call the
high school of patience in impatience."

"Ah, how very pretty, my child! A charming *aperçu*.
I see that you add to your other talents no small aptitude
for metaphysics."

"I am a Weimarese," Adele repeated. "It is con-
tagious. It is not so wonderful, is it, when one speaks
French after ten years in Paris? And in our Muses' Circle
we are as much devoted to philosophy and criticism as
to poetry. Not only our poetry do we share with each
other; we also write and read essays, the result of research and analysis, the subject-matter of which is always the very latest thing in the realm of mind, as we
used to say. Nowadays we say culture. But the old Geheimrat would best hear nothing of these meetings."

"No? Why not?"

"There are several objections. In the first place he
has an aversion to blue-stockings; he is sarcastic on the
subject and we dread to have him laugh at activities so
dear to our hearts. One can certainly not say that the
great man is disinclined to our sex — that would be hard
to bear out. Of the *naturel* of women he has thought
and uttered the highest praise a man of his character could

ever have spoken: namely, that it is 'closely related to art.' What do we want more? And yet in his attitude to the feminine there is something overbearing, I might almost say coarse — a masculine prepossession that would deny us access to the lofty realms of poetry and intellect, and enjoys laughing at the things dearest to us. It may or may not be pertinent, but one day he saw some ladies picking flowers in a garden plot and he said they were like sentimental nanny-goats. Do you think that was good-natured?"

"Not precisely," answered Charlotte with a smile. "It makes me smile," she explained, "because in its malicious way there is something about it that hits the mark. But one ought not to be malicious, of course."

"It does hit the mark, just that," said Adele. "There is something deadly about such a remark. I cannot take a walk and bend down to take some of spring's children to my bosom without seeming to myself like a sentimental nanny-goat, and even when I write down a poem in my album, either by myself or somebody else, I feel the same."

"You should not take it so much to heart. But why else must Goethe not hear of your and your friends' æsthetic aspirations?"

"Dearest Frau Councillor, because of the first commandment."

"What do you mean?"

"The one that says: 'Thou shalt have no other gods before Me.' We are here, dearest lady, once more arrived at the subject of tyranny. Not a harsh tyranny, but a natural one, probably inseparable from a certain dominating greatness; one does well to condone and respect it, while not actually yielding to its behests. He is great, and old, and little inclined to value what comes after him. But life goes on, it does not stop even at the greatest, and we are children of the new life, we Muselines and Julemuses, a new stock, not at all sentimental nanny-goats. We are independent and progressive minds, with the courage of the new times and new tastes. Already we have found and love new gods: painters like the good Cornelius, and Overbeck — I have heard the master say he would like to fire a pistol at his pictures — and the heavenly David Caspar Friedrich, of whom Goethe says he might just as well look at his paintings upside down. 'It should not be allowed!' he thunders. Real Jovian thunder, of course; we in our Muses' Circle just let it rumble away — in all respect, of course, while we copy down Uhland's verses in our poetry note-books and enchant ourselves with reading aloud the splendid grotesque tales of Hoffmann."

"I do not know these authors," Charlotte said soberly. "You do not mean to say that with all their grotesquerie they can rival the works of the author of *Werther*?"

"They do not rival him," responded Adele, "and yet — forgive me — they surpass him; simply because they are farther on in time, because they represent a new stage, nearer to us, more familiar, more akin, have things to tell us that are closer to our hearts than we can get from a commanding and forbidding greatness towering up like some ancient granite boulder amid the new life of the time. I beg you not to think us irreverent. It is the time which is that, rejecting the old and bringing in the new.

Certainly, what comes after is a smaller growth. But it fits the time and the children of the time, the living and present; and with that we must deal, with an immediacy that leaves no room for reverence, but speaks to the hearts and nerves of those who are of it because it has brought them forth with itself."

Charlotte preserved for a moment a reserved silence.

"Your family, Fräulein," she said, after a little, abruptly and with a rather forced cordiality, "it comes, I hear, from Danzig?"

"Quite right, Frau Councillor. On the maternal side altogether, on the paternal in a way just as much. The grandfather of my deceased father was a business man who had settled in the Republic of Danzig; but the Schopenhauers are of Dutch origin, and my papa was an Englishman at heart, a great amateur of everything English and a perfect 'gentleman.' His country-house in Oliva was built and furnished entirely in the English style."

"Our family, I mean the Buffs," Charlotte remarked, "has had an English origin ascribed to it. I have not been able to find any evidence to that effect, though for obvious reasons I have gone into the family history and have collected some documents—especially since the death of my dear Hans Christian has given me time for genealogical research."

Adele's face was blank for a moment; she did not at once understand the "obvious" grounds for such research. Then she brightened and cried out:

"Ah, how splendid, how praiseworthy are these efforts of yours! You are preparing for a posterity in need of exact information about the origins and native surroundings of a woman of your election and your significance for the history of the human heart."

"Precisely that," said Charlotte, with dignity, "is my conception too. Or rather it is my experience, for I see that even today scholars are occupying themselves with research into my origins, and I feel it my duty to help all I can. In fact, I have succeeded in following my family back in all its branches beyond the Thirty Years' War. A postmaster, Simon Heinrich Buff, lived from 1580 to 1650 at Butzbach in the Wetterau. His son was a baker. But one of the baker's sons, named Heinrich, born in 1640, took to wife Petri, daughter of a clerk of the court, became a chaplain and in the course of time *pastor primarius* in Münzenberg. Since then the Buffs have most of them sat as clericals and *consistoriales* in provincial manses, at Crainfeld, Steinbach, Windhausen, Reichelsheim, Gladenbach, and Niederwöllstadt."

"That is important, that is invaluable, that is most interesting!" cried Adele, all in one breath.

"I assumed that it would interest you," Charlotte replied, "despite your penchant for the lesser literary *nouveautés*. In passing, I have also succeeded in setting right an error about myself which threatened to survive uncorrected. The 11th of January has always been fixed on as my birthday. Goethe accepted that date; he probably still does. But actually I was born on the 13th and baptized on the following day—as the Wetzlar parish register clearly shows. As sponsors are entered a Madame Bodenburg, born Weissenbruch, from Schiffenberg, a Felicitas Wetzel, born Buff, a half-sister of my father, and lastly a Demoiselle Feyler, my mother's sister."

"Everything must be done," Adele said, "and I myself will do my best, to spread the truth on this point.
Above all, the Privy Councillor himself should be enlightened; your visit here, dear Frau Councillor, affords
an excellent opportunity. But those precious achievements of your maiden hand, worked under his eyes in
those immortal days, the unfinished temple of Amor and
the rest—for heaven's sake what has become of these
sacred relics? We unfortunately digressed—"

"They still exist," answered Charlotte, "I have taken
care that these objects, in themselves quite insignificant,
should be preserved. I have charged my brother George
with the task—in my father's last days this son occupied
his official position, and he became his successor in the
house of the Teutonic Order. I have given these souvenirs into George's keeping: the temple, one or two gar-
landed mottoes, some little embroidered purses, the
sketch-book, and other such trifles. We must realize that
they may have a museum value in the future, like the
house itself, the living-room on the ground floor, where
we so often sat with *him*, and the corner room upstairs
on the street side. We called it the Good Room; the wall-
paper had pictures of the gods and there was an old clock
on the wall with a landscape in the dial. How often
he listened with us to its tick-tock and striking the
hour! This Good Room, to my mind, would be more
proper than the living-room for a museum, and if I had
my way all the souvenirs should be collected there,
under glass."

"Posterity," asserted Adele, "the whole of posterity,

not only the fatherland but the reverent pilgrim as well, will be grateful for your forethought."

"I hope so," Charlotte said.

The conversation halted. The visitor's culture seemed to be running dry. She gazed on the floor, moving the tip of her parasol to and fro. Charlotte awaited her adieux, though not wishing for them so much as one might have thought, considering her situation. Indeed, she was better pleased when the young girl began to speak again, as volubly as ever.

"Dearest Frau Councillor — or may I say honoured friend? — my soul is full of self-reproaches; the most oppressive of them is for having accepted all too unscrupulously the gift of your time. But almost as much so is the knowledge that I am using this gift so ill. I am guilty of wasting a great opportunity. You know the legend, where a man has three wishes, and three times wishes something quite silly and trifling, without thinking of what he really most desires. I prattle on, in seeming carelessness, about this and that, about anything but the subject closest to my heart. Yet that it is — let me confess at last — has driven me to you, because I pray for and count on your aid and advice. You must be astonished, even annoyed, that I take up your time chattering about trifling subjects like our Muses' Circle. I would never have mentioned it if it were not linked with the trouble and anxiety I so unspeakably long to pour out to you."

"What sort of trouble and anxiety is it, my child? What does it concern?"

"A dear human soul, Frau Councillor, a beloved

friend, my only one, my treasure, the finest and noblest of creatures. She is deserving of happiness; but she is entangled in the meshes of a fatal destiny — a quite unnecessary, yet apparently quite inevitable fate. It is driving me to despair. In a word, I am speaking of Tillemuse."

"Tillemuse?"

"Pardon me, that is my darling's name in our circle. I spoke of it before; it is the name of my Ottilie, Ottilie von Pogwisch."

"Ah! And what unhappy fate is it threatens Fräulein von Pogwisch?"

"She is about to be married."

"And pray tell me — if I may ask — to whom?"

"To Herr Kammerrat von Goethe."

"You do not tell me! To August?"

"Yes, to the son of the great man and the Mamsell. — The decease of the Frau Privy Councillor makes possible a union that in her lifetime was wrecked on the opposition of Ottilie's family and of society in general."

"And wherein do you see the ill consequences of such a union?"

"Let me inform you," Adele begged. "Let me solace my anxious heart by confiding in you; let me implore your interest for a dear and endangered creature — who would be angry with me if she knew of my intercession, richly as she deserves and needs it."

And with that the Demoiselle Schopenhauer began her revelations, rolling up her eyes to the ceiling to disguise their squinting, while as she talked the moisture gathered in the corners of her large and eloquent mouth.

CHAPTER FIVE

"On her father's side my Ottilie comes of a Holstein-
Prussian military family. Her mother was a Henckel
von Donnersmark, and the marriage with Herr von
Pogwisch was a love match, in which unhappily reason
played too small a part. At least, that was the view of
Ottilie's grandmother, a noblewoman of the real old
eighteenth-century kind. She had a downright, ruthless,
objective understanding, and was intellectual in a rough-
and-ready, caustic style, which abhorred all pretence.
She had no patience with her daughter's surrender to a
feeling as ill-advised as it was romantic and beautiful.
Herr von Pogwisch was poor, and so was that branch
of the Henckel family; that may have been the reason
why the Countess, two years after the Battle of Jena,
went into court service at Weimar and became Mistress
of the Robes to our new Princess Royal from the eastern
provinces. The Countess sought a similar post for her
daughter, and had good prospects of success. At the
same time she bent all her efforts towards the dissolution
of a union whose happiness bade fair to be choked in
ever increasing material calamities. The small pay of
the Prussian officer of that time made a proper standard
of living impossible; the effort to sustain it even toler-

ably led to constant debt and insecurity. In short, the difficulties of the wedded pair finally brought about the triumph of the mother's wishes. There was a separation, a parting by common consent, though at first without judicial action.

"No one knows the state of the father's heart at leaving behind, in the charge of the partner of his adversity, their two charming little daughters, Ottilie and her younger sister Ulrike. He may have been nerved to the painful resolve by a fear of having to abandon his beloved and hereditary military calling. His wife's heart bled; it is probably not too much to say that she never knew a happy hour after that capitulation to necessity and the pressure of her indomitable mother. As for the daughters, their father's handsome knightly figure was indelibly printed on their hearts — particularly on the deeper and more romantic nature of the elder. Ottilie's whole emotional life, her attitude towards public affairs and the problems of the age, were entirely conditioned, as you will see, by her memory of the parent she had lost.

"After the separation Frau von Pogwisch spent some years with her daughters in retirement at Dessau. She lived there through the days of shame and disgrace, the wreck of Frederick the Great's army, the ruin of the fatherland, and the inclusion of the western and southern states of Germany in the frightful Corsican's power system. In the year 1809 the old Countess was able to redeem her promise to get her daughter a court position; and the latter moved to Weimar in the quality of lady-in-waiting to the Duchess Louise.

"Ottilie was then thirteen years old, a child of the loveliest and most original gifts. She unfolded in an atmosphere of tension and irregularity; for the service of princes is not compatible with domestic tranquillity. The mother was preoccupied, the child left much to herself. She lodged at first in an upper storey of the Schloss, and afterwards with her grandmother. She spent her time by turns with her mother and with the old Countess, in having all sorts of lessons, and in company with friends — among whom, though a little older, I came to belong. Often she took her meals at the house of Oberkammerherr von Egloffstein, with whose daughters I was on a most friendly footing; and there it was we formed ourselves into a band of chosen spirits. Among us, it seemed, age was not reckoned by years, so full they were of stimulation to rapid growth; during them we turned from fledglings to mature human beings. My love for Ottilie makes it easy for me to acknowledge that her original character and precociously developed ideas made her in a way the leading spirit of our group.

"This was especially true in the field of politics. Such things are of less moment today, to the individual and to society, now that our world has more or less returned to a stable state after the trials and shocks it underwent at the hands of the monster and man of destiny. We are now protected by the forces of the sacred order of things — all the rest has retreated into the background, in the general as well as in the individual mind, leaving more room for purely human concerns. But then politics dominated almost exclusively the intellectual scene. And to politics Ottilie was passionately devoted, in a sense and spirit sharply differentiating her from her environment. Yet she might not breathe a word, save to me, her most intimate friend, of her secretly hostile attitude. Me she could imbue with all her own ideas and emotions, and draw me with her into the world of her beliefs and hopes, where we revelled in all the joys of secrecy.

"What secrets were these? We lived at the very heart of the Rhenish Alliance. Our Duke had been pardoned by the Corsican monster, and ruled as Napoleon's loyal ally. Everywhere there reigned unshaken faith in the genius of the conqueror and his mission as bringer of a new world-order, as the organizer of the Continent. We were, if not enthusiastic, yet inured to resignation. And yet, in this environment, my Ottilie was a fanatical Prussian. Undaunted by the defeat of the Prussian arms, she was permeated by a belief in the superiority of the northern stock over the Saxons and Thuringians. Among these she was, as she put it, condemned to live; and to them she dedicated a contempt the stronger for enforced concealment. In me she confided. This dear child's heroic soul was dominated by a single ideal: the Prussian officer. Needless to say, this cult-image bore more or less clearly the traits glorified by the memory of her lost father. Though more general sympathies were in play as well, the aptitudes of her race and blood. These opened her ear to distant events while the rest of us were still unaware; she alone was in touch, she alone alertly hearkened, in a way that to me seemed prophetic and was soon to show itself so in sober fact.

"You can easily guess what events I mean: the moral

reawakening and revival following on the collapse in the land of her origins; the resolute scorn, rejection, and extirpation of every tendency, no matter how charming or refined, suspected of having contributed to the downfall. There was a heroic purification of the body politic from all the tinsel and trumpery of such customs and ideas; a steeling of it for the unique and glorious day which should bring in the rebirth of freedom and the destruction of the foreign tyranny. There was a conscious acceptance of fate's decrees; an acceptance of poverty, involving the other monastic virtues of chastity and obedience; involving renunciation, sacrifice, universal discipline, a life regimented by devotion to the fatherland.

"All this, then, was quietly going forward; the conqueror knew as little of it as of the accompanying rehabilitation of the army. And our little world knew nothing at all. It had attached itself to the triumphal car, it acquiesced in the prevalent mood — without much distress, even with some conviction, though groaning at times over the burdens and compulsions laid upon it by the victor. In our circle, only Ottilie — secretly, of course, but with fanatical devotion — was in touch. True, here and there teachers and men of the learned professions, belonging to the younger generation, attached themselves eagerly to the movement; with these Ottilie was soon in contact, and a lively exchange of ideas went on. In Jena, for instance, there was the history professor, Heinrich Luden, an excellent man, imbued with the loftiest patriotic feelings. All his property and scientific

equipment had been destroyed in the day of our downfall and disgrace — he and his young wife returned to an
utterly devastated and unmentionably filthy house. But
he was not crushed. He declared that he would joyfully
have borne every loss; that if only we had won he would
have stood up stripped and beggared to exult after the
retreating foe. He kept his faith in the fatherland's cause,
and he knew how to inspire his students by the fire of
his words. Then further there was Professor Passow in
Weimar; a Mecklenburger, broad and strong of speech,
a man of great learning, who dwelt in the loftiest realms
of thought. He was enthusiastic for freedom and fatherland. He taught Greek (my brother Arthur had private
coaching from him at one time), æsthetics, and the philosophy of language; but his method was novel and peculiar to himself: by his instruction he sought to build
a bridge between knowledge and life, between classical
antiquity and the attitude of a bourgeois in a free German fatherland. In other words, he aimed to present the
significance and practical application of Hellenism for
the politics of the present day.

"With such men as these, then, Ottilie kept secretly
in touch, I might almost say she maintained an intrigue.
At the same time she led the life of an elegant member
of our francophile high society. I had the private impression that she revelled in this double life. And as her
friend and confidante I shared in its romantic charm and
the equivocal fascination it purveyed; it is my conviction that such feelings as these played an important and
regrettable part in the romance in which for the last four

years I have seen my darling involved — a romance cost-
ing me such unspeakable chagrin that I would give my
life to free her from its toils.

"It was early in the year of the Russian campaign that
August von Goethe began to pay court to Ottilie. He
had come back the year before from Heidelberg and
entered almost at once into the service of court and State.
He was a gentleman-in-waiting, and acting assessor of
the ducal Kammer-Collegium. But his activities in this
office were limited by the tact of His Serene Highness
to such as he could perform compatibly with his work
for his august father. Goethe had to be relieved of all
sorts of daily cares and petty domestic details; not only
these, but August had to represent him at formal func-
tions and even on journeys of inspection to Jena. Also
he acted as his father's secretary and keeper of his collections, especially after Dr. Riemer left, as he did about
this time, to marry the Demoiselle Ulrich, who had been
companion to the Frau Privy Councillor.

"Young August undertook all these obligations and
performed them with meticulous care. In particular he
dealt with the domestic problems in a pedantically cal-
culating spirit, which indeed was characteristic of him;
for the moment I will call it a sort of jejuneness, though
so pronounced and indefatigable as to be almost more
than that. I am in no haste to enter upon the mysteries
of his character — I shrink from doing so out of feelings
which are a mixture of pity and repugnance. I was not,
nor am I now, the only one to be thus impressed by the
young man. Riemer, for instance, told me himself that
he felt actual fear of him; indeed, his resolve to set up

his own establishment was hastened by the return of the one-time pupil to the parental roof.

"Ottilie by that time had begun to go to court, and it may well be that August first made her acquaintance there. They also met, very likely, in the Frauenplan, at the Sunday concerts given during some years by the Privy Councillor and at the rehearsals before the performances. For my friend possesses among her other gifts and attractions a charming voice; she was a member of the choir which practised once a week at Goethe's house and sang on Sunday afternoons during dinner and afterwards before the guests.

"This gave her the privilege of personal contact with the great poet; and he seems to have had his eye on her from the first. He liked to talk and jest with her, and by no means concealed his penchant for the 'little person,' as he called her. I have made as yet no attempt to paint you a picture of her charms — how could I, indeed, in words? And yet the exceptional character of this girlish charm needs to be emphasized, it is important and significant. A speaking blue eye, abundant brown hair, a rather small figure, anything but Junoesque, instead quite light and dainty and appealing — in short, it is the type which always had the good fortune to flatter a certain personal taste. It has conferred upon its possessors the highest honours in the realm of feeling and poetry. I will say no more. At most I will remind you that there was once a most lovely if worldly variation of this type, and there was actually a betrothal. It had no sequel; but it is said to have caused acute annoyance to the guardians of the established social order.

"Well, now, the son of that would-be bridegroom of yore began to be interested in the lovely Ottilie: the extra-marital scion of a very recent ennoblement, in a von Pogwisch-Henckel-Donnersmarck. And the conservative aristocracy of Weimar felt very much as their class in Frankfurt had felt before them. They could hardly say so. The case was so exceptional, the recent ennoblement so very imposing that its pretensions could scarcely be brushed aside. It might well feel a conscious satisfaction in asserting its claims on a son's behalf. I am here expressing only my own personal opinion; but it rests on painstaking observation and is not likely to deceive me. I feel sure that the father was the first to be interested in Ottilie, and that the interest he displayed was what drew the attention of the son. It rapidly developed into a passion — and the passion displayed the father's taste. In fact, August displays the father's taste in more respects than one — if one can speak of tastes, for in sober truth the son appears to have no tastes at all, being wholly dependent upon the father's pattern, particularly in his relations with the sex. But of that later on — and even then early enough, in all conscience! Let me rather speak of Ottilie.

"At the time of the dear creature's first meeting with Herr von Goethe, her state of mind might be characterized by a single word. It was expectant. Even at a tender age she had had suitors; she was much courted, and showed herself at times coy, at others playfully receptive. Her heart, as it were, was swept and garnished to receive the all-compelling god; and now, in the feelings inspired in her by her strange, anomalous, aristocratic wooer, she thought to recognize the divine presence. Her reverence for the great poet was naturally most profound. The favour he showed her immensely flattered her; what wonder that when the son came wooing, with the father's definite sanction and as it were in his name, she found him irresistible? It was almost as though the father himself, his youth renewed, sued for her hand in the guise of his son. Young Goethe loved her, and she — she scarce hesitated, she saw in him the awakener of her dreams, her man of destiny. She doubted not that she loved him in return.

"And she was, I think, the more convinced of her destiny by the very strangeness of the form it assumed. She knew that love is capricious, an irresponsible, sovereign power, liking nothing better than to play tricks on the reason and assert its dominion over judgment and understanding. She had imagined quite otherwise the man of her choice; she had thought of him as created more after her own likeness, more light-hearted and high-spirited, with a gayer nature than August's. It seemed to her a romantic confirmation of the genuineness of her feeling that he so little corresponded to her preconceived ideas. August had been no very agreeable child or unusually promising youth. No one had expected him to survive. As for his mental parts, the impression was general among the friends of the house that they showed no great promise. Then he had outgrown the slight weediness of his boyhood and settled into a good, stout, sturdy figure of a youth: a little heavy and gloomy, a little dull. I am thinking of his eyes when I use that adjective — they might have been fine if their

look had possessed more direction or concentration. I
am speaking in the past tense, trying to see him at a distance and judge him objectively. But all I have been
saying is true of the man of twenty-seven, even more
than of the youth he was when Ottilie first met him.
He was not socially agreeable or animated. His mind
seemed hampered by reluctance to use it; by a melancholy better described as hopelessness, that spread a
sort of desolation where he went. This lack of cheer-
fulness, this dumb resignation, had its source in his
position as a son, to his fear of the imminent, unnerving comparison with his father. All that was plain to
any eye.

"To be the son of a great man is a high fortune, a
considerable advantage. But it is likewise an oppressive
burden, a permanent derogation of one's own ego. —
When August was a boy, his father had given him an
album. In the course of years it filled up with names
and sentiments inscribed by all sorts of celebrities, German and foreign, here in Weimar and in the places they
visited together — Halle and Jena, Helmstädt, Pyrmont
and Karlsbad. Hardly one but emphasized a quality of
the youth most impersonal to him but foremost in the
minds of everybody else: his quality as a son. It might
be inspiring — but at the same time it was embarrassing —
to a young mind, to have Professor Fichte, the philosopher, set down: 'The nation makes great demands upon
you, unique son of the unique man of our time.' And
how can one tell the effect of the pithy sentence inscribed by a French official: 'Seldom do the sons of a
great man count for much to posterity'? Should he

take it as a challenge to become the exception? Even that would be bound to weigh upon his spirit; while the alternative, though less far-fetched, was in the sense of the inscription Dante placed above the entrance to his Inferno.

"August seemed sourly bent on forbidding the fatal comparison to be so much as raised. He brusquely and explicitly — almost bitterly — disclaimed any poetic ambitions or any connection with the world of the intellect. He deliberately sought to pass for nothing but a practical everyday person, a sober, materialistic man of business, of no more than average understanding. One might see much to praise and respect in this resolute protest, this renunciation of higher things — as though, even if they were present in him in the germ, he must deny and repress them, in order at all costs to prevent the deadly parallel from being drawn. But his self-distrust, his discontent and moodiness, his suspicions and irritability, were not calculated to win people to him; at the same time one could not think of him as actuated by pride. The truth was, he was sick with broken pride. He had reached his station in life with the aid of all the easements afforded, or rather forced upon him, by his origins. He had submitted to them unwillingly, yet without being able to prevent them from gnawing away his manhood and self-respect. His education had been sporadic, irregular, and undisciplined. The offices he held had fallen to him without his needing to prove his fitness; he was quite aware that he owed them to nepotism, not to his own capacity. Another man might have accepted complacently such advantages; he was so made

that he suffered under them. That was honourable — yet
at the same time he did accept them.

"There is something else we must remember: August
was not only his father's but his mother's son. A dilemma
and a conflict were inevitably created — as regards both
his own self-respect and his position in the world. There
was a conflict between two kinds of rank: on the one
hand he was noble, on the other irregular. True, the
Duke, at the instance of his great friend, had conferred
upon the eleven-year-old lad a decree of legitimization
propter natales, with the title of nobility attached. It
made no difference at all, nor did the parents' marriage,
six years later. He was a 'love-child'; that was firmly
fixed in everybody's head — in August's too, no doubt,
as firmly as the phrase 'the unique son.' Once there had
been something of a scandal, when he appeared at a ball
in honour of the Duchess's birthday, in all the attractive-
ness of his thirteen years, in the character of Amor, and
presented the exalted lady with flowers and verses. 'A
love-child,' people said, 'should not have appeared as
Amor among respectable people.' Did the reproach reach
his ears? We do not know. But such obstacles he must
have encountered often in later life. His position was
cloaked by his father's fame and authority and the favour
of the Duke; but it remained equivocal even so. He had
friends — or what one calls friends — at school, in his
office and through his service at court. He was too reserved, too mistrustful, too conscious of his own special
position in both directions. His society had always been
mixed; what came to him through his mother was a little
bohemian: many theatre folk, many carousing young

people — and he himself, at an incredibly early age, was inclined to drink. Our dear Baroness von Stein told me that once in a jolly group of his mother's friends the eleven-year-old lad had drunk not less than seventeen glasses of champagne; she herself, she said, had difficulty, when he visited her, in restraining him from taking too much. It was, she thought — however strange it was to say so of a child — an impulse to drown his sorrow! On that one occasion it had been a quite definite sorrow; for he had received the shock of having his father weep at sight of him. That was the time of the master's serious illness in 1800, when whooping-cough and varioloid together brought him to the brink of the grave. Painfully convalescing, he wept much out of weakness; but especially whenever he saw the lad — and then August found it did him good to drink his seventeen glasses. The father would not have had much to say against it, for his relation to the divine gift of the vine had always been one of blithe and grateful acceptance, and he had probably made his son free of the same at an early age. The rest of us, however, could not help ascribing many of August's defects, his wild, morose, unmannerly, and irritable traits, to his early and regrettably increasing inclinations to the joys of Bacchus.

"In this young man, then, who paid her his not exactly attractive, not exactly engrossing attentions, Ottilie thought she saw the embodiment of her destiny. She thought she returned his love — however improbable, or just because it was improbable, as I said before. Her own nobility of soul, her poetic sense of the tragic and pathetic side of his life, strengthened her belief. She dreamed of herself as his good angel, the exorcist of his evil spirit. I spoke of the romantic charm she discovered in her double life as Weimar lady-in-waiting and secret Prussian patriot. Her love for August made her savour this charm in a new and concentrated form; for the contradictions between her own opinions and those prevailing in the home of her suitor heightened the paradoxical nature of her love-affair and made it seem more like one than it really was.

"I cannot say that our intellectual hero, the pride of Germany, the glorious pinnacle of our national renown, had ever shared either the sorrow of its noble hearts over the downfall of the fatherland or the enthusiasm that almost burst our souls as the hour of liberation approached. I cannot but say that he held himself coldly aloof from such emotions and, so to speak, left us in the lurch in face of the foe. What had to be had to be. We had to suffer and forget, to allow our feelings to be submerged in the admiration we had for his genius and the love we cherished for his great personality. The disaster of Jena had brought with it serious inconvenience, not alone at the hands of the victorious French soldiery but even before the battle from the Prussians billeted in Weimar: they broke into his garden house and smashed up doors and furniture to kindle their fires. In all that followed he certainly bore his share. They say the visitation cost him fully two thousand thaler, not to mention twelve casks of wine; and the *marodeurs* molested him even in his sleeping-chamber. But he was not plundered, for a guard was early stationed before his house, and he had marshals lodging with him: Ney, Augereau,

Lannes, and finally even Monsieur Denon, well known to him from Venetian days, now Inspector General of the Imperial Museums and Napoleon's art-adviser in the appropriation of works of art in the conquered countries.

"To have this man quartered on him was very pleasant for the master; and he afterwards seemed to wish to give the idea that he was but little affected by the whole affair. Professor Luden — who had suffered so much — told me that four weeks after the sack of the city he had met the master at Knebel's. The catastrophe was mentioned, and Herr von Knebel burst out several times: 'Horrible! Monstrous!' Goethe muttered some unintelligible words; and when Luden inquired how His Excellency had fared during the days of shame and disaster, the other replied: 'I have nothing to complain of. "As a man from a firm cliff looks down upon the raging sea and can bring the shipwrecked no help, while he himself cannot be reached by the raging surf" — that, according to one of the classic authors, can be even a pleasant feeling —' Here he paused, trying to recall the name of the author. Luden, who of course knew the quotation, refrained from helping him out; but Knebel, despite his earlier outburst of feeling, supplied the name, Lucretius. 'Yes, yes, Lucretius,' the master said, and added: 'Thus I stood calmly and let the raging storm pass over my head.' Luden said he felt an icy shiver through him as he heard the words, spoken as they were with a certain satisfaction. He felt the same shuddering several times; for when he made some further tremulous remarks about the fatherland's distress and shame, and his religious faith that it would rise again out of its ashes,

Knebel repeatedly cried out: 'Bravo!' but Goethe gave
not a sign. Knebel, then, after his 'Bravo's!' changed
the subject and talked of literary matters, and Luden
soon afterwards took his leave.

"Such was the excellent Luden's report. But with
my own ears, in my own mother's salon, I heard the master take our Dr. Passow, the schoolmaster, to task for
his opinions. I was a very young girl, but I felt resent-
ful. Passow spoke eloquently of the ardent faith, on
which his whole soul leaned, that by revealing Hellenic
antiquity, by developing the Greek spirit in the bosoms
at least of individuals, there might be reimplanted the
love of freedom and fatherland which Germany as a
whole had so shamefully lost. Let me point out in passing that such men as Passow opened their hearts to
Goethe without suspicion or reserve, because they could
not even faintly imagine how anybody could object
to ideas they found so desirable and so sound. It took
long for them to perceive that the great man disagreed
with them utterly and they must not talk before him.
'Listen to me!' said he on this occasion. 'I flatter myself that I too know something of the classic authors. But
the love of freedom and the fatherland which you think
to deduce from them is always in danger, always on
the point of becoming absurd.' I shall never forget the
icy bitterness of that last word — it is always the cruellest
condemnation he can utter. 'Our civic life,' he went
on, 'is very different from that of the ancients, our relation to the State is quite other than theirs. The German,
instead of confining himself to himself, must take in the
whole world in order to have an effect on the world. Our

goal must be, not hostile separation from other peoples, but rather friendly association with all the world, cultivation of the social virtues, even at the expense of our inborn feelings or even rights.' This last he uttered with his voice raised commandingly and tapping with his forefinger on the table before him. He added: 'To resist a superior, to oppose a conqueror just because we have Greek and Latin in our bones and he knows nothing of them, is childish and in poor taste. That is academic pride; it makes a man absurd, and injures him in proportion.' Here he paused, and turning towards young Passow, who sat there quite abashed, he finished in a more friendly yet a serious tone: 'Nothing is less my wish, Herr Doctor, than to hurt your feelings. I know you mean well. But it is not enough to mean well, or even nobly. One must also be able to see the consequences of one's activities. I shudder at yours, because they are the first manifestation, as yet quite high-minded and harmless, of something frightful, to be displayed some day by us Germans in the form of the crassest follies. You yourself, if you could know of them, would turn in your grave.'

"Imagine the universal bewilderment, the wave of horror that swept the room! My mama found it difficult to set going a harmless conversation. But so it was: at the time he behaved like that; he wounded by his words and his silences our sacredest feelings. We must probably lay it all to his admiration for the Emperor Napoleon, who distinguished him so markedly at Erfurt in 1808 and conferred on him the Legion of Honour. Our great poet always expressly referred to it as his most precious decoration. He saw in the Emperor the Jupiter, the world-regulating head; the new German states and the inclusion of the southern, old, and genuinely German regions in the Rhenish Alliance seemed to him a fresh and hopeful structure, promising for the growth and purification of German intellectual life in fruitful association with the French culture to which he always said he owed so much. You remember that Napoleon urged him, nay, summoned him, to remove to Paris. For a long time Goethe seriously entertained the idea, and made various practical inquiries. After Erfurt there was further personal contact between him and the Emperor; the conqueror treated him as an equal, and the master may have felt that he had nothing to fear from him, in his intellectual kingdom or as a German; that Napoleon's genius was not antagonistic to his own, however much ground the rest of the world had for trembling.

"Perhaps you will call that an egoistic security and friendliness. But in the first place, we must admit that the egoism of such a man is not a private affair, but justified of its results to the world at large. And in the second place, did he really stand alone in his opinions and convictions? By no means. For instance, His Excellency Minister von Voigt, our Chief of Cabinet, maintained that Napoleon would soon have laid his last enemy by the heels; however heavy the burden now, after that had happened a united Europe was sure to find peace beneath his sway. More than once I have heard him say that, in company. And I still remember how he condemned the risings in Prussia in 1813: they were trying, he said, to turn it into another Spain, *invito rege*. 'The good King!'

he cried. 'How one pities him — and how he will suffer for it, however innocent himself! The rest of us will need all our prudence and cleverness to remain calm, non-partisan, and loyal to the Emperor, if we do not want to be destroyed ourselves.'— Thus the shrewd and conscientious statesman who still governs us today. And His Highness the Duke himself? Even after Moscow, when the Emperor so swiftly raised new forces and our Prince rode out with him towards the Elbe, whither he was riding to defeat the Prussians and Russians (they having, contrary to expectation, combined against him, when shortly before we had thought nothing else than that the Prussian King would march with the Emperor against the barbarians), even then Karl August came back from that ride full of enthusiasm, quite beside himself with admiration for 'that truly extraordinary being,' as he called him. He seemed to the Duke like a Mohammed, like a man 'filled with God.'

"But after Lützen came Leipsic, and no more was heard about being 'filled with God.' No more enthusiasm for the hero; it was all, like Passow's, devoted to freedom and fatherland. I must say I find it amazing how quickly and easily men change their views, when the course of events and the misfortune of a man they had believed in give them better instruction! Even stranger and more difficult to grasp is the sight of a great and pre-eminent man put in the wrong by the event, while many much smaller and more modest folk turn out to have known better than he did. Goethe had always said: 'Rattle your chains all you like, you good people, the man will always be too big for you!' Lo and behold, the chains fell off, the Duke put on Russian uniform, we drove Napoleon across the Rhine, and the men the master had so condescendingly called 'You good people,' the Ludens and Passows, stood up against him as victors and upholders of the righteous cause. Anno 13, that was the year of Luden's triumph over Goethe — one cannot express it otherwise. And he admitted it, in shame and regret, and wrote his Berlin Festspiel, *Epimenides*, where the lines occur:

> 'I blush for all my hours of leisure,
>   With you to suffer had been gain;
> Since by that suffering your measure
>   Of greatness over mine is plain.'

And again:

> 'What from the pit so boldly mounted
>   By iron foredoom and edict stern
> With half a globe o'errun and daunted
>   Must to the pit again return.'

You see? He sends back to the pit his Emperor and peer, the ruler of the world — at least he does so in a play, for privately, I believe, he still says: 'You dear good people.'

"Well, his son, August, Ottilie's suitor, copied his father's political attitude to the life, he was nothing at all but the father's echo. He was entirely for the Rhenish Alliance, seeing in it a unification of the cultural elements of Germany, and had nothing but scorn for the northern and eastern barbarians. Such views became him less than they did the elder Goethe. For he had in his nature more than a trace of the barbaric, I mean of the extravagant and crude, mingled with a melancholy that

was not subtle but only morose. In 1811 the Emperor
sent an ambassador to Weimar, a certain Baron de Saint-
Aignan. He was a charming man, a humanist, and a great
admirer of Goethe. The two were soon on the most
cordial terms. August, for his part, had nothing better
to do than to adopt as his friend the Baron's secretary,
Herr von Wolbock. I mention him in the first place
to show you in what quarters the young man sought his
friends; and in the second because when Napoleon, on
his return from Moscow, passed through Erfurt, on De-
cember 12th, it was this Herr von Wolbock who conveyed the Emperor's greetings to Goethe. August too
was gratified by the occurrence, for he practised what
amounted to a cult for the person of the tyrant—no
very becoming one, in my view, for it had no intellectual
justification. Even today he keeps a collection of portraits and relics; the father contributed to it his Cross of
the Legion of Honour, when the time came that he could
no longer wear it.

"Seldom indeed, one may say, have the bonds of love
united two hearts of more unequal beat. August worshipped Ottilie as he worshipped Napoleon—I cannot
avoid the comparison, however odd it sounds. And my
poor darling—as I saw with horror and misgiving—listened with tenderness to his clumsy wooing, convinced of
the power of the almighty god of love, who triumphs with
a laugh over opinions and ideas. It was harder for her
than for him, who might openly avow his convictions,
while hers she had to hide. But what she called her love,
her sentimental, inconsistent feeling for the son of the
great poet, she did not hide, nor did she need to, in our

little world where feeling and the cult of feeling are tenderly cherished and always strike a sympathetic chord. As for myself, I was her anxious confidante, faithfully accompanying her through the stages and episodes of her romance. But also to her mother she was able to unbosom herself, the more openly since Frau von Pogwisch herself had been for some time in a similar case, and met her child's confidences as woman to woman. She had an affair with the handsome Count Edling, from South Germany, now court marshal and Minister of State. He was her daughters' guardian and jestingly spoke of himself as their adopted father. He was on the most intimate footing in Frau von Pogwisch's house, a friend of the family, who might one day be even more. Her hopes were not without foundation, but the actual proposal hung fire. Thus Amor gave mother and daughter abundant matter for mutual confidence, when they discussed the daily hopes and fears, the raptures and despairs of their common state.

"August and Ottilie met at court, at the theatre, at his father's house, and at many other social gatherings. But in addition the lovers met privately, in the grounds of the two garden houses on the Ilm, the one belonging to Goethe, the other to Ottilie's grandmother. Here they found a safe and secluded rendezvous. I was always by my darling's side on these occasions, and could only marvel at the blissful sighs she breathed at parting, the blushing embraces she showered on me in thanks for my assistance. I cannot believe it was solely my ungrateful rôle as third party and chaperon that made me find the meeting so unprofitable, the talk so forced and barren.

It revolved, heavily and with many halts, about the last cotillion, the latest court gossip, a journey taken or about to be taken. Its nearest approach to liveliness came when the young man spoke of his service to his father. But Ottilie would not admit embarrassment or boredom. She behaved as though in these arid sessions and strolls she had discovered her soul. Certainly she told her mother that such was the case — presumably receiving in exchange the news that all signs pointed to a speedy declaration from the Count.

"Thus things stood when a certain event occurred in the dear child's life. I cannot speak of it without vibrating in sympathy; for in that experience was summed up for us both all the beauty and greatness of the time, endowed with personal meaning.

"The year 1813 dawned. As I have said, we got but few, faint echoes of the glorious events in Prussia, the patriotic rising, the triumph of the new idea over the King's hesitations, the establishment of the volunteer corps, to which the best youth of the land resorted in throngs, ready to renounce all comforts and culture, panting to risk their lives for the fatherland. Yet there always subsisted a sensitive connection between my friend's soul and the sphere of her lost father. I have already mentioned it; it may be that it was sustained by definite information reaching her through her Prussian relatives. Her lovely form thrilled; she glowed from her contact with coming events. Living in our idyllic midst, she had long desired and long foreseen them. She felt by blood and spirit akin to the heroic folk now rising to shake off the chains of foreign tyranny. Her whole being dissolved in enthusiasm. And just as her people, by its example, was kindling all Germany to take part in the struggle for freedom and honour, so she carried me away with her and made me wholly a partisan of her hatreds and her burning hopes. In neither of these emotions did she stand so much alone as formerly in our city. The fatherland conspiracy was alight here already, under cover of loyalty to Napoleon and the Rhenish Alliance. Young noblemen like Chamberlain von Spiegel and Councillor von Voigt had a hazardous secret understanding with the Prussians in Jena to keep them informed of events in Weimar. Ottilie had soon got in touch with them, she shared their passions and their secrets. She played with her life. Then, half to hold her back, half out of genuine feeling, I became her fellow in these political secrets as I was in those of her maiden heart and her meetings with August von Goethe. I know not which of them gave me more concern.

"On the military side, of course, things did not look rosy at first. True, Ottilie soon had the joy of seeing Prussian uniforms in Weimar. At the middle of April, the 16th, I remember as well as though it were today, a division of hussars and rifles executed a *coup de main* on our city. They seized the few French soldiers quartered here and took them along as prisoners when they withdrew. On hearing the news Imperial cavalry came over from Erfurt. They found no Prussians in the city and went back again — too soon, it seemed; for the next morning — imagine my Ottilie's rapture — some of young Blücher's troops, together with more hussars and some green rifles, rode into the city and were received with acclaim by the populace. There was a dancing and carousing, a reckless rejoicing, that made the judicious grieve and reaped its reward in a few hours. The word went round: 'The Frenchmen are coming!' Our deliverers rushed from the revel to arms. General Souhon's troops, in overwhelming strength, forced their way into the town, and after a brief struggle the French were once more masters of the place. We sat in our chambers trembling for the lives of the heroes we had but now feasted and wined. We peered through the curtains at the tumult in the streets, we heard crashing gun-fire and the braying of horns. The fighting soon passed from the streets to the park and presently beyond the city limits. The enemy, alas, won his accustomed victory. And actually, against our wills, it seemed to us like a triumph of order over rebellion — a childish and foolish rebellion, as the event had proved.

"Order and quiet are good — no matter to what one owes them. We had to provide for the billeting of the French troops, and the town was straightway burdened to the utmost limit of its capacity. Not only heavy but long was the burden laid upon it. Still, there was peace; the streets were open till sundown, and the citizen might go about his business, under the oppressive protection of the victors.

"Led by some mysterious intuition, Ottilie fetched me next day soon after dinner to take a walk with her. The night had been rainy, and the April day allured us with its fresh and tender air, sun-drenched and full of promises of spring. Our curiosity emboldened us to walk in the streets but yesterday the scene of horrid conflict. We shuddered to see its traces, the bullet-marks on the

houses, the blood-splashed walls. And with our shuddering mingled the admiration felt by the weaker sex for
the prowess of the stronger one.

"We came from the castle and the market square to
the Ackerwand; then, in search of greener, more open
spaces, struck out in the direction of the Ilm. Once
there, we walked by field-paths and overgrown ways
near its shore, past the 'Borkenhaus' towards the 'Roman house.' Trampled ground, a weapon or piece of
accoutrement here and there betrayed that the fighting,
the flight and pursuit had reached this point. We talked
of what had happened and what was to come; of the expected occupation of Saxon cities by the easterners; of
Weimar, precariously placed between the Imperial
stronghold at Erfurt and the oncoming Prussians and
Russians; of the awkward situation of His Highness the
Duke, and of the departure of the Grand Duke for neutral Bohemia and some of the French legates to Gotha.
We spoke of August too, I recall, and of his father, who
had yielded to family pressure and left the threatened
city. Early on the previous day, just before the Blücher
raid, he had gone off in his carriage to Karlsbad. He must
have met them on the road.

"To venture farther seemed unsafe, and we were
about to turn back when a loud sound, half groan, half
cry, struck into our talk and rooted us to the ground.
We started, we stood listening. Again the groaning cry
came, from the bushes beside our path. Ottilie had seized
my hand in alarm; now she dropped it, and together,
with throbbing hearts, we broke a path through the
budding undergrowth, calling out as we went: 'Is any-

one there?' And there in the wood, in the wet grass,
lay the handsomest of youths—a wounded soldier, one
of the heroes who had been driven out of Weimar. His
curly blond hair was ruffled and sticky with damp. He
had a stubble of beard on his well-featured face, and his
fever-red cheeks were an alarming contrast to the waxen
whiteness of his brow. His soaked and earth-stained
uniform was stiffening as it dried—on the part next the
ground with his own blood! The sight was horrid yet
sublime, and fit to rouse one's deepest feelings. You can
imagine our quavering voices, our trembling emotion as
we overwhelmed him with questions about his wounds.
'Heaven sent you hither!' he replied. His accents were
harsh north German, fetched out between chattering
teeth. When he moved he drew in his breath, and his
comely face was drawn with pain. 'I got one in the
thigh in yesterday's little fracas; it was all up with me
in a minute, I had to give up the idea of walking on my
two pins. I could only crawl as far as this; it wasn't so
bad, only a bit damp when it rains as hard as it did last
night. I've been pegged out here since yesterday morning, and I'd be better for a bed, for I seem to have a bit
of fever.'

    "In such light-hearted student fashion did the hero
describe his dire predicament. And in fact he was a student, as he went on to tell us, his teeth still chattering:
Ferdinand Heinke, law student from Breslau, now volunteer in the rifles. 'But what can the ladies do with
me now?' He might well ask, for seldom was good
counsel harder to come by. We were put in a flutter
at the sight of our Prussian idol in the flesh, with the

bourgeois name of Heinke and expressing himself in student slang. It deprived us of our presence of mind. What were we to do with him? You can picture the shrinking of two young females from the idea of taking actual hold of an actual hero, wounded in the thigh — and such a handsome hero too! Should we lift him up and carry him? Whither? Not into the city, it was full of Frenchmen. Temporary shelter, for instance the Borkenhaus, was nearer, yet too far for our strength as well as for his. He said his wound had nearly stopped bleeding. But the leg was very painful; he could not possibly walk, even with our aid. We decided — and he agreed — to leave him where he was, in his more or less sheltered retreat among the bushes, and to go back to town. There we would reveal our precious secret to trustworthy persons and take counsel with them as to safe and secret measures. Above all else Ferdinand dreaded being taken prisoner. He was firmly bent on getting well and then striking down 'Noppel,' as he called the Corsican, freeing the fatherland and reducing Paris to ashes.

"He talked about these projects and seemed to ignore the practical difficulties of the present situation. He was plagued with thirst, and Ottilie found a few peppermints for him in her purse. A smelling-bottle I had with me he waved away with manly scorn, but allowed us to leave him our shawls, the one as a pillow, the other as a most insufficient covering. He bade us good-bye with the words: 'Well, ladies, just see what can be done to get me out of this damned hole. Sorry to lose your esteemed company meantime. My word, it was a pleasant interruption in my little nook!' Thus, with heroic sang-froid, did he speak, hovering as he was between life and death! We curtsied to him as he lay, and he responded with a movement, as though clicking his heels. We hurried off.

"I know not how we got back to the city. On wings of excitement, of course, of exaltation and fear. But we had to take care lest our state be remarked. We ourselves were incapable of making any plans for the rescue of the heroic youth. Chief among our distracted thoughts was that he must not lie a second night out of doors and helpless, but be fetched under a roof and given nursing and care. Yet scarcely less urgent was the wish to share the nursing. We considered taking our mothers into our confidence. We were certain of their sympathy, but, after all, what could they do to help? Masculine aid was indispensable. We fixed at last on Chamberlain von Spiegel. We knew his sympathies — besides, he had been one of the instigators of the fatal Prussian sally and had every reason therefore to succour this victim of it. He was then at liberty. As a matter of fact, he and his friend von Voigt were arrested some days later, through the denunciation of some advantage-seeking citizen, and would have paid with their death for their reckless patriotism if Napoleon, when he was next in Weimar in person, had not pardoned them out of courtesy to the Duchess.

"This in passing. In what follows I will try not to lose myself in detail. Enough that Spiegel did not disappoint us, but proved both energetic and efficient in our affair. He set to work at once, with the necessary caution. A stretcher was conveyed, secretly and in sections, to the park. Dry clothing and food were soon procured; a surgeon visited our hero. He changed into civilian clothes and when twilight fell he was conveyed to the castle by a roundabout route. There the Chamberlain had arranged lodgment for him in a little room high up under the roof in the old part, the gate-house of the so-called bastille.

"Here, hidden from all the world, our brave friend kept his bed for many weeks. Added to the festering wound he had taken a chest cold from exposure and had a severe cough, increasing the fever and pain. His case might have alarmed the doctor if the patient's youth and his equable, cheery temper, only marred by impatience to return to the fray, had not given warrant for his cure. The doctor paid regular visits, the old castellan brought the patient his meals. We two, Ottilie and I, shared the nursing, daily climbing the crumbling stair to his enchanted aerie to bring him wine, jam, and other little delicacies. We read aloud for his distraction, and had long talks so soon as his condition permitted. We wrote his letters. He called us his good angels. Behind his brusque and careless way of talking he had a very soft heart. He did not share our literary interests, putting them by with a smile, for beyond his jurisprudence he had nothing in his head but the fatherland—for the sake of the one, indeed, he had deserted the other. We gladly conceded that one may scorn poetry when one is embodied poetry oneself. In fact, as just that, as the fulfilment of our most poetic dreams, did we regard this noble and handsome human being. And so, in the course of time, it naturally came about that Ottilie, descending the stair after one of our visits, gave me a silent, most eloquent embrace, while I, in response to her confession, returned her kiss from the bottom of my heart. The exchange of feeling, in the ancient and crumbling state of the stair, almost cost us both a fall.

"Those were weeks of emotional exaltation. They gave a most beautiful content to our maidenly lives. Ours was the task of saving this heroic youth for the fatherland; and gratifying past words it was to see how, after some anxious hours, he steadily improved from visit to visit. We shared in that joy, as indeed in all the emotions we dedicated to our glorious charge. Our own intuitions will tell you that tender inexpressible feelings mingled with our charity and our patriotism. Yet here, too, my own feelings only seconded those of the lovely Ottilie, while leaving her, so to speak, the *pas*. That lay in the nature of things. A measure of Ferdinand's gratitude might light upon unbeautiful me, but I did well to hope for no more. His intellectual simplicity became him well, even with lustre. But there was a consequent utter indifference to such gifts as I might have entered in default of outward beauty. I wisely contented myself with the rôle of confidante in this romance. To that my nature was suited. I was saved from jealousy not only by my love for my friend, my tender pride in her charms, but also by the fact that Ferdinand treated us quite alike. I was human enough to be glad that he never varied from a key of brisk friendliness, even towards my darling. And another source of satisfaction I had too: the hope that this new, undreamed-of experience might help to wean Ottilie from August von Goethe and from that unhappy, to me most unlucky affair.

" I made no bones of my satisfaction and relief when upon my bosom she confessed that her feelings for Ferdinand were different from all her heart had previously known. Life had now taught her, she said, the difference between friendship, however deep and sympathetic, and true love. My joy was only dampened by the thought that Heinke was not of noble birth but quite simply the son of a Silesian fur-dealer, and certainly no match for an Ottilie von Pogwisch. Whether the knowledge of this was all that held him to his key of gay friendliness was another matter.

"During Heinke's convalescence the season came to an end. The Comédie was still open, but the court invitations, and the balls where the French officers had shone so brilliantly, were few and far between. We saw August von Goethe less·often than in the winter-time. But the walks, and the rendezvous in the gardens, did not quite cease, though the elder Goethe's absence increased his son's tasks. Ferdinand's story had been kept a closely guarded secret; no one but the initiated knew of our foundling in his sleeping-beauty retreat. But Ottilie felt bound to reveal the situation to the Chamberlain Assessor. Primarily, of course, out of loyalty to the friendship; but she had, it seemed to me, a certain curiosity to see how he took the news of our adventure and how he would behave about it. His manner was unconcerned, even light, especially after he had informed himself more or less about Heinke's family, and learned his bourgeois origins. He showed so little curiosity or interest, almost as though he preferred to remain aloof, that we afterwards referred to the subject only briefly, and thus August remained in deliberate ignorance or half-knowledge of the actual situation, of the happy recovery of our hero, his further brief stay in Weimar, and his temporary absence from it.

"But I have got a little in advance of my story. Sooner than we thought, Ferdinand could leave his bed and try his legs by limping about on a stick in his lofty chamber. The spring had entry to him only through a mansard window; yet it favoured his cure. And soon a change of quarters was effected, that he might better profit by the mild air. A brother of the castellan had a cobbler's shop in the bowling-alley behind the royal mews and was ready to receive the convalescent in a room on the ground floor. On one of the first June days he left his romantic retreat, supported on stout shoulders, and now he could sit sunning himself on a bench by the river, or even cross the bridge and gain the open, the green woods round the shooting-box, and the Tiefurter Allee.

"There had been a quiet interlude in world affairs. The truce was to last only into the middle of the summer—I cannot call that a misfortune, for the coming events were to lead us, though through great horrors and prolonged sufferings, to glory and freedom. For the time, life in Weimar was pleasant, despite the continuous burden of billeting—we accommodated ourselves to that as best we might. We were moderately sociable up until the early summer. Our warriors, their cheeks visibly rosier and plumper, took part with reserve, in modest civilian attire. At our mothers' houses, at the Egloffsteins', in the salon of Frau von Wolzogen, and elsewhere we spent many hours, gaily, yet in an at-

mosphere of deep feeling. Our young hero was everywhere well and cordially received, on account of his
youthful good looks and soldierly simplicity. Dr. Passow especially was all fire and flame for the young man;
conformably to his tradition, he saw in him the embodiment of Hellenic beauty united with heroic patriotism and love of freedom. With much justice, of
course. Yet for a man he went rather too far for my
taste in his admiration of our hero. Not for the first or
last time I made the observation that the warlike national spirit is connected with an increased enthusiasm
of man for his own sex. The phenomenon is an inheritance from the customs of the ancient Spartans. It has
a strange, harsh flavour not very acceptable to us women.

"Ferdinand, for his part, preserved towards everybody alike his even, sunny manner — towards us as well.
Herr von Goethe would have had no occasion for jealousy about Ottilie, even if the two young men, as different from each other as day from night, had ever
met. But that Ottilie knew how to prevent. It was plain
that her feelings for the hero gave her a sense of guilt
towards her gloomy lover. She seemed to regard them
as a default of her obligations to August, and suffered
pangs of conscience in the presence of both. However
much I admired these moral standards, they made me
shudder as I realized that there was no hope her attachment to Heinke might loosen the awkward bond
with the son of our great man. 'Yes, Adele,' she said
one day to me, with a dark shadow in her blue eyes, 'I
have known happiness, light, and harmony, they have
been revealed to me in the form of our Ferdinand. But

however noble their visage, the claims of darkness and suffering upon our magnanimity are even greater. In the depths of my soul I recognize my destiny.' 'May heaven keep you, my darling!' was all I could answer, feeling a chill at my heart, as one does when fate fixes upon us its awful, unalterable eye.

"Heinke took his leave. We were destined to see him again; but now, after a stay of seven weeks, he left for his Silesian home, to visit his dear ones, the fur-dealer and his family, while his leg grew completely strong. When that was accomplished he rejoined the army at once. Ottilie and I wept together at our loss, but consoled ourselves by exchanging vows that our friendship from then on should be a unique cult of his heroic memory. He had been to us the ideal presentment, in flesh and blood, of the German youth on fire for the fatherland, as portrayed by the singer of *Lyre and Sword*. But as flesh and blood always conflict to some extent with the claims of the ideal, a disappointment with these is inevitable. Frankly, it is an advantage, a clarification of the ideal, when flesh and blood are absent. Ferdinand had been wearing civilian garb. When he left he restored to our mind's eye the image of him clothed in the former military splendour which had so enhanced his masculine charms. After he left, the image grew daily brighter to our eyes. On the other hand, as you will see, the figure of August veiled itself in ever darker shadows.

"On August 10th the armistice expired. During it Prussia, Russia, Austria, and England had united against the Emperor. In Weimar we got but scant and indefi-

nite news of the triumphs of the Prussian generals,
Blücher and Bülow, Kleist, York, Marwitz, and Tauent-
zien. But we knew that somewhere our Ferdinand had
a share in those triumphs, and our maidenly hearts beat
faster with pride. The thought that his young blood,
pledged to the fatherland, might somewhere be dyeing
the sward made us tremble. We knew almost nothing.
The northern and eastern 'barbarians' were drawing
near — that was the only word. But the nearer they drew,
the less were they called barbarians, the more the sympathies and hopes of society and the people veered
towards them and away from the French. That of
course was partly because we began to see in them the
victors one might hope to placate — even from a distance.
But even more it was because we human beings are by
nature submissive. We need to live in harmony with
outward events and situations. We need to come to
terms with power — and now fate itself seemed to be
giving the signal for the change. In the space of a few
days the barbarians, the rebels against civilization, turned
into liberators. Their successful advance brought to a
bursting-point the general enthusiasm for folk and
fatherland.

"Shortly after the middle of October, with mingled
admiration and horror, we beheld Cossacks in Weimar.
The French Embassy fled. If they were not insulted
before they left, that was only because it was not yet absolutely certain what fate really intended, or just how
we were to make sure of being in harmony with power
and success. But in the night of the 20th to the 21st a
whole five hundred of these Huns rode into the town.

Their colonel — von Geismar was his name — went by night to the castle and stood by the Duke's bed, his cap cocked over one ear. He came to announce the allies' great victory at Leipsic. He was sent, he said, by Czar Alexander, for the protection of the ducal family. Then His Serene Highness at last understood what time of day it was. Like a wise prince, he was fain to adjust himself and get in line with the march of events.

"My dear lady, what days those were! The din and shock of battle resounded in our very streets. Cossacks, Prussians, Magyars, Croats, Slavs — an endless variety of savage faces. When the French retreat to Erfurt gave our residential city to the allies, they poured into it straightway, and there burst upon us such a flood of billeting as strained all households to the uttermost and beyond, no matter what their size. The city was jammed; we beheld much brilliance and greatness: two Emperors, the Russian and the Austrian, and the Prussian Crown Prince as well, held court there. Chancellor Metternich arrived, and the air was thick with generals and honourables. Only the poor, with nothing to give, had time to gaze their fill. The rest of us, squeezed into the narrowest quarters, worked night and day. Breathless with the absorbing tasks laid on us, we should have been more than human to think even of our next-door neighbours. Usually we did not know until afterwards how they had fared.

"Yet even so, there was one difference among us, despite our common burdens: some of us carried them more cheerfully and easily because we were repaid by the triumph of our cause. That helped us to bear the

rudeness and arrogance of these allies of ours, these Cossacks, Bashkirs, and hussars from the east. Both our
mothers, Ottilie's and mine, were housing the high command with their adjutants and servants, and we daughters became literally handmaidens to our imperious
guests. But my darling rejoiced in the freedom of showing herself at last a Prussian unashamed; she was radiant,
despite every burden. To me, rather more inclined to
faint-heartedness, she imparted her enthusiasm for this
great, this glorious time. In secret we shared its private
aspect, which bore the lineaments of our heroic youth.
Somewhere, we knew, he was doing his part to consummate the sanguinary task of freedom.

"So much for our feelings, distinguished but little
from the general and public temper. How different was
the tone in the famous house connected with my Ottilie
in a way so disturbing to my peace of mind! Our great
German poet was the unhappiest man in Weimar, in the
dukedom, very likely in the whole delirious fatherland.
He had not been half so wretched in 1806. Our dear
von Stein thought him melancholy. She warned us all
against talking politics with him. To put it mildly, he
seemed not to share our enthusiasm. This year of our
exaltation, a red-letter one in all our annals, he spoke of
as the 'sad,' the 'frightful' year. Yet certainly he had
been spared more than most of us the worst of its horrors. In April, when the theatre of war had threatened
to be transferred hither, Prussia and Russia were occupying the surrounding heights and there was prospect
of a battle, with fire and pillage to follow. And Goethe
was a man of sixty-three, enduring, it is true, but always

ailing, and long since inured to habits he could not break. The Frau Councillor and August could not see him exposed to hardships probably even more severe than those of 1806. They advised him a speedy departure to his beloved Bohemia, to Töplitz, where he might be safe and lead his regular life, working on the third volume of his Recollections, while mother and son bowed to the fury of the storm. That was all in order, I say nothing against it — not I. I will not conceal that there were others to condemn his going and see in it only the egoistic self-preservation of the grand seigneur. That was not the view of the oncoming army of Blücher. He met the troops just outside the town; they recognized the author of *Faust* and perhaps they did not think he was just out for a drive. They surrounded his carriage and blithely and confidently asked his blessing on their arms. After some demur he gave it, in a few cordial words. A pretty scene, was it not? Only slightly ambiguous, a little awkward, on account of the absurd misunderstanding at the bottom of it.

"Until the middle of the summer Goethe remained in Bohemia. Then it was no longer safe there and he came back, but only for a few days. At that moment it looked as though the Austrians were marching on Weimar from the south-west, and August again urged him to move. He went to Ilmenau and stayed there until early in September. From then on, indeed, we had him in our midst; and whoever loves him must agree that he shared enough and too much in our heavy lot. It was the worst time of the billeting. Even his beautiful house, though we had hoped it might be spared, was perforce turned into a hostel. For a full week he had twenty-four persons at table every day. The Austrian Chief of Ordnance, Count Colloredo, was there—you must surely have heard about it, for there was a great deal of talk. Goethe—in a strange unconsciousness, or perhaps defiance, or the conviction that great gentlemen like the Count and himself lived in their own sphere, remote from the passions of the mob—Goethe advanced to greet him with the Cross of the Legion of Honour on his dress uniform. 'The devil!' cried Colloredo coarsely. 'How can anyone wear such a thing?' This to him, to Goethe! He did not understand. To the Count he said nothing. But afterwards, to others, he spoke: 'What! Because the Emperor has lost a battle, shall I no longer wear his Order?' He was a puzzle to his oldest friends— and they to him. The Austrian was succeeded by Minister von Humboldt; Goethe and he had shared their intellectual interests for many years. He was even more cosmopolitan than the poet himself, always preferring life abroad to life at home. But since 1806 he had been a good Prussian, as they say—meaning that he was no longer anything else. Napoleon had brought that about— one must admit that he changed the Germans very much. He turned their milk - that is to say, their homely, pious ways of give and take—into boiling dragon's blood; and he even made a grim patriot and soldier of freedom out of the versatile humanist von Humboldt. Shall we account it a merit or a crime in Cæsar, that he changed our minds and brought us to ourselves? I will not judge.

"Reports trickled through of the talks between Goethe and the Minister. Things were whispered about.

Humboldt, in the atmosphere of Berlin, had ever since the spring expected that, like young Körner, the sons of Goethe and Schiller would take arms for the fatherland. In Weimar he tried to learn his old friend's views and August's intentions. But August displayed only gloomy indifference, while the father demurred and doubted, about all the things the rest of the world admired. Liberation? That was simply freedom to go under, Goethe bitterly said. The remedy was worse than the disease. Napoleon conquered? He was not yet, not for a long time yet. He was, to be sure, a stag at bay; but that he enjoyed, and it might still be that he would throw off the pack. But suppose he was beaten. What then? Were the people really roused and did they know what they wanted? Did anybody know what would come after the great man's fall? Russian hegemony instead of French? Cossacks in Weimar? For his part, that was not quite his heart's desire. Did they behave so much better than the French? These friends of ours would plunder and lay waste, precisely as our foes had done. They took the transport, that was so hard to get, away from our soldiers, and our wounded were plundered by their own allies on the field. That was the truth, disguise it as one would with sentimental fables. The poets ruined themselves mixing in politics. They and the people were simply in a state of disgusting and indecent heat. In short, it was awful.

"Awful, dear lady, indeed it was. And the worst of it, the real wound to our sympathies, was that the daily and hourly evidence of our senses spoke on Goethe's side. It is true: the French retreat and the allied pur-

suit resulted in the most frightful destruction and con-
fiscation. We had a Prussian militia colonel, a regular
fire-eater, at the head of the regiment, as well as a Russian and an Austrian commandant. And the troops of
various countries were constantly inflicted upon us,
either in billets or on the march. The wounded came in
streams from beleaguered Erfurt; the maimed, the fever
and dysentery patients crowded our hospitals; soon the
population of the city began to sicken. In November
we had five hundred typhus cases — in a population of
six thousand souls. There were no doctors, they were all
stricken. Johannes Falk, the writer, lost four children
in one month; his hair turned white. In some houses not
a soul survived. The terror, the fear of contagion, suppressed every sign of life. Twice daily the streets were
fumigated with a smudge of white pitch. But the hearse
and basket still plied their gruesome trade. There were
many suicides, people killed themselves for fear they
would starve.

"That was the outward picture of things, the reality,
if you like. If you could not rise above it to the ideal
of freedom and fatherland you were in a bad way. Yet
many could; at their head Professors Luden and Passow,
and with them Ottilie. That our prince of poets would
not or could not join was of all our woes perhaps the
bitterest. We got from August only too clear a picture
— he was, of course, no more than his father's echo. This
childishly exact adhesion to the father's point of view
had something touching about it; but it did seem a little
unnatural, and oppressed us above and beyond the pain
the words themselves gave. Ottilie received them with

bent head, only lifting to him once or twice a glance from her blue eyes swimming in tears. In a cutting voice he repeated as though they were his own the opinions his sire had uttered to von Humboldt and others about the trials and errors of the times. Also about their absurdity and folly. And the opinions were right; if one chose, if one set oneself to it, one could see the absurd, the ridiculous side of the way the excited, delirious people were going about, emotionally exalted and mentally diminished by the passion uniting them. In Berlin, Fichte, Schleiermacher, and Iffland went armed to the teeth and made their swords ring on the pavement. Herr von Kotzebue, our famous dramatic poet, wanted to form an amazon troop; and I do not doubt that Ottilie, if he had succeeded, would have been capable of letting herself be persuaded to join. She might even have drawn me in, however fantastic the idea now seems to my cooler head. It was definitely not a period of good taste. People who set store by that, or by culture, sobriety, discipline, or self-criticism, got little out of it. Certainly they got little out of the poetry produced by that distracted time. Today we should even find it offensive, though then it brought tears of sensibility to all our eyes. Everybody scribbled verse; we swam, we wallowed, in apocalyptic visions, prophecies, blood-and-thunder rhapsodies of hatred and revenge. A clergyman wrote a satirical poem on the destruction of the Grand Army in Russia, offensive in its details as in its idea. My dear friend, enthusiasm is beautiful. But not without enlightenment. When hysterical citizens revel metaphorically in the shedding of blood, because the historic hour has given the rein to their evil passions, the sight is painful to behold. I must admit that things got beyond a joke; they got beyond reason and decency. The country was flooded with ravings in rhyme, vilifying and insulting the man the ravers had so lately worshipped and feared. What made it worse was that very often the verses were directed not so much against the tyrant as against the upstart, the son of the people and the Revolution, the herald of the new time. Even Ottilie was embarrassed by these hymns of hate, as clumsy as they were venomous, addressed to 'Nicky the journeyman tailor.' She said nothing, but I could see. How then could the Augustus of German culture, the author of *Iphigenie,* have failed to be distressed over his fellow citizens' state of mind? 'Unless a thing sounds like a Lützow campaign,' he complained — we heard him through August's mouth — 'nobody will listen to it.' It wounded us. We should have realized that the reproach was addressed not only to those clumsy and ferocious versifiers but to the gifted singers of freedom, Kleist and Arndt, as well. He condemned the bad example they set. And from the downfall of his hero he augured nothing but chaos and the reign of barbarism.

"You perceive that I am trying — however oddly it becomes me — to defend the great man and to excuse him for his too apparent aloofness. I do so the more gladly because I know his intellectual isolation must have cost him many a pang — even considering that as a poet he was used to feeling remote from the popular point of view. But what I can never pardon him is what he did at that time to his son, and the heavy, agonizing consequence to that already darkened soul — and therewith to Ottilie's love.

"At the end of November in that great and dreadful year the Duke, following the Prussian model, sent out a call for volunteers. Actually, it was in response to the popular demand, in particular the ardour of the Jena professors and students, who were all on fire to shoulder muskets. They had an exalted patron in the lovely reigning favourite, Serenissima Frau von Heigendorf, or rather Jagemann. Other advisers of the prince were against the idea; Minister von Voigt thought it would be better to damp the students' youthful fire — it was not necessary or desirable, he thought, for educated men to join the army. Young peasant lads could do the work, and do it better. The most eager of the students were just those who were the most gifted and promising. They should be restrained.

"That was the view of our master as well. We heard him talk about the matter with displeasure and utter words about the favourite which I could not possibly repeat in your presence. He had great respect, he said, for the professional soldier. But the volunteer, fighting on his own and outside the ranks, was a presumptuous nuisance. In the spring he had been in Dresden, at the Körners'. The young son of the house had ridden with the Lützowers, without the permission, certainly without the approval, of the Elector, who still clung to his allegiance to the Emperor. That, Goethe said, was flat rebellion. And this whole arbitrary activity of volunteer soldiers was a blunder, which could only give the authorities trouble in the end.

Thus the great man. His distinction between regular and volunteer service was rather artificial, and probably it was a pretext, since his heart was not in the fatherland's cause. Yet we must grant one thing. In the matter of the volunteers he was entirely in the right — actually, if not ideally. Their training was superficial, they accomplished little or nothing and were to all intents and purposes superfluous. Their officers were incapable, desertions were numerous. For a long time they did not even take the field. And when the cause triumphed in France, the Duke sent them home with a letter of thanks couched in the most general terms, referring to the popular and poetic conceptions of their warlike prowess. Last year, before Waterloo, they were not called up at all. But this only in passing. Lacking enthusiasm as our great poet did, he saw well and clearly in this matter. Of course, he was from the very outset against the volunteer system, and accused the Heigendorf behind her back of wanton and silly infatuation with the military — there, some of his harsh epithets have escaped me after all! But granting all that, the fundamental reason — however much it grieves me to state it — was that at the bottom of his heart he was opposed to the War of Liberation altogether, and to the agitations it brought in its train.

"Suffice it to say, the exalted summons went forth, enlistment began. Fifty-seven cavalry and as many as ninety-seven infantry rifles assembled. All our cavaliers enlisted, the whole of our younger social world. Von Gross, Gentleman of the Bedchamber, von Seebach, of the Household, not to mention the gentlemen von Helldorf, von Häseler, District President von Egloffstein,

Chamberlain von Poseck, Vice-President von Gersdorf
— in short, everybody. It was the fashion, it was *de rigueur*. Patriotic duty received the social cachet of good form. And that was the fine and splendid thing. August von Goethe could not avoid joining — it was not a question of personal opinions but of honour and *chic*. He enlisted, rather late, as fiftieth infantry rifle, without his father's consent. And once he had done it, it seems there was a tremendous to-do. They said the father called the son feeble-minded, unfilial. For days, out of sheer vexation, he did not speak a word to the poor soul — who after all had certainly not acted out of enthusiasm for the cause!

"The truth was, Goethe really needed his son; and there was nothing in his heart to have made the inconvenience easier to bear. Dr. Riemer had married the Ulrich and left the house — not least on account of August, who had behaved with unpardonable rudeness to the sensitive man. After he left, a certain John had acted as secretary; a not very agreeable or capable person, and it is quite true that the father had serious need of his son, for his writing and a thousand other services. But it is just as true that the thought of doing without him excited the father quite disproportionately. Of course this lack of proportion was due to his animosity against the volunteer service — and that in turn was due to, or served as a handle for, the other and more far-reaching objection. At no price would he have August go into the field. From that moment he bent all his powers to prevent it. He applied to Minister von Voigt, to His Serene Highness the Duke himself. The letters he wrote

— we learned of their contents through August — one can only describe as Tasso-like. Their inordinate and desperate terms displayed all the extravagance of that other ego of his. The loss of his son, he wrote, the forced entrance of a stranger into his intimate correspondence, his creative work, and all his personal affairs, would make his situation, his very existence, intolerable. It was all fantastic. But he threw his own weight into the scale — such a powerful counterbalance that it could but bear down anything on the other side. The Minister and the Duke hastened to meet his wishes. Not that August had actually to remove his name from the rolls. They could scarcely wish to disgrace him. What Voigt proposed, and His Serene Highness acceded to, not without a grimace at August's compliance, was this: the young gentleman should first go with Kammerrat Rühlmann to Frankfurt, the headquarters of the allies, where negotiations for financing the campaign were proceeding. After that he would take up an equally nominal adjutancy with the hereditary Prince Karl Friedrich, nominal head of the volunteer corps, and thus remain at his father's service.

"So it was arranged, and so, alas, it fell out. At New Year's August went to Frankfurt, simply not to be in Weimar on the day — at the end of January 1814 — when his fellow members of the rifles, cavalry and infantry, were sworn in at the town church. The week after they marched off to Flanders, he came back to take up his service as adjutant to the prince. Like the prince, he put on the uniform of the rifles, and his father called that 'following the horns.' 'My son has followed the horns,' he declared, and he acted as though everything was now just as it should be. Alas, it was not. There was quite general shrugging of shoulders over the twenty-four-year-old man who had remained at home. Everybody censured a father who not only so utterly failed himself to share the new patriotic life of the German people, but even forced his son to remain aloof. His false position vis-à-vis his comrades in arms, the volunteers facing danger in the field, was clear from the outset. When they got back, they were destined to be his official and social companions. Between him and them were any good relations possible? Would they concede him respect and friendship? The reproach of cowardice was in the air. I have another situation in mind as I speak, a contrast betraying the profound injustice of life and the way it will punish one person and indulge another, for precisely the same conduct. I know, human nature is very various. On profoundly personal grounds conditioning our moral and æsthetic judgments, a thing may be wrong in one person and quite right in another. In the one something may even look like painful perversion, while in another it is allowed, as fitting and natural. I have a brother, my dear friend, named Arthur. He is a young scholar, a philosopher, though not by tradition, for he was intended for a business life and came late to his actual career. I think I told you he attended Dr. Passow's Greek classes. A good head-piece, without a doubt, but a little bitter in his judgments of the world and men. I know people who predict a great future for him — though no greater than he anticipates for himself. My brother too belongs to the generation that dropped its studies to fling itself into the struggle for the fatherland. But nobody suggested such a course to him; not a single soul even thought of it. The singular reason is that Arthur Schopenhauer himself considered it not for a moment, it never entered his head. He gave money for the equipment of the volunteers, but he did not think of joining them. In the most matter-of-course way he left that to the kind of men he calls 'nature's ready-mades.' And nobody was surprised. People accepted his position with a perfect equanimity that amounted to approval. Never was it clearer to me than on this occasion that what satisfies us, morally and intellectually, what we really like, is harmony, is being in tune.

"But people looked down their noses and were scandalized at August. I can still hear our dear Frau von Stein: 'Goethe does not want his son to go with the troop! What do you say to that? The only young man of station in the place who has remained at home!' And Frau von Schiller: 'At no price, for nothing in the world, would I have stopped my Karl from going! His whole life, his disposition, would have been spoilt — the lad would have become melancholy.' Melancholy. Was not our poor friend that? Indeed, he always had been. But from this unhappy time on, his poor turbid soul grew more and more clouded, his trouble showed itself by harmful indulgence in tastes to which he was already prone — I mean the immoderate use of wine, the intercourse — forgive me for speaking of it — with light women. His requirements in this direction have always been considerable. A person of sound mind is fain to ask how such tastes harmonize with the melancholy that

overshadowed even his love for Ottilie. I should not like
to say how much I feel that in these debauches he tried
to prove the manhood society had questioned in other
fields.

"I had, if I may say so, the most mixed feelings about
all this. Pity and disgust strove together in my heart.
Great reverence of course I had, for his wonderful father.
But mingled with it—and not alone in me—was disapproval of his father's untimely course in forbidding his
all too docile son to follow the call of a whole generation's heart. Even so, I cherished the hope that August's
disgrace, his injured repute, might estrange my darling's
feelings. Perhaps I might at last be relieved of my distress over this unsuitable, dangerous connection; perhaps
Ottilie would end by giving up a young man whose behaviour was so contrary to her holiest convictions, and
whose course at that time was so little honourable. My
dearest lady, my hopes were blasted. Ottilie the patriot,
the admirer of Ferdinand Heinke, she clung to August,
she stuck to her friendship with him, she always ex-
cused him, on occasion she defended him in society.
When people repeated evil of him she either refused to
believe or she explained it in the sense of a romantic
melancholy, a kind of possession. I think the dear child
felt herself called to reclaim him. 'Adele,' she would
say, 'believe me, he is not a bad man at all, however much
people condemn him. I despise them, and I wish he
knew better how to return their scorn. Then he would
give them less occasion for their malice. In a conflict
between a cold, hypocritical man and a lonely soul, you
will always find your Ottilie on the side of the lonely

one. Can one doubt that nobility resides in the soul of
such a father's son? And he loves me too, Adele, and I,
I owe him my love. I have enjoyed the great happiness —
our great happiness — of knowing Ferdinand. I continue
to cherish it in my memory, yet I cannot help accounting
it a debt I owe to August. I must pay the debt — his
melancholy gaze admonishes me. Yes, I am guilty
towards him. Suppose the stories that make me shudder
are all true. Then are his acts not due to despair on my
account? For you know, Adele, so long as he trusted
me he was not like that.'

"More than once she said such things to me, and my
feelings were again divided. I suffered to see she could
not get free of the unhappy man. The thought of giving herself to him for ever, by the desire of his great
father, sat like a barb in her heart. Yet some of my
other misgivings were stilled as I listened. Her Prussian
ideals, her militaristic and nationalist views, had sometimes made me ask myself what sort of hard, barbarian
little soul might inhabit that delicate frame. But now
her attitude towards August, the scruples she felt on
account of her tenderness for the fine, heroic figure of
our simple friend Heinke, made me recognize the nobility and refinement, the sensitive discriminations of her
soul. And I loved her the more, while my distress was
at the same time redoubled.

"In May of that year August's troubles reached their
climax. The campaign was over, Paris was conquered,
on the 21st the Weimar volunteers came home. They
had not precisely covered themselves with glory or
merited the fatherland's highest rewards. But still they

entered the city crowned with the laurels of victory. This moment I had always dreaded, and rightly, as the sequel proved. The young gentlemen did not hesitate to show their scorn and contempt for their stay-at-home comrade — and that in the most unvarnished terms. They were cruel. Once more I confirmed to myself my scepticism about the feelings men put forward as guiding them in their actions. For men do not act quite of themselves. They act in response to an outward situation, and on being presented with an opportunity to conform to a pattern. If the pattern gives licence to cruelty, so much the better. They take advantage of the licence so thoughtlessly, so thoroughly, that it becomes perfectly clear: the generality of mankind are only waiting for the chance, only waiting for outward circumstance to sanction brutality and allow them to be cruel and brutal to their heart's content.

"August was so naïve — or possibly so defiant — as to greet his comrades in the uniform of the volunteers. He had, of course, the right to wear it, as adjutant to His Highness, the honorary commander of the troop. But of course it was a deliberate challenge to the warriors, and a defiance of any scorn they might feel. And Theodor Körner had not written his lines in vain:

> 'Fie on the fellow who crawls under benches,
> Skulks behind lackeys and scullery-wenches,
> Shame on the pitiful, cowardly wight!'

The lines were too good a fit — they were quoted far and wide. A certain cavalry captain, von Werthern-Wiese, distinguished himself in extracting the last ounce out of such a heaven-sent chance. He it was who referred to August's birth and antecedents. These quite explained, the captain said, his cowardly and unchivalrous conduct. Herr von Goethe would have fallen upon the man with his unfleshed sword had he not been seized by the arms. A challenge, under the most drastic conditions, was the outcome of the scene.

"The Privy Councillor was established at Berka, a near-by resort, composing his *Epimenides*. He had been invited by Iffland, the Berlin intendant, to write a festival piece for the return of the King of Prussia; and the offer had so much tempted him that he put aside his other work to draft that extraordinary, ambiguous, seven-sleeper allegory, so highly individual and different from all other such occasional pieces in the world. 'I blush for all my hours of leisure,' he was writing; and 'Back to the pit he must return.' And there in Berka he got a letter from Frau von Wedel, a female admirer and lady of the court, warning him of August's situation, the encounter with the captain and the impending duel. The illustrious parent took immediate steps. As I know him, he got — above and beyond his concern for August's life — a certain satisfaction from using his influence and staking his own importance to save his son from the duel as he had from military service. Always he was on the side of aristocratic privilege, and making distinguished exceptions to rules.

"He asked Frau Wedel to mediate, he wrote to the Minister-President. A high official, Privy Councillor von Müller, came to Berka. The situation was explained to the prince, to the Duke himself. The captain was forced to apologize, the quarrel was smoothed over. August, protected from on high, became invulnerable, and the critics were hushed. But not entirely silenced. In effect, the abortive duel rather increased the popular disbelief in August's courage. People shrugged their shoulders and avoided him. No further comradely intercourse was to be thought of between him and his peers. Herr von Werthern had received a sharp rebuke from the highest authorities, he was even punished by arrest. But he had succeeded in bringing to the fore the half-forgotten facts about August's irregular birth and his—so to speak—mongrel antecedents. They accounted, people said, for his reprehensible conduct. Where else, they asked, would he get it? One had to admit that the Frau Privy Councillor had never paid much attention to the serious side of the times we lived in. Her love of pleasure had always given food for comment—it was not actually bad, but undignified, even ridiculous.

"Yet, after all, Ottilie's uncouth wooer displayed a sense of honour that did him credit. He took the whole matter very much to heart. His way of showing it, however, was singularly indirect: it was manifested in an obstinate and increasingly passionate reverence for the conquering hero, the man in Elba. He was fanatically loyal, he poured scorn on the renegades who refused to remember that they had but now been celebrating Napoleon's name-day as the greatest day in the year. In this way he gave proof of his pride and defiance. And we understood—for was he not suffering with and for his hero? Was he not disgraced because he had not entered the lists against him? In the guise of loyalty to the

Emperor he could openly express his sense of the disgrace
he smarted under; and he did so to his father, himself
exalted above the moods of the day. He did so, too, to us,
ruthlessly treading on Ottilie's sensibilities. She let him
talk, she bore with his egotistic excesses, though the tears
stood in her lovely eyes. For it did him so much good
to talk, regardless, or even glad, of the pain he was giving. But I doubted that even her conscientious scruples
could hold out for ever against such mistreatment; and
I felt fresh hope in my secret heart. Of course, there was
something more in this insistent Napoleon cult; something hid behind it, used it as pretext, yet sometimes came
out quite baldly and nakedly. That something was
jealousy of young Heinke. Yes, Ferdinand was again
among us, and August continually mocked at him in our
presence, as the archetype of the Teutomaniac, the ally
of the barbarians, who had thwarted great Cæsar's designs for the salvation of the Continent.

"Yes, our protégé was again in Weimar — or, rather,
he was here again for the second time. After the battle
of Leipsic he had served for some weeks in the city as
adjutant to the Prussian commandant. He mingled in
society and enjoyed universal popularity. Now, since
the fall of Paris, he had come back again, decorated with
the Iron Cross. Our feelings, of course, were worked up
to fever pitch by seeing this sacred badge upon his
breast. Especially Ottilie's feelings. But we admitted to
each other that they were a little dampened by his manner. We saw him often, and he was as always cordial,
grateful, and friendly. Yet we found him a little reserved. His feelings seemed to be not quite a match for

ours. And before long we received the rather sobering explanation. Ferdinand told us what for some reason or other he had previously concealed. He now felt it his duty to disclose that at home in Prussian Silesia a dearly loved bride awaited him, and he thought very soon to lead her to the altar.

"You can readily guess that we were embarrassed by the news. I do not speak of pain or disappointment: such sentiments could scarcely be borne out, since all we had felt was enthusiastic devotion to an ideal, mingled, of course, with a sense of the claims we had, as his rescuers, upon his very agreeable person. He was to us, in truth, more a personification than a person. That is a difficult distinction; perhaps after all it may be just the qualities of a person that enable him to become a personification. Here, indeed, it will be better for me to retire my own feelings to the background and speak only of Ottilie's. Hers, at any rate, could never have had any foundation of hope or even of desire, considering Ferdinand's simple origins, as a fur-dealer's son. Indeed, I sometimes thought it was rather myself who might have entertained such ideas. In my weaker moments I conceived that Ottilie's unattainable charms might speak in favour of a bond with my much lesser ones. Then I would shrink in horror from the dangers of such dreams — or, again, I would contemplate them with a literary eye, as a theme on which a Goethe might employ his great powers in a subtle portrayal of conflicting feelings and standards. In short, we were not entitled to indulge any feelings of disappointment or betrayal. We responded to his confession with the warmest congratulations, and were merely a little chagrined that he had seen fit to spare us so long — though in truth we would gladly have been spared still longer! We were certainly embarrassed, our feelings were hurt, we suffered unacknowledged pain over Ferdinand's lost and affianced state. Some undefined, indefinable dreamlike hope had sweetened our friendly intercourse with the young man, and now it fell away. Implicitly, by common consent, we sought to lessen our discomfiture by including his betrothed in our admiration and enthusiasm; we set up a double cult of our young hero and his German bride, and would admit no doubt of her worthiness of her election. We pictured her to ourselves half Thusnelda, half — or even more than half — Goethe's Dorothea; though of course with blue instead of black eyes.

"How shall I explain that we concealed the fact of Heinke's betrothal from August, as long as Heinke himself had concealed it from us? Ottilie would have it so; we did not even explain it to ourselves. I must say, I was surprised. After all, she had felt guilty towards August on the score of her patriotic *tendresse* for our young warrior. Yet she would not explain that her feelings in that direction were entirely without prospects, quite aside from their social awkwardness. They formed no actual threat to her melancholy swain — and yet she would not tell him so. The knowledge would most certainly have done him good, might possibly have made him indifferent to Ferdinand, or even friendly. I readily followed her whim. August's disagreeable, spiteful way of alluding to the young man did not deserve consolation. Besides, his continual irritation might one day lead him too

far, his constant insults to Ottilie's tenderest feelings
might one day end in the hoped-for breach.

"My dearest listener, it so came about. At least, and
for the time, things began to move in the direction of
my private hopes. The meetings and intercourse with
Herr von Goethe grew more and more difficult and precarious. Scene followed on scene. August's face was
black, he smarted under his disgrace and his jealousy.
He outdid himself in reproaches to us for the betrayal of
our friendship with him in favour of a numbskull with
a good figure, a proper German Michael. Ottilie never
mentioned Heinke's Silesian commitments, but she was
deeply wounded in her loyalty, and dissolved in tears
upon my breast. At last the explosion came; and when
it did, it mingled, as usual, the political with the personal. One afternoon, in the Countess Henckel's garden,
August again gave voice to his fanatical worship of
Napoleon. The epithets he hurled at the Emperor's de-
tractors were quite obviously directed at Ferdinand as
well. Ottilie replied: she gave free rein to her abhor-
rence of the scourge of Europe; and when she portrayed
the heroic uprising of youth against the tyrant, the
lineaments of Ferdinand were all too plainly visible in
the picture she drew. I seconded her. August was pale
with rage. His voice choked as he declared that all was
over between him and us. He would know us no more,
from that time on, we were as nothing to him. He left
the garden, consumed with fury.

"I was much shaken at finding myself thus at the goal
of my desires. But I confessed the truth openly to
Ottilie and sought with all my eloquence to console her

for the breach. I told her that the relation with him could
never in all the world have come to good. My darling
felt her position most cruelly, and I was inexpressibly
moved. Think of it! The youth whom she so fondly
loved was another's; and now he to whose redemption
she had meant to dedicate her life repulsed her in the
most savage way. Even that was not all. She would
have turned for consolation to her mother's breast; but
alas, that mother's heart had just been stricken too with
a frightful blow. She herself was in too great need of
comfort to have any left to give. Ottilie, after the crushing scene with August, had taken my advice and gone
for a few weeks to relatives in Dessau. There she received a message which brought her flying home again.
Frau von Pogwisch had confidently, and justifiably,
counted on receiving the proposals of Count von Edling,
the adopted father of the family, and the handsomest man
in the Duchy. Now, all of a sudden, and without giving
a word or a thought to the expectations he had aroused,
he had married a visiting Princess Sturdza from Moldavia.

"What an autumn and winter we had, my dear lady!
Not only because in February Napoleon escaped from
Elba and we had to defeat him all over again. We had
also the disaster to Frau von Pogwisch's and Ottilie's
hopes, and the strain put upon their fortitude and self-
control. Fate had dealt the same blow to both. Fran von
Pogwisch had to meet the Count almost daily at court,
very often his young bride too. She had to smile and be
friendly, with death at her heart; this under the eyes of
a malicious world very well aware of her shattered hopes.

Ottilie had been sent for to sustain her in this humanly almost impossible situation. Now she herself was compelled to bear with what grace she could summon the *brouillerie* with Herr von Goethe. That too was soon known to society, and watched by sharp and eager eyes. He deliberately and ostentatiously cut her. It was my office to twist and turn my heart-sick way through all these vexed complications; and I was desolate too, for shortly before Christmas Ferdinand left us, to return to Silesia and lead to the altar his Thusnelda or Dorothea — actually, the girl's name was Fanny. I had never had a title to any hopes on his account. Stepmotherly nature had always cast me for the rôle of confidential friend — though she did not spare me the pain of his loss. Yet she did, in my case, somewhat soften the blow, by giving me a certain sense of relief, even a mild feeling of satisfaction. I, in my unlovely person, found it easier now to share with my lovely friend the cult of our dear departed hero, being no longer made uneasy by his physical presence.

"So I got some welcome peace of mind from our young man's departure and his union with another, notwithstanding all the renunciation it involved. There was hope of peace for Ottilie too, growing out of the breach with August. It had brought much pain and social embarrassment. Yet she confessed to me that it did her good, it was a relief and a liberation. Now that all was over between them, her heart might find a neutral sort of repose after the unnerving strain of the relationship. She could give herself to the sacred memory of Ferdinand, and to the consolation of her unhappy mother. I was glad to hear it. Yet somehow I could not feel quite secure. August was a son — that was the distinguishing characteristic of his life. In him one was dealing with his great father. And the father certainly had not approved the breach with the 'little person'; the son had simply brought it about himself without Goethe's consent. Just as certainly the father would use all his authority to heal it. That he desired and furthered the ill-omened connection I knew. Indeed, August's sorry passion for Ottilie was but the expression, and the result, of the father's desires. The son loved in her the very type of the father's election; his love was imitative, traditional. It was bond-service, and the breach was revolt, an act of attempted independence. I did not estimate very highly its strength or persistence. And Ottilie? Had she really freed herself from the son of such a father? Could I really regard her as free? I doubted it — and with reason.

She received with agitation the reports of August's increasingly irregular mode of life. I saw my doubts justified. Events had conspired to rob the young man of his moral fibre and make him seek oblivion in certain vices — indeed, his nature had always been inclined to them, for he was only deceptively robust, and withal sensual in a strange, melancholy sort of way. There were the social ostracism of the enlistment scandal, the break with Ottilie, his own inner conflicts, and probably open disagreement with his father as well. I mention them all, not for the purpose of condoning the dissipated course now the theme of common gossip in Weimar. Yet they do, in a way, explain much. We heard talk from all sides, among others from Schiller's daughter Karoline and her brother Ernst. People complained of August's intolerable behaviour; it was grossly rude and quarrelsome. It was said that he drank immoderately, and one night in a drunken condition was involved in a disgraceful brawl and taken up by the watch. For the sake of his name he was not held, the bad business was hushed up. The whole town knew of his intercourse with women one can only call creatures. The Privy Councillor had turned over to him the pavilion on the Ackerwand, to house his minerals and fossils — for August imitated his father in a passion for collecting. This pavilion, it seems, now served him in his questionable doings. He was carrying on an affair with a hussar's wife, the husband winking at it for the sake of the presents the woman brought home. She was a tall, lanky creature, though not actually ill-favoured. There was much laughter over the tale, repeated out of vanity by the woman herself, that August had sworn to her she was the day-star of his life! Something else people laughed at, that was shocking and yet rather touching as well: the old poet was supposed to have met the pair in the garden one evening, and hastily disappeared, with the words: 'Children, don't disturb yourselves.' I cannot vouch for the story, but incline to think it is genuine, for it tallies with a certain moral *laissez-faire* — to call it by no other name — characteristic of the great man. I refrain from passing judgment upon it.

"But I must try here to express something I have often thought about, though often with misgivings about the propriety of dwelling on such ideas — either for my-

self or anyone else. This is what I mean: certain traits
of the famous father seem to me faint foreshadowings of
characteristics so unhappily and destructively developed
in the son. It is not easy to recognize them as the same,
and reverence and loyalty would shrink from the task.
In the father's case they are held in an equilibrium so
happy and so creative that the world has joy of them.
But in the son they reveal themselves as coarsened and
sensualized, and all their moral offensiveness stands out.
Take for instance that glorious work *Elective Affinities*.
It is enthralling, even from the point of view of its ethical
problem, and highly subtle in its treatment. But it is a
novel about adultery, and philistines have often condemned it as immoral. Classical sentiment and standards
have of course shrugged their shoulders or even rejected it
as partisan and bald. Neither criticism is at all in place.
No one could, on his conscience, deny that the book
contains a morally equivocal element, a something complaisant, or even false — forgive me the word. It plays a
very questionable game of hide-and-seek with the sanc-
tity of marriage, and yields too much, and too fatalis-
tically, to a sort of natural mysticism. It even deals with
death in a way that. . . . We are taught to regard death
as the means by which our moral nature preserves its
freedom. Is it not here felt and portrayed as the last and
sweetest refuge of concupiscence? Ah, I well know how
absurd, how even blasphemous it must seem to compare
August's irregular and dissipated character with the gifts
that created the novel and gave it to mankind; to see in
him an unlovely manifestation of the same powers! I
have already spoken of my scruples and doubts, my mis-

givings on the score of truth: whether it really is something worth striving after, and all knowledge of it a duty and an obligation — or whether there are such things as forbidden truths. . . . To return to Ottilie: she was obviously far too much agitated by the current gossip. I could not believe she was disinterested. Her hatred of the hussar's wife was so violent as to tempt one to give it a more precise name. There must be a bottomless depth in the feelings of a pure woman when a man whom she regards confers his favour on such a creature and puts her in a position of preferment, no matter with how base an object. On the one hand, a good woman must feel such a rival to be so far beneath her that her own self-respect is unscathed. But on the other, jealousy — that special variant of the vice of envy — makes her lift up her rival to her own plane, to hate her there as an equal by the power of sex. Again, the man's immorality, despite all the horror it makes her feel, may perhaps exercise a profound and awful fascination on such a pure feminine soul. It might fan to flame an expiring love. And as to the pure all things are pure, it might even evoke the desire to reclaim him, to bring him, by surrender and sacrifice, back to his better self.

"In a word, I was anything but convinced that my darling would not welcome a renewal of August's suit. He, in his turn, would very likely be forced, sooner or later, to make such a move, urged by that other will behind his own, which he had defied when he broke with her. My expectations, my fears, were realized. In June of last year — I recall the evening as though it were yesterday — four of us were standing in the Hall of Mir-

rors at court: Ottilie and I, our friend Karoline von
Harstall, and a Herr von Gross. I had seen August hovering in the background and listening. At length he came
up and entered into the conversation. At first he spoke
to no one in particular. But after a while—it was a very
tense moment, demanding much self-control from us
all—he addressed some questions and remarks directly
to Ottilie. His words were conventional, they revolved
round the war and the peace, the lists of the fallen, his
father's autobiography, the Prussian ball and its excellent
cotillion. But he spoke with a forced enthusiasm ill
suited to the subject-matter of the talk. And when we
parted from him, with a curtsy — for we had been about
to leave — he rolled up his eyes.

"'Did you see him rolling his eyes at you?' I asked
Ottilie on the stair. 'I saw him,' she answered, 'it distressed me. Believe me, Adele, I do not want him to
return to his old love. It would only give me back my
old torments, in place of my present comfortable indifference.' That was what she said. But the ice had been
broken, the open feud was a thing of the past. At the
theatre, and elsewhere in society, Herr von Goethe renewed the contact. Ottilie avoided private conversation
with him. But she confessed that she often felt strangely
touched by the look in his eyes. The infinitely wretched
expression he wore recalled old times and stirred old
feelings of guilt in her heart. In response I spoke of my
own anxiety, and of the mischief I foresaw in renewed
intercourse with such a disturbing, undisciplined nature.
No friendship with him was conceivable, I told her; he
would always demand more than, if I understood her

aright, she was prepared to give. But she responded: 'Be calm, dear heart; I am quite free again, and shall remain so. Look, he has lent me a book, Pinto's *Wonderful Trip round the World in Twenty-one Days*. I have not even looked at it yet. If it were Ferdinand, I should know it by heart.' That was true. But was it a sufficient safeguard or consolation? I still saw that she was under his spell, that the thought of being his charmed her, she was like a little bird before a snake.

"My head went round when I thought of her as August's wife. And yet what other end could there be? Things happened, incomprehensible things; they rent my heart. My conviction that this unhappy man would destroy her seemed true even in advance. Last autumn my poor darling fell seriously ill, probably in consequence of her inner conflict. Three weeks she lay ill with jaundice, being treated with tar—it is supposed to be good for this ailment to keep a vessel of tar under the bed and mirror oneself in it. But when she recovered and once more met him in society, he seemed not to have missed her at all, nor to have remarked her absence. At least, not a syllable escaped him to the contrary!

"Ottilie was beside herself, she suffered a relapse and had to mirror herself in the tar for another week. 'I could have given up my hopes of heaven for him,' she sobbed on my breast, 'and he betrayed me! Can you believe it?' Two weeks later she came to me, deathly pale, poor creature, and with staring eyes told me that August, with perfect calm, had spoken of their approaching union, as though it were a settled fact! Can you imagine anything more uncanny? What do you say to it? He had not declared himself, nor asked for her love; you cannot even say he had talked about his marriage with her. No; with paralyzing casualness he simply *referred to it*. 'And you?' I cried. 'I beg you, Tillemuse, my dearest, tell me what you replied to him!' My honoured friend, she confessed to me that she had been speechless.

"You can understand I was outraged, I was in revolt against the sinister fate that so coolly and calmly opposed her. One obstacle still stood in the way: the existence of a woman, the Frau Privy Councillor, Christiane, the Demoiselle. If Herr von Goethe, as he must in the end, asked the consent of Ottilie's mother and grandmother, his own mother would be a serious drawback to the match. My dearest friend, she died last June. The obstacle was done away. Nay, more, the situation was even worsened; for now it is August's duty to lead a new mistress to his father's house. During the period of mourning, and because the season was coming to an end, he saw Ottilie but seldom throughout the summer. But something else happened. I can give you no precise account, because partly as a jest, partly out of embarrassment, Ottilie has shrouded the event in mystery. At the beginning of August she had a meeting on the Ackerwand with the Privy Councillor, Germany's great poet.

"I repeat, I must omit any account of this meeting, for I possess none myself. With a playfulness that had about it nothing in the least playful, Ottilie refused to give me any. It pleases her to shroud the affair in a partly teasing, partly solemn mystery. When I urge her she tells me, with a smile: 'You know, Adele, he will never be expansive on the subject of his conversation with the Emperor. The memory is a jealously held possession, kept from the world and even from his friends. Forgive me if I take him for my pattern; let it be enough if I simply say, he was charming to me.'

"He was charming to her. So much, dearest lady, I can repeat to you. And with the information my story ends. As you see, it is of that delightful kind that ends with a betrothal. If no miracle happens, if heaven does not intervene, then court and city may expect the event at Christmas or at latest by New Year's Eve."

CHAPTER SIX

THE CONVERSATION with Mademoiselle Schopenhauer
has been related as though it took place without inter-
ruptions. But actually there were two: in the middle and
again near the end the flow of her voluble broad-Saxon
accents was arrested, both times by Mager, the waiter.
Obviously suffering under the necessity, and with most
fervid apologies, he appeared in the parlour to make further announcements.

The first was a message from Frau Geheimrat Ridel's
maid. She was downstairs, he said, urgently inquiring
after the Frau Councillor and how long it would be before she came to the Esplanade, where they were greatly
disturbed about her, and the dinner was getting spoiled.
Mager had tried in vain to explain that important callers
had delayed the arrival of the Elephant's illustrious guest
at her sister's house, and that he, Mager, was not the man
to interrupt them. But the mamsell had insisted vigorously and, after waiting some time, she had forced him
to come upstairs and announce her presence. She had
strict orders, she said, to get the Frau Councillor and
fetch her back home, where impatience and hunger were
both mounting.

Charlotte had got up, very red in the face. Her manner and her gesture seemed definitely to say: "Yes, it is inexcusable. What time is it? I must go. We must interrupt ourselves, for the time." But, surprising to say, after that she sat down again and said just the opposite of what might have been expected.

"Very good, Mager, I know, you do not like bursting in on us like this. Tell the mamsell she should wait — or else go; perhaps it would be best if she went and told the Frau Chamberlain not to stay dinner for me; I will come as soon as affairs permit. She must not worry about me, there is no ground for that. Of course, the Ridels are upset; who would not be? I am, myself, for I have no idea what time it is, and everything has turned out quite differently from what I thought. But things are as they are: I am not a private person, and I have higher claims to satisfy than that of a spoilt dinner. Tell the mamsell to say that I had to have my portrait taken, and then discuss important matters with Herr Doctor Riemer. Say that I am now just listening to a report from this lady and cannot get up and go away in the middle of it. Tell her to say all that, and about the claims on me, and the annoyance, to which I am no stranger myself, but I must deal with things as I can and I ask them to do the same."

"Very good, I thank you," Mager had answered, quite satisfied and understanding. He went away and Mademoiselle Schopenhauer resumed her tale, at about the point where the two young maidens went townwards on the wings of their enthusiasm after making their discovery in the park.

When Mager knocked the next time, she was at the moment in her narrative when she introduced the hussar's wife and discoursed about the *Elective Affinities*. He knocked with more firmness than before, fully justified of the interruption and having no scruples about it. With self-assured mien he announced: "Herr Chamberlain von Goethe."

It was Adele who sprang from the sofa at the announcement. Charlotte remained seated, indeed, but not because she was calm, merely that her limbs refused their office.

"*Lupus in fabula!*" cried Fräulein Schopenhauer. "Ye gods, what now? Mager, I must not meet the Herr Kammerrat. You must see to that, my man. You will have to smuggle me past him somehow. I rely on your discretion."

"Quite right, Fräulein," responded Mager, "quite right. I had expected something of the kind, for I know the delicacy of the social relations and how you can never tell what may happen. I told the Herr Kammerrat that the Frau Councillor was occupied for the moment, and invited him into the tap-room below. He is having a glass of Madeira and I set the bottle at his elbow. So I am in a position to ask the ladies to conclude their talk at their leisure and then give me the privilege of conducting the Fräulein downstairs to the entry before I tell the Herr Kammerrat that the Frau Councillor will receive him."

He was assured of the approval of both ladies for his foresight and discretion, and departed once more. But Adele said:

"My dear madam, I realize the importance of the moment. The son has come — that means a message from the father. He too, whom it concerns most of all, is aware of your arrival. And it could not be otherwise; it is a great sensation, and Weimar's Fama is a goddess fleet of foot. He has sent to you, he is presenting himself in the person of his son. I am so much moved, shaken as I already was by the events I have put before you, that I can scarcely refrain from tears. This advance is so incomparably more important and pressing than any visit of mine that I could not think of asking you — in consideration of the circumstance that the Kammerherr is well provided with Madeira — to hear my tale to the end before you receive him. I could not think of it, honoured friend, and my departure must prove —"

"Stay, my child," Charlotte had answered with decision, "and do sit down again, I beg." The old lady's cheeks had a pastel tint and her mild blue eyes a feverish glaze. But she sat extraordinarily upright on the sofa, alert and self-controlled. "The gentleman," she said, "who has announced himself can wait a little. By listening to you I am also occupying myself with his affairs; and in my own I am accustomed to preserving due order and sequence. Go on, I beg of you. You were speaking of the filial inheritance, of a pleasing balance —"

"Quite right," Adele took up her thread, sitting down again with speed. "Take such a glorious performance as —" And in increased tempo, with the most flowing cadences and incredible glibness of tongue Adelmuse brought her story to an end. She only took breath after the last word; indeed, it was almost without a pause, only with a certain shift of intonation, that she went on:

"Such are the matters, my dear lady, that the news of your presence impelled me to put before you. The desire to do so was one with the wish to see you to pay my homage. And thus I have been guilty of a subterfuge before Line Egloffstein: I did not tell her of my purpose and kept her away from this interview. Dear and most honoured friend! The miracle I spoke of—it is one I hope you may perform. If, as I said, heaven does intervene to prevent a perverse and perilous union that weighs upon my very soul, it might well, so it seems to me, make use of you as its instrument, and may have brought you hither to that end. In a few minutes you will see the son, and in a few hours, I suppose, his august father. You might use your influence, might warn, might presume to do so. You might be August's mother. You are not, because the course of your life was otherwise decreed, because you would have it otherwise. Bring here in play that power of reason, that clear and sober sense of what is right and fitting, that actuated you in that earlier time. Save my Ottilie! She might be your daughter, she looks as though she were; and just because of that, she is today in the same danger you once escaped by opposing to it a deliberate and dignified rational sense. Be a mother to this image of your own youth, for that she is, and as such is she beloved, by and through a son. Protect this "little person" as the father calls her; on the ground of what you once were to the father, save her from being sacrificed to a fascination that makes me so inexpressibly afraid! The man whom in your wisdom you chose is gone, the woman who became August's mother is now no more. You are alone with the father, with him who might be your son, and with the dear child who might be your own daughter. Your voice would be like to a mother's voice — lift it, then, against this wrong, this destructive course! This is my prayer, my invocation — "

" My dear good child," Charlotte said, " what are you asking of me? How would you have me intervene? As I listened to your story, with mixed feelings, it is true, but with the liveliest interest, I never dreamed that such a suggestion, such a responsibility, would be linked with it. I am bewildered — not alone by your request, but by the way in which you prefer it. You would plunge me into situations — you would lay on me obligations, you would make me, an old woman, envisage a return to my former self. . . . You seem to suggest that with the Frau Privy Councillor's death my relations with the great man whom I have not seen for a lifetime are entirely altered — and in such a way that he would grant me maternal rights over his son! Confess that such an idea is both shocking and absurd. It would appear that even this journey of mine — but probably I have misunderstood you. I beg your pardon. I am weary from all the impressions and trials of the day, and, as you know, there are still more to come. Farewell, my child, and my cordial thanks for your communicativeness. You must not think that this leave-taking means I repulse you. My attention as I listened must assure you that you had turned to no unsympathetic ear. Perhaps I may really have the opportunity to help and advise. You will understand that I cannot know before I receive the

message; I cannot know whether I shall be in a position
to aid you."

She remained seated, putting out her hand with a
friendly smile to Adele, who had sprung up to make her
curtsy. Both were flushed and excited, Charlotte's head
bobbed above the young girl as Adele imprinted a re-
spectful kiss upon her hand. Mademoiselle Schopenhauer left the room. Charlotte was a few minutes alone
and sat there with bent head on the reception-room sofa;
then Mager came and repeated: "Herr Kammerrat von
Goethe."

August entered. His brown, close-lying eyes were
bright with the eager gaze he directed towards Charlotte, yet he wore a shy smile. She looked towards him
with an urgency she tried to soften by smiling too. Her
heart was in her mouth, her cheeks glowed. All that
might come from the strain she had been under; but
for a sympathetic observer the sight, if a little absurd, was also, we may hope, appealing and charming.
Surely there was not such another schoolgirl of sixty-
three in the world! He was twenty-seven — four years
older than in the long-ago time. In her confused thoughts
it seemed as though only those four years divided her
from the young Goethe of that time. Of course it was
absurd, it had been four-and-forty! For her a great span
of years, a whole long lifetime; without much variety,
yet withal so rich, so full of feeling! Rich, that is to
say, in children; eleven hard and happy childbeds, eleven
periods of nursing at the breast. Twice the breast had
been heavy with milk in vain, the poor suckling had been
too feeble, they had given it back to earth. Then the

time of her widow- and matron-hood, already sixteen
years long, without her mate and father of her brood,
who went before and left vacant the place beside her.
That was her idle time; she was no longer busy with
bearing and cherishing, with the actual present that was
stronger and more real than the past and outweighed all
thought of the "might-have-beens" of life. Now she
had time — time to think and recall, to conjure up memories and imaginings of her other personality, the shadowy
one that had nothing to do with being a mother and
doing her duty by society, but was a legend and a symbol, and from year to year had played an ever greater
part in the thoughts and imaginations of mankind.

Ah, time! And we, time's children! We faded in her,
we drooped and dropped to earth; but life and youth
were always above earth. Life was young, youth was
always alive, with and beside us as we dropped away.
There was yet a space when time was still ours while already it belonged to youth. When we could still see
youth and kiss its smooth brow, that was our own youth
returned; and it had been born out of us. The man before her was not hers, she had not borne him — but she
might have done: a thought not so remote since the death
of that other who forbade it. The place beside her own
was empty now; so was that other place, beside the
father, the youth of long ago. She measured him with
her eyes, this fruit of that other one. She looked at him
critically, jealously, to see how much better, perhaps,
she might have done. No, the demoiselle's work had been
fair enough. He was impressive, he was almost handsome, if you liked. Did he look like his mother? But

she had never seen the sharer of Goethe's bed. Perhaps
it was from her he got his tendency to portliness — he
was too heavy for his age, though his height carried it
off well. The father had been slighter in her time, that
vanished time that had fashioned and dressed its children
so differently from this, more formally, with rolled and
powdered hair and ribboned queue behind, or else more
unconventionally, with loose-flowing locks and lace-
trimmed shirt romantically open. This youth wore his
bushy brown locks in the unpowdered, natural, post-
Revolution style, covering his forehead and running
down in curled side-whiskers inside the high, pointed
shirt-collar. The soft round chin nestled with almost
comic dignity within it. Certainly he looked more formal, more socially presentable, even official, in his high
stock that filled the opening of the collar. He wore a
brown frock coat wide open in front as the fashion was;
the shoulders were built up and on one of the sleeves was
a mourning band. The waist fitted snugly and correctly
about his rather plump form. He stood with his elbows
elegantly drawn in, holding his top hat bottom side up
before him. And yet this impeccable conventionality,
free from any trace of the *outré*, seemed as though meant
to counteract and obliterate something else, something
not quite *comme il faut*, not quite irreproachable from a
bourgeois point of view, though perhaps fine in itself.
The eyes betrayed it; they were soft and pensive, they
had a more humid brilliance than is quite acceptable, so
to speak. They were the eyes of the Amor who had
been a scandal when he presented the birthday verses to
the Duchess — the eyes of a love-child.

It was the dark-brown hue of these eyes, so like the elder Goethe's, set close together and with a something just not quite right about them, that suddenly made her receptive for August's likeness to his father. It happened during the few seconds it took the young man to enter, make his bow, and move towards her. The likeness was universally recognized, and as striking as it was hard to analyse in detail. The forehead was lower, the nose less aquiline, the mouth smaller and more feminine. Yet none the less a likeness asserted itself — shyly worn, tinged with melancholy as though by the consciousness of being a little debased; worn, indeed, with an air of apology. But unmistakable; there was the carriage of the body, with shoulders thrown back and torso thrust forward, either in imitation or else a genuine and constitutional inheritance. Charlotte was deeply moved. She saw before her an effort, not quite successful, on the part of life to repeat itself by variation, to be uppermost again in time and in the present; a manifestation evoking many memories, and peer of that earlier one only in respect of youth and presentness. It agitated her very much; her breathing became almost a gasp as Christiane's son bent over her hand. He exhaled an odour of wine and eau-de-cologne.

Suddenly she recalled that as it stood before her in its present form, youth also represented the rank of nobility.

"Welcome, Herr von Goethe," she said. "I greatly esteem your attention and am rejoiced to make, so soon after my arrival in Weimar, the acquaintance of the son of a dear friend of my youth."

"I thank you for your kind reception," he answered,

and for a moment showed his small, white, youthful teeth in a conventional smile. "I am come from my father. He has received your letter, and instead of answering it, he preferred to have me welcome you in his name, Frau Councillor, to Weimar. Your presence, he said to me, will be most enlivening."

In the midst of her emotion and embarrassment she had to smile.

"That is expecting a great deal," she said, "from a tired old woman. And how is our honoured Privy Councillor?" she went on, indicating one of the chairs where she and Riemer had sat. August took it and placed himself near her, with ceremony.

"I thank you for asking," he said. "He is so-so. We must be content. On the whole he is in good condition; there is always ground for concern or caution, he has his ups and downs and is liable to many ailments. Great regularity is always desirable. May I in turn inquire about the Frau Councillor's journey hither — it was without mishap, I trust? And you are well accommodated here? My father will be gratified to learn it. We hear you are come to visit your sister, Frau Privy Councillor of the Board of Domains. That will indeed be a source of great and heart-felt gratification in a family whose head is highly esteemed by the authorities and universally respected by his subordinates. I flatter myself that I myself sustain the most harmonious relations with him, personally and officially."

Charlotte found his language old-fashioned and artificial. The phrase "most enlivening" had been odd

enough; "heart-felt gratification" and "harmonious relations" made her smile too. Riemer might have said
that sort of thing, but in the mouth of a young man it
sounded even stranger, it was eccentric and pedantic.
She felt that his manner of speech had been acquired —
of course he was quite unaware of any affectation. Her
features twitched involuntarily; but she was convinced
that he did not notice it, since any reason for smiling must
be remote from his mind. She could not help contrasting
his stiffness and dignity with all that she had just heard
about him, all that had poured from the wide mouth,
from between the humid lips of Mademoiselle Adele.
She thought of the hussar's wife, of August's weakness
for the bottle, of the time he had been accosted by the
watch; and of Riemer's departure from the house, af-
fronted by his rudeness. She thought of his precarious,
artificially protected social position since the affair of the
volunteer troop; of the ill-suppressed charges of cowardice and unchivalrous behaviour. And above all there
was the thought of his gloomy penchant for Ottilie,
the "little person," the fair blonde maiden. That love
did not now seem to Charlotte in contradiction to his
singular way of expressing himself, but immediately and
far-reachingly connected with it. Yet at the same time
it was connected also with Charlotte herself, the old
Charlotte, or rather with the larger, the abstract presentment of herself; and this, indeed, in a way that disturbed her and complicated the present situation. It
made her confuse the two characters, that of the son and
that of the lover; though all the time the son remained

the son, pre-eminently therein that he behaved like his father. "My God! " Charlotte thought, looking into the rather handsome and so familiar face, "My God! " And into the soundless cry she put all her feeling, all the pitying tenderness the young man aroused in her, as well as all her sense of the absurdity of his manner of speech.

She thought again of the mission with which she had been charged, the plea that she would enter the lists in the present situation to prevent a certain thing from taking place. She was either to talk the "little person" out of sticking to her lover, or the lover out of sticking to the "little person." Certainly she felt no urge or vocation to do so. It was too much to ask her to intrigue against the little one in order to rescue her. As Charlotte looked at it, it was the little one's own business; she ought obviously to drive the hussar's wife from the field, and all other rivals as well. And from this point of view, Charlotte, the elderly woman, felt great solidarity with the little one.

"I am glad to hear, Herr Kammerrat," said she, "that two such able men as you and my brother-in-law are on such excellent terms. It is no news to me, of course. In correspondence " (she repeated the words involuntarily, almost as though she were assuming one of his ludicrous habits of speech), "in correspondence I have had the same report from my sister. May I take the occasion to congratulate you on your recent advancement in office and at court? "

"I thank you most humbly."

"Of course you merit it," she went on. "I hear much

praise of your earnest and conscientious services to our
land and our prince. For your years, if I may say so, you
have heavy responsibilities. And I am aware too that besides all else you are of great and praiseworthy assistance
to your father."

"I rejoice," he said, "that I can still be that, in addition to the rest. Considering his serious illnesses, in 1801
and 1805, it is a wonder that we have him still with us.
Both times I was very young, but I well remember our
terror. The first time it was smallpox brought him to the
edge of the grave, complicated as it was by a bronchitis
that would not let him lie in bed for fear of choking.
He had to fight it out standing up. For a long time his
nerves were shattered. And eleven years ago he had
asthma, with attacks that made us fear for his life for
weeks and weeks. Dr. Stark of Jena treated him. After
the crisis he had a long, slow convalescence, and Dr.
Stark advised a trip to Italy. But my father said he was
too old to bring himself to such an undertaking. He was
at the time fifty-six years old."

"He was giving up too early."

"You agree with me? And we think he has given up
his journeys to his Italy on the Rhine as well, though last
year and the year before they did him so much good.
Had you heard of his accident?"

"No — did something happen to him?"

"Oh no, he suffered no harm. This summer, after my
mother's death —"

"My dear Herr Kammerrat," she interrupted, again
with a start, "I have till now refrained — I scarcely know
why myself — from offering my condolences for this

grave, this irreparable loss. But you are already aware, without words, of the sympathy of an old friend — "

He gave her one quick shy look from his dark, humid eyes, then dropped them again.

"I thank you most warmly," he murmured.

There was a fitting silence of a few seconds.

"But at least," she continued after a little, "that harsh blow from the hand of fate did not succeed in doing serious damage to the health of our dear Privy Councillor."

"He himself was unwell in the last days of her illness," resumed August. "He had hastened back from Jena, where he was working, when the news became alarming; but on the day she died he was kept in bed by a fever. My mother died of convulsions, or perhaps during convulsions — a very hard death. Even I was not allowed to go to her, none of her friends were about her at the last. The Riemers, the Engels, and the Vulpiuses had withdrawn. The sight was probably more than one could bear. We had two nurses from outside; in their arms she breathed her last. It was — I scarcely know how to express it — it was a business for women only, like a difficult and awful miscarriage or a stillborn childbed, a — a birth of death. That was the way it seemed to me. Perhaps it was the convulsions made me think of it, and that they would not let me in. And my father, with his delicate constitution, that always had to be spared all sad or disturbing sights — how much more had they to protect him from it, even if he had not been ill abed! He kept his bed when Schiller was dying, too. His nature makes him avoid contact with death and the tomb; it is partly deliberate, I should say, and partly involuntary. Did you know that four of his brothers and sisters died in infancy? He survived, he lives — one might say he lives to the highest degree. But several times since his childhood he has been close to death — momentarily or during a given period. By the last expression I am referring to the Werther phase." — He bethought himself, somehow confused, and added: "But I was thinking rather of the physical crises, the hæmorrhage in his youth, the serious illnesses in his fifties, besides the attacks of gout and the stone, that made him when still so young begin to visit the Bohemian spas. Then there have been times when, without anything definite ailing, everything was at sixes and sevens with him, and society would not have been surprised to hear any day of his death. Twelve years ago we were watching him with anxious eyes, that was when Schiller died. Beside him, the invalid, my mother always seemed in blooming health; yet it was she who died, he who is alive. Very much alive, despite all threats to his existence; I often think he will outlive us all. He will not hear of dying, he ignores the idea, simply passes it by. I am convinced that if I were to die before him — and I might; I am young, of course, and he is old, but what is my youth beside his age! I am nothing but a by-blow of his nature, and gifted with indifferent energy. I am convinced that if I died, he would say nothing, do nothing to let people see his feelings, and never mention my death. That is what he would do, I know him. You might put it that he is on uncertain terms with life, and for that reason so consistently avoids deathbeds and burials and the macabre in general. He has never been able to attend funerals; he would not see Herder in his coffin, or Wieland, or our beloved Duchess Amalie, of whom he was so fond. I had the honour to represent him at Wieland's obsequies, in Osmannstaedt, four years ago."

Charlotte cleared her throat, feeling a mental unease that almost amounted to a revulsion. She blinked rapidly, then she said: "I have a little note-book where I set down quotations that I love. I put in it this: 'Since when does Death encounter thee in frightful guise, when thou hast lived all thy life tranquilly with his changing shapes as with all the other wonted forms of earth?' That is from *Egmont*."

"Yes, *Egmont*," said he; and that was all. He stared on the ground; suddenly lifting his eyes to look at Charlotte with wide and searching gaze, then casting them down again. She had the impression, afterwards, that he had purposely aroused the emotions she was struggling with; if so, the quick glance should have assured him of his success. At least, he seemed to relent and seek to soften the effect of his words, for he said:

"My father did of course see my mother as she lay dead, and took a most affecting leave of her. We have a poem he wrote then; a few hours after the end he had it copied down. He dictated it to his attendant, as I was otherwise occupied. Only a few lines, but most expressive:

> O sun, in vain thou seek'st
> The gloomy clouds to sever:
> My life's whole content now must be,
> To mourn her ever."

"H'm," went Charlotte again. She nodded with hesitant sympathy. But within herself she confessed that she found the lines on the one hand insignificant, on the other exaggerated. And again she got the impression — and read it with some conviction in the look he bent on her — that he had repeated the poem to challenge just that opinion. Not, of course, that she would express it, but that she would have it, and that they would read it in each other's eyes. She cast down her own, murmuring some inarticulate words of praise.

"You agree?" said he, though he had not understood. "It is of the highest importance," he went on, "that the poem exists; I rejoice at it more every day, and I have given out several copies. Society will see — with chagrin, yet it will not hurt it to see at last — how truly and deeply my father loved my mother, despite all the freedom and independence he had of course to preserve. He honours her memory with profoundest emotion, the memory of a woman pursued by society with hatred, malice, and slander. And why?" he asked himself, with increasing warmth. "Because when she was well she liked to have a little distraction, to dance and drink a glass of wine in cheerful society. What a reason! Father has always laughed about it; he liked to joke with me sometimes over Mother's rather lusty love of life. Once he even wrote some verses describing the joyous circle that always made Mother their centre. But it was all in a friendly spirit, and quite approving. After all, he always goes his own way, he was more away from us, in Jena and at the baths, than he was at home. Sometimes he even stopped at work in the castle at Jena over Christmas — that means

my birthday too — and only sent presents. But Father
well knew how Mother cared for his physical well-being,
at home or abroad; how she carried the burden of the
house on her shoulders and kept everything from him
that could disturb his difficult and important work. She
never pretended she could understand it — I should like
to know if the others do either — but she always showed
it the greatest respect. He was grateful, and society
should have been grateful too if they had truly respected
it themselves. But respect is just what they have not
got in their mean little souls. They preferred to heckle
Mother and make spiteful remarks because she was not
ethereal enough, not sylphlike, but fat, with red cheeks,
and could not speak French. In heaven's name! It was all
sheer envy and nothing else, just green-eyed jealousy,
because quite unconsciously she had been fortunate, and
become the presiding spirit and wife in the household of
the great poet and Minister of State. Just envy, just
envy. And so I am glad that we have this poem on
Mother's death; it makes society go into fits of rage, because it is so beautiful and so full of meaning." His voice
had risen, he spoke wildly and furiously, his fist was
clenched, his eyes dark; the veins stood out on his forehead.

Charlotte saw that she had before her a young man in
a rage, liable to excesses.

"My dear Herr Kammerrat," said she, leaning towards
him, and taking the fist that lay shaking on August's
knee. Gently she loosened the clenched fingers. "My
dear Herr Kammerrat, I can quite feel with you, the
more that I am heartily pleased that you so loyally sup-

port your dear departed mother, instead of contenting yourself with your justifiable pride in your great father. It is not an easy thing to be a good son to a father like yours. I esteem most highly in you your chivalrous attitude in upholding against the world the memory of your mother, even though she was made, like the rest of us, of commoner clay. I myself am a mother, I even might, as a matter of age, be yours. And the envy you speak of — ah, how much I agree with you there! I have always despised it, and kept myself free of it with all my strength, and I may say I have succeeded. What folly, to be envious of another's lot! As though we all had not to pay for being human — and then to make the mistake of wishing enviously for some other person's destiny! And besides that, how pitiably weak! To unnerve ourselves by idle coveting of others' fortunes, instead of being the architect of our own! "

August took back his hand, with an embarrassed smile, and a slight bow, in thanks for the motherly little service she had done him.

"The Frau Councillor is right," he said. "Mother had suffered enough. Peace be with her. But it is not on her account alone that I am bitter. It is for Father's sake too. It is all over now; it has passed, as life passes, and all is still. The stone of stumbling is now safely under the earth. But what a stone it once was, always in the way of the self-righteous and the Pharisees, the moral guardians of society! How they always badgered my father and found fault with him because he dared to rebel against the social code and take a simple girl from the people and live with her before their faces! How they always made me feel it wherever they could, and looked at me out of the corners of their eyes! They shrugged their shoulders, with taunts or else a censorious kind of pity for the freedom to which I owed my very existence! As though a man like my father had not the right to live according to his own lights, by the fundamental, classic law of moral self-government! But these Christian patriots, these exponents of enlightened virtue, would not grant him that. They moaned over the conflict between genius and morality — as though the law of free and self-governing beauty were a matter of art only and not of life as well! But that would never occur to them; they preferred to keep on giving little pin-pricks about inconsistency and bad examples. All female tittle-tattle! And did they even give credit to the genius and poet in him, if not to his personality? Certainly not. The *Meister* was a mass of pornography, the *Elegies* a sink of iniquity, and the 'God and the Bayadere' and the 'Bride of Corinth' a lot of priapic indecency. No wonder they began by finding the *Werther* itself immoral and corrupting! "

" It is new to me, Herr Kammerrat, that anyone should have dared—"

"They have, Frau Councillor, they have. They dared to call the *Elective Affinities* lascivious. You little know human beings if you think they do not dare. And if it had only been the crowd, the common people! But everybody who was against the classic, against the law of æsthetic autonomy — Klopstock and Wieland, Bürger and Stolberg and Nicolai and the rest of them, they quarrelled with all my father's works and ways, and

looked askance at my mother because he chose his own
path and had her live with him. Herder was his old
friend, and President of the Consistory. It was he who
confirmed me. Even Schiller, who collaborated with my
father on the *Xenien*, even he; he wrote, as I happen to
know, a poem about my mother and privately blamed
my father about her — actually, I should think, because
he chose a woman beneath his station instead of one of
noble birth, like Schiller himself. Beneath his station!
As though a man like my father had a station — as though
he could have a rank, when he is unique! Intellectually
a man like him must choose beneath his station — then
why not socially too? Schiller himself was the first to
extol the superiority of merit above superiority of birth;
he made much more of it than my father ever has. Then
why did he make a wry face at my mother, who, it seems
to me, achieved superior merit by her care of my
father! "

"My dear Herr Kammerrat," Charlotte said, "humanly speaking, I quite understand what you mean;
though I must confess I do not know what æsthetic autonomy is, and have my doubts about taking up the
cudgels against such worthies as Klopstock, Herder, and
Bürger, or indeed against morality and patriotism! I
should not like to do that. But even such a reservation
does not need to prevent me from being on your side
against all those who pick quarrels with our dear Privy
Councillor or attack his renown as the great poet of the
fatherland."

He had not been heeding. His great dark eyes were
starting out and rolling from side to side. robbed of all

their beauty and softness by the fresh attack of fury which seized him.

"And was not everything regularized in the end?" he went on in a choked voice. "Father married my mother and made her his legal wife; and even before that I had been legitimized by ducal rescript and declared the legal heir of Father's patent of nobility. But the thing is that the nobility simply burst with rage at the idea of ennoblement for merit. That is probably why a man like that cavalry puppy seized the first opportunity to insult me about my mother. Only because in deference to Father's wishes I did not take the field against the Emperor. Simple arrest was much too mild a punishment for such blue-blooded insolence towards genius. He ought to have had a judge and a jailer and a branding-iron —"

His face was scarlet, he pounded his knee in an access of rage.

"Dear Herr Kammerrat," Charlotte said soothingly, as before. She bent towards him, but drew back a little as the fumes of cologne and Madeira saluted her nose. They seemed to be accentuated by his anger. She waited until the trembling fist relaxed and then gently laid her mitt-clad hand upon it. "We must not be so warm. I scarcely understand your words; but I almost feel that we are losing ourselves in fanciful imaginings. We have got off the track. Or rather, you have. For I have still in mind the mention you made of an accident your dear father suffered — or escaped, as you gave me to understand, else I should long since have insisted on hearing the rest. Pray tell me about it."

He still panted a little, but presently was able to smile at her for her kindness.

"The accident?" he asked. "It was nothing, let me reassure you. An accident of travel; it came about in this way. My father did not know where to go this summer. He seemed to be tired of the Bohemian spas, he visited them last in that melancholy year of 1813, when he was in Töplitz. It is a pity. The cure here at home is nothing by comparison, nor are Berka and Tennstädt. Karlsbad would probably be better for the rheumatism in his arm than the Tennstädt sulphur baths he last visited. But he has been put off the Karlsbad springs since 1812, when he suffered an attack of kidney trouble while taking them, the most severe for a long time. So then he discovered Wiesbaden, and went to the Rhine and Necker country for the first time in 1814. It did him good beyond all expectation. For the first time in many years he was once more in his native city — "

"I know," nodded Charlotte. "How sad it is that his dear, unforgettable mother was no longer alive! I know that the Frankfurt *Postoffice Gazette* published a fine article in honour of the city's great son."

"Yes. That is, it was when he came back from Wiesbaden, where he had spent some time with Zelter and Mines Commissioner Cramer. He went to see the Chapel of Saint Rochus, in the neighbourhood, and when he got back he made us a delightful sketch for an altar-piece: Saint Rochus leaves his father's castle as a young pilgrim and distributes his goods and gold to children. It is full of charming feeling. Professor Meyer and our friend Luise Seidler of Jena painted it."

"A professional artist?"

"Quite right. A connection of Frommann, the book-seller, and a close friend of Minna Herzlieb—"

"A suggestive name—you utter it without explanation—who is she?"

"Pardon, she is the Frommann's foster-daughter; my father was a frequent guest at the house while he was writing the *Elective Affinities*."

"Of course," Charlotte said. "I think I do recall hearing the name. The *Elective Affinities!* A work full of the most delicate perceptions. One can only regret that it did not have such an enthusiastic, world-wide reception as *The Sorrows of Werther*. But let me not interrupt you. Tell me about this journey."

"It was very happy, very successful, a real renewal of youth for my father, and he seemed to expect that when he undertook it. He spent several jolly days with the Brentanos in their nook on the Rhine, Franz Brentano, you know—"

"I know. Maxi's stepson. One of the five children of good old Peter Brentano's first marriage. I know. They say she had remarkably fine black eyes. Also that she was lonely, poor thing, in her husband's big old merchant house. I am pleased to hear that her son Franz is on better terms with Goethe than her husband was."

"As good as his sister Bettina in Frankfurt. She it was who was so useful in getting material for Father's autobiography; sitting down daily with my departed grandmother and coaxing from her reminiscences of his childhood and youth, which Bettina took down for him. It is a consolation to think how many of the present gen-

eration feel an inherited love and reverence for my father
—in all the changes that have taken place in their opinions and views."

She had to smile at the distant way in which he referred to his own generation. But again he did not mark
the smile.

"The second time, in Frankfurt, he stopped with the
Schlossers; the Assessor's wife, you know, was a sister of Georg, who married my poor aunt Cornelia; her
sons Fritz and Christian are two good lads, full of sensibility, and perfect specimens of the thing I just spoke
of. They are hopelessly romantic and prey to the absurd
humours of the time; they would like best of all a return to the Middle Ages, just as though there had been
no Enlightenment. Christian has already embraced
Catholicism, and Fritz and his wife will not be long in
following him. But the traditional love and admiration
for Father, among all this yielding to the fashion, has
never failed them, and that may be the reason why he
excuses them and seems to feel very much at home with
these young people."

"A mind like his," Charlotte said, "is always able to
understand every point of view, if only it is held by people he can respect as human beings."

"Quite," responded August, with a bow. "But I
think," he added, "that he was glad to shift to the Gerbermühle, the Willemer estate on the Upper Main, near
Frankfurt."

"Yes; it was there my sons sought him out and finally
made his acquaintance. He was very kind to them."

"I am sure. He went there first on September 14th,

and again during the next month, coming from Heidelberg. In the brief interval came Privy Councillor Willemer's marriage to Marianne Jung, his foster-daughter."

"That sounds like a novel."

"Yes, it was romantic. The Privy Councillor was a widower, with two young daughters; a capital man, a philanthropist, a pedagogue, a political mind — even a poet, and an enthusiastic friend of the drama. Well, ten years before and more he had taken into his house Marianne, the child of actors in the Linz theatre, to save her from the dangers of stage life. The sixteen-year-old girl with the curly brown locks grew up with the daughters of the house. She is charming, she sings ravishingly, she presides capably and delightfully at an evening party; in the end the pedagogue and philanthropist becomes a wooer."

"Only human. The one does not exclude the other."

"Of course not. But even so, the domestic situation left something to be desired. Who knows how long it would have gone on if Father had not intervened and used his influence to put things in order. To that was certainly due the fact that when he came back, at the beginning of October, from Heidelberg, the foster-father, only a few days before, had made the foster-child his wife."

She stared at him, and he at her. Her flushed and weary features were drawn with an expression half of uncertainty, half of pain. She said:

"You seem to suggest that this change in the situation was somewhat of a disappointment to your father?"

"Not in the least," he answered, astonished. "On the

contrary, his pleasure as a guest in that charming spot could only come about against a background of a clear, settled, and regulated position. There was a splendid terrace, a shady garden, a wood close by, a refreshing view of water and mountains, and the freest and most generous hospitality. Father has seldom felt himself so fortunate. For months afterwards he raved about the mild sweet-scented evenings when the wide Main lay rosy in the sunset glow and his young hostess sang his own songs to him: 'Mignon,' 'The Bayadere,' and 'To the Moon.' You can fancy the pleasure felt by the newly wed husband at the friendship with which the great man honoured the little bride whom he himself had discovered and introduced to society. He regarded it, from all that I can hear, with a lively pride; and certainly he could not have done so if the situation had not first been clarified and regulated. In particular my father spoke with enthusiasm of the evening of the 18th of October, when from the Willemer's lookout tower they all enjoyed the bonfires lighted to celebrate the battle of Leipsic."

"That enjoyment, my dear Herr Kammerrat," said Charlotte, "refutes much of what has been said about your father's lack of patriotic feeling. In those days nobody suspected that a few months later Napoleon would escape from Elba and plunge the world into new confusion."

August nodded. "Yes, and entirely upset my father's plans for his next year's holiday. He thought and spoke of nothing else all winter but of repeating his expedition to that charming neighbourhood. And everybody felt that Wiesbaden had suited him better than Karlsbad.

He had not got through a Weimar winter so well for a long time. Aside from a rather violent catarrh that troubled him for a month, he felt well and young. Probably something else helped too: I mean his new field of study and poetic activity. Ever since that trying year of 1813 he had been immersed in Oriental, particularly Persian poetry; and a whole great corpus of songs and aphorisms in the most extraordinary and novel style had gradually accumulated in his portfolio. Many of them purport to be by an Oriental poet called Hatem, dedicated to a fair one named Zuleika."

"That *is* good news, Herr Kammerrat! The lover of poetry must rejoice to hear it, and admire a persistence, a power of renewal of the creative gift, as a direct boon from heaven itself. A woman, a mother, must look with envy, or at least with admiration, at the masculine power of endurance, so much greater than hers; at the great advantage of the creatively intellectual over the passively feminine. To think that it is no less than one-and-twenty years since I gave birth to my Fritz, my youngest child! "

"Father told me," said August, "that the name of the Dionysiac poet supposed to have written the verse, Hatem, means 'richly giving and taking.' You too, Frau Councillor, if I may say so, have been a richly giving one."

"But it is all so sadly long ago! " said she. " However, do go on. The god of war upset Hatem's plans? "

"He was driven from the field," replied August. " He was defeated by another god, and after some delays all went according to the heart's desire. At the end of last

May Father went to Wiesbaden, where he made the cure
until July, and while he was there the war threshed itself
out, no matter how; there were no political clouds in
the sky and he could enjoy the remainder of his summer on the Rhine."

" On the Main? "

" On the Rhine and on the Main. He visited Minister
von Stein at Burg Nassau and drove with him to Cologne,
having lately become interested in the work on the cathedral. He gave us a delightful description of the return
journey via Bonn and Coblenz, the city of Herr Görres
and his *Rhenish Mercury*, which was promoting the
Stein plans for a Constitution. It would surprise me to
know that he felt particularly in harmony with such
plans — more, indeed, than to hear that he fell in with
the ideas for the completion of the cathedral, which had
been shrewdly suggested to him. I ascribe the good mood
he was in during all this time rather more to the fine
weather and his pleasure in the delightful landscape. He
was again in Wiesbaden, also in Mainz, and then, in August, reached Frankfurt and was welcomed at the comfortable country estate, where affairs had long since got
into a settled train. There for five weeks he realized his
dream amid that generous hospitality and tasted once
more the immense well-being of the previous year. August is his birth month. It may well be that there is a
sympathetic bond between a man's temperament and the
time of year that brought him forth; that each recurrence has power to heighten his spirit. But I cannot forget that August is also the birth month of the Emperor
Napoleon, so lately celebrated as a high day and holiday

in Germany. I marvel, or rather I rejoice, to think of the
advantage the man of heroic thought has over the man of
heroic deeds. The awful tragedy of Waterloo had made
the way free for my father to enjoy the hospitality of
the Gerbermühle. Of the two who had conversed in
Erfurt, one sat chained to a rock in the middle of the
sea; whilst the other was left free by a favouring destiny
to enjoy the moment to his heart's content."

"I see but justice in it," Charlotte remarked. "Our
dear Goethe has done naught but good and friendly
deeds to men, whereas the other chastised them with
scorpions."

"Still," answered August, throwing back his head,
"no one can persuade me that my father too is not a
tremendous and dominating force."

"No one would try," responded she, "and no one
would dispute it. But it is like Roman history, where
we read of good and bad emperors. Your father is one
of the good and mild ones, while the other was a blood-
reeking demon. Their diverse destinies mirror the difference you so aptly point out. So Goethe stopped for
six weeks in the home of the newly wedded pair?"

"Yes, until September, when he went to Karlsruhe,
and by commission from His Serene Highness visited the
famous mineral collections. He went expecting to meet
Frau von Türckheim, the former Lilli Schönemann of
Frankfurt, who sometimes came over from Alsace to
see her relatives."

"After so many years, then, there was a meeting between him and his former betrothed?"

"No, the Baroness did not come. It may have been illness that prevented her. I may tell you privately that she is consumptive."

"Poor Lilli," said Charlotte. "Still, not very much came of that episode. A few lyrics, but no great world-stirring work."

"The same illness," Herr von Goethe added to his former remark, "carried off that poor Brion, Friederike of Sesenheim, three years ago now. Her grave in Baden is not very far from where Father was staying. Her sad life ended in retirement at the home of her brother-in-law, Pastor Marx. I asked myself if Father visited or was tempted to visit that near-by grave. But I did not like to ask, and think it unlikely; he says in his confessions that on account of their painfulness he has no memory of the last days before the final farewell."

"I pity the poor girl," Charlotte said; "she had not the strength of purpose to rouse herself to a happy and honourable life, to wed some honest and capable man there in the country and love him as the father of her children. To live on memories alone is the privilege of age, after life's tasks are done. In youth it means death."

"You may be sure," responded August, "that what you say about strength of purpose is quite after my father's heart. He has said, in just this connection, that youth speedily triumphs over illnesses and wounds, no matter where the blame for the suffering lies. He counsels physical exercise, riding, skating, fencing, and so on, as aids in helping one pluck up one's heart. But the happiest means to resolve and to banish all one's own personal problems is of course the gift of poesy. In that confessional lies power to spiritualize our memories, to convert them into terms of universal humanity and make them issue in enduring works of art."

The young man had put the tips of his fingers together and with a movement of the elbows was mechanically swaying the two hands thus joined to and fro in front of him as he talked. His forced smile contradicted the wrinkles and red patches on his brow.

"Memory," he went on, "is certainly a strange thing. I have often thought about it; my life with a man like my father gives rise to many and varied reflections, some of them quite natural and proper, some not so much so. Memory must play an important part in the poet's life and work, the two being so interwoven that one may properly call them one, and speak of the poet's work as his life, his life as his work. It is not alone that the poetry is conditioned by the memories of the past; not alone that in Faust, in the two Maries in *Götz* and *Clavigo* and the bad figure their two lovers cut, the memories recur as an *idée fixe*. No, as I see it, memory becomes an *idée fixe* of life as well. Let us take, for instance, the theme of resignation. Painful renunciation, or what the poet in the confessional scourges as disloyalty and betrayal, is actually the initial, decisive, and inevitable factor. If I may so express it, it becomes the pattern and principal theme of life, and all the later renunciations are only a result and repetition of the same thing. Ah, how often have I thought of all this, and my spirits grew big with fear (there *are* such fears, that enlarge the soul, I assure you), as I realized that the great poet is a ruler of men; that the course of his fate, his work, and his life is effective far beyond the confines of his person, and conditions the character, the culture, and the future of the nation! My heart grew big with dread at a certain picture, indelible, stamped on all our hearts. Were we not all present, were there only two there at that fateful scene? The lover, mounted to depart, reaches down his hand to the daughter of the people, the maiden who loves him with all her soul. His dæmon demands of him that cruel parting; her eyes are full of tears. Those tears, madame — even with my mind and heart at their biggest with dread, I still do not understand the meaning of those tears."

"For my part," Charlotte retorted, "I am intolerant enough to say that that good child, the daughter of the people, would have only been worthy of her lover if she had had enough resolution to carve herself out a real life after he was gone, instead of surrendering to the worst fate of all and pining away. My friend, the worst thing of all is to pine away. She who knows how to avoid it must be grateful to God; but — unless all moral judgments are sheer presumption — she must be blamed who yields. You speak of renunciation. Well, the little one over there in her grave had ill learned how to renounce; for her, renunciation and self-destruction were the same thing."

Young Goethe separated his finger-tips and brought them together again. "The two," he said, "are close neighbours; it would not be easy to keep them apart anywhere, in one's life or in one's work. I have thought about this too, when the meaning of those tears stretched my heart nigh to bursting. I do not know whether I can put it in words. I thought of the actual; by that I mean the known, and how it came to pass; and I thought of the possible, that which we do not know but can only divine. It makes us sad, with a sadness we conceal from ourselves and others, out of respect for the actual. We banish it to the depths of our hearts. For what is the possible in comparison with the actual; and who would dare speak up for it, knowing he runs a risk of disrespect towards the actual? And yet I often think there is a kind of injustice here — an injustice due to the fact (yes, it is possible in this connection to speak of facts) that actuality takes up all the room and attracts all the admiration to itself. On the other hand, the possible, the unfulfilled, is only an outline, a guess at what might have been. And considering that sort of 'might have been,' we may easily fear lest we lack respect for the actual — resting, as it must, in good part, upon the perception that all our work and all our life are by nature a product of renunciation. But where the possible still exists, if only in the form of longing and intuition, of an adumbration, a whisper of what might have been — that is the sign-manual of destruction, of 'pining away.'"

Charlotte shook her head. "I am, and always shall be, on the side of resolution, for holding stoutly to the actual and leaving the 'might have been' to shift for itself."

"Sitting here beside you," he said, "as I have the honour to do, I cannot quite bring myself to believe you have never even felt that pull towards the possible. It is so natural, it seems to me: the very preponderance of the real and actual is what tempts us to speculate on the possible, the thing that did *not* happen. The actual gave us great things, and why should it not, with such creative powers? It would succeed in any case, and it did, magnificently enough; it even created something out of renunciation and unfaithfulness. But still, a man asks himself — he has a right to, even considering the sovereign and splendid significance of the work and the life, for all life and all the future — what would have happened. Might we not all have been much happier if this idea of renunciation had not been in control, if there had never been that early picture of the parting and leaning down from the saddle to clasp hands — or those unforgettable tears? It was thinking of them and of all that, made me wonder whether Father, when he was at Karlsruhe, thought of that little grave in Baden, still not so very old."

Charlotte replied: " We must highly esteem the idealism which sides with the possible against the actual — despite, or perhaps because of, the greater advantages of the latter. But we must, I think, let it remain a question which of the two is morally superior, between idealism and resolution. We might easily be unjust; for idealism has great charm, though perhaps resolve reaches a higher moral plane. But what am I saying? My tongue seems to run on today. And it is usually the part of the woman to admire and nothing else, and wonder at all the things such a man can think of. But you might be my son, by your years, and a good mother does not leave her son to struggle alone. Hence I prattle on, however I may offend against the feminine proprieties. But now let us leave the possible in peace in its grave and apply ourselves to the actual, I mean the enjoyable travels of your father on the Main and the Rhine. I should gladly hear more of the Gerbermühle; that was the spot where Goethe made the acquaintance of two of my children."

"I cannot, alas, tell you anything of the meeting," replied August. "But I know that the visit there, as seldom in actual life, resulted in a complete restoration to health; it was better for my father than even the first visit had been. That was due to the social talents of an elegant young hostess, and the host's inexhaustible hospitality — all against a background of well-ordered amenities. Again the Main glowed in the rosy sunset, the air was sweet, the lovely Marianne sang Father's songs, accompanying herself on the piano. But this time, and on these evenings, he not only richly took but richly gave. He consented, he even offered to read aloud from the increasing store of his songs to Zuleika, addressed by Hatem to his Rose of the Orient; the wedded pair were duly conscious of the honour he paid them. The young wife seems not to have been one of those women who confine themselves to wondering at all the things such a man can think of. She in her turn did not limit herself to receiving. Susceptible to the honour, she began to reply in kind to the passionate addresses in Zuleika's name; and her husband listened like a complaisant host to the antiphony."

"He must be an estimable man," said Charlotte, "with a healthy sense for the rights and advantages of the actual. But the whole story, familiar as it is to me, is a good illustration of what you said about memory: that it insists on repetition. And at the end? The five weeks came to a close, and the illustrious guest departed? "

"After a last moonlight evening, when the air resounded with song; at its close, I am told, the fair hostess herself almost inhospitably urged the guest to depart. But even here the desire for repetition found ways to gratify itself; and in Heidelberg, whither Father had gone, they met again. The husband and wife found themselves there unexpectedly; and there was a last and final moonlight evening, when the little bride, to the surprise and joy of her husband no less than her friend, produced another poem, of such beauty that it might have been written by Father himself. We should take care how we attribute advantages and rights to the actual over the poetic. The poems Father composed then in Heidelberg and later for his Persian *Divan* — they are the very height of the actual, the actual's very stuff. I have the advantage of knowing them earlier than anyone else, and of possessing some of them. Dearest lady, they are remarkable, they are uncanny, they are inexpressibly wonderful. There never was their like. They are Father through and through; but Father from a new and entirely unsuspected side. I might say they are a mystery, yet must hasten to add that they are childishly clear. It is — what shall I call it? — the mystery, the esoteric of nature: most personal, yet with the charactertistics of the heavenly firmament, so that the universe takes on a human visage, and the ego looks out with eyes of stars. I keep having two lines from one of the songs in my mind — listen! " He recited, in a voice low and trembling with awe:

> " ' And thou sham'st like sunrise blushes
> Of these heights the sober face — '

"What do you say to that?" he asked, his voice still shaking. "Say nothing until I add that he rhymed his own name in the verses: that is to say, the next line has Hatem, but the rhyme makes it clear that he was referring to his own great self. What do you think of that? Is it not simply touching, all this conscious greatness, kissed by youth, put to the blush by youth?" He repeated the lines. "My God, what sensibility, what majesty!" he cried. He sat bent forward, did young Goethe, with his forehead resting on his palm, the fingers rumpling his hair.

The emotional gesture and pose were more offensive to Charlotte than the young man's previous anger. She said, with reserve, that the public would surely share his enthusiasm, when the collection appeared. But it was unlikely such jestingly allusive poetry would ever win the universal admiration of the world, like that novel which had soared on the wings of the poet's own youth. "One may perhaps regret the fact. And the repeated visits? You have tumbled your hair, I will lend you my little comb if you like. Ah, it seems these same fingers that tumbled it can put it to rights again. So the repetitions came to an end at last?"

"They were to come to an end," answered August. "This summer, after Mother's death, Father could not make up his mind where he should go for his cure. Should it be Wiesbaden, Töplitz? We saw that he was tempted westwards, to the Rhine; it was as though he awaited a sign from a favouring deity, such as last time had smitten the hand of the god of war, that he might follow his inclination. And the sign came. His friend

the enterprising Zelter was going to Wiesbaden and in-
cited him to follow. However, he would not accept the
omen at once. 'Let it be the Rhine, then,' he said, 'but
not Wiesbaden, rather Baden-Baden, and the route via
Würzburg, not Frankfurt.' Very good; they did not
need to travel directly to Frankfurt to arrive there in the
end! In short, Father set out on the 20th of July. He
chose for his companion Professor Meyer, the art-historian, who was immensely flattered, and boasted of his
election. But what happens? The favouring deity may
have been offended, for he played them a trick. Two
hours out of Weimar the carriage upsets – "

" My goodness me! "

" – and both the occupants are rolled out on the road
chosen with so much self-control. Meyer bled freely
from the nose. No matter for him, he was just paying
for the joys of vanity. But it is humiliating, and at the
same time it makes one smile, a wry sort of smile, to
imagine greatness, so conscious of itself, so long accustomed to stately and deliberate conveyance, now tum-
bling, with disordered clothing, in a muddy ditch."

" My goodness me! " said Charlotte again.

" It was nothing," August went on. " The mishap, the
bad joke, if you like, did no harm at all. Father was quite
unscathed. He lent Meyer his handkerchief and took him
back to Weimar. He gave up the journey – not only for
this summer; for apparently he has forsaken the Rhine
once and for all, in obedience to the omen. This I gather
from his remarks."

" And the album of songs? "

" They do not need the further stimulus of a Rhine

journey. They have been waxing and flourishing, they are a mighty and marvellous achievement, quite without that, perhaps better without it — indeed, it may be the mocking but favouring deity knew that all the time! Perhaps it merely wanted to demonstrate that certain things are permissible and justifiable only as a means to an end."

"As a means to an end," Charlotte repeated. "I cannot hear you use the phrase without misgiving. The honourable and the dishonourable are so confounded in it that there is no distinction between them, and one does not know where one stands."

"And yet," answered August, "in the life of a dominating personality — an emperor, whether a good or a bad one — there are many things which one must place in this debatable category."

"Very good," said she; "but one can always take everything more than one way; it depends on the point of view. And any good and resolute means can make an end out of itself. But I do envy you, dear Herr Kammerrat," she went on, " your private knowledge of this wonderful collection before its publication. It is a privilege to turn one's head. Your father confides a great deal in you? "

"One may well say so," he answered, with a short laugh, showing his small white teeth. "Riemer and Meyer pride themselves no end on their intimacy, and flatter themselves they know this or that sooner than the rest of the world. But of course with a son the position is quite different from that of such chance devotees. A son, by nature and station, is his father's aid and representative. So soon as he is old enough, there fall to his lot all sorts of diplomatic negotiations and the cares that belong to the head of a family, when that head must be spared them because he unites in one person the dignity of genius with the dignity of age. There are household accounts and dealings with tradespeople; visits to be received or declined — and all sorts of other arrangements and obligations. For instance, attending funerals. Then there is the curatorship of the well-arranged and constantly growing collections, the cabinets of minerals and medals, cut stones, engravings and prints, all of them a delight to the eye. I may have to dash into the country somewhere because a valuable quartz or a fossil has been found in a quarry. No, my head and hands are never empty. Perhaps, Frau Councillor, you are informed of the situation in the administration of our theatre? I am about to be called in an adjutatory capacity."

"Adjutatory?" she asked, at once startled and amused by the word.

"Yes indeed. This is the situation: Father is the First Minister in order of seniority; but for a long time, actually since his return from Italy, he had not administered any of the departments. He is a regular adviser in the affairs of the University of Jena, but does not wish to be burdened with the title or duties of a curator. There are only two departments which, until quite recently, he still supervised: the direction of the court theatre and the overseership of the court institutions of art and science — the libraries, the drawing-school, the Botanical Garden, the Observatory, and the natural-science collections. These were originally founded and supported by the ducal house, and Father still insists on their being strictly distinguished from the rest and kept separate from the property of the State. He considers that theoretically he is not responsible to anybody but His Serene Highness for an accounting. In short, his overseership, in a way, is a relic of past times. He uses it to make a demonstration against the new constitutional State, which he prefers to ignore — I use the word advisedly, you understand."

"I can readily understand. He clings to the old relations, by nature and habit he conceives his service to the Duchy as service from one person to another."

"Quite so. And I find it wonderfully befits him. What sometimes disquiets me — pray do not be astonished at my opening myself to you so frankly — is the light that falls on me, his natural aide in these occupations. For I have to do many things in his stead, execute many a commission, ride to Jena when there is building going on, to get the views of the professors — and things like that. I am not too young for it, I am seven-and-twenty, a mature man. But I am too young for the spirit in which it happens. I am sometimes fearful of putting myself in a bad light by playing assistant to an obsolete overseership, which cannot be inherited, because it disqualifies the heir by making him seem to be hostile to the new order of things."

"You are too scrupulous, my dear Herr Kammerrat. What man, in the performance of such natural services, need be prey to such fallacious ideas? And now you are also to be adjutatory in the administration of the theatre?"

"That is so. My mediation is necessary here most of

all. You cannot imagine the vexation Father has always suffered in this supposedly pleasant task. All the follies and pretensions of the actors, the authors, the public — to speak of nothing else. There are the whims and demands of the court, worst of all in the case of those persons who belong to both the court and the theatre. I refer, by your leave, to the lovely Jagemann, Frau von Heigendorf, whose influence with the Duke can always outweigh my father's own. In short, there are complications. . . . And Father himself, one must admit, has never been what one could call a steady man — in this field no more than in others. Every year he would be absent for many weeks during the theatre season; travelling, visiting the baths, giving the theatre not a thought. There was and is in him a curious mixture of zeal and indifference, passion and contempt. He is no theatre man at all, believe me; anyone who knows him realizes that he cannot get on with theatre people. To do that, no matter how high you are above them, you must have some theatre blood in you — and certainly Father. . . . But enough; I dislike even to think of it. With Mother it was different; she knew the key, she had friends, both men and women, among them; and I was often with them, even as a child. So then Mother and I had to be buffers between him and the troupe. But soon he took an official from the Chamberlain's office as assistant, Kammerrat Kirms; and the two of them co-opted certain persons, to protect themselves still more. That led up to a corporate administration, and now, under the Duchy, it has become a Board of Management, consisting of Father, Kirms, Councillor Kruse, and Count Edling."

"Count Edling — is he not married to a Princess from Moldavia?"

"Ah, I see, you are well informed. But, believe me, Father is often in the way of the other three. It is almost comic — they are subject to an authority to which they would always yield, if they did not realize that authority knows itself too well to exercise pressure. He would like to get rid of it — and it is true that he has always needed freedom and privacy — but then again he does not quite want to give it up altogether. So then the idea came up of taking me in. It came from His Serene Highness himself. 'Let August come in,' he told my Father; 'then you can still have a hand in it, old fellow, and yet not be bothered.'"

"Does the Duke call him 'old fellow'?"

"Yes, he does."

"And what does Goethe call him?"

"He says 'my gracious Lord' and 'Your Serene Highness's humble servant.' It is not at all necessary; sometimes the Duke laughs at him for it. In my mind, however, it is associated with a comparison — perhaps an unsuitable one — but it might interest you: Mother always said 'you' to Father, but he said 'thou' to her."

Charlotte was silent for a little while; then she said: "It is an odd detail, touching, and after all quite understandable. But let me not forget to offer you congratulations on the new appointment."

"My position," he remarked, "will be rather delicate. There is considerable difference in age between me and the other gentlemen on the board. And I shall represent to them an authority which knows itself only too well."

"I am convinced that your tact and *savoir faire* will know how to deal with the situation."

"You are very kind. Does it bore you to have me recite the tale of my responsibilities?"

"I listen with the deepest interest."

"There is a good deal of correspondence on matters rather beneath my father's dignity; for instance, the fight over the pirated editions competing with our complete edition in twenty volumes. Then just now Father would like to get an honorary dismissal of the claims for deductions on the money he inherited from Grandmother. It consists of property in Frankfurt, on which he has to pay taxes. And if he gives up his citizenship in Frankfurt and transfers the capital to Weimar, he will have to pay as much as three thousand gulden if they don't let him off. He is petitioning the city to remit the tax — in consideration of the honour he has just paid it by the charming description in his reminiscences. Of course, he will be giving up his citizenship; but certainly he has conferred undying honour already on the place. Naturally, he cannot boast of that or refer to it; he leaves it to me and I carry on the correspondence. It takes patience and shrewdness, and reaps no little vexation of spirit. What do they answer me — or him, whom I represent? The city authorities say that the proposed remission amounts to robbing the other citizens of Frankfurt. What do you think of that? Is it not a perverted sense of justice? I am only too glad I do not have to deal by word of mouth — I cannot vouch for it that I should be either cautious or restrained. Well, we are going on with it, the end is not yet. I will be both patient and per-

sistent in my rejoinder; and I shall not be satisfied until
I get both the printing rights and the remission of the
tax. Father's income is not commensurate with his genius. It is at the moment not small, of course. Cotta is
paying sixteen thousand thaler for the collected edition,
and that at least is an adequate sum. But position and
renown like Father's ought to be convertible in quite
another way. Humanity, so richly rewarded, should pay
proportionate tribute to the giver, and the greatest man
ought to be also the richest. In England — "

"As a practical woman, and a housekeeper of many
years' standing, Herr Kammerrat, I can only commend
your zeal. But suppose we could — as we cannot — establish an exact relation between the gifts of genius and
its economic recompense; then there would be no more
room for expressions of enthusiasm from a grateful humanity."

"I grant the two realms are incommensurable. And
people do not like it when a great man behaves as they
do themselves; they demand from genius that it should
behave with lofty indifference towards worldly advantage. They have a craving to look up to the great; it
seems to me both silly and egotistic. I have lived with
great people ever since I was a child; and I have never
found that a man of genius has that attitude. On the contrary, his business sense seems to be just as high-flying
as his intellect. Schiller's head was always full of money
matters. That is not true of Father — maybe because his
intellect is not so high-flying either — and also because
he does not need money so much. When *Hermann and
Dorothea* had such popular success, my father told

Schiller that he ought to write a play in the same vein; it would bring in a pot of money, and the author himself need not take the thing seriously at all."

" He was not to take the play seriously? "

" No. Schiller began something at once, and Father encouraged him. But it came to nothing."

" That was because he did not take it seriously."

" It may be. But the other day I copied out a letter to Cotta in which it said that he ought to use the present favourable patriotic exaltation to push the sale of *Hermann and Dorothea*, a poem so greatly in harmony with the times."

" A letter from Goethe? " Charlotte paused a moment. " That shows," she resumed with emphasis, " how wrong it is to accuse him of estrangement from the spirit of the times."

" Ah, the spirit of the times! " said August contemptuously. " Father is neither estranged from it, nor is he its partisan and slave. He stands high above it and looks down on it — he can even regard it with the eye of commercial advantage! He long ago rose above the individual, temporal, national point of view, to the human, universally applicable one — that was where the Klopstocks and Herders and Bürgers could not follow him. But their position was not half so bad as that of the people who imagine themselves far in advance even of the timeless! There are our romanticists, our neo-Christians, our neo-patriotic fanatics — they all think they are further on than Father and represent the very latest thing in the intellectual realm, which he does not even understand. There are asses among the public who think the same.

But can anything be worse than the spirit which would like to see the downfall of the eternal and the classic? You may be sure Father gives it to them; only he does it privately, and outwardly he behaves as though he did not notice the insults. Of course, he is too clever and dignified to let himself in for literary squabbles. But privately he takes his revenge, both now and in the future; not only for the opposition and the time spirit but for his own elegant restraint as well. You see, he has never liked to offend, or confuse the minds of what he indulgently calls 'the majority of good men.' But in private he has always been quite other than the great monument of propriety the public likes to see in him. He has always been incredibly free and bold. People see the Minister and courtier — but in reality he is audacity itself. And why not? Would he have risked writing *Werther*, *Tasso*, or *Wilhelm Meister* and all the other novel and unheard-of productions if he had not had a gift and penchant for the daring thing? Often I have heard him say that actually the thing we call talent consists only in this. He always kept a secret archive of strange productions, and the beginnings of *Faust* and the *Wandering Jew* and *Hans Wurst's Wedding* lay in it side by side. Even today he has a 'Walpurgis-sack' full of doubtful or even offensive matter; for instance, I have seen a poem in rhymed lines called the 'Diary,' an Italianate piece that is a very pretty mixture of eroticism, moralizing, and, with your permission, obscenity. I am in charge of all that, posterity may rely on my taking care of it. It is to me they have to look, for there is not much dependence upon Father. His carelessness with manuscripts is incredible, it seems he does not care if they get lost; takes the greatest chances, and if I did not prevent him would send to Stuttgart something of which we have no copy. So I have to look after things and preserve them: the unpublished, the not to be published; the private papers, the truths about his dear Germans, the polemics, the diatribes against intellectual opponents and against the follies of the time in religious, political, and artistic fields."

"A good and loyal son," Charlotte commented. "I rejoiced, dear August, to make your acquaintance — and with more reason than I knew. A mother, an old woman like myself, must be greatly touched by this beautiful filial devotion, this absolute unity with him against oncomers possessing the impudence of the age. One cannot enough praise — "

"I do not deserve it," interrupted the Kammerrat. "What can I be to my father? I am an average man, with a bent for practical things; far from intellectual or learned enough to give him support. Actually I am not much together with him. To be loyal to him in my heart and to serve his interests is the least I can do, and I am ashamed to be praised for that. My dear Frau Schiller always makes me blush with her kindness and her sympathy, because I have the same literary tastes as she has — as though it were a virtue, and not simply a matter of personal pride to stick by Goethe and Schiller and let other young people take up with the new fashions."

"Indeed, I know very little of these new fashions," answered Charlotte, "and I assume my years would shut me out from understanding them. These pious painters and impious writers — well, I don't know them, and I don't feel the loss. Of one thing I am sure: their works cannot rival those that were created in my own time and conquered the world. Yet you may say, in a way, they do not need to rival them in order to excel them. I am no person to make paradoxes, all I mean is this: the new things are the expression of the present time, and so they speak more immediately and satisfyingly to the youth, the children of the time. And the satisfaction is the important thing."

"The question of where one finds it," answered August, "is important too. There are those who seek and find it in pride, honour, and duty."

"Good, excellent. And yet experience has taught me that a life of duty and service to others often results in a certain harshness of temper and does not tend to affability. You are attached to Frau von Schiller, you say, by bonds of confidence and friendship?"

"I will not boast of a favour which I do not owe to my qualities, but rather to my opinions."

"Oh, surely they belong together. I feel something like jealousy to find already occupied a position to which I felt some pretensions — that of a second or substitute mother. You will forgive me if I cling to the pretension so far as to ask if you have other friends and familiars among persons somewhat nearer your age than Schiller's widow?"

She bent towards him as she spoke. August looked at her; his eyes expressed both gratitude and shyness. It was a melancholy, emotional gaze.

"They have been hard to come by," he replied. "We

mentioned before that there are many diverse views and
aspirations among my own generation; they stand in the
way of a genuine rapprochement and would always lead
to embarrassment, even without the reserve which I consider my proper attitude. There is a Latin quotation —
I find it most appropriate to the times we live in: ' The
victorious cause is pleasing to the gods, the defeated to
Cato.' I admit that the lines have long struck a sympathetic chord in me. I like the way in which reason calmly
saves its dignity from the vicissitudes of blind chance.
It is the rarest thing in the world; shameless disloyalty
to the *causa victa* and a capitulation to success, these are
the far more usual attitude, and it embitters me more
than anything else. Ah, what contempt the age teaches
us to feel for the flunkeyism of the human soul! Three
years ago, in the summer of 1813, we had persuaded
Father to go to Töplitz, and I was in Dresden, then occupied by French troops. The population celebrated Napoleon's birthday, illuminating their windows and setting
off fireworks. As late as April, illuminations and troops
of white-clad maidens had been saluting the Majesties of
Russia and Prussia. The weathercock had only to turn
around again — it is too pitiable for words! How shall
a young man keep his faith in mankind when he has seen
the perfidy of the German princes and the criminal conduct of the famous French field-marshals who left their
Emperor in the lurch — "

"But shall we become embittered, my friend, over
what cannot be altered, and fling away our faith in human kind because men behave like men towards one who
was not a human being at all? Loyalty is excellent, run-

ning after success is not. But a man like Buonaparte
stands or falls according to his success. You are very
young; I wish for you the maternal wish that you should
take an example from your great father. He cheerfully
celebrated the Battle of Leipsic, there on the Rhine or
the Main, and took no exception when that which had
so audaciously risen from the abyss had to return to it
at last."

"But he did not allow me to enter the field against
the man of the abyss. And, let me add, in so acting he
paid me a fatherly compliment; for I know and despise
from the bottom of my heart the kind of youth who flung
themselves into it and were just fit for it — those puppies
of the Prussian League of Valour, the ecstatic, empty-
headed donkeys, like a row of peas in a pod — I cannot
listen to their silly student jargon without almost bursting
with rage — "

"My friend, I do not mix in the political quarrels of
the time. But I confess that I am, in a way, saddened by
your words. Perhaps I ought to be glad, as our dear
Frau Schiller is, that you bide with us elders; and yet it
pains me, it almost alarms me, to hear how the tiresome
politics of our time isolate you from your contempo-
raries, from the young folk of your own generation."

"But after all," replied August, "politics is not something by itself. In a hundred ways it is indissoluble from
one's views, one's religion, one's convictions. It is a factor in everything — bound up with the ethical, the
æsthetic, with things apparently intellectual and philo-
sophic. Those times are fortunate when politics is innocent of all these, when it lives in its own limited world,

and no one save its own adepts even speaks its language. In such supposedly unpolitical periods — periods, let me say, when politics are dormant — it is possible to love and admire the beautiful, independently of the political, with which, even so, it remains in silent contact. It is not, alas, our lot to live in such a mild and tolerant time. Ours is one that casts a sharp and ruthless light, which brings out the political inherent in everything, in all beauty, all humanity. I am the last person to deny that much pain ensues, much loss, many bitter partings."

"You mean that you yourself are not unacquainted with that bitterness?"

"Perhaps," answered young Goethe after a brief silence, looking down at the tip of his boot as he moved it to and fro.

"And would you care to speak of it to me, as a son to his mother?"

"Your kindness," he responded, "has drawn from me the general statement, I may as well let the particular follow. I knew a young man, a little older than I, whom I would gladly have made a friend. His name was Arnim, Achim von Arnim, of the Prussian nobility. He had a handsome person — that gay, ardent, gallant image stamped itself early on my heart, and remained there, even though I saw him only at long intervals of time. I was only a boy when we first met, in Göttingen, whither I had accompanied my father. He was a student, and called our attention to himself by cheering my father on the street after our arrival. Of course that made the liveliest and most pleasant impression on us; the twelve-year-old lad never forgot it, sleeping or waking.

"Four years later he came to Weimar. He was by then not unknown to the world of poetry. His tastes ran to the romantic and old-German; he was given to a certain witty exuberance — or exuberant wit. And while he was in Heidelberg he and Clemens Brentano had compiled and published that collection of folk-songs called *The Boys' Magic Horn*. It was received with an emotion and gratitude not surprising when one thinks how kin it was to the tendencies of the time. The author paid my father a visit and was warmly praised for the charming contribution of himself and young Brentano. We two youths struck up a friendship. Those were happy weeks. Never had I been so glad to be my father's son as then; that advantage outweighed my lack of years, education, and merit and attracted the young man's attention, regard, and liking. It was winter-time. He was proficient in all physical sports, far beyond my own powers, save in one; there to my great joy he could be my pupil. He had never skated, and I could teach him. Those hours of brisk movement, in which I excelled my admired friend and could instruct him, were the happiest of my life. Quite frankly, I expect no happier in the future.

"Again it was three years before I saw him again — in Heidelberg, whither I went in 1808 to study law. I had introductions to several important and intellectual families, in particular that of the famous Johann Heinrich Voss, the Homeric scholar, a friend of Father since his Jena days; his son Heinrich had sometimes substituted for Dr. Riemer as tutor in our house. I will admit that I did not care much for the younger Voss. His idolatry of my father bored rather than won me. Such natures are both enthusiastic and prosaic — there is such a combination. And he had an affliction of the lip which even when I was in Heidelberg was preventing him from lecturing. It did not make him more attractive. His father, the rector of Eutin and author of *Luise*, was another odd combination: a writer of idylls and a controversialist. A good-natured, domesticated sort, petted and coddled by a most capable wife and housekeeper; but in scholarly, literary, and public matters a perfect fighting-cock. He had a passion for disputation, for rushing joyously into print with biting articles against anything that he found antagonistic to his position of enlightened protestantism, his classic and lucid humanity. The Voss house, so intimately connected with my own, became a second home in Heidelberg, and I was like a son of the family.

"It was with a joyful start and some embarrassment and misgiving as well that, soon after my arrival, I unexpectedly met in the street that idol of my dreams, the partner of those delightful crisp wintry days. I might or ought to have expected the encounter and reckoned with it inwardly. For I knew that Arnim lived here, and published his *Hermit's Gazette*, a witty sheet with an unworldly reactionary point of view, the organ of the young, romantic generation. Actually, I knew in my heart that the idea of seeing him again was my first thought when it was decided that I should go to Heidelberg. Now he stood before me in the flesh, and my heart contracted with pleasure and shyness, I think I went red and white in the face. All the discords of the time and the generation were heavy on my conscience. I well knew what the Vosses thought about the religious cultivation and enhancement of the German and Christian past. And Arnim was more and more prominent as the representative of just this tendency. I saw that my childhood days, when I was free to move between the two camps, was a thing of the past. My friend was handsomer, more gallant than ever; and his very cordiality embarrassed as much as it enchanted me. He seized me by the arm and took me to Zimmer's book-shop, where he had a desk. At first we talked about Bettina Brentano; I had been seeing her at my grandmother's house in Frankfurt. But after that our conversation gradually dragged, and I suffered under the impression I must be giving him of a heaviness ill-suited to my years. His looks, his involuntary head-shakes soon betrayed the worst, and I was in despair.

"In my parting handshake I sought to express some of the longing and hopelessness, some of the tenderness in my boyish heart. But at the Vosses', that same evening, I could not help mentioning that I had seen him — and I found the situation even worse than I had suspected. The old man was about to launch a polemic against 'these fellows,' as he called them, 'these corruptors of youth, these obscurantist apologists for the Middle Ages.' He was writing a tract which he hoped would spoil their influence and even their sojourn in Heidelberg. His hatred of the malicious, light-headed, insidious, and inimical activities of these romantic poetasters exploded in blustering words. He called them impostors, without any sense of history or philosophical conscience. Their piety was mendacious; they impudently falsified the texts they discovered, under pretext of restoring them. In vain I objected that my father had given a friendly welcome to the *Boys' Magic Horn.* Voss answered that my father was too good and too tolerant; but that his honour and esteem for the national folklore was of a different character entirely from that of these Germanizing scribblers. His old friend and patron, said Voss, held the same view as himself of these patriot pietists and neo-Catholics, whose glorification of the past was nothing but spiteful defamation of the present. Their reverence for the great man was highly suspect and had the single purpose of using him for their own ends. In short, if I set store by his, the rector's, fatherly friendship, his love and sympathy, I would do well to cut loose from intercourse with Arnim and not see him again.

"What more shall I tell you? I had to choose between this good man, my father's old friend, who gave me an asylum in a strange city, and the doubtful joys of a forbidden friendship. I gave in. I wrote to Arnim that the position I held, by birth and conviction, in the party strife of the time forbade me to see him. I dropped a boyish tear on the paper; it showed me that the fancy I now renounced belonged to an outgrown stage of my life. I sought and found compensation in the companionship of the younger Voss, Heinrich. His bad lip and his boresomeness were made up for by the certainty that his enthusiasm for Father was entirely disinterested."

Charlotte was at pains to thank the narrator for his little confession and to assure him of her sympathy for a trial which, one might say, he had stood like a man. "Like a man," she repeated. "It is a very manly story that you have told me — out of a man's world — I mean a world of principles and ruthlessness; we poor women look at it half with respect, half with a laugh and a shake of the head. We are children of nature, children of toleration, compared with your strict conceptions; I am afraid we seem to you like elemental beings. But perhaps a good share of the attraction our poor sex has for you rests on the relief from your principles which you get from us. If we have the good fortune to please you otherwise, your strictness of principle can shut one eye and prove not to be so rigid after all. We have stories of old feuds and family quarrels, inherited disagreements and so on; they never interfere with passionate love-affairs between the children of such traditional enmities. Indeed, the lovers find an additional charm in being able to spite them and go their own way."

"That may be, then," said August, "the point in which love differs from friendship."

"Of course. And now, let me ask you a maternal question: your story had to do with a thwarted friendship. Then you have never loved?"

The Kammerrat looked at the floor — and then at her.

"I am in love," he said, very low.

Charlotte was silent, her face showed concern.

"Your confidence," said she, "touches me as much as the fact itself. Confidence for confidence! I will confess why I was so bold as to ask. August, you have told me about your life, your devoted, praiseworthy, filial conduct. You are a faithful aide to your father, you smooth his path, you take care of his writings, you are a buffer between him and business cares. I too know what suffering and resignation mean; you must not think that

I do not know how to estimate the moral value of such a life of selflessness and love. And yet may I tell you that as I listened, my feelings were not quite unmixed? Something like concern, misgiving, dissatisfaction, came into them — a revulsion, such as one feels against something that seems not quite natural or according to the will of God. He, I feel, did not create us, He did not give us life, in order that we should give it up, or pour it all into the life of another human being, no matter how noble or beloved. We must lead our own lives — not in selfishness, not regarding others solely as means to an end, but also not quite selflessly; rather independently and by the light of our own thoughts, in a reasonable balance between our duties to others and those to ourselves. Am I not right? It is not good for our souls, not even good for the gentleness and mildness of our characters, to live altogether for others. I must say to you straight out, I should be happier if what you tell me betrayed some sign of an intention to emancipate yourself from the paternal house. It would befit your years. You ought to have your own establishment, you should marry, August."

"I have the intention to marry," said the Kammerrat, with a bow.

"Capital!" she cried. "Then I am speaking with a bridegroom?"

"That is saying too much as yet, perhaps. The affair is not yet *publique*."

"Even so, I am delighted. I ought to be angry that you have only now given me the opportunity to congratulate you. May I know who is the chosen one?"

" A Fräulein von Pogwisch."

" Her Christian name? "

" Ottilie."

" How charming! Like a story-book! And am I Aunt Charlotte to you both? "

" Do not say Aunt. She might be your daughter," responded August. His gaze at her had become not merely staring, but strangely glassy.

She started and blushed. " My daughter — what are you thinking of? " She was stammering, possessed by an uncanny feeling at the recurrence of this word, and at the accompanying stare. She had the impression that he had spoken involuntarily and given utterance to a subconscious thought.

" Yes indeed," he answered, with a lively gesture. " I am not jesting — or scarcely. I was not speaking of an actual likeness, that would be strange indeed. I meant a kinship — and that happens thousands of times in the world. Let me say, Frau Hofrätin, that you belong to those whose fundamental appearance the years can but little affect. Such people change little with time. Or rather, their mature appearance is transparent, so that the youthful one shines through it. I would not presume to tell you you look like a young maiden. But one needs no second sight to see through the mask of dignity the lineaments of the young girl, almost the schoolgirl you once were. And all I would say is that this young girl might easily be Ottilie's sister. What do we mean by a resemblance? I do not mean a similarity of single features, but the likeness as a whole, the identity of type. It is the same: delicate, charming, slender — in both; and this it is could make you sisters, or make Ottilie your daughter."

She gazed at him in her turn, she seemed to have been infected with his very own kind of glassy staring, though even more pronounced.

"Von Pogwisch, von Pogwisch," she repeated mechanically. Then she realized that she might easily seem to remember the name and its associations. "That is from the Prussian nobility, is it not?" she queried. "Then it is a marriage of the sword and the lyre. I have sincere respect for the Prussian military temperament — its point of view, its love of honour and the fatherland. To these qualities we owe our liberation from the foreign yoke. And in this tradition your betrothed — if I may so call her — grew up. I suspect that under the circumstances she is not precisely an admirer of Buonaparte or the Rhenish Alliance."

"Such questions," August said distantly, "have been overtaken and decided by the course of events."

"Heaven be praised!" said she. "And the marriage has been sanctioned by the approval and fatherly consent of Goethe?"

"Entirely. He is of the opinion that it holds out the fairest prospects."

"Yet he will lose you — or a considerable part of you. You recall that I myself advised you to set up an independent life for yourself. But when I put myself in the place of the old friend of my youth, our dear and honoured Herr Geheimrat, — he will feel the loss of his familiar helper and excellent adjutator, when you leave his house."

"Such an idea has not occurred to us," August replied. "Let me reassure you: nothing will be altered to my father's disadvantage. He will not lose a son, but gain a daughter. We shall occupy the former guest suite in the second storey, charming rooms looking out on the Frauenplan. But Ottilie's sway will not be confined to them. She will assume the rôle of hostess and entertain in the salons below. It is among the advantages to be hoped for from my marriage that it will at last restore to the house a mistress and female head."

"I understand — and I can only marvel at the conflict of my feelings. Just now I was concerned for your father — but at this moment I am equally so for the son. My good wishes for him bid fair to be realized in a way that — I frankly confess — is somewhat disappointing, while reassuring to me on your father's account. Perhaps just for that reason. I am not certain if I have understood you correctly: you mean the young lady has given you her word?"

"It is one of the cases," responded August, "where there is actually no need of words."

"No need? And 'of words'? Words? My friend, you are devaluating something very solemn when you change the singular to the plural. The 'word' is something quite different from 'words.' And it is only given after mature consideration and even hesitation. As he learns who binds himself by it. You love; you have confessed it to me, an old woman who might be your mother, and I am deeply touched. I do not doubt that you are loved in return; your native merit is the securest guarantee for that. But I must ask — and with a certain maternal jealousy, indeed — if you are truly loved, loved for your own personal qualities of mind and heart? When I was young, I used often to put myself in the place of many a rich and much courted maiden. I realized with alarm that such a one is in the position to choose as she will among the youth of the land. But she could never be completely certain whether the homage she received was paid to her or her money. Suppose she had some physical defect — a squint, a limp, some little deformity. There is no end to the tragedy that could ensue in the soul of the unhappy girl. A tragedy of yearning to believe, conflicting with her perpetual gnawing doubt. It shocked me to think that such a young girl would be driven to think of her riches as a personal advantage and say to herself: 'Even if he loves only my money, yet the money is mine, it is inseparable from me, it compensates for my limp, and so he loves me despite my limp.' Forgive me; such thoughts as these, this inescapable dilemma, is an old *idée fixe* of mine; my girlhood days were full of such anxious, pitying dreams, and now in my old age I still prattle about them. But it was only, dear August, because I suddenly saw you as the rich youth who can make free choice among the daughters of the land, yet is compelled to question the reason for his being chosen. Is it truly for himself alone, or for some advantage possessed by him? This little person — forgive me the familiarity, but your own vivid description makes me call her that, and the daughter-sisterly relation to myself you have brought in, gives me a certain right to refer to her as I might to myself . . . again, forgive me, for I no longer feel quite clear about what I am saying. This whole day has been a strain on me, socially, and on my mental powers — I cannot remember its like before in all my life. But I must finish what I began. This little one, Ottilie, does she love you in your setting, so that in fact she loves you for your father's sake? How carefully you must test such love before the bond is knit! I might be your mother, and it is my duty and my task to tell you of my misgivings. For you also said I might be her mother; and that in Goethe's eyes the marriage holds out the most decided prospects — if that was the way you or he expressed it. So perhaps — since I myself was once the person who found favour in those eyes, and since in a sense I might have been your mother too — the question must be asked whether it is you yourself she loves, or whether here too you are acting as your father's representative. You loved young Arnim, and would gladly have been his friend. If it had so fallen out, that would have been altogether your own affair, and the affair of your generation. But this, it seems to me, is perhaps only a matter between us elders. Hence my misgivings. Pray do not think I have no appreciation of the advantages of a marriage wherein, if I may put it thus, youth would realize and make good what its elders had neglected and sacrificed. And still I must insist upon the doubtful side of an affair which, so to speak, is one between brothers and sisters — "

She lifted one hand, in its crocheted mitt, and laid it over her eyes.

" No," said she, " pardon me, my child; I have already said that I am not longer in full control of my words, or even of my thoughts. You must forgive an old woman —

I can but repeat that I have never before had a day that demanded of me such things as this has done. I am actually giddy — "

The Kammerrat had been sitting for the last few minutes stiffly on his chair; he started up hastily at her words.

"My God," he said, "what have I been doing! It is unpardonable, to have worn you out so. We have been speaking of my father, that is my only excuse. For on such a theme, though one could never exhaust it, it is difficult to leave off. I will take my leave — " here he struck his forehead with the flat of his hand — " and had nearly gone without delivering you the message which was my only excuse for troubling you." He resumed his self-control and went on, in a low voice: "I have the honour to convey to the Frau Councillor my father's greetings and welcome to Weimar; also his regret that, because of the rheumatism in his left arm, his freedom of motion is somewhat limited. He would feel it an honour and pleasure if the Frau Councillor, with her family, her daughter, Herr Kammerrat Ridl and his wife, would take the midday meal with him, in the family circle, on next Friday — that is, on the third day from now — at half past two o'clock."

Charlotte had also risen, and stood there slightly swaying.

"Very gladly," she answered, "provided that my family is free on that day."

"Then I will take my leave," he said, with a stiff bow, and offering his hand.

She moved towards him, still slightly swaying. Then she took his head, with the little side-whiskers and the bushy locks, between her two hands and kissed him tenderly on the brow. She could reach it quite easily as he stood bent towards her.

"Farewell, Goethe," she said. "If I have talked nonsense, forget it, for I am weary. Rose Cuzzle and Dr. Riemer were here before you, and little Schopenhauer; then there was Mager, and the whole Weimar populace before that, and it has all been a little too much for me. Go now, my son. In three days I will come and dine with you — why not? How many times did he not eat bread and milk with us, in the House of the Teutonic Order? If you like each other, you young ones, then marry, for his sake, and be happy in your upstairs rooms! I have no call to talk you out of it. God keep you, Goethe! God keep you, my child! "

CHAPTER SEVEN

ALAS, that it should vanish! That my bright vision of
the depths must so soon be gone again — as though the
whim of a genie gave it and as suddenly snatched it away
— it fades into nothing, I emerge. So lovely it was! And
now what? Where are we? Jena? Berka? Tennstädt?
No, this is the Weimar coverlet, the silken one, here the
familiar hangings, the bell-pull. . . . What, what?
Here's a brave showing, forsooth! Good for you, old
man! Be not dismayed, blithe oldster that thou art! No
wonder either, after all: what glorious limbs, how the
goddess' bosom, fine resilient flesh, lay pressed into the
shoulder of her handsome huntsman! How chin nestled
to neck and slumber-rosy cheek, ambrosial little hand
twined round the wrist of the glowing vigorous arm
clasping her in its strong embrace! How little nose and
mouth sought the breath from his dream-relaxed lips!
And Cupid there beside them, half angered, half triumphant, swinging his bow, Halt there, halloo! While on
the other side the bright-eyed beagles gazed and gam-
bolled! At sight of that splendid picture how your heart
leaped in your breast! But whence? Aha, I have it, of
course, the l'Orbetto, the Turchi, from the Dresden
Gallery, Venus and Adonis. Think they'll restore the

Dresden paintings, do they? Take care, my children!
May turn out badly, if you want a quick job, and let
bunglers try their hands. Lots of bungling in this world,
deuce take it! They don't know how hard perfection is,
don't even want it — just want to get off easy. Must tell
them about the Academy of Restoration in Venice, with
a director and twelve professors shut in to their delicate
dangerous task. Venus and Adonis. . . . The "Cupid
and Psyche" was to have been done, long ago; some well-
meaning friend reminds me, now and then, I gave the
order, never tells me where to find the time. Must look
at the copperplate Psyches by Dorigny in the Yellow
Room, to refresh my idea — then just put it off again!
Good to put off, things always get better by waiting, no
one can steal your thunder, no one take your ownest-
own, no one get ahead of you, even trying to do the
same.

What does subject-matter amount to? Material —
world's full of it, lies about in the streets. Go ahead, children, take it, I need not present it to you, as I did Schiller
the Tell, to make his high-flown revolutionary play —
and all the while kept it for myself, the real, easy-going,
epic, ironic thing, the Herculean Demos, caring not a fig
for politics or power, and the comfortable Tyrant having his fun with the women of the country. Do it yet, I
will, just wait a bit: hexameters mellower, more married
to the words, than even in Hermann or in Reineke. To
grow, to grow! Grow like a tree, your crown ever broad-
ening, so long you are young. The way I now am, at
my present stage, with all my being beautifully broad-
ening out, now would be the time to go at the "Cupid

and Psyche." Power, experience, dignity of age, youth's
kiss fresh on my lips — what lightness, what loveliness
might not follow! No one could dream how lovely, till
it came out. Maybe in stanzas? Alas, there's too much
to do; in the press so much must perish! I wager even the
Reformation cantata will languish. Thunder on Sinai.
. . . Wide solitary space and breath of morn — so much
I have fast. For the chorus of warrior shepherds Pandora might help. Sulamith, the beloved afar — Beyond
compare is my joy — in his love day and night. All that
would be sport. But the central figure Himself, and the
higher teaching, mind, ever misunderstanded of the mob;
isolation, soul's utter anguish — yet ever consoling and
giving strength. They shall see the old pagan got more
out of Christianity than all the rest of them put together.
But who shall play the fiddle to my words? Who understand, who hearten and praise, before it come to the
birth? Without it I lose my zest, I warn you — then I
should like to know what you will have to celebrate the
day! Alas, were He but here, who years ago departed —
ten years it is, he turned his face away — to spur me on,
to challenge, stimulate! Did I not fling you down the
Demetrius, on account of the senseless difficulties you
made me with the production — however much I wanted
to finish it, make it the most splendid memorial performance on any stage? Gave it up in a rage, because of your
uninspired insistence on the commonplace; have yourselves to blame he died once again and once for all, and
was dead to you and to me, when I gave up trying, with
all the inner knowledge I had of him, to make him live
again! How wretched I felt! More wretched than per-

haps one ever is for others' faults. Did my zeal belie me?
Did my own secret heart resist, my true intent? Did I
make outward obstacles the excuse and sulk like Achilles
in my tent? He, if I had died first, would have been up
to finishing the Faust. God forbid! — I ought to have
put a clause in my will! — But it was and remains a bitter
grief, a bad *rifiuto*, a shocking defeat. Whereat my un-
quenchable friend here can do naught but droop for very
shame.

What is it of the clock? Did I awake to darkness? No,
light from the garden peers through my blinds. Must
be seven or near, by time-honoured rule; 'twas no genie
snatched away my lovely scene, only my own seven-
o'clock will, calling me to the business of the day, my
will, awake and alert down there in the pregnant vale,
like well-trained hound gazing wide-eyed on love-lorn
Aphrodite, with look both understanding and remote.
See you, he is Saint Gotthardt's in the flesh, the same
who snatches the bread from his master's table to succour
the starving Saint Roch. Must put down the saws for
Saint Roch's day in my note-book — where is it? Left-
hand drawer of the secrétaire: When April's dry The
peasants sigh. When the willow-wren sings ere the vine
doth sprout — a line of verse. And the one about the
pike's liver — what's that but a reference to inspection
of entrails, genuine soothsaying, most primitive kind!
Ah, the folk! The folk-nature, part of nature itself, elemental, earthy, pagan, full of folk- and nature-wisdom,
fruitful soil of the unconscious, nourishing vale of renewed youth! How good to mingle with them at their
immemorial feasts, fontanalia and maypole games, or like

that time at Bingen, when we drank our wine at the long
table 'neath the awning — smoke of melting fat, smell of
fresh bread, sausages roasting over glowing ashes! That
was a Christian feast, yet how mercilessly they strangled
the stray badger and tore its bleeding flesh! Man cannot
tarry long in his conscious mind; must take from time to
time refuge in his unconscious, there his being has its
roots. Maxims. Our dear departed friend knew or would
know naught of all this. Haughty invalid, aristocrat of the
conscious mind, touching he was, in his greatness and
helplessness, and daft about freedom. They took him —
absurd, it was — for a man of the people, me for the courtly
courtier — whereas he knew nothing whatever about the
people, and less than nothing about the Germans. Well,
and I liked him for that, nobody can get on with the
Germans, be it in triumph or defeat. Simply stood out, in
all the purity of his sensitive soul and sickly body, incapable of getting down among them, for ever trying in
all his mildness to think of baser souls as one with
himself and lift them as in the arms of the Redeemer up
to himself and the life of the mind. Yes, he had much
of Him whom in the cantata I seek to interpret. Childlike — and self-important too, had ambitions to play the
man of affairs. Childlike indeed — yet very much the
man too, too much, and more than is in nature to be; for
the essentially man — intellect and free will — they are
not nature. That made him, in the presence of the female, simply absurd. His feminine characters are laughable, and he thought of sexuality as a goading cruelty.
Horrible, offensive and horrible! But what a gift withal,
what soaring boldness of thought, what knowledge of the

good, how far above and beyond the vile and vulgar
herd — my equal, my only kindred soul, I shall not look
again upon his like. What good taste, even in the tasteless, what sure feeling for the beautiful! Owned to all
the gifts of fluency and elegance, incredibly bore witness to his freedom from his own physical state. Understood the said or only half-said, answered with utmost
shrewdness; would call you to yourself, instruct you in
your own thoughts, assert himself critically, make comparisons, even to being wearisome. Yes, yes, of course,
the speculative and the intuitive mind, provided both
have genius, can meet halfway; of course, the point was
that this man who was not nature, who was nothing else
but man, could be a genius, was a genius and stood beside
me as an equal — the high place was the thing, and the
equal rank — also, and just as much, to escape from poverty and be able to give a year for each play. A disagreeable, wily man, a climber. Did I ever like him? Never.
Not his stalking gait, or his red hair, his freckles, his
stoop, his hectic cheeks, his hooked nose for ever red
with a cold! But never, long as I live, shall I forget his
eyes, so deep a blue, so mild, so piercing, eyes of a Redeemer, Christ-eyes, speculator-eyes, both at once. How
I mistrusted him — saw he wanted to exploit me. Wrote
me that devilishly clever letter, to win the " Master " for
the *Horen* he had just, on purpose, founded. Smelt the
rat, you did! Came privately to an agreement with Un-
ger. Insisted on having the Faust for the magazine and
for Cotta. All most vexing, since he of all of them could
understand the business of the objective style, after Italy,
knew I had changed and the clay got hard. All most an-

noying. Kept at me, kept pushing me, because *he* was in a hurry. But time alone can bring things to pass.

Yes, time one must have. Time is mercy — a kindly, unassuming boon, to him who will honour it and fill it diligently out. Unbeknown she does her work, quietly she brings dæmonic intervention. I wait, and time encircles me. Doubtless she would perform her task more swiftly, were he still here. Yes, who can I talk to about the Faust, now that the man has taken leave of time? Knew all my problems, all the impossibilities, all the ways and means as well. Immensely quick-witted he was, lively, flexible, had a keen appreciation of the great joke, and emancipation from prosy solemnity. After Helena had come in, did me good to have him praise my distillation of ghost and gargoyle into the classically beautiful and tragic; thought the union of the high and grotesque, the pure and fantastic might well produce a poetic tragelaph not to be despised. He saw Helena before he died, heard her first trimeters, his noble mind was impressed — that ought to cheer me on. Knew her, as well as did Chiron the rover, from whom I inquired of her. Smiled as he listened and heard how I had managed to imbue each word with the classic spirit:

> Much have I witnessed, e'en tho' the ringlets
> Youthfully cluster over my temples,
>
> . . . .
>
> Through all the clamour of warriors thronging
> Thick in their dust-clouds, heard I the frightful
> Voices of discord, gods in their anger
> Brazenly rising, ring through the field,
> Rampartwards!

He smiled and nodded. " Capital! " said he. That much had his sanction, so far my mind is at rest, it need not be changed, he found it capital — smiled, so that I had to smile too, my reading turned to smiles. Not German here either, smiling at excellence — no German does so. They put on a grim face, not knowing culture is parody — love and parody. . . . He nodded and smiled too, when the Chorus called Phœbus " the Knower ":

> Yet mayst thou boldly stand forth;
> For he beholds never the ugly,
> Nor hath his hallowed eye
> Ever the shadow seen.

That pleased him, he recognized himself in it, it had his stamp. Then he turned round and began to carp: it was wrong to say shame and beauty ne'er together hand in hand their way pursue. Beauty, said he, was always shamefaced. Why should she be? asked I. Because, he said, she knows she rouses desire, and that conflicts with the spiritual, which she represents. I answered him: Then desire ought to be ashamed; but she is not, perhaps because she is aware that she herself represents longing for the spiritual. He laughed at that, we laughed together. Now there's no one to laugh with. He left me behind, confident I should find my way through, discover the right hoop to bind in all the multifarious matter of my design. He saw all that. Knew Faust had to be brought into contact with active life — easier said than done, and did the good man imagine it was news to me? Long ago, when the whole plan was vague, still cloudy as a child's dream, did I not make my Faust translate not

In the beginning was the Word, or Sense, or Power, but In the beginning was the Deed!

Dunque, dunque! What's for today? Gird thyself up to seize the joyous task, thyself to industry arouse; late resting in the shade of leisure, now find in labour stern thy pleasure, in duty see thy sweetest joy. Tinkle, tinkle, there goes the "little Faust," the magic flute, where Homunculus and offspring are still one in the gleaming little phial. . . . Well, and what does the day demand of me? Oh, yes, devil take it, I have to render Serenissimus my judgment on the Isis scandal, wretched business! How one forgets down there! Yes, now comes up the spectre of the day to haunt me: must do the draught of the birthday Carmen to His Excellence von Voigt. Or rather, bless my soul, it must be written out and copied fair, his birthday is the 27th. And I've not got much yet, actually only a few lines, one of them good: Nature at last might aid herself to fathom. That's good, reads well, has my mark, can carry the polite rubbish the rest of it has to be. That's what society wants of you, when you have a "gift for poetry." Ah, that gift for poetry! To the deuce with it! People think it's the main thing. As though a man wrote the Werther at four-and-twenty years and then lived and grew another four-and-forty without outgrowing poetry! As though a man of my parts had stopped where he was and was still satis-fied with poetry-writing! Shoemaker, stick to your last — yes, if you are a shoemaker. The fools say I have for-saken poetry to waste my time in dilettante dabbling. How do they know it isn't the poetry that's the dab-bling and the serious work lies somewhere else, namely in the whole of life? Quack, quack, let them quack, silly geese! The fools don't know a great poet is first of all great and after that a poet. Don't see it's all the same whether a man writes poetry or fights battles, like the battles of that man I met at Erfurt. His lips smiled and his eyes were stern; behind my back, quite loud, for me to hear, he said: "That is a man." Not "That is a poet." Yet the fools think it is great to write the Divan but not at all great to produce the colour theory.

Confound it, that reminds me of something else: the Pfaff book, the professorial opus against the colour theory. Pfaff is the wretch's name. Sends me, "with his compliments," his impudent diatribe, has the cheek to send it here to my house! Typical Teutonic tactlessness; if I had the say, such people would be socially ostracized. But why should they not vent their guts on my scientific work, when they have already vented all they had on my poetry? Compared my Iphigenie with Euripides until there was nothing left of it, abused the Tasso, made the Eugénie hateful with their drivel about "smooth and cold as marble." Schiller too, Herder too, and that cackling de Staël woman — not to mention the bass-string of lowness, Dyck was the scribbling bass-string's name. Shame on me for remembering it or him! In fifteen years he will be as dead as he already is today, but I have to know him, because he lives with me in time. . . . That they dare to judge! That anybody may judge! It ought to be forbidden. A matter for the police, in my opinion, like Oken's Isis! Listen to their judgment and then tell me I ought to be for the States-General and the franchise and the freedom of the press, and Luden's Nemesis and the broadsheets of the Teutonic Students' League, and the People's Friend of Wieland's *filius*! Simply monstrous. When the masses fight, they are respectable; but their opinions are not delectable. Put that down, stick it away — hide, hide! Why should I publish and give myself over to their mercy? One can still care only for what one keeps to oneself and for oneself. When it has all been handled over and chattered over, one has no more courage to go on. Could have done you the most wonderful sequel to the Eugénie, but however ready I was, you did not want to be pleased. I'd be glad to write just to entertain them — but they can't be entertained; a sour, unhumorous lot, no understanding of life. Don't know there can be no life, without give-and-take and bonhomie, one has just to shut one's eyes and trust God and let things be, so they can go on somehow or other. What does all man's work amount to, either the deeds or the poetry-writing, without love, and the stimulus of taking sides? Just so much dross. But they go on as though they were here to demand the Absolute, and had the vested right to it in their pockets. Damned spoil-sports! The stupider they are, the crabbeder! And yet one keeps on spreading out one's all before them, so trustfully — " and may it find favour in your eyes! "

There now, there goes my cheery morning mood, all clouded over, blown on by gnawing corrosive thoughts. How do I feel? How is my sore arm? Bites shrewdly when I bend it. I always think a good night will mend matters; but sleep has no more its old power, one must just forget it. And the eczema on my leg? Adsum! as sure as morning dawns. Neither skin nor joints want to

play the game. I wish I were at Tennstädt, in the sulphur baths. Once I used to yearn for Italy, now I yearn
for hot water to loosen my stiffening joints. So age alters
our desires and brings us down, so man must come to his
second fall. But what a wonderful thing it is about this
fall, this growing old! A blessed invention of the ever-
lasting Goodness — man fits into his circumstances and
they into him, so that he is at one with them and they
are his as he is theirs. You get old, you get to be an old
man, and look down with contempt, albeit with benevo-
lence, on youth, on the young fry about you. Would
you care to be young again, the young cockerel you once
were? Wrote the Werther, did the young cockerel,
with absurd facility, that was certainly something, at his
years. But to go on living, to get old — there's the rub.
All the heroism lies in enduring, in willing to live on and
not die. And greatness only comes with age. A young
man can be a genius, but he cannot be great. Greatness
comes only with the weight, endurance, power, mental
equipment of age. Mind and power are products of age,
they are what make up greatness. Love too comes only
then; what is any youthful love beside the spiritual and
intellectual strength of love in age? What a callow,
green-sickly thing is the love of youth, beside the head-
turning flattery paid to lovely adolescence singled out
by maturity and greatness — her tenderness exalted and
adorned by the force of his mighty emotions! What beside the glowing bliss of age when the love of youth
confers on it the boon of new life? Eternal Goodness,
I thank thee! Life for ever fairer, richer, more instinct
with joy and meaning, hence for ever more!

That's what I call restoration, renewal. If sleep can bring it no longer, then thinking can. So now let's ring for Carl to fetch the coffee. Before he is warmed and refreshed the good man cannot properly tell how he feels, nor what he will be able to do. At first I wanted to malinger, stop in bed and let things slide. So much that infernal Pfaff did to me, and the thought that they won't let my name be entered in the history of physics. But my good mind knew how to get me on my legs again, and the hot drink may do the rest. . . . Every morning I pull the bell-rope I am reminded the gilt handle is out of place here. A fine show-piece, ought to be in one of the reception-rooms instead of here in my cloister of the austere intellect, burrow to crawl in, kennel of care. Good that I arranged my quarters here, my quiet, spare, serious kingdom of the mind. Good for the little one too, so she could see the rear of the house was to be a *retiro*, not only for her and her family but for me as well, though on other grounds. That was — let's see, summer of '94, two years after we had rebuilt the house I had been presented with, and moved back into it. Period of my contributions to the science of optics — oh, *mille excuses*, my gentlemen of the guild, I mean of course only to the theory of colour, for how should a man venture to attempt anything in optics, unversed in geometry and yet daring to contradict Newton? A wrong-headed, sophistical man, consummate liar and protector of scholastic error — traduced heaven's own daylight, held that its purity was composed of cloudy ingredients, its clarity a combination of elements each darker than itself. Evil-minded fool, darkener of

counsel, stiff-necked teacher of false doctrine — we must
not weary in assailing him. When I had grasped the
opaque medium and understood that the utmost transparency was already the first degree of opaqueness, when
I had found out that colour is modified light, then I had
my fingers on the theory of colour; at least the foundation and cornerstone were there, the spectrum could
make me no more trouble. As though it were not an
opaque medium, the prism! Well I remember how I held
the thing in front of my eyes in the room with the white-
washed walls. Contrary to the theory, they remained as
white as ever, nor did the pale-grey sky outside show
any trace of colour. Only where something dark impinged on the white did any colour show: the cross-bars
of the window came out in brightest colours. So there
I had the rascal fast, for the first time I said the words
aloud: the theory is false! And my very inwards leaped
for joy, just like that other time when I saw so clear
what I had known before by virtue of my good understanding with nature, that the little intermaxillary bone
was the forerunner of the incisors in the human jaw.
They wouldn't believe it, they won't believe it now
about the theory of colour. A happy, painful, bitter
time. Of course I made myself a burden, with my querulous insistence. Had I not shown, with my little bone
and my metamorphosis of plants, that nature had not
refused me a glimpse or so into her workshop? But they
would not grant my calling, turned away their heads,
shrugged their shoulders, behaved small. You were a
disturber of the peace. And so remain. They all make
thee their salutations and each one hates thee to the death.

Only the princes — they were something else. Unforgettable, how they respected and fostered my new passion. His Highness the Duke, kind as ever, offered me room and leisure to follow my *aperçu*. Ernst and August at Gotha, one lent me his physics cabinet to work in, the other sent to England for my beautiful compound achromatic prisms. Gentlemen they are, gentlemen! The pedants brushed me aside for a dabbler and troublemaker; but the Prince Primas in Erfurt followed all my experiments with the most gracious interest and did me the honour to make marginal notes in his own hand in the copy I sent him of my essay. Gentlemen, that is, have a feeling for dilettantism. To work for love of the work is aristocratic, the aristocrat is an amateur. On the other hand, the guild, the trade, the profession, they are all common. You talk of dabbling, you philistines — but have you ever dreamed how dilettantism is related to genius and comes close to the dæmonic, just because it is not bound but free, so made as to see a thing with new eyes and an object not as tradition sees it but in its purity just as it is; not as the herd sees it, which always, whether the thing is physical or moral, always gets a second-hand view? I came from poetry to the arts, and from them to science; soon painting and sculpture and architecture were to me like mineralogy and botany and zoölogy — and so I must be a dilettante! Just as you say! When I was a lad I made the observation that the spire of Strassburg Cathedral was to have had a five-pointed finial, and the designs bore me out. But I am not to make observations on nature! As though the universe, the All, were not all one! As though only he who had unity would not be the one to understand it — as though Nature herself would not yield her secrets to him alone who was of her!

The princes, and Schiller. He was a nobleman too, from head to foot, despite all his notions about freedom; had the naturalness of genius too, even though so wrong-headed, and behaving towards nature with such culpable arrogance. Yes, he was sympathetic, he believed, encouraged me with his responsiveness. When I sent him the merest first draught of the history of the colour theory he had the vision to recognize in it the prototype of a history of the sciences, the romance of human thought, which would grow out of it in eighteen years. Ah, yes, he could see, could understand! He had the eye, the quality, the soaring imagination — were he still here, he could prick me on to write the Cosmos, the all-embracing history of nature I always felt I had to write, beginning with the geology so long ago. Who can do it, if not I? I say that of everything — but I cannot do it all, under conditions that make up my life and rob me of it at the same time. Time, time, give me time, good Mother, I will do it all! When I was young I remember someone saying to me: You act as though we all lived a hundred and twenty years. Give it me, kind, slow-moving Mother Nature, give me only that little space of all the time thou hast to give, and I will take from others all those tasks thou wouldst see done, I can do them best of all.

Two-and-twenty years I have had these rooms, and not one single change, save moving the canapé out of the study to make room for my piles of papers. And yes,

the first lady-in-waiting, the Egloffstein, gave me the
arm-chair here by my bed. Otherwise no change — yet in
this unchanging setting what all has not happened, what a
raging storm of labour, effort, birth-pangs, creation, has
passed through it! What power to take pains has God
given man! That thou honestly hast striven, whate'er
cometh, God He knoweth! But time, time always went
on over my head. The blood mounts to my temples, always, when I think of it. Two-and-twenty years —
something has come of them, we have accomplished
something in that time; but it is almost a lifetime, almost
the whole life of a man. Hold fast the time! Guard it,
watch over it, every hour, every minute! Unregarded it
slips away, like a lizard, smooth, slippery, faithless, a pixy-
wife. Hold every moment sacred. Give each clarity
and meaning, each the weight of thine awareness, each
its true and due fulfilment. Keep book of the day, account its each and every use. *Le temps est le seul dont
l'avarice soit louable.* Music, now: has its perils for the
clear mind. Yet a magic spell, to hold fast and stretch
out the time, give it its own peculiar meaning. When
my little one sings The God and the Bayadere, she ought
not to sing it, it is too much her own story. When she
sings Knowst Thou the Land? — tears came to my eyes,
to hers too, the lovely beloved, whom I had dressed in
turban and shawl — she and I, we stood among our
friends and saw each other through the shining of our
tears. And she, the clever little treasure, said in her singing voice: " How slowly goes the time when music plays,
and what manifold living and experience she compresses
within a little space! Yet when we listen absorbed, a

long time seems to have passed. But what is time, that
seems so long and so short? " I praised her greatly for
her *aperçu* and agreed with all my heart. I answered:
" Love and music, both are brief, and both eternal."
Some such nonsense as that. I read Seven Years' Sleeper,
The Dance of the Dead, then Only This Heart Abideth,
then Never, Never Will I Lose Thee, then Mistress, Say,
What Is't Thou Whisper'st, then at last So on Rosy
Wings of Morning I Was Borne to Thy Sweet Lips.
The moon was full, the night grew late. Albert slumbered, Willemer slumbered, his hands, good man, folded
across his stomach, and was made a mock. It was one
o'clock when we parted. Felt so lively I had to take
Boisserée out on the balcony and show him, with a candle, the experiment of the coloured shadows. Saw her
standing on her terrace, listening. 'Neath the moon to
meet at evening have you made most sacred pledges —
" Avanti! " He might have stayed away a bit longer!

" Right good morning to Your Excellence! "

" H'm, yes, yes. Good morning. Set it down. Yes,
good morning to you too, Carl."

" Thank you, kindly, Your Excellence. It's no great
matter to me; but I hope Your Excellence slept well."

" Fairly, fairly. Odd, it seemed to me again, as you
came in, that you were Stadelmann. Just habit. The
Carl I had for years, you took the name from him. Must
seem strange to you to be called Carl, when your real
name — when actually your name is Ferdinand."

" I never notice any more, Your Excellence. We're
used to that, in my profession. Once I used to be called
Fritz. And for quite a while Battista."

"*Accidente!* That's what I call a versatile career. Battista Schreiber — that's a good name for you, Carl, you're a good scribe."

"Thank you kindly, Excellence. Always at Your Excellence's service. Would Your Excellence like to dictate something lying in bed?"

"Can't tell yet. Let me drink my coffee first. But draw the blinds, so I can see what sort of day it is. The new day. I've not overslept?"

"Not a bit of it, Your Excellence. It is just past seven."

"Already past? That's because I lay awhile and thought my thoughts. — Carl?"

"Servant, Your Excellence."

"Have we still a good enough supply of the Offenbach zwieback?"

"Well, Your Excellence, that depends on what Your Excellence means by 'good enough' — good enough for how long? We have enough for a few days yet."

"Quite right, I expressed myself badly. But the emphasis lay on the word 'supply.' 'For a few days' — that is not a supply."

"It is not, Your Excellence. Better say an almost exhausted supply."

"There, you see? In other words, not enough for a supply."

"Just so, Excellence. After all, Your Excellence always knows best."

"Yes, in the end it would mostly come to that. A supply that is giving out, so that you see the bottom of it, has something alarming. Mustn't let the well run dry.

Must take care to be able to dip from a full spring. In every field it is important to look ahead."

"Your Excellence never spoke a truer word."

"Good, glad we agree. So now we must write to Frau Assessor Schlosser in Frankfurt and tell her to send us a good fat boxful. My parcels are always franked. Don't forget to remind me to write. I enjoy these Offenbachs immensely, they are the only thing tastes good this time of day. Fresh zwieback, you know, is flattering to us old folk, it is crisp and seems hard, yet it is tender and easy to chew; so we get the illusion that we still bite as hard as sweet youth itself."

"But, Your Excellence, Your Excellence does not need such illusions. Your Excellence, if anybody does, is still dipping from a full spring, permit me to say."

"Yes, you may say so. Ah, good, the pure fresh air blows in, the morning air so sweet and virginal, and fans one round, so loving and familiar. How heavenly it is, new every morning, this rebirth of the world out of the night, to us all, old and young! It is a saying that youth goes with youth; yet this fresh young nature comes readily to us old folks too. Canst thou be glad, then I am thine, thine more than youth's. For youth has no right understanding for youth, only age has that. Frightful it would be, if only age came to age! Must not come in, must stop outside by itself. . . . How goes the day? Rather dark?"

"A little dark, Your Excellence. The sun is overcast, and here and there higher up we have — "

"Wait a bit. First go over and look at the barometer

and thermometer outside the window. And use your eyes."

"Yes, Your Excellence. The barometer stands at 722 millimetres, Your Excellence, and the thermometer at 13 degrees Réaumur, outside temperature."

"Look at that. Now I can picture the troposphere. The breeze coming in seems rather damp, west-south-west, I should say, and my arm tells the same story. Five or six cloud-banks; the overcast sky may have looked earlier like a downpour, but the wind has come up, the clouds show that, they are moving rapidly out of the north-west, as they did last night. It will soon scatter them and send them flying. There are long banks of cumulus heaped in the lower region — is that right? Above them slight cirrus and cirro-cumulus and cirro-stratus, like sweepings, with patches of blue between. Have I got it more or less right? "

"Perfectly correct, Your Excellence. I recognize the sweepings — they are sort of brushed along by the wind."

"I assume, then, that the wind in the upper regions is easterly; even if lower down it blows from the west, the cumulus will eventually break up into the prettiest little shoals of mackerel. Towards midday we may get a clear sky, by afternoon it may turn cloudy again. A changeable, contrary-minded day. I must practise judging the cloud-formation from the barometer. Used to be no proper interest in these variables in the upper regions; now a man has written a whole book about them, with an entire new terminology. Contributed a term myself, *paries*, for a bank of cloud. So now we can nail down these

changeable humours and tell them to their faces what
species and class they belong to. That is man's prerogative on earth: to call things by name and put them in a
system. They cast down their eyes before him, so to
speak, when he calls them by name, for to name is to
command."

"Shouldn't I take that down, Your Excellence? Or
have you told it to Dr. Riemer, for him to make note
of?"

"Tut, tut, you mustn't pay so much attention."

"But things must not be let get lost, Your Excellence,
no matter how great the supply. That book on the
clouds, I saw it lying next door, of course. A man is
simply amazed at all the things Your Excellence takes
notice of. The sphere of Your Excellence's interests
must be called universal."

"Simpleton! Where do you pick up such expressions?"

"It's the truth, Your Excellence. — Shall I just look
to see what your fine specimen of milkweed caterpillar
is doing, and whether it is still eating?"

"It won't eat any more, it has eaten enough, first outside and then since I have had it under observation. It
has already begun to spin itself in; you will see, if you
like to look, how the gland secretion is forming the
cocoon, soon it will be a chrysalis; still, I wonder if we
shall see the transformation and the psyche slip out to
live the brief and fluttering life it ate so much for when
it was a worm."

"Yes, Your Excellence, these are the marvels of nature.
But now what about the dictation?"

"Right, yes, so be it. I must prepare the opinion for His Royal Highness the Duke in that accursed journal business. Be so good as to take this away and hand me the pages of notes and the pencil, I put them ready yesterday."

"Here, Excellence. If I might be so bold and tell Your Excellence the truth, your copyist, Herr John, is here already and asked if there is anything for him. But I should like it so much if I might just stay and take down the opinion. There will be enough for the Herr Secretary to do after you get up."

"Yes, you may stay, just get ready. John always comes soon enough — though as a matter of fact he is nearly always late."

"Thank you very much indeed, Your Excellence."

Pleasant fellow, well set up, nice manners serving and about my person. His flattery is not calculated — at least not wholly; some of it comes in part from real devotion and need to love something, mixed in with a little vanity. Good-natured, sensitive, fond of the women. I suspect he is going to quacks because he got an infection after we came back from Tennstädt — if I am right, then I cannot keep him. Must speak to him, or tell August to — no, no, not August, better Rehbein. In the bordello the lad meets again the girl he loved, who tormented and tyrannized over him to the top of her bent. So now he gets his own back. Quite a pretty revenge. Something striking might be made out of it, light and hard, in perfect style. Ah, if one only lived in a free, intellectual society, what powerful, extraordinary things one could write for it! Art's natural ruthlessness is shackled and limited by all sorts of petty considerations. But it may be good for her; maybe she is all the more feared and loved, mysterious and powerful, wearing a veil instead of going naked, and only now and then giving a startling and rapturous glimpse of her native brazenness! Cruelty is one of the chief ingredients of love, and divided about equally between the sexes: cruelty of lust, ingratitude, callousness, maltreatment, domination. The same is true of the passive qualities, patience under suffering, even pleasure in ill usage. And five or six other perversities — if they are perversities — that may be a moral judgment — which, without adding anything else, are the chemical components of love. What if sweet love itself were put together out of nothing but sheer horrors, and the very purest just a compound of shadinesses we dare not confess to! *Nil luce obscurius!* Nothing darker than light — was Newton right after all? Well, no matter; at least the novel of European thought sprang from such ideas.

Besides, one could not say light was ever the occasion of so much error, disorder, confusion, so much laying bare of the indispensable proprieties, as everywhere and every day love is! Karl August's two families, the children — this Oken is attacking the Prince in the political field; will he stop there if we stir him up and keep on stirring him up, will he hesitate to attack in the private as well? Must make my master understand, quite baldly, the suppression of the sheet, the surgeon's knife, is the only reasonable and effective means. No rebuke, no threat, certainly no stirring up the fiscal to inveigh against this impudent Catiline — no bringing a suit, as the

good presiding officer of the Ministry would like. They
want to pick a quarrel with brains, poor souls. Much
better leave it alone. They don't understand. He will
talk just as cleverly and impudently as he writes; give
them replications — if he takes the trouble to answer the
summons — much better than any they could ever parry
with; then they will have to choose between arresting
him and letting him carry it off in triumph. Improper
and insufferable anyhow, for a writer to be given a
dressing-down like a schoolboy. Injurious to our culture and doesn't help the State. He is a man of merit and
brains. If he starts undermining the State, we have to
take away his tool, and *punctum*. But no threats, to make
him sorry and act better in the future. Punish a leopard
to make it change its spots! A man by nature bold and
impudent — where shall he get modesty and restraint?
He will simply go on as before, or else take refuge in
irony, and in face of that you will be quite helpless. You
do not know the resources of the mind. Force him, by
half-measures, to greater subtlety — that will profit him
more than it will you. Imagine the authorities following
up his little games with charades and logogriphs — playing the Œdipus to a sphinx like that! I should blush all
over for them.

And the fiscal's charge? They want to haul him up
before the Sanhedrin — and what is the *causa*? High treason, they say. Where is the high treason? Can you call
high treason what a man does in all openness as a citizen?
Get things clear in your own heads before you cross
swords in the name of law and order with such a shrewd
and able *destructeur*! He will publish your charges with

comments to show that he can prove all he says down to the smallest detail, and nobody can be punished for telling the truth! And where, in these divided times, is the tribunal you could entrust with the case? Are there not people sitting in the higher courts moved by the same revolutionary spirit as your culprit himself? Would you like to see him leave the court acquitted or even commended? It would look finer still to see a sovereign prince submitting these internal problems to a jurisdiction whose morale is shattered by the subversive times! No, it is no matter whatever for the courts, it must not be made so. It must be dealt with by the police, quietly, without publicity. Ignore the publisher entirely, attack the printer, make him liable if he prints the sheet. A silent, thoroughgoing rooting-out of the evil — and no revenge. You actually talk about avenging yourselves and do not see the monstrousness of the admission. You, with your wrong-headed service to law and order! Do you want to add fuel to the flames we see about us, and give barbarism a free rein? Chastise with whips a man like that, deserving of a brilliant rôle in science — and how can you be sure that stupidity, once up in arms, will not chastise him with scorpions? May God forbid — God, and the eloquent and moving judgment I mean to render! — " Ready, Carl? "

" Ready, Your Excellence! "

" I have at all times made it my first care to carry out as quickly and exactly as lay in my power Your Royal Highness's gracious commands — "

" Just a little slower, if I might beg Your Excellence — "

"Get on with it, butter-fingers! Abbreviate as best you can, else I will call John!"

"And so forth. Your Royal Highness's most faithful and obedient servant. — There is the first draught. I have crossed out all that I had in my notes. You can just put it tidy a bit, it is not finished, it still says too much, composition not just what I want. When I have it before me I will put it in order and soften it down. Make it so I can read it, if possible before midday. Now I'll get up. I can dictate no more letters now, this has taken up too much time, and I have so much for tomorrow. *Une mer à boire* — and every day just a few swallows. At noon I want the wagon, tell them in the stables. There will be no nimbus formation, it won't rain today. I will go with Herr Head Architect Coudray to inspect the new buildings in the Park; he may come back to dinner with me, and maybe Herr von Ziegesar too. What are we having today?"

"Roast goose and pudding, Excellence."

"Have plenty of chestnuts in the stuffing, they are filling."

"I will see to it, Your Excellence."

"Possibly one or two professors from the academy too. Part of the school is moving from the Esplanade into the hunting-lodge. I must go and inspect it. Put my dressing-gown here on the chair; I'll ring when I want you to do my hair. Go now. And Carl! Have my breakfast ready a little before ten, or not a minute later. Some cold partridge and a good Madeira. I am not my own man till I take a little something to warm the heart.

Morning coffee is more for the head, it's the Madeira strengthens the heart."

"Of course, Your Excellence — and for poetry one needs them both."

"Be off, you rascal! "

Holy water, pure and cold — holy not less in thy soberness than is the boon-and-blessing, sun-and-fire-combining gift of the vine! Hail, water! Hail, fire! Hail to the strong and simple hearts, the simple-heartedness which each day enjoys, like an adventure brave and new, that pure, first-given element, original refinement custom-staled! And hail to that refinement simple-heartedness can so mightily, so joyously embrace! For only here is culture, greatness. Fish in it fly, birds in it sky — pretty. Birds in it sky — quite a spacious, elemental little jest! Put it down. Might serve some time to show how one gets a happy thought. — Flow, water, flow, while earth stands fast! Stream free, O light, O love! O fire, leap up! Celebration of the elements already in the Pandora, that's why I called it a festival play. They will enrich and enhance the festival in the second Walpurgis Night. Life is growth, what has been lived is weak, strengthened of the spirit it must be lived anew. Be the Elemental Four honoured now and ever more! I will keep that, it shall be the closing chorus of the mythological-biological ballet, the satiric nature-mystery. But only the light touch, the light touch! Last and highest effect of art is charm. No scowling sublimity — even at its best and most brilliant, even in Schiller, it falls tragically exhausted, betrays itself the product of moral feeling. No, no, the

depths must laugh! Profundity must smile, glide gently
in, and smiling yield itself to the initiate alone — that is
the esoteric of our art. For the people, gay pictures; for
the *cognoscenti* the mystery behind. You, my good man,
were a democrat, you thought to offer the highest and
best direct to the many, noble — and bald. But culture
and the crowd, they do not square. Culture is the pick
of society, understanding, agreeing, discreetly smiling.
And its augur-smile is for the mischievous parody-nature
of art, that utters shameless things with utter dignity,
resolves the hardest riddles with an easy jest.

This sponge — I have had it a long time: handy specimen of deep-seated animal life, from the primeval Tha-
letic slime. Long before the coming of man, that was.
In what bottom didst thou shape thyself and nourish
thee to thy increase, strange skeleton for life, without
life's tender little soul? In the Ægean, perchance? Hadst
thou thy place on the Cyprian's throne of iridescent
shell? I blind my eyes with the stream gushing from thy
pores, and they see the Neptunian triumph, the dripping
rout: hippocamps, sea-dragons, ocean graces, Nereids,
Tritons blowing short notes on wreathèd horns — surrounding Galatea's rainbow car they stream through the
watery realm. . . . Good habit, that, to squeeze out the
sponge on the back of your neck — hardens your whole
body, if you can bear the shock without losing your
breath. But for the neuralgia in my arm I would bathe
in the river — as once, young mannerless fool, I would
rush up by night with dripping hair and like an apparition startle the late-going goodman! All do the gods
give, the Eternal, to their favourites, all! Long gone is

the moonlit night when, stirred to thy depths, thy flesh and being all intoxicate, thou mountedst from the flood and gavest out the lines into the silver air. — In that self way the water streaming over your neck conjured up the vision of Galatea. Inspiration, fancy, idea as gift of physical stimulation; healthy excitation, free and happy flow of blood, Antæan contact with nature and the elements. Mind, product of life, life that again in mind first truly lives. Each includes the other. Each has life from the other. What matter if the thought springing from joy of life thinks better of itself than it is? It is the joy that counts, self-satisfaction makes a poem of it. Certainly there must be care in the joy, one must take care too, and thought for the right. Thought, indeed, is not thought the care and pain of life? Then would the right be son of care and joy. From mother the blithe joy of life. . . . All seriousness springs from death and is reverence for it. But dread of death is despair of the idea — it is the stream of life run dry. We all go down in despair — honour, then, to despair! It will be your last thought. To eternity your last? Piety would have faith, that into the black renunciation of the life-forsaken soul might some time break the joyful ray of a higher life. . . .

With the dust the spirit not dispersèd. . . . I could like piety, if it were not for the pious. Piety would be good, and the secret hoping and trusting and honouring of the mystery — if only the fools, in their arrogant conceit, had not made a fetish of it, and a " movement," a bare-faced youth-triumph, neo-piety, neo-faith, neo-Christianity — and tied it up with all sorts of hypocrisy and fatherland rubbish and bigoted, malcontent croak-

ing, into a kind of green-sick philosophy, sinister indeed.
Well, well, we too were arrogant in our day, Herder and
the rest of us in Strassburg, and inveighed against everything old; you celebrated Erwin and his Minster and
stoutly refused to let the flabby doctrine of new schools
of beauty weaken your sense of the strong and crude
and characteristic. That would be just after the hearts
of the moderns, and flatter all the Gothic pietists; that
is just why I suppressed it and kept it out of the collected works. But then Sulpice, my good, trusty, intelli-
gent Boisserée, appealed to my conscience on the score
of the omission and rejection, and put me in wholesome
touch with the revived tradition and my own early attitude. Praise be to the higher favour and my own inborn
good fortune, that what might have been offensive and
annoying came to me in such fine, upright guise, the
good, reverent, cultured youth from Cologne, with his
loyalty to old-German architecture and painting and the
value of folk- and ecclesiastical art. Opened my eyes, he
did, to a lot I had not wanted to see, Van Eyck and the
artists between him and Dürer, and Byzantine lower-
Rhenish art. Youth comes to topple us old ones from our
seats; I had tried to protect myself and shut out impressions of a new, upsetting kind. Then, all at once, in the
gallery at Heidelberg, with Boisserée, there opened a
whole new world of form and colour, and pushed you
out of the old rut of sensations and opinions — the old
as youth, youth in the old — you learned what a good
thing it is to give way when it means conquest, and to
submit when submission spells freedom, because freedom
has brought it about. Said as much to Sulpice. Thanked

him for coming in all modesty and honest friendliness
to win me over, to hitch me to his car — of course, they
all come for that — to his plans for the completion of the
Cologne Cathedral. He took all possible pains to make
clear the national character and originality of old-German architecture, and how the Gothic had been more
than just the result of Greek and Roman decline.

> Here the grotesque they find,
> Creation of a clouded mind,
> To be the highest in its sphere.

Went about his affair so cleverly and neatly, did the lad,
was so clear and courteous, so sincere in all his diplomacy,
I took a liking to him — and to his subject too. What a
fine thing it is, to see a man love his subject like that!
Makes him and his subject both worth while, even if it is
nothing in itself. I smile when I recall his first visit, in
1811, we worked together over his copperplates from the
lower Rhine, the Strassburg and Cologne designs and the
Cornelius illustrations to Faust, and Meyer comes in and
catches us at it. Casts an eye over the table, and I shout
out: "Look, Meyer, how the old times actually live
again in these!" Couldn't trust his eyes when he saw
what I was so taken up with. Grumbles and growls at
the faults young Cornelius had faithfully taken over from
the old-German style; opens his eyes wide at me several
times when I calmly pass over his disapproval and praise
the Blocksberg and Auerbach's cellar and say that the
movement of Faust's arm as he offers it to Gretchen is a
good invention. Looks quite dashed, gasps for breath,
when he sees I don't sweep all that barbarous Christian

architecture off the table, but find the designs for the spires quite amazing and consent to admire the size of the pillared nave. Growls, looks at the designs, then at me, comes round, gives in, does the Polonius act — " It is back'd like a camel " — just a hanger-on, a snubbed and betrayed retainer, left in the lurch. Is there anything more diverting than to snub your satellites? Any better stolen pleasure than to run away from them, make fools of them? Any better joke than the sight of their dropped jaws when one finally has the courage to give them the slip? Of course, it's easy to misunderstand, may look as though one had got on the wrong side; the pious may well think you are as pious as they. Actually, we can take pleasure in the absurd too, but only when we learn something from it. Folly is of interest too, we must keep our minds open to everything. Asked Sulpice to tell me something about the Protestant converts to Catholicism. Should like to understand the workings of their minds, how they came to do it. He thinks Herder had a good deal to do with it, and his philosophy of the history of humanity; but the times had contributed too, the tendency of the age. That I ought to know, we have something in common there, in fact there is always something in common even with fools, only it looks very different and has different results. The tendency of the age — thrones are shattering, empires quaking — well, I ought to know something about that, unless I mistake I have been through it too. Only the experience enables one man to span the centuries, gives him a millennial point of view, as it were, and another it makes a Catholic. Certainly that millennial point of view has something to do with tradition, if we only understood it. But the fools try to bolster up tradition with history and scholarship — as though that weren't the death of all tradition! Either one accepts it and concedes something to it from the beginning, or one does not accept it at all and is a regular carping philistine. But the Protestants — so said I to Sulpice — feel there is something missing, so they set up a sort of mysticism; because when something has to be born and can't be, that is mysticism. How absurd they are! Don't even understand how the Mass came into existence, and behave as though one could manufacture a Mass. If that makes you laugh, you are more pious than they. But then they think you are playing the pious with them. They will claim for themselves your little old-German pamphlet on the Main and the Rhine and the history of art there in the Dark Ages; they will lose no time in threshing out your little harvest and making a patriotic harvest-festival parading about with the empty straw. But no matter for them; they know nothing about freedom. To give up existence in order to exist — certainly the trick will have been done. But it takes more than character, it takes mind, and the gift of renewal through mind. The beast's life is short. But man can experience recurrence, he knows youth in age and the old as youth; it is given him to relive what he has lived, his is the heightened rejuvenescence that comes after the triumph over youthful fears, impotence, and lovelessness, the circle closes and shuts out death.

Brought it all to me, the good Sulpice, so mannerly, so charmingly full of his theme, and only minded to hitch me to his car. Did not guess how much he brought, nor

could have brought it had not the lamp been waiting for
the light it kindled, had I not been ready for this chance
that brought so much in its train and led to so much more
than just the little old-German book. It was *anno* '11 he
was with me; year by year after that came the Hammer
translation with the introduction on the poet of Shiraz.
Came the gift of inspiration, the recognition as in a glass,
the blithe and mystical dream-play of metempsychosis,
the all-embracing millennial spirit he invoked, the Corsican Timur, my mighty and sinister friend. Came my absorption in the history of mankind — when faith was
great and reason small — my fruitful journey downwards
to the patriarchs, then that other journey into my mother-
land, taken in foreknowing readiness: yet shalt thou love.
Came Marianne.

Needs not to know how all that hangs together, I have
not told him, how it began with his coming, five years
ago, it would not be right, might put ideas in his head,
who himself was but an instrument and my tool, though
minded with all due respect to make me his. One day he
even had the idea of learning of me how to write, that he
might better advance the idea he had at heart; even
wanted to stop the winter in Weimar, to look over my
shoulder and get some hints. Better not, my friend, said
I. My pagans here are often too much even for me, who
am myself a pagan. Would be no good for you, you'd
have no one but me to fall back on, and that would not
be much, for I cannot always be with you. Spoken in
all affection, like other such things I said. Praised his
little writings and pronounced them good and well done,
for they had the right note, that is always the chief

thing. I could probably not do half so well, I have not a godly mind. Read aloud from the Italian Journey, where I praise Palladio to my heart's content and curse everything German including the climate and the architecture. Had tears in his eyes, the good lad. I hastily promised to strike out the offending passage, so he might see what a good soul I am. And just to please him I took out of the Divan the diatribe against the crucifix, the amber cross, that folly of the west and north. He found it too harsh and bitter, begged me to reject it. Good, said I, seeing it's you, I will cut it out. I will give it to my son, like other such things that might offend the public. He will enjoy it, and preserve it faithfully. So I will compromise between burning and offending. . . . But he loves me none the less, and was so pleased with my sympathy for his balderdash, not only for the sake of his own affair but for mine as well. A listener *comme il faut* — how charmed he was with the Shortest Night and the windy sighs of love-smitten Aurora for her Hesperus, when I read it to him in the cold room, on our Neckarelz trip! What a good soul! Said the prettiest, most intuitive things about the relation of the Divan to Faust; was at all times an excellent travelling-companion and confidant, I relished opening my bosom to him as we drove or when we put up, told him things about my own life. Remember the journey from Frankfurt to Heidelberg, while the stars came out and I talked about Ottilie and how I loved and suffered for her — rattled on out of excitement, cold, and want of sleep — I think I frightened him. . . . Fine road from Neckarelz up into the chalk hills, where we found petrifactions and fossil shells.

Oberschaflenz, Buchen — we ate at midday in the inn garden at Hardtheim, and there was that young waitress who looked at me with her heart in her eyes, and I demonstrated to him how youth and Eros can make up for beauty. For she was not pretty, yet uncommonly attractive, and got more so as she grew excited and blushed, and pretended disdain, when she saw, as she was meant to do, that the strange gentleman was talking about her. He saw too, of course, that I was only talking so she could see I was talking about her, yet his bearing was perfect, neither embarrassed nor coarse — that was his Catholic culture — his presence was altogether acceptable and happy when I gave her the kiss, the kiss on the lips.

Raspberries, with the sun on them, unmistakable smell of warm fruit. Are they making preserves in the house? No, not this time of year, must be in my own nose. Lovely fragrance, beautiful berries, swollen with juice under their dry velvety skin, warm with living fire, like women's lips. Love is the best of life, and of love the best the kiss: poetry of love, seal of ardent desire, sensual and platonic, sacrament midway between spiritual beginning and fleshly end, sweet commerce, held in a higher sphere than the other and with the purer organs of breath and speech — spiritual because still discriminating, still individual. . . . Bent back between thy hands that one and only head, beneath the lashes that serious, smiling gaze dissolving in thine; thy kiss says to it: I love thee, and I mean thee, precious particular of the divine All, expressly thee in all creation. For the other, procreation, is something else, anonymous, animal, at bottom without choice, shrouded in darkness. The kiss is joy, procreation is lust — God gave it to the worm. Well, in my time I have wormed it enough too; but after all the kiss is more my line, and the joy of the kiss, that fleeting visitation of conscious desire to fugitive beauty. There is the very same distinction between art and life. For the consummation of life for the human being, the making of children, is no affair of poetry's, or of the spirit-kiss on the world's raspberry lips. . . . Lotte's lip-play with the canary-bird — the sweet way the little creature pressed its bill to her sweet lips and then made contact from one mouth to the other with its pretty picking — how daintily depraved, how shatteringly innocent! Well set-up, gifted young fool, already knew as much about art as about love and privately meant one when he made the other! A mere young cockerel and already quite prepared to betray love and life and human beings to his art! My loves, my outraged friends, it is a *fait accompli*, it has to come out for the Leipsic fair, forgive me if you can! I must be your debtor, yours and your children's, good souls, for the evil hours my — call it what you will — brought down upon you. Bear with me, I beseech you! — It was about this time of year I wrote it, in those misty, far-off times. Came back to me, the very letter, when I had the first edition again in my hands this spring and went over the whole crazy invention for the first time in so many years. No chance that, it had to happen, reading it supplied the last link of all that began with Sulpice's visit. Belongs to the recurring phase, the blithe celebration of the recurrent feast. . . . Capital, too, brilliantly done, congratulations, young popinjay! The in-

terwoven psychological motive, the solid richness of
intuitive material. Picture of autumnal strayings and
flower-pickings — good too. Very neat the letter where
the young lady cons the list of her friends and can yield
him to no one, in each finds some flaw. Might be out of
Elective Affinities. So much skill and pains, along with
so much vagrant uncontrolled feeling, such tempests of
yearning and revolt against the limitations of the individual, the prison walls of the human soul — no wonder
it was a success; the man who began with it was certainly
no small beer. How easy something is to do, he knows
who thinks of it and puts it through. Easy and happy as
art, by virtue of the epistolary form, makes it immediate,
beginning over again from the beginning each time — a
whole reference system of lyrical units. Takes talent, to
make a thing hard for yourself and then see how to make
it easy. Same thing with the Divan — marvellous, how it
always is the same. Divan and Faust, yes, but Divan and
Werther are even more closely related — same thing on
different levels, ascent to a climax, repetition and refinement of life. So may it ever be, so go on *ad infinitum* —
gain through penitential striving, at eternities arriving
. . . much talk of kissing in both poems, early and late.
Lotte at the piano, never so charming her lips as then,
they seemed to open thirstily and drink in the sweet
tones. Was she not already Marianne to the life, or,
rather, was Marianne not Lotte, when she sang Mignon,
and Albert sat there too, sleepy, complaisant? Really like
a recurrent feast, this time; celebration and imitation of
the original, solemn performance, timeless memorial rite;
less life too than before, yet more, more intellectualized

life. . . . Well now, the high and holy season is past,
that reincarnation I shall see no more. Would, but have
been shown I may not; that spells renunciation, ever abiding in hope of renewal. Only abide, the beloved will return to be kissed, ever young — rather haunts me, though,
to think somewhere she still lives, old, her shape subdued
to time; scarce as comforting and acceptable as the
thought that the *Werther* lives on beside the *Divan*.

But the *Divan* is better, it has got beyond the pathological and ripened into greatness, the lovers are a consummate pair, soaring together towards higher spheres.
Blood goes to my head when I think of all the young
popinjay dragged in, in his frenzied search for motivation: social rebellion, offended bourgeois pride — why
did you have to bring that in, young simpleton, a bit of
political tinder that takes away from the whole thing?
The Emperor was quite right to condemn it: Why did
you do that? he asked me. A good thing nobody paid it
much heed, just swallowed it along with the other fiery
excesses and felt sure it was not meant for direct effect.
Silly, immature stuff, moreover subjectively false. My
attitude towards the upper classes was always very well-
affected — must certainly dictate a passage in the fourth
part of the Life, that, thanks to the Götz, I stood well
with the aristocracy, however much the work offended
established literary conventions. . . . Where is my
dressing-gown? Ring for Carl to dress my hair. The
readiness is all — somebody might come. Nice soft flan-
nel, pleasant to my hands when I fold them across my
back. Wore it mornings when I walked up and down
in the arcade by the Rhine, at Winkel with the Brentanos

and on the terrace at Willemer's Tannery. No one dared
speak to me, not to disturb my thoughts — though sometimes I hadn't a thought in my head. Fine to be old and
great; reverence there must be. Yes, where all has not
the good coat been with me, familiar domestic habit on
my travels, to assert my own permanent self and stand
out against stranger ways! Like the silver cup I pack and
carry with me everywhere and the wine I have tried and
found good, so that I shall not lack them where I go.
Enjoy the others and their ways, profit by them, yet
prove that I and mine are no less good. Cling to your
own, stand on your own legs — they may accuse me of
being set in my ways — it is a silly reproach. Clinging
stoutly to your ego, preserving your personal unity —
that is one thing, renewal and rejuvenescence are another,
but there is no inconsistency — *all' incontro:* one finds
these only in unity, in the closed circle of personality,
that bids defiance to death. . . . " Make me fine, Figaro,
Battista, whatever your name is; dress my hair, I have
scraped away the stubble-field. You take me by the nose
when you go at my lips, I cannot bear it, it is an uncouth
practice. Do you know the old story about the student
who was a practical joker and laid a wager with his mates
that he would pull an exalted old gentleman's nose? He
introduced himself to the worthy as a barber and calmly
proceeded, before everybody, to take him by the beak
and turn the exalted head to and fro — the old gentleman
took a fit out of sheer chagrin, and his son challenged the
joker to a duel and gave him something to remember the
joke by all his days."

"I never heard the story, Your Excellence; but it de-

pends on the spirit in which a man takes another by the
nose — I assure Your Excellence — "

"Never mind, I like better to do it myself all the same.
There isn't much to shave, from one day to the next. But
dress my hair and powder it, and put the tongs to it here
and there. You feel like a different man when your hair
is put in its place, away from forehead and temples; then
the frigate is stripped for action, and the head is clear.
For the hair and the head inside it hang together, and
what good is an uncombed brain? The neatest dressing,
you know, was the old bag-wig and cadogan; you never
saw it, you came in the middle of the Swedish period.
But I begin farther back — I've gone through so many
stages, short hair, long hair, formal hair, floating side-
locks — I seem to myself like the Wandering Jew, passing
through the ages, himself always the same, customs and
costumes changing on his very body, while he takes no
heed."

"That must have become Your Excellence very well,
the queue and the hair rolled over the ears, and the embroidered coat."

"Let me tell you, it was a good age, with decent and
proper conventions; a little craziness had its value in the
background, more than it has today. Tell me what freedom is, I always say, if it isn't becoming free. You
mustn't think there were no human rights then. Masters
and servants, yes, but those were ranks divinely ap-
pointed, each one worthy in its way. The master himself
had respect not only for his own rank but for the servant's too, as being fixed by the hand of God. The more
withal because in those times the view was more general

that whether high or low, everybody had to put up with being human."

"Well, Your Excellence, I'm sure I can't say. It seems to me the little fellows always have more to submit to, in practice it is safer not to have to depend too much on this respect of the high rank for the low."

"Maybe you are right. Would you have me quarrel with you — and me with my head in your hands so you can pull my hair or burn me with the tongs if you don't like what I say? I would do well to hold my tongue."

"You have very fine hair, Your Excellence."

"Thin, I suppose you mean."

"It is only beginning to be a little thin on the forehead. No, I mean each single hair is fine; soft as silk, one seldom sees it like that in a man."

"Very good. I am of the stuff God made me of."

Was that indifferent or dissatisfied enough? Objective about my own parts? *Parucchieri* must always flatter — the man takes on the manners of his trade, tries to feed my vanity. Doesn't realize that even vanity has manifold sources and forms. How should he know it can be a profound preoccupation, serious and contemplative absorption in the self, passion for autobiography, compelling curiosity about the why and wherefore of one's physical and moral being, nature's devious ways, the hidden secrets of her dark laboratory, that produced this being which is you, to the wonder and admiration of the world? A light word of flattery for my physical parts — he would think it just pleasantly tickled my ego. Actually, it refers to a mystery so joyful and profound, only to think of it brings my heart into my mouth! I am of the stuff nature made me out of. That is all there is to it. I am as I am and as I live. Well I know we get farther by acting unconsciously, like a bolt into the blue. And the autobiographical urge? Maybe not very consistent with the bold principle I just set out. But suppose it only applies to the process, to the edifying demonstration of how a genius develops (and that may be just scientific vanity). At bottom the curiosity is always there, the itch to understand the essence of the process, of the being not only as it is but as it has been, the far-flung sources of its life and experience. If thinkers think about the thought-process, why shall not also the worker think of him who works, if a work does come out of it — considering that all work may be nothing but a very vain preoccupation with the worker as a phenomenon — a highly egocentric performance, in short? Very fine, superfine hair. Here is my hand, resting on the powdering-cape. Doesn't go with the fine hair, not a slender, spiritual, aristocratic paw at all. Broad and firm, a workman's hand, shaped by generations of blacksmiths and butchers. What mixture of power and delicacy, strength and weakness, coarseness and frailty, madness and common sense, the impossible and triumph over it — what all must not have mingled by happy chance, as the centuries ran, to produce the phenomenon, the genius, in the end? In the end. Out of a series of bad things or good things there is finally born the phenomenal thing to amaze the world and bring it joy. Half-god and prodigy, marvel and monstrum — when I wrote that, I thought of them as one, I took one for the other, knew that there is always some amazement in joy, always in the half-divine a touch of the mon-

strous. Good or evil — what does nature reck, who recks
so little of disease and health, and can make the morbid
give birth to joy and healing? Through myself, nature,
do I first of all know thee, through myself feel thee most
profoundly. — You taught me that an ancient stock, before it dies out, can produce an individual holding in
itself all its ancestral qualities, uniting all talents previously isolated or undeveloped, giving them for the first
time full expression. Neatly formulated, carefully set
down for the better instruction of mankind: natural science, deliberately decanted from your own not too canny
essence. Egocentric, you may say. But shall he not be
egocentric who knows himself to be the goal, the fulfilment, the consummation, the apotheosis, last and highest
result of nature's uttermost extreme of care and pains?
Take this whole process of pairing and breeding of stocks,
crossing and mating of clans throughout the centuries:
the journeyman who comes from the next county to woo
the master's daughter; the wench of the count's tailor
or lackey, who marries the sworn surveyor or educated
bailiff. Was all this hodgepodge, this *quodlibet* of mixed
bloods, so especially privileged and favoured of the gods?
But so the world was to find it, in me, its issue; for in me
the most dangerous native tendencies have been subdued,
civilized, purified, applied and compelled to good and
great ends, by dint of a character sprung from somewhere
else altogether. My ego — a balancing trick, only just
achieved; a lucky stroke, just lucky enough; a sword-
dance poised between difficulty and love of facility; a
just barely possible that achieves genius — who knows,
perhaps genius is always just barely possible! They value

the work, when it costs enough, the life nobody values. Try doing it yourselves, see if you don't break your necks!

What about my fear of marriage, my half-conscious sense that it was wrong and foolish to continue in the bourgeois ancestral pattern, and struggle on after the goal was already reached? There is my son, issue of an easy compromise, fruit of a light and lickerish union frowned on by society — who knows better than I that he is a by-blow and an after-clap? Nature pays him no heed — yet I have taken the notion to act as though I could and might begin again in him. As though marrying him to the little person, she being of the stock that made me turn tail, could inoculate us with Prussian blood and make an after-play at which Nature herself would yawn and shrug and go home to bed! I know it all. But knowing is one thing, feeling another; and feeling will have its rights, *quand même*, whatever cold knowledge knows. It will look all pleasant and presentable at first; there will be a Lilli to preside over the house and smile at the old man's gallantries, if God please there will be grandchildren, curly-haired ones — shadow grandchildren, seed of the void in the heart. They will be loved despite faith or hope, simply out of feeling.

She was without faith or hope or love, Cornelia, sister of my heart, my female alter ego. She was not born for wifehood. Her revulsion against her husband probably corresponded to my fear of wedlock. A nondescript human being, a riddle to others and herself, wandering aloof and bitter on this earth, a crabbed votary. Strange it was, how in that first unnatural, detested childbed she passed away and died! Such was my sister in the flesh, the only other one of four children to survive — alas for her — those early days. Where are they now, that lovely little maid, and the strange, willful, silent lad who was my brother? Gone long ago, vanished and scarce bewept, so far as I recall. Dreams, and three parts forgot, I should not know them again. Fate willed that I should stay and you should pass; you went before, and little was your loss. I live on in your stead, at your expense, and roll the stone for five. Am I so egoistic, so avid of life, that I murdered you by sucking up what you might have lived on? Profounder and more secret sins there are than those we actually and consciously weigh ourselves down with. This strange childbed bore fruit of one really unusual life and four deaths — perhaps that was due to the father's being twice as old as the mother when he wooed her. Blest pair, vouchsafed to give a genius birth! And yet unblest! My blithe, happy-natured little mother — she spent her best years as nursing sister to a decrepit tyrant. Cornelia hated him — perhaps only because he gave her life. But was he not otherwise hateful? A querulous hypochondriac, who felt every draught of air a disturbance of the order of things; a cross-grained half-wit, too eccentric for any profession, a tedious pedant in any sphere. You took after him in many things: his size, his bearing and ways; his love of collecting, his formality, his manysidedness, his pedantry — but you transmuted it. The older you grow, the stronger that shadowy form will come out in you. You will recognize and confess him, more and more proudly, consciously and defiantly assume and honour the father-image. Feeling, feeling — I believe in, honour it. Life could not be borne unless we glozed it over with warm, deceptive feeling. Yet beneath it always lies the icy coldness. You make yourself great, make yourself hated, telling the ice-cold truth. And anon do penance and appease the world by merciful, heartening lies. My father was a shady character, late-born child of elderly parents, his brother definitely out of his mind and died an imbecile — as did my father too, in the end. My grandsire Textor was a ladies' man; yes, that came of his light-hearted, aspiring temperament; a jolly rake, a callous, deliberate petticoat-chaser, always getting into trouble with outraged husbands. But a clair-voyant too, had the gift of prophecy. Extraordinary mixture! Perhaps I had to kill off all my brothers and sisters to get the blend transmitted to me in some more tolerable, milder, more pleasing shape. Enough craziness left in me too, underneath all the brilliance! If I had not inherited the knack of order, the trick of saving myself, a whole system of protective devices — where should I be? Madness I loathe — abhor from my soul, beyond all power to utter, hate in my bones all crack-brained geniuses and near-geniuses, all emotionalism, eccentric gesturing and posturing, extravagance! Boldness, yes, audacity, boldness is all, the one indispensable thing — but quiet, decorous, wedded to the proprieties, velvet-shod with irony. That is how I am, that is what I will. There was that chap — what was his name? Sonnenberg, they called him the Cimbrian. Came from Klopstock, rolling his eyes and tearing his hair — at bottom quite a decent fellow. His great affair was a poem on the Last Judgment, daft undertaking, without polish in its daftness. Formless,

apocalyptic — he used to recite it like one possessed of
the devil. Intolerable. Made me sick. The end was, the
genius threw himself out of the window. Farewell, farewell! And *absit omen!*

Good, now; he has put me to rights, made me dignified
and elegant, a little like older, statelier times. When company comes, I will talk of trifles in a measured voice,
soothing to both sides. Not a trace of the dark, inscrutable genius these poor dear mediocrities love to gaze at and
draw edification from their delicious shudders. My phiz
must give them enough to talk about: my brow, and my
belauded eyes — those, to judge from the pictures, come
quite direct from my mother's mother, born Lindheymer,
Textor's wife, as well as the shape of my skull and mouth,
and my Mediterranean skin. The husk, the outward features, they were there a hundred years ago, with no more
significance than just a female, a buxom, clever armful of
a brunette. In my mother it slumbered, she being of quite
another cast. Then it came out in me, became the shape
and person of that which I am. Took on an intellectual
significance it never had before and never needed to get.
How inevitably does my physical self express my mental?
Couldn't I have these same eyes without their being just
Goethe's eyes and nobody else's? I mean to stick by the
Lindheymers — probably the best thing in me. Pleasant
to think their early seat, whence they took their name,
lay close to the Roman wall, in the slope of the watershed,
where the blood of ancients and barbarians has always
mingled. Thence it comes, from there you get the eyes,
the skin — your aloofness from the Germans, your perception of their vulgar strain; that scurvy misbegotten

race, out of it, in spite of it, you take your life, your antipathy for it gnaws at a thousand roots that feed your very being. So you lead this unspeakably precarious, painful life, called to their instruction, isolated not only by your station but from the very outset by your instinct; grudgingly respected and honoured, picked flaws in wherever they can! Don't I know they find me a burden, one and all? How could I appease them? I have moments when I would so gladly do so. It should be possible — sometimes it has been. For in your bones there is so much Sachs and Luther marrow; you even take a defiant pleasure in the fact, yet the very stamp and seal of your mind drives you to lift and lighten it with all your gift of irony and charm of words. So they mistrust your German soul and you, they feel it an abuse, your fame is a source among them of hate and anguish. Sorry existence, spent wrestling and wrangling with my own blood — yet after all it is my blood, it bears me up. It must be so, I will not whine. That they hate clarity is not right. That they do not know the charm of truth, lamentable indeed. That they so love cloudy vapouring and berserker excesses, repulsive; wretched that they abandon themselves credulously to every fanatic scoundrel who speaks to their baser qualities, confirms them in their vices, teaches them nationality means barbarism and isolation. To themselves they seem great and glorious only when they have gambled away all that they had worth having. Then they look with jaundiced eyes on those whom foreigners love and respect, seeing in them the true Germany. No, I will not appease them. They do not like me — so be it, I like them neither, we are quits. What I have of Germany I will keep — and may the devil fly away with them and the philistine spite they think is German! They think they are Germany — but I am. Let the rest perish root and branch, it will survive in me. Do your best to fend me off, still I stand for you. But the thing is, I was born far more apt for appeasement than for tragedy. Appeasement, compromise — are they not all my striving? To assent, to allow, to give both sides play, balance, harmony. The combination of all forces makes up the world; each is weighty, each worth developing, each gift reaches perfection only through itself. Individuality and society, consciousness and naïveté, romanticism and practical sense, each equal, each alike complete. To accept, to refer, relate, to be the whole, to shame the partisans of every principle by rounding it out — and the other side too. . . . Humanity universal, ubiquitous; parody secretly directed against itself, the highest, the irresistible pattern, world-dominion as irony and blithe both-sided betrayal! So then the tragedy falls away, falls down below where no mastery yet is, where my Germany yet is not, for my Germany consists in this very dominion and mastery, she represents it — for that sort of Germany is freedom, is culture, universality, love. All this no less true because as yet they do not know it. Tragedy between me and this people? Ah, yes, we may bicker and brawl. But above it all I celebrate an exemplary reconcilement; harping deftly yet profoundly, I will marry the rhyming magic of the cloudy north with the trimetric spirit of the eternal azure sky — and from

the embrace genius shall come. But say then why my
words so sweetly flow. What comes with ease must issue
from the heart —

"Did Your Excellency speak?"

"What? No — did I say anything? If so it was not to
you. Must have been talking to myself — that comes, you
know, with age, people mumble to themselves."

"It cannot be your age, Excellence, it must be just the
liveliness of your thoughts. I wager you sometimes did
it in your youth as well."

"Right there too. Much oftener than I do now I am
old. Talking to oneself is silly, youth is a silly time, so
it is fitting, but very likely not to age. When I was young
I rantipoled about — when something throbbed inside my
breast I gave the nonsense words and 'twas a verse."

"Yes, Your Excellence, that must be what people call
the inspiration of genius."

"May be, for aught I know. Who haven't it call it
that. Character and good intentions have to make up
afterwards for the native foolishness; what they do is at
bottom better and more comprehensible. — Well, are
you done at last? Can't go on for ever, you know. From
your point of view quite right — you take your own
work for the most important thing; but these little trap-
pings of life must keep their proper place."

"I see that, Your Excellency. But, after all, everything
has to be *advenant*. And a man knows who it is he has
under his hands. — Here is the hand-glass, if you —"

"Very good, very good. Give me the cologne for my
handkerchief. Ah, how good! What a pleasing, refreshing invention! They had it back in the time of the bag-

wig. I've loved it all my life. The Emperor reeked of it
from head to foot. Let's hope he still has it on St. Helena.
You see the little comforts and satisfactions of life become most important when the heroic deed, even life
itself, is all over and done with. What a man, what a
man! They have shut up that rebellious, intractable spirit
in the impregnable wastes of ocean, so that we here can
have peace and cultivate our gardens. . . . Quite right,
too. The age of arms and épopées is past, the king takes
flight, the burgher is on top. We are in for a practical
era, you will see: money, brains, business, trade, pros-
perity — we may come to hope and believe that even Nature herself has turned sweet reason, renounced for ever
all her fevers and fulminations, and perpetual peace is on
the cards at last. Quite a refreshing idea — nothing whatever against it. But when you think how an elemental
force like that must feel, with its powers all choked
among watery wastes, a giant paralysed, chained to a
rock, an Ætna smothered with ashes, boiling and seeth-
ing down below with no outlet for its fires — and you've
got to remember that if lava destroys, it fertilizes too —
when you think of all that, you feel such distress that you
are almost tempted to pity — though pity is not a feeling
proper to such a case. At least, one may hope he has the
eau-de-cologne. — I will go over now, Carl. Tell Herr
John he may come."

Helena, Saint Helena, that he should be sitting there,
that so it should be called, by that name, her name whom
I seek, my single craving, lovely as charming, charming
as desired — that she should share the name with that

rock of Promethean torture, my daughter and darling, all mine, belonging not to life and not to time! That longing 'tis chains my creative powers to this lifelong task, as yet unmastered — how strange a fabric is this weave of life, these destinies! Here now my work-room, morning sober, fresh and cool, abiding my next assault. Here my *subsidia, stimulantia*, sources, tools to lay the world of science under tribute to my creative aims. How burningly interesting all knowledge can become, when it serves to enrich and sustain a new creation! All irrelevant to its purpose the mind rejects — yet the mass of the relevant grows ever greater. The older one grows, the farther one spreads afield; go on at this pace, soon there will be naught left outside! This treatise on plant diseases and malformations, must read more of it, this afternoon if I can, or this evening. Freaks and sports are full of meaning to the friend of all life! Maybe the pathological teaches us most about the norm; comes to me sometimes, setting out boldly on the track of disease we might best pierce the darkness of living forms. . . . And here what joy in store for the discerning: Byron's Corsair and Lara, fine proud talent, must read more, in the Gries translation of Calderon too; the Ruckstuhl Treatise on the German Language has some stimulating things, must certainly give farther study to Ernesti's Technologia Rhetorica. That sort of thing clears the mind and brightens the flame. These Orientalia — the ducal library has waited a good while for their return, the dates are long since past. Shall not have a single one of them, cannot give up my tools while I am on the Divan; make pencil marks in them too, nobody will dare grumble. *Carmen panegyricum in laudem Muhammedis* — deuce take it, the birthday poem! Begins: "Fanned by the mountain air, as fine as ether, On rocky summits of the wooded gorges" — pretty stiff combination that, the top of a hollow! Never mind, let it go, it is a bold, rousing figure; if their gorge rises at it, let them swallow! "Of these heights the sober face" was the same kind of thing. Then comes the poet's bower, not so pleasant, with cupids shooting arrows through the air. Thirdly we have intellectual society, shattered by Mars. Lastly sweet peace returns, even so our minds right-about-face, turn and turn again, make a virtue of necessity, get back at *last* to our *past*, to ancient *tradition*, and then the *position* of the *crowd*, who will have their claims *allowed* — good, if you settle down to it after dictation you'll get it together in twenty minutes.

All this raw material and underpinning, never thought of itself as raw, but something in and of itself, with its own meaning and purpose, not just there for somebody to come along and squeeze out one drop of attar of roses and throw the rest away! Where does a man get the cheek to consider himself a god, and everything about him just trumpery, to exploit as he sees fit? To think of himself as the only mirror of the universe, and even of his friends — or those he regards as friends — as so much paper to write on? Sheer impudence and *hubris*? No, it is nature and character, laid on one and borne in God's name — enjoy it and forgive, it is there for your pleasure. . . . Waring's Trip to Sheeraz, very useful; Memorabilia of the Orient, by Augusti, helpful in some ways; Klaproth's Storehouse of Asia; Treasures of the

Orient, edited by a society of amateurs — wonderful find for a society of dustmen! Must go over the couplets of Sheik Jalal-uddin Rumi, bright pleiades of the Arabian sky; the Repertorium of Biblical and Oriental Literature will be most useful for my notes. Here's my Arabic grammar, must practise the florid script a bit, helps to get into closer contact. Contact, good word, expresses how you bore and burrow into some beautiful new world you have seized upon, dig away like possessed, till you know its secrets and can speak its tongue. And nobody sees the difference between imitated and invented detail. Queer sort of possession! Would surprise people to know how many books of travel and description a poet had to feed on for one little book of verses and sayings. Not just a mark of genius, they would think. When I was young, Werther was just making a sensation, there was a boorish chap named Bretschneider got worried about my conceit. Told me the root-and-branch truth about myself — or what he thought it was. Don't think so highly of yourself, my lad, said he. You're not so big a fish as you might think, with all the noise about that little tale of yours. What kind of brains have you got, when you come down to it? I know you: your judgment is mostly wrong; at bottom you know that unless you take a long time to consider, your intelligence is not reliable; you are clever enough, with people you think have insight, to back down at once and not enter into serious discussion; you wouldn't run the risk of giving away your own weakness. That is the way you are. And you are an unsteady kind of fellow, won't stick to any one system, go jumping from one extreme to the other, you could be talked into being anything, a pietist as easy as a free-thinker, you are so easily influenced it cries to heaven! And yet you are overweeningly vain, you consider everybody a weakling but yourself, whereas you are the weakest of all — quite incapable of judging the few people you think have brains, you cannot test them and have to follow the opinion of the common herd. Once for all I tell you: one grain of ability you have, your gift for poetry. When you have carried some stuff round with you a very long time and mulled over it, and scraped together everything about it that might be useful — then it works, then something may come of it. You get an idea, it sticks in your head, or in your feelings; it is like a lump of clay in your hands, you try to work everything into it that you see, you think and dream of nothing but this one thing. That is the way you get it done, that is all your genius comes to. Don't let your popularity put bees in your bonnet! — I can hear him still, queer chap, stickler for the truth, crank about knowledge, not spiteful at all, most likely suffered himself from his own keen critical insight, the ass! Clever ass, sharp-eyed, pessimistic ass — wasn't he right after all? Thrice right, or at least twice and a half, in all he rubbed into you about your inconsistency, your lack of independence, your suggestible soul? And about your genius, that it was only good for getting impressions and carrying them a long time, finding *subsidia* and knowing how to use them? Would all this material have been here if the age had not had a weakness for Oriental studies before you came on the scene? Did you discover Hafiz on your own? No, Hammer did it for you, gave you a proper translation, and when you read it, *anno* Russia, you were fascinated by a book which was the intellectual vogue of the day. But you can read nothing without being affected by it, it gets into your blood and makes you want to do the same kind of thing. A new experience like Hafiz makes you feel creative. So you began writing poetry in the Persian style and sucking up whatever served your turn in that ravishing new field, for the new masque you meant to put on. Independence — I'd like to know what it is! Enough that he was an original and, being one, did just as other fools have done! I was twenty years old then, but I left my hangers-on in the lurch and laughed at the " genius " school and its caricature of originality. I know why I did. Originality! That kind is just crazy, distorted, art minus creation, barrenness, vanity, petty dried-up spinsterishness! I loathe and despise it. What I am after is the productive, male-female force, conceiving and procreating, susceptible in the highest degree. Not for nothing do I look like that sturdy brown ancestress. I am the Lindheymer in male form, womb and seed, androgynous art, quick to receive, yet myself begetting, enriching the world with that I have received. So should Germans be, I am their image and pattern. World-receiving, world-giving, hearts wide open to admire and be fructified. Great in understanding and in love, mediating spirits — for mediation is of the spirit too — so should Germans be, and such their destiny. Not this pig-headed craving to be a unique nation, this national narcissism that wants to make its own stupidity a pattern and power over the rest of the world! Unhappy folk! They will end in a smash. Do not under-

stand themselves, that makes the rest of the world laugh
at them, at first; but after a while the world hates them
for it, and that is dangerous. Fate will smite them, for
betraying themselves and not wanting to be what in fact
they are. She will scatter them over the earth like the
Jews, and justly. For their best always lived in exile
among them; and in exile only, in dispersion, will they
develop all the good there is in them for the healing of
the nations, and become the salt of the earth. . . . Somebody coughing, yes, there's young Phthisicky a-knock-
ing at the door. "Come along, come in, for heaven's
sake! "

"Your humble servant, Herr Privy Councillor! "

"So it's you, John. Come along, how are you? — out
of bed betimes today! "

"Yes, indeed, Your Excellence is always early at
work."

"No, no, I mean you. You are up and out sooner
than usual."

"Oh, I beg pardon, I did not venture to suppose I was
the subject of remark."

" Why not? Your misunderstanding is over-modest,
seems to me. Is my son's schoolmate, the good Latinist
and law student, my faithful and fluent calligrapher, not
worth mention? "

"I thank Your Excellence most humbly. But even so,
I could not expect that the first words of greeting from
those revered lips should be a reproof. How else can I
interpret the comment that today I reported early? The
state of my chest and my long coughing fits before I can
fall asleep sometimes force me to lie a little longer, but I

thought I was safe in assuming that Your Excellency's humanity — and besides, I see that you preferred Carl's services to mine, although I did announce my presence."

"Oh, get along with you, man! Stop uselessly darkening your own morning. First insinuates that I have been too harsh in my words, and then is insulted because I have been too gentle in my actions. I only dictated something to Carl as I lay in bed, because he happened to be there. It was only official business. I have something much better for you. I meant no wrong by my words, I had no thought of hatchelling you. How could I help respecting your unfortunate weakness and making allowance for it? After all, we are all Christians, I hope. You have shot up so, I have to crane my neck as I stand, and then all the sitting over papers, among dusty old books — no wonder you wheeze! It's only a disease of youth, you will outgrow it. When I was twenty I spit blood myself, yet here I am, quite sound on my old pins. I like to stand with my hands clasped behind my back, chest well thrown out and shoulders back, like this. You let your shoulders sag and your chest cave in, you give up too easy, I tell you so in all Christian charity. You ought to find something to offset all that dust, man. Whenever you can, shake the dust from your feet, get out in the open, under the sky, ride, walk — I did that, it was the making of me. A man belongs out of doors, with the bare ground under his feet so that strength and power can run into him from the soil, like sap, and he can raise his eyes to the birds skied overhead. Civilization and culture are good things, great things, we are the last to dispute it. But without contact with the soil, the Antæan compensation, if I may so call it, they are plain ruin to a man. They put him in a morbid state; he even gets to be proud of being morbid, and clings to his ailment as though it were something honourable and advantageous. For there are advantages, let me tell you, even in illness. It sets you free, excuses you, much must be forgiven you for Christ's sake. If an ailing man makes pretensions, is finicking about his food, drinks too much; if he lacks self-discipline, seldom keeps to regular hours; he can count on your Christian forbearance not to reproach him, though he may worsen his lungs with tobacco smoke until the fog of it penetrates the whole house and he becomes a nuisance to other people who cannot stand it — I mean the smoke does, of course, not you, for I know that despite it all you are fond of me, I am dear to you, and it hurts you to have me complain of you."

"Grievously, Your Excellence, most grievously. I implore you to believe me. I am shocked to learn that the smoke from my pipe has penetrated the cracks despite all my precautions. For I well know Your Excellency's aversion — "

"Aversion. An aversion is a weakness. You turn the talk to my weaknesses. But we were talking about yours."

"Exclusively, Your Excellence. I deny none of them, and make no subterfuge to excuse them. I only beg you to believe me: if I have not overcome them, it is not that I presume upon my weak chest. I have no ground to presume upon my chest, I ought to beat upon it — my breast, I mean — instead. Your Excellence may smile at that, but I say it in all seriousness. My weaknesses, yea, my

vices, are inexcusable. Yet I yield to them from time to
time, not because I am ill, but because of the confusion in
my miserable suffering soul. My patron has such vast understanding of the human soul — it would be presumptuous in me to remind him that sometimes a young man will
suffer from an emotional crisis that upsets the regular
conduct of his life. He may go through a period when
all his opinions and convictions are in a transitional stage,
due to pressure from a new and compelling environment
— until he no longer knows whether he is losing or finding himself."

"Well, my child, you have not betrayed much sign
of such a crisis up till now. But I can make a guess what
you are driving at. I will be frank with you, my friend.
I knew nothing of your political flights or your Icarian
passion of perfectionism. I did not know you were the
author of that reckless anti-aristocratic broadside against
the forced labour of the peasantry and in favour of a
highly radical form of government. If I had, I would not
have received you into my household, in spite of your
good education and excellent hand. In fact, I have been
censured for so doing by men of high position surprised
at my action. Now, if I understand you — and my son
has dropped hints to the same effect — you are about to
come out of your fog, give up your revolutionary errors,
and honestly try, in matters of State and practical government, to turn your mind towards the good and traditional way of life. But I think you should be proud to
ascribe this process of enlightenment to your own stout
heart and lively understanding, not to any outward influ-
ences or deliberate pressure. I believe it cannot account

for your moral qualms and distracted behaviour; anything so obviously healing should be accompanied by benefit to both body and mind. For the two are so closely connected that nothing can affect the one without the other, for better or worse. How can you think your revolutionary humours and excesses had nothing to do with your lack of the Antæan compensation, the healthy contact with nature and the soil? To me, your invalidism and weak chest were the physical counterpart of the morbid notions in your mind. It all goes together. Give your body exercise and fresh air, avoid spirits and strong tobacco, and you will find your brain dwelling on ideas making for order and authority. Above all, get rid of that wretched spirit of opposition. It is contrary to nature to want to reform the world. Cultivate your own garden instead, aim at wholesome efficiency inside the existing order, and you will see your body, too, will gain robustness and become a stout and sturdy vessel for the enjoyment of life. There's my advice, if you want to listen to it."

" Oh, how could I not, Your Excellence? How could I fail to accept with deepest gratitude such wise, experienced advice? It is borne in upon me that in time these comforting assurances will take actual shape and bear fruit. But in the meantime I confess my present confusion and bewilderment. In the lofty and enlightened atmosphere of this house I have been passing laboriously through a period of transformation of all my thoughts and convictions; and if it has been attended by the pangs of parting I might perhaps claim some indulgence. Yet claim is not the word — for how could I claim aught? I can at most humbly express my hope. For such conversion in a man means resigning himself to the loss of much greater hopes — unripe and childish perhaps, in painful rebellion to his surroundings, yet sustaining and comforting, lifting his soul up to harmony with a higher reality than the present. Idealists cherish a fond belief in a revolutionary cleansing of the nations, in a purified humanity united for freedom and the right; in short, in a kingdom of happiness and peace on earth under reason's rule. To give up all that, to reconcile oneself to the bitter if tonic fact that ever and always the blind pitiless forces will sway to and fro, alternately overcoming each other — that is not easy, it must always set up inward conflicts. And when, in the throes of such growing pains, a young man does resort for cheer to the bottle, or seeks to veil his troubled thoughts in the comforting haze from his pipe, may he not count on mild judgement from those, no matter how highly placed or powerful, who can sympathize with his struggles? "

"Come, come, I call that rhetoric! You should have been a lawyer, so well you know the arts of special pleading. Maybe you will still become one. Perhaps not only a lawyer, an orator, but a poet, you have the art of making your pains interesting to others. No, not a poet; political fervour does not become them, politicians and patriots make poor poets, freedom is not a poetic theme. Your gift of words might well make you a writer and popular speaker. But let me tell you, you do ill to use it to put me in a bad light. As though contact with me had robbed you of belief in humanity and made you cynically hopeless of the future! Do I not wish you well? Can you blame me for thinking more of your personal welfare than humanity's? Does that make me a Timon? Do not misunderstand me. I consider it perfectly possible, even probable, that our nineteenth century will not be merely a continuation of the eighteenth. It may open towards a new era, when we may rejoice at the sight of humanity pressing onward to new heights. Though actually things look as though an average level of culture would prevail, a mediocre culture, one of whose features will be that many people who ought not to will concern themselves with problems of government. At the lowest level we shall have the young folk, deluded with the idea that they must have their say in affairs of State; at the highest, an attitude which yields more than is proper, out of weakness or exaggerated liberalism. I am instructed in the weaknesses and dangers of a liberalism that so releases individual demands and desires that in the end you are at a loss to know which should be granted first. You will always find that too much kindness and moral sensibility from above will not do in the long run, when a mixed and often mischievous society has to be kept within the bounds of law and order. The law in all its severity must be enforced. That is essential. We have even begun to take a lax view of the responsibility of criminals. Medical testimony and expert opinion often contrive to help the wrongdoer escape just punishment. It takes a strong character to remain firm in face of general laxity. I give due credit for his strength of purpose to a young medical officer named Striegelmann, lately commended to me. A short time ago we had a case of a woman who killed her new-

born child, and the court questioned her responsibility
for the deed. Striegelmann gave his opinion that she was
indeed fully responsible."

"How I envy Dr. Striegelmann Your Excellency's
commendation! I shall dream of him, I feel sure, draw
encouragement from his strength of purpose, intoxicate
myself with the thought of it. Yes, intoxicate! Ah, I
have not said all when I confessed to my benefactor the
difficulties of my own conversion. I am impelled to make
a clean breast, as to a father or a confessor. My change
of heart, my new relation to law and order and tradition
involved many pangs at parting from my immature and
futile dreams. But there was something else — *pénible*
it is to utter it. There was a new, a dizzying, breath-tak-
ing ambition — and as before, so now, it drives me to my
bottle and my pipe, to drown its voice, or, again, with
their help to plunge deeper into the glowing depths of
my new visions."

"H'm — ambition? And what kind?"

"It springs from the thought of the great advantages
a convinced acknowledgment of authority and law have
over the spirit of revolution. Revolution is martyrdom.
Whereas acquiescence in authority means we are willing to serve power and to receive our share of its benefits.
These are the new heart-swelling dreams which, in this
process of change and growth, have driven the old ones
out. My acceptance of authority carries with it my service; this easily makes clear to Your Excellence that I am
eager to put theory into practice. The unexpected boon
of this private talk emboldens me to make my request."

"Which is — ?"

" Surely I need not protest how much I prize my present employment, due to a school friendship with your honoured son. I appreciate to the full the advantages I have for two years enjoyed in a household so highly esteemed by me and all the world. On the other hand it would be absurd to imagine myself indispensable. I am one among many employed by Your Excellence for subsidiary tasks: the Kammerrat himself, Dr. Riemer, the librarian Kräuter, and your valet Carl. Again, I am well aware that I have given Your Excellence cause for complaint of late on account of these distractions of mine, and my chest trouble — all together I do not feel Your Excellence particularly values my services. Perhaps my exaggerated height, my spectacles and pock-marks come into it too."

" Come, come, as far as that goes — "

" My idea, my ardent wish is to exchange Your Excellence's service for that of the State; more specifically, a department affording favourable opportunity to apply my new and chastened convictions. There is a certain Captain Verlohren, a patron of my poor but worthy parents, living in Dresden and with personal contacts with several of the heads of the Prussian Censorship. If I might humbly beg Your Excellence to put in a word for me with Captain Verlohren, indicating my change of views, he might receive me for a time and in his turn recommend me to the proper authorities. In that way I might gratify my urgent wish to make my way up the ladder of the Censorship. And my gratitude to Your Excellence, so great already, would indeed become boundless."

" Well, John, that can certainly be done; I have no objection to writing the letter to Dresden, and I should rejoice to help persuade the authorities in charge of the preservation of law and order to decide favourably on your case despite your former offences. I cannot say I am quite pleased with what you say of the ambitions connected with your change of heart. However, I am used to being not quite pleased, in a number of ways, about you, and you may well be glad of the fact, since it makes me readier to help you onward. I will write — let me see how to put it: shall we say I shall be glad to see time and space granted an able person to acknowledge his errors, avoid them, and redeem them by honest effort; and that I only hope this benevolent enterprise may succeed and lend conviction and courage for similar ones in future. Will that do? "

" Splendidly, Your Excellence! I am utterly and completely — "

" And do you think we might now for the present leave your affairs and come on to mine? "

" Oh, Your Excellence, it is quite unpardonable — "

" I have been standing here turning the pages of the Divan, they have increased by a few good things of late. I have put them in order and filled them out here and there, but there was enough already to divide into books, as you see: Book of Parables, Book of Zuleika, Book of the Cup-bearer — well, now, I am supposed to give some of them to put into a Ladies' Album. But I don't want to. I do not like to break the jewels from the chaplet as it rounds out, to display them singly between my fingers. I doubt if the single piece will show to advantage, it is the whole that counts, not the parts. I see it as a revolving dome, a kind of planetarium; besides, I hesitate to put any of these fabrications before an astonished public without the notes, the commentary I am writing to instruct the reader in the traditions and linguistic practices of the Orient from a historical point of view, by way of preparing them for my offering. On the other hand, one does not like to be mock-modest, and one does like to respond to the public demand by coming out with one's own little novelties and personal experiences turned into light verse. What do you say — what shall I put into the Ladies' Album? "

"Perhaps this, Your Excellence: ' Tell It Only to the Wise Ones ' — it is so pregnant."

"No, not that one. I could not bear to. It was prompted by a singular inspiration, and is caviar to the general. It is all right in the book, but it is nothing for the Ladies' Album. I agree with Hafiz, who was convinced that you please only by singing what people like to hear and can understand; now and then you may venture to slip in something a bit more difficult. Not even art can get on without diplomacy. And this album is for ladies. 'With Woman deal forbearingly ' — that might do, if not for the line about the crooked rib: ' If you would bend her she breaks, Leave her alone she grows the crookeder ' — that is offensive, it can only pass in a book with other things. ' May from this my writing-reed Only charming things proceed ' — that's the sort. The lighter, simpler, gayer ones; for instance: 'Young Adam was a lump of clay,' or this about the frightened little drop that was vouchsafed hardness and permanence that it might become a splendid pearl in the Emperor's crown. Or this that I wrote last year: 'In Paradise by full moonlight,' about God's two loveliest thoughts. What do you say?"

"Very good, Your Excellence. Perhaps also: 'Never, never would I lose thee'—with the fine lines: 'Thou my simple youth adorning With thy passion's mighty power.'"

"H'm, no, that is the feminine voice. I imagine the ladies prefer to hear the man's and poet's. For instance, the one just before it: 'If she find a heap of ashes She will say, he burned for me.'"

"Very good. I confess I should have liked to choose just one—but I must content myself with cheerful acquiescence. Yet at least let me put in a warning about 'The Sun, the Helios of the Greeks'—the rhyme you use smacks of dialect, the lines are in need of revision."

"Oh, let it stand! The bear must growl as his forbears did. Well, we shall see. But come now, let us sit down, I will dictate from my Life."

"At your service, Your Excellence."

"My dear fellow, do stand up again! You are sitting on your coat-tails. If you do that for an hour they will look dreadful—wrinkled and crushed, and all in my service. Let them hang down from your chair, I beseech you."

"Thank you very much for your concern."

"Now we can begin—or rather go on, beginning is harder. At this time my position vis-à-vis the upper classes was most favourable. Although in Werther the unpleasantnesses attending on contact between two different spheres . . ."

Ugh! I'm glad he's gone; good that breakfast came to interrupt us. Can't abide the chap, God forgive me! He could not take up a position that would not go against my grain! I like the new one even worse than the old. If it had not been easy going today, with Hutten's letter to Pirkheimer that I had among my papers, and about the goodwill of the aristocracy of that time, and the state of things in Frankfurt, I could not have stood him. He left a bad taste in my mind, let me have another good gulp of this liquid sunshine here with my bird's wing. Why did I promise him that letter to Dresden? Vexes me that I did. The idea of draughting it tempted me, of course — danger in this love of expression and the well-turned phrase; makes us forget that words imply action, it is like a play, you make up opinions for a character who might or might not have them. Did I have to help him further his nauseating ambitions? Now he will most likely turn into a zealot for law and order, a perfect Torquemada of legality. He will hound down the youth who are having the same dreams of freedom he once had. Had to save my face and praise him for his conversion; but the whole thing is a confounded nuisance. Why am I against the sweet freedom of the press? Because it only makes for mediocrity. Legal restrictions are good, an opposition without them goes stale. Limitations make it use its wits, a big advantage. A man entirely in the right need not mince his words; but a party is never entirely in the

right, else it would not be a party. It has to use the indirect method, the French are models and marvels at that,
whereas the Germans think their hearts are not in the
right place unless they express their opinions straight
from the shoulder. You don't get far that way, in indi-
rection! Oh, yes, culture! But all I mean is, necessity
is the mother of invention, and this fellow John is a phthisicky fool. Government or opposition — six of one and
half a dozen of the other — he actually thinks this silly
shuffle of his is a soul-stirring event.

That was a disgusting talk, *pénible*. I feel it more and
more now it is over. Like a harpy, fouling my meal with
his filth. What does he think I am? What does he think
I think? Does he think he now thinks as I do? Ass, ass!
But why do I work myself up over him like this? Can
it be my annoyance, or what amounts to actual suffering,
is the same kind as the soul-searching misgivings I really
only have, not for such as him, but for my work, including every shade of doubt and fear and anxiety —
because my work is my objective conscience! The pleasure of activity, that's it! The fine, the great deed, that's
the thing. (What does he think of me?) Faust must be
brought into active life, into public life, he must serve
mankind. His striving, which shall bring him redemption, must take shape in a large political sense; the other,
the great Phthisicky, he saw it and said it, and was not
telling me anything new. Easy for him to say it, though,
the word " politics " did not set his teeth on edge like sour
apples, the way it does mine. But why have I got Meph-
istopheles? I can use him to make up to myself for
having to have the spirits of fame appear to Faust and

praise the great deed. "Oh, fie on you for yearning after fame!" Notes in the desk, let's see. "By no means, this terrestrial sphere Gives ample scope for deeds of daring, Amazing things are e'en preparing, I feel new powers for bold employ. . . ." Good. "Bold employ" is capital — if it did not, unfortunately, refer to something unpleasant. But I must and will show that this tempestuous, disillusioned soul has to turn from metaphysical speculation to practical idealism if he is to fathom the human spirit as he saunters irresponsibly through the world of experience at his diabolic mentor's side. What was he, and what was I, when he lurked in his lair and tried to storm the heavens by dint of philosophizing? Then had the poor pathetic affair with the little grisette? The song, and its hero — they had both to outgrow their boyish limitations and talented trifling, and become objective, actively human and mature. From the scholar's vault, the gallery of glooms at the Emperor's court . . . hating all bounds, yearning beyond the height of the possible, here too the eternal seeker must play his constant rôle. But how reconcile his maturity and worldly wisdom with the rebelliousness of former days? Political idealism, panaceas for universal betterment — but he remains a starveling, hungering and thirsting after the unattainable. Hungering and thirsting — good, let me put that down, I'll use it somewhere. That is realism, that is aristocratic, truly German to censure German ways with German words. . . . Make a bargain with authority, then so act as to establish a better, nobler, higher order of things on earth. Of course he fails to inspire Kaiser and court, they almost die of ennui, the Devil has to come in and save the

situation with brag and bounce. The political enthusiast
is reduced to the rank of *maître de plaisir*, court engineer
and contriver of fireworks. The carnival will be great
sport. I can make a fine procession of masks, mythological figures and witty tomfooleries — sort of thing to give
for Serenissimus' birthday or an Imperial visit, only it
would cost too much. Should end on a note of bitter
irony. But at first he must be in earnest, must want to
govern for the good of the people — must find the right
key for the expression of his faith, find it, of course, in
my own breast. Where have I got it? Here: "The human hearing's very keen, And splendid deeds can follow
one clear word. Only too sore man feels his human need,
And gladly counsel he will heed." I like that. God Himself, the Positive Principle, the creative Goodness, might
answer the Devil in those very words, and I agree, I side
with the positive. Never had the misfortune to be in the
opposition. Not my view, either, that Mephisto should
talk in the Palatinate. Faust will not let him cross the
threshold of the audience-chamber. Refuses to let magic
or hocus-pocus in word or deed appear in the Imperial
presence. The black art is at last to be cleared from his
path, here as in the Helena scenes. She too is only allowed by Persephone to revisit the earth on condition
that all shall come about naturally and humanly, and her
wooer win her love by the power of his passion alone.
Fits wonderfully. I know of somebody who would be
awake to the necessity, if he were only not asleep,
alas! . . . And another condition there is too, everything depends on it, the absolute, all-important technique, the only hope of giving new life to the outworn

theme of age and youth. I mean the light touch, simplicity, playfulness. Faery is the only wear. If I just
think "my little jokes," then I can finish it. And what
could even you, my friend, have against witty light-
mindedness and the comic element? You always liked
to talk about "unpoetic seriousness." And your edu-
cational essays, with the authority of your philosopher,
praised almost pedantically the æsthetic value of playfulness. Light though it be, not lightly is it done. And
where you take lightness seriously, you may also take the
serious lightly.

There, or nowhere, is the place for my work. The
classical Walpurgis Night . . . ay, my thoughts slip
easily away from the political, I am not loth to forget it,
I feel at bottom I should be better off if I decided to
leave it out — just as I felt when I was talking with young
Phthisicky and getting worked up about it, if only because it is a pity about the verses already written. The
classical Walpurgis Night — to return to the happiest and
most heartening thing I can think of — ah, what a grand
game, how far beyond any court masquerade that shall
be! A comedy, fraught with ideas, life-mysteries, witty,
fantastic, Ovidian interpretations of man's origins — no
solemnity, graceful, light-footed style, Menippian satire
— is there a Lucian in the house? Yes, in the next room, I
know exactly where, a *subsidium*. I will read him again.
Moves my very entrails to think how the homunculus
came to me, quite unexpected, in a kind of dream-inspira-
tion — and I got him right — who would have thought
he could be brought together with her, the loveliest, in
the frame of life's vast mystery; made the playfully scien-

tific, Neptunian-Thaletic basis and motivation for the appearance of the highest type of human beauty? " The final product of ever advancing nature is the human being." Yes, Winckelmann knew something about beauty and the humanism of the senses. He would have rejoiced in the audacity of including the biological prehistory of the beautiful in its manifestation. Would have liked the idea that the power of love helps make an entelechy of the monad, beginning as a little clot of organic mud at the bottom of the ocean, running, through uncounted time, the gamut of life's lovely metamorphoses, finally attaining its highest and finest form. The greatest intellectual feat in drama is the motivation. You did not care for it, my friend, you considered it beneath you, made bold to contemn it. But you see there is a kind of motivation daring enough to escape the reproach of pettiness. Has ever the entrance of a character been prepared like this? Of course, it represents beauty itself, so there had to be special preparation. And it goes without saying it must all be suggested and implied, not expressed. All depends on the use of mock mythology and travesty. Anything like abstruse natural philosophy would jar on the requisite lightness of form. So in the Helena scenes a stately or severe classical delivery would be a satirical contradiction to the intrigues and illusions of the plot. Parody — I love to dwell on it. Much to think on, much to muse on in the slender strand of living — and of all the matter for musing there is in art, I find this the most strangely gay, the tenderest. To destroy without hatred, to abandon with a smile . . . imitation, yet a jesting mockery. To reproduce the admired, the beloved, old

and sacred pattern, on a plane and with a content that sets
the stamp of parody — a product like the late, loose,
ironic forms of post-Euripidean tragedy. . . . Strange
existence, solitary, unfriended, uncomprehended; coolly
taking on myself in the heart of an uncultured folk to
embrace all the culture of the world, from the age of
faith to the conscious decline!

Winckelmann . . . "Precisely speaking, one may say
there is but one single moment in which the beautiful human being is beautiful." Extraordinary sentence. We
capture in the metaphysical that instant in the life of the
beautiful when, much admired and censured much, it
appears in all its melancholy perfection. The eternity of
the moment, as our departed friend painfully immortalized it in a phrase. Dear and all too clear-sighted enthusiast and lover, with your intellectual absorption in
the senses! Do I guess your secret, the moving spirit behind all your knowledge? The worship today without
its votaries that bound you to Hellas? For your *aperçu*
only applies to masculine adolescence, to that exquisite
moment in the life of the youth, captured only in marble. Lucky for you, when we say "man," we mostly
mean male; you could conceive your beauty as masculine as you liked. Whereas for me it came in youthful-
feminine guise . . . yet perhaps not quite — for I can
understand your device, and recall in all candour and
enjoyment that comely blond waiter last summer on the
Gaisberg, Boisserée was there that time too, with his
Catholic discretion. Sing thou only to the others, to the
cup-bearer be silent. . . .

In the whole moral and sensual world the thing whereon

my whole life long I have most dwelt with horror and
desire is seduction — inflicted or borne, active or passive,
sweet and terrible, like a command laid on us by a god;
the sin we sinlessly commit, guilty as tool and victim
both; for to withstand it does not mean we cease to be
seduced. It is the test no one withstands, it is so sweet,
even to endure it spells defeat. It pleases the gods to send
us sweet temptation, to make us suffer it, as its instru-
ments, as patterns of all temptation and guilt, for the one
is already the other. Never heard of a crime I could not
have committed. Not committing it, you escape the
earthly judge but not the heavenly. For in your heart
you have committed it. Seduction by one's own sex —
that might be a revenge, a mocking retribution for seduction practised by oneself — Narcissus, for ever deluded
by his own image. Revenge for ever bound up with seduction, trial not overcome by victory — that is the will
of Brahma. Hence my horror and my desire, thinking
on it. Hence the creative awe as I think of the poem
dreamed and planned since early days, always and still to
be put off, the poem of the Brahman's wife, the Pariah-
goddess. There in all the accents of horror I mean to
proclaim and celebrate seduction. Postponed it, kept it
buried in my breast to dwell and grow, that proves to
me its worth. Will not put it from me, nurse it to ripeness
and beyond, bear it within me through all the ages of
my life; some day the seed so young conceived will bear
a late-born child, great with the weight of mysteries it
holds, tempered, condensed, refined, like a Damascus
blade forged from the finest steel — so I imagine its final
form.

Know right well the source, so many years ago, the
same that brought me the God and the Bayadere: the German translation of the Journey to East India and China — a
musty volume, yet stimulating, must be mouldering somewhere among my traps. Hardly remember what itself
was like, only how my mind seized on and shaped it for
my own ends. A picture of women, holy, noble, pure,
walking down to the river daily for fresh water, needing
nor jar nor ewer for the task, for in their pious hands the
water rounds into a splendid crystal ball. How I love
this crystal ball, carried by the pure wife of the pure
Brahman in daily joyful ritual to her home: clear concrete symbol of untroubled clarity, untouched innocence, and its simple power. In the poet's sinless hand
Water shapes a ball — yes, I am bent upon it, my crystal
ball shall be this poem of seduction: the poet, much seduced, the tempting-greatly-tempted, he has the power
and the gift, the pure hand that shall shape the crystal
ball. But not so the woman. The river mirrored for her
the image of the divine youth, she lost herself in gazing, the
unique divine apparition seized upon her soul and shook
it. Then the water denied her, would not form the ball.
She stumbles homeward, her high lord sees her guilt and
cries out for revenge. Drags the stricken guilty innocent
to the sacrificial mound, strikes off her head. But the son
threatens the avenging father to follow his mother to
death, as widows do their husbands. It shall not be! Lo,
truly the blood has not dried on the sword, it still flows
fresh. Quick, join again head to body, say the prayer,
bless the union with the sword, she will arise. So said,
so done. Alas, alas! For on that mound of sacrifice two

bodies are confused, the mother's noble form and the corpse of a condemned woman of the pariah caste. In his haste the son placed his mother's head on the out-cast's body and healed it with the sword of judgment. A giant goddess arises, the goddess of the impure. — Make a poem of this, round and compress it to a crystal ball of words, pellucid, resilient. What more pregnant task? She became a goddess, but among gods, wild her 'haviour, wise her willing. Before the eyes of the pure woman the vision blissful of the youth will hover, heavenly tender; but sinking down into her impure heart it kindles lust and madness and despair. Ever endures temptation. Ever will it be repeated, the divine distracting vision, brush her garment as it passes, ever rising, ever sinking, ever brightening, ever fading — so hath Brahma willed. She stands before Brahma, the terrible goddess; warns him gently, rages at him, from her racked and heavy-laden, sore-bewildered heart — and in the mercy of the Highest all suffering creatures share.

I think Brahma fears the woman, for I fear her, fear her as my own conscience when she stands before me, wishing wisely, doing wildly — just so I dread the poem, put it off through the decades, knowing some day I must write it. — I ought to tinker at the birthday carmen, and put some more of the Italian Journey together. But this good aloneness, at my desk, the good warmth of the Madeira in my bones — they tempt me to more secret, curious tasks. In the poet's sinless hand —

" Who is it? "
" A right good day to you, Father."

" Oh, it's you, August, come on in."

" Am I disturbing? I hope not, you are putting away your papers so fast."

" Oh, my child — what is disturbing? Everything disturbs; the question is whether the disturbance is welcome or not."

" Yes, and that is just the question now. I cannot answer it, it must be addressed to the message I bring, not to me. Without it I should not have broken in on you at this hour."

" Glad to see you, but what is it? "

"Since I am here, let me first ask if you have had a good night."

" Thank you, I feel refreshed, so far as that goes."

" Enjoyed your breakfast? "

" Heartily. You question me like Rehbein."

" But I ask for the world. May I ask, too, what you were doing just now? Something interesting? The Life? "

" Not precisely. The life it always is. But what is it you have brought? Must I drag it out of you? "

" There is a visitor, Father. Somebody has come, from away, from out of the past, and is stopping at the Elephant. The town is on the *qui vive* about it. I heard the news before the letter came. An old acquaintance."

" An acquaintance? Old, eh? Don't make such a pother over it."

" Here is the note."

" ' Weimar, the 22nd — look once more upon a face — become so well known — née Buff.' H'm. Curious. I call that a curious thing to happen. Don't you? But wait a bit: I've something to show you too, to make you open your eyes and congratulate me. Look here! . . . Well, how do you like it? "

"Marvellous! "

"Makes you open your eyes, doesn't it? Worth staring at, I tell you. Feast for the eyes. Present from Frankfurt for my collection. Some other minerals came too, from Westerwald and the Rhine. But this is much the finest. What should you say it is? "

"A crystal."

"I should say so! A hyalite, a hyaline quartz, wonderful specimen both for size and purity. Ever seen such a piece before? I cannot look at it and think about it enough. What light, what transparency, what perfection! It is a work of art, or rather a work of nature, a revelation of the cosmos, of immaterial space, that projects its eternal geometry upon it and gives it dimensions. Nothing but shining facets and exact angles through and through, I call that perfect structurality. Just one single and entirely determining form and structure throughout, from within outwards, continuously reproduced, determining its axes, its crystallographic system. That is what gives the transparency, the affinity of such molecular bodies for light and the transmission of light. Want to know what I think? I think the gigantic and massive geometry of planes and angles in the Egyptian Pyramids had this same hidden meaning: their relation to light, to the sun. They are sun-monuments, giant crystals, mammoth imitations by man of cosmic immaterial concepts."

"That is vastly interesting, Father."

"I should say! Has to do with duration too, time and

death and eternity, for we observe that mere duration is only apparent triumph over death and time, mere dead being, with no growth since the beginning; because in it death ensues upon procreation. These crystalline pyramids last on through time and outlive millennia, but have no life or meaning — dead eternity, with no life-history. What happens to a thing, its biography, is what matters; and the biography of anything so early completed is poor and brief indeed. You see, such a *sal* (a salt, as the alchemists called all kinds of crystals, including snow-crystals, though our specimen is not a proper salt but a silicate), such a *sal* has just one single moment of growth and development, when the crystal lamella is thrown down by the mother-liquor and makes the point of departure for other lamellæ, producing the geometric shape accordingly, faster or slower, to a larger or smaller size, that does not matter, for the smallest is as perfect as the largest and its biography was finished when the lamella was born. It just lasts on into time, like the Pyramids, even a million years; but time is outside it, not inside, and that means it grows no older — not such a bad thing, if it were anything but mere lifeless persistence. The reason it has no time-life is that there is no breaking down to correspond with the building up, no disintegration to match the integration. True, the very tiniest crystals are not yet geometric, they do not have planes and surfaces, they are roundish and rather like organic nuclei. But the resemblance is only apparent, for the crystal is entirely structure from the very first, and as such is light, transparent, something to look at. The hitch is, it is death, or leads to death — in the case of crystals death follows immediately upon birth. Never death and eternal youth, as it would be were there an even balance between form and loss of form, between building up and breaking down. No, the scale does not balance; from the very beginning of life structure holds first place, in the organic world as well, and so we too crystallize and endure only in time, like the Pyramids. Empty duration, continuance in outer time, with no inner time, no biography. Animals are like that too, once they are full grown and structurally mature. Alimentation and reproduction go on mechanically and always the same, like crystalline accretion — all the rest of the time they live they are standing at the goal. Animals die early too — probably out of boredom. Can't stand completion and perfection and being at the goal. Everything, my dear boy, is tiresome and monotonous that has its being in time, instead of having time within itself and making its own time; not making straight ahead towards a goal but moving in its own circle, always at the end, yet always at the beginning. That would be the true kind of being, working in and on oneself, so that being and becoming, working and work, past and present were one and the same thing, and produced a permanence that would be endless progress, growth, and perfectionment. And so on thenceforth. Well, take all this as comment on the clear little text you are looking at, and forgive me for preaching. — How goes the haymaking in the big garden?"

"It is done, Father. But I am crossways with the farmer, he does not want to pay. He says the mowing and carting away balance the account, or actually leave something still owing. I will not let the fellow get away with it so easily, be sure of that. The second crop is worth money, and I will get it if I have to take him to court."

"Good, good, you are in the right of it, one needs to watch out. *A corsaire, corsaire et demi.* Have you written to Frankfurt about the tax money? "

"Not actually written, Father. My head is full of draughts, but I still hesitate to put my hand to it. That must be no milk-and-water letter, to refute their absurd claim that we are robbing the citizens of Frankfurt! It must be a crushing combination of dignity and irony, and force them to come to their senses. That takes some thinking out."

"You are right, I would postpone it too. You have to wait for the propitious moment. I have hopes of getting the remission. If I could only write myself, directly — but I must not appear."

"Certainly not. In all such matters you must be protected. That is a special need — and I was born to fill the gap. — What does the Frau Hofrätin say? "

"How are things going at court? "

"Oh, they are breaking their heads over the Prince's first redoute, we are to practise the quadrille again this afternoon. Nothing has been settled about the costumes to appear for the first time in the polonaise. We do not even know whether the polonaise is to be a go-as-you-please affair, or whether everybody is to conform to a single idea. At the moment people's wishes are very individual, probably because of what they can get hold of for a costume. The Prince declares he is going to be a noble savage; Staff wants to be a Turk, Marschall a

French peasant, Stein a Savoyard. Madame Schumann insists on a classical costume and Frau Registrar Rentschin on being a rustic maiden with a rake."

"Hark ye, that is *du dernier ridicule*. A rustic maiden — Frau Rentschin ought to know what becomes her years. We'll have to stop her — a Roman matron is the most we can allow. If the Prince has decided to be a savage, that makes his intentions clear: he will amuse himself with the ancient gardener-girl and there will be a scandal. Seriously, August, I have a good mind to take things in hand myself, at least the polonaise. I am not for a lively go-as-you-please at all, there should be a central idea and a free kind of order and meaning. Just as in my Persian poetry, here too, and everywhere: there must be something as a guide, what we Germans call the leading spirit, if general satisfaction is to result. I have a masque in mind, and I'd be glad to play the director and herald. It needs some brief introduction, some music as well, mandolins, guitars, and theorbos. Yes, gardener-girls, if you like — pretty Florentine ones, in arbours, selling gay artificial flowers. To each girl a bronze-skinned gardener, with a great market-basket full of fruit — the bowers must run over with the whole year's harvest, bud and blossom, flower and fruit, to feed the eye and fancy. Then fishermen and fowlers, with lines and nets; they mingle with the maidens and there follows a charming game of flight and pursuit, of capture and escape — interrupted by a boisterous train of wood-cutters, representing the inevitable element of rudeness and coarseness ever present in the charm. Then the herald invokes certain figures of classical mythology: on the heels of the

Graces, dispensing loveliness as an odour, follow the grave Parcæ, Atropos, Lachesis, and Clotho, with spindle, distaff, and shears; close upon the three Furies — but mark me, these must not look a wild, repulsive crew, more like three comely young females, only with something snake-like and malign about them — there must lumber in a mountainous thing, a perfect colossus hung with carpets and topped by a little tower; in short, an elephant, with a slender female perched on its neck, driving it with a goad, and on the very tip the goddess sublime — "

" Yes, but — Father! Where could we get an elephant, and how could it get into the — "

" Don't be a spoil-sport! It would be easy to contrive some sort of frame, shaped like an animal, if one wanted to, with trunk and tusks — it should move on wheels. The winged goddess on top would represent Victory, presiding deity of the scene. Beside the elephant must walk two stately female forms; the herald must announce them as Fear and Hope, laid in chains by Common Sense, who denounces them to the audience as bitter foes of mankind."

" Is Hope to be an enemy too? "

" Yes, is she not, with quite as much justice as Fear? Consider how she weakens mankind, deluding them with sweet false thoughts, lulling their ears with whispers of life without care and good beyond their wildest dreams. — As for the Victory, she becomes the target at once of Thersites' slavering spite, till the herald can stand it no longer, but must fall upon him with his staff. The dwarf-ish figure writhes and shrieks, rolls into a ball that turns before their eyes into an egg, it swells and bursts, out creep a grisly pair, otter and bat, one crawls away on all fours, the other flaps up shadowy to the roof — "

" But my dear, good Father, how ever could we represent all that, the exploding egg, the otter and bat? "

" Dear me, with a little goodwill and inventiveness it could be done! But that should not be the end to the surprises. Next comes in a splendid car, drawn by four horses, driven by a perfect cupid of a boy; on it must sit a king, with round moon face under his turban. The herald does his courtly office and presents them: Moonface is King Pluto, god of riches; the lovely boy, with jewelled spangles in his raven locks, who should he be but Poetry, in its quality as lavish giver, enriching the feast for Pluto King? Has but to snap his fingers, the rogue, and from them fall in glistering strings pearls and ouches, combs and crowns and priceless brooches — see how the base crowd struggle for the things! "

" All very well for you, Father, with your pearls and ouches, of course you are thinking of ' I scratch my head and rub my hands ' — "

" They could just be trumpery gawds and counters; all I want is an allegorical representation of the relation between poesy and riches, giving and spending — calls up a picture of Venice, art flourishing like a bay tree in the rich soil of trade. The turbaned Pluto must say to the lovely boy: ' This is my beloved son, in whom I am well pleased.' "

" But, Father! He could not possibly say it like that — it would be — "

" We might even try to contrive little tongues of flame, springing up from heads here and there, sign of the greatest gift in the hand of the charioteer: flames of the Spirit, leaping up on one head, dying down on another, leaping, blazing, seldom lasting, on most heads too soon consumed: Father, Son, and Holy Ghost."

"But, Father, that would never do, never in the living world! Quite aside from the practical difficulties. It would upset the court, offend the pious — it would be blasphemy."

"Why call you such graceful, reverent allusion blasphemous? Religious symbolism is a cultural treasure-house, wherein we have a perfect right to dip when we need use the familiar images to make visible and tangible some general aspect of spirit."

"But not just the same way as the other symbols, Father. You yourself may be capable of taking that view of religion, but the average spectator will not be, nor the court either, at least not in these times. The town follows the court, true, but the court also follows the town, and today, when religion has come back into its own, in society and among the young — "

"Very well, *basta!* I will pack up my little puppet-play again, and my little spirit-flames, and say to you as the Pharisees said to Judas: 'See thou to that!' And all sorts of fine things were to come: a procession of the great god Pan, the wild rout, prick-eared fauns and shrunk-legged satyrs, friendly dwarfs and nymphs and giants from the Harz — well, let be, I must see to use it in some other place, where I'll not be troubled with your modish scruples. If you have no sense of humour, then I'm not your man! What were we talking about?"

"We were speaking of the letter I brought you,

Father. We ought to consider it and come to some decision. What has Frau Councillor Kestner written?"

"Oh, yes, the letter. You brought me a billet-doux. What does she say? But wait: I wrote something too, just read it first — *un momentino*, here it is, it is for the Divan."

"'They say that geese are silly things, The proverb is but hollow; For one of them just turned around And beckoned me to follow.' Very neat, Father, very nice — or not so very nice, as you look at it. At any rate, it is no good as an answer to the letter."

"No? I thought as much. Then we must think up another, in prose of course, the usual thing to distinguished pilgrims to Weimar: an invitation to dinner."

"That much at least. — The note is very well written."

"Oh, very. How long do you think the poor soul worked over it?"

"People must look to their words when they write to you."

"Chilling thought."

"That is the cultural discipline you exact."

"And when I am dead they will say 'Ugh!' and go back to grunting as before."

"I very much fear it."

"Don't say 'fear.' Don't grudge them the right to follow their natural bent. I do not want to crush them."

"Why do you talk about crushing? Or about dying, indeed? You will remain to us for many years to come, our benevolent tyrant leading us onwards and upwards towards the Good and the Beautiful."

"Think so? I do not feel so extra well today. My

arm hurts. And I had trouble with Phthisicky, and on top of it I dictated a long time, it affects the nervous system."

" In other words, you do not want to go and pay your respects to the writer of this letter; and you would rather not decide what to do about it."

" In other words, in other words. You have a way of drawing conclusions — not very gentle, you drag them out by the roots."

" Forgive me, I am only groping in the dark, to find out how you feel and what you want."

" Well, and so am I. And in the dark, one is likely to see ghosts. When past and present become the same thing — they have always tended to do that, with me — it is not surprising that the present should seem to be haunted. Very fine — in a poem. In life, rather terrifying. — You say the affair is making a stir in the town? "

" Quite a considerable one. Naturally enough. Crowds gather in front of the inn, they want to see the heroine of Werther. The police have their work cut out to keep order."

" What a silly lot! But, after all, the cultural level in Germany must be high if a thing like this can rouse such curiosity. — *Pénible*, son. A *pénible*, an execrable business. The past conspires with folly against me, to make trouble and create disorder. Why could not the old woman have spared me this? "

" That is more than I can say. You see, Madame Kestner is quite within her rights. She is visiting her dear relatives, the Ridels."

" Of course. Of course she is visiting them. She has a

sweet tooth, she wants to taste a little more fame; little she knows how close together fame and notoriety lie. To begin with there is this stir amongst the common folk — but how Weimar society will love it and feed on it, gape and ogle and whisper and sneer! We must do all in our power to put a stop to it, we have to think the thing out carefully and act with decision. We will give a dinner for a small company, with her relatives; but otherwise keep aloof and give sensation-mongers nothing to feed on."

" When shall the dinner be for, Father? "

" In a few days. Some time shortly. The proper distance, the due proportion. On the one hand we must have time to look at the situation and get used to it from a distance; on the other, better have it behind us than look forward to it too long. — Just now the cook and housemaid are busy with the washing."

" It will all be back in the presses by the day after tomorrow."

" Good, then three days from now."

" Whom shall we have? "

"Our nearest friends, with a few others — our usual circle slightly enlarged. Mother and daughter and their two relatives; Meyer and Riemer and their wives, Coudray or Rehbein perhaps, Hofkammerrat Kirms and Madame Kirms — who else? "

" Uncle Vulpius? "

" Certainly not, you are crazy! "

" Aunt Charlotte? "

"Charlotte? You mean the Stein? Another absurd idea. Two Charlottes are a bit too much. I told you we must be circumspect. If she come, there will be a strained situation. If she decline, that will make talk too."

"Any of our neighbours? What about Herr Stephan Schütze?"

"The writer? Good, ask him. Engineer Werner, the geognost, from Freiburg, is in town, you might ask him, then there would be somebody for me to talk to."

"That makes sixteen."

"Some people may decline."

"Oh, no, they'll all be there. What sort of dress?"

"Formal. The gentlemen full dress with decorations."

"As you wish. It is a gathering mostly of intimates, but the number will justify some formality. And it is a courtesy to the guests from away."

"So it seems to me."

"And we shall enjoy the opportunity of seeing you again with the White Falcon — I had almost said the Golden Fleece."

"That would have been a quaint slip, much too flattering to our infant honours."

"But I almost said it — probably because this meeting has an air of being a postscript to Egmont. In the Wetzlar days you had no Spanish court dress or decorations to appear to your Clärchen in."

"You seem to be in high spirits — they do not make for good taste."

"And a too fastidious taste may sometimes seem like fretfulness."

"I imagine both of us have other things to do this morning."

"Your first one being to write a reply to the note?"

" No, you must call. That will be both more and less. You will present my compliments and greetings. I have the honour to beg her presence at dinner."

" A great honour to me, to represent you. I have seldom done it on a more pregnant occasion. Except perhaps at Wieland's funeral."

" I will see you at dinner."

CHAPTER EIGHT

ARRIVED at the Ridels' on the Esplanade, as she had, at last, on that 22nd of September, Charlotte Kestner found no difficulty in explaining and excusing her certainly immoderate delay. Once on the spot, at length received into the arms of her youngest sister, with the husband standing by, his face alight with pleasure, she was dispensed from further accounting for the events that had cost her the forenoon and even part of the afternoon as well. Only in the succeeding days, in private talk and from occasion to occasion, did she partly volunteer and partly relate in answer to questions some account of that morning's interviews. Even the invitation for the third following day, brought by the last of her visitors, she remembered only after the lapse of hours. Then, certainly, she was not behindhand in urging upon her family their assent to the letter of acceptance she addressed, after her arrival, to the famous house on the Frauenplan.

"I thought not last," said she to her brother-in-law, "and perhaps even first, of you in the matter. I see no reason for not taking advantage of connections useful to one's relatives, however antiquated they may be."

The Privy Councillor of the Finance Board, that is, aspired to the position of head of the ducal Finance

Chamber; largely because since the days of the French invasion he was without private means and dependent upon his salary, and a considerable increase to the latter would accrue with the new position. He smiled gratefully. In fact, this was not the first time that the friend of his sister-in-law's youth had favoured his advance in life. Goethe esteemed him. The young Hamburger had been tutor in a count's family, and Goethe had got for him the same office for the young Hereditary Princess of the Saxe-Weimar house. He had held it for some years. In the salon of Madame Schopenhauer he had often been in the company of the poet, but never, so far, in the famous house; the occasion afforded by Charlotte's presence was thus more than welcome.

The Ridels received that same evening a written invitation to dinner at the Frauenplan. But in the following days the affair was glanced at only lightly; it was as though it was hardly in the family's mind, and mentioned, if at all, with a certain cursoriness of attention. Only the married pair were bidden, not their daughter; and this, as well as the indication that dress should be worn, suggested that the party was not merely a family one. The fact was touched on in talk; then came a slight pause, as though to weigh whether this were a pleasurable occasion or no; then the subject shifted again.

The sisters had been so long parted, and the medium of letters been so inadequate to bridge the gap, that there was much to talk of from both sides. Children, brothers and sisters, and brothers and sisters' children must have their doings and their present status canvassed. They had to mourn for many a member of the little group that had pressed around Lotte as she cut the bread and thus received a blithe poetic immortality. Four sisters had already passed away, the first to go being the eldest, Friederike, Hofrätin Dietz, leaving behind her five sons, all of them in excellent positions in the courts or the magistracy. The fourth sister, Sophie, had died unmarried, now eight years gone, in the house of her brother George, a very fine man. Charlotte, despite an expressed wish from another quarter, had named her eldest son after him. He had married into a wealthy Hannover family and succeeded his father, on the death of the elder Buff, in the official position at Wetzlar, where he gave general satisfaction.

All together, the masculine portion of that immortalized little troop had proved themselves more tenacious, more capable of life, than had the feminine — always excepting the two old ladies who now sat in Amalie Ridel's sitting-room and over their sewing discussed past and present events. The eldest brother, Hans — the same who had been on so cordial a footing with Dr. Goethe and had such exuberant and childlike joy in the Werther book on its arrival — Hans was director of finances for Count von Solms-Rödelheim, a respected and well-rewarded post. Wilhelm, the second, was a lawyer; another, Fritz, a captain in the Dutch army. Amid the rattle of wooden needles or the pricking of embroidery, the sisters spoke of the Brandt girls, Annchen and the Junoesque Dorthel. Had aught been heard of them? Yes, now and then. The black-eyed Dorthel had not accepted the circumspect wooing of that Councillor Cella of yore, though it had not gone unremarked in the lively circle — in particular a certain young student, himself susceptible to the charms of black eyes, had made rather rudely merry over it. She had chosen instead a physician, Dr. Hessler, and after his early death had now for a long time been housekeeper to a brother in Bamberg. Annchen had been Frau Councillor Werner for five-and-thirty years; and a third sister, Thekla, had entered on a satisfying existence at the side of Wilhelm Buff.

All these, living and dead, came to mention. But Charlotte grew truly animated, the delicate pastel tint that so became her visited her cheek and she had to check the nodding tendency of her head, only when her own sons were the theme; men themselves now in the forties, with such dignified careers as Theodor, the professor of medicine, and August, the Councillor to the Legation. Their visit to the friend of their mother's youth at the "Tannery" was once more referred to; all together, the name of the mighty neighbour — a name so loftily remote, yet so inwoven with the life and lot of this whole family circle since its early days — crept anon, though seemingly shunned, into the sister's talk. For instance, Charlotte recalled a journey she had made with Kestner, forty years ago, from Hannover to Wetzlar, when they had stopped off to pay a call on the mother of their whilom friend. They had got on so famously, the Frau Councillor and the youthful pair, that she had claimed the privilege of standing godmother to the youngest Kestner girl. The man who once had said he would dearly love to hold each child, as it came, over the christening font was at the time in Rome. The mother had just been surprised by a brief intelligence of his visit

there, and now betrayed her inward pride by descanting
at length upon her extraordinary son. Lotte remembered
her words and now retailed them to her sister. How
fruitful, Frau Aja had cried, how advantageous, how
highly rewarding must be such a sojourn to a man of such
keen-eyed vision for all that was good and great — how
rich in blessing, not alone for him, but also for all those
privileged to live in his sphere and under his spell! It had
fallen to this mother's lot to celebrate loudly and openly
the good fortune of those lucky ones belonging to the
circle of her own son. She had quoted the words of a
friend, the deceased Frau Klettenberg: "When your
Wolfgang comes to Mainz, he brings more than others
from Paris or London." The proud and happy mother
said he had promised her, in her letter, to visit her on his
homeward way. Then he must tell all his experiences
down to the very last straw; friends would be asked to
the house, there would be splendid, lordly entertainment,
game and roast and fowl would be as the sands of the sea.
Probably nothing came of all that, Amalie Ridel sur-
mised; and her sister, who thought she had heard the
same, turned the talk back to her own sons: they had
been brought up to be dutiful and make due and regular
visits, she said, taking occasion in her turn to sing the
praise of her own.

She probably was aware that such talk in time grew
tedious to her sister. And so, since they would naturally
consider the matter of their toilets for the coming event,
Charlotte privily revealed the jest she proposed: the
choice of a frock on the model of the Volpertshausen
ball-gown, with subtraction of the pink bow. It came up

when she inquired of her younger sister's plans, and then, being asked in turn, first shrouded her own in smiling, smirking, hesitant silence, then finally came out with her literary, suggestive little joke. Moreover, she secured herself beforehand against her sister's judgement, by demanding her censure of young Lotte's cold and critical strictures upon the idea. So that it meant little to have Amalie say she found it charming — with a facial expression not actually in accord with her words. She even added, as it were consolingly, that in case the master of the house did not remark the allusion, one or other of his family would surely do so and call his notice. She did not enlarge further upon the subject.

So much anent the discourse of the reunited sisters. It is certain that the first few days of Charlotte Buff's sojourn in Weimar were passed in the bosom of the family. Society, however curious it might be, had to wait for her appearance; the public glimpsed her on the short walks she took with the Frau Kammerrat through the rural little city and the park, to the Templars' house, the Lauterquelle, and the Klause; very likely too as she was fetched at evening by her maid and returned to the inn on the square, accompanied from the Esplanade by her daughter and perhaps by Dr. Ridel as well. She was often recognized — if not immediately in her own person, then by inference from her company; often, proceeding onwards with the blue eyes directed in mild hauteur straight before her face, she was perforce made aware that people passed her with suddenly lifted brows and a smile, then shuffled and turned round behind her back to stare. She had a stately and dignified way of returning salutations meant for her companions but improving the occasion to include her as well. It was almost majestic, and much remarked.

So came on the day, or the afternoon, mentioned with such reserve beforehand, awaited, indeed, with silent constraint: the day of the command invitation. The hired coach stood before the door; Ridel had bespoken it out of respect for the ladies' toilets and his own shoes, if also in part for the occasion as well, since this momentous day of the 25th of September threatened rain. The family had partaken, late in the forenoon and with scant appetite, of a cold second breakfast; they mounted the coach towards half past two, under the eyes of a half-dozen inquisitive provincials who had gathered, as for a wedding or a funeral, round the waiting hackney-carriage, to question the driver on the goal of the drive. On such occasions the admiration of the gaping crowd for the actual participants in the function is mostly equalled by the envy of the latter for the free and easy outsiders in their everyday clothes. And the outsiders too are privately aware of their own good luck; so that on both sides there is a mixture of feelings: on the one condescension mingles with an unexpressed " You lucky beggers! " and on the other admiration with malicious satisfaction.

Charlotte and her sister took the well of the coach. Dr. Ridel, his top hat on his knees, in tails, with white neckerchief and the fashionable padded shoulders, a small cross and two medals on his chest, with his niece by his side filled the hard back bench. Scarce a word was exchanged on the brief drive along the Esplanade, and through the Frauenthorstrasse to the Frauenplan. On

such occasions there mostly obtains a certain remission of
individual animation, a state of inward preparation like
that behind the scenes of a theatre; and here there were
special circumstances to becloud or lower the general
mood.

The married couple respected Charlotte's silence.
Four-and-forty years. They thought of them with feelings of sympathy, now and then nodding and smiling at
their dear one, even touching her caressingly on the
knee, a gesture giving her opportunity to nod back and
thus to disguise or justify that intermittent and touching
sign of age, the trembling of her head, sometimes so
strongly apparent, again scarcely present at all. Anon
they stole glances at their niece, sitting there in a deliberate and obvious aloofness from the whole undertaking
almost amounting to a reproach. Young Lotte's sober,
virtuous, and self-sacrificing course of life made her a
person to be respected, her satisfaction or dissatisfaction
weighed in the scale; thus the straight line formed by her
firmly closed lips played its part in the general tendency
to silence within the coach. That her severity concerned
the misguided apparel of her mother, now concealed beneath a black wrap, they were all aware; Charlotte most
clearly of all, and that single phrase of approval from her
sister had not been enough to reassure her of the excellence of her little idea. More than once she had lost heart
for it herself, and only stuck by it out of obstinacy, having once conceived it. She told herself, to her own consolation, that it had taken very little to summon up that
long-ago picture, since everyone knew she always wore
white by preference and had a perfect right to do so now;

only the pink bows and the absence of the breast-knot
betrayed the schoolgirl trick she meant to play. She sat
there with her ash-grey hair dressed high, confined by
a gauze band and falling in ringlets to her neck; and despite some feeling of envy for the others' unobtrusive
garb, the very thought of that trick made her heart beat
with a stolen and defiant throb of expectancy.

Their wheels rattled over the uneven cobblestones of
the square, then came the Seifengasse, and then there
stood the great house, a long façade with slightly diag-
onal wings — Charlotte had already passed it several
times, with Amalie Ridel. A parterre and a bel-étage,
with windows in the moderately high mansard roof; in
each wing a yellow-painted porte-cochère, and shallow
steps leading up to the front door in the middle. The
family alighted; other guests were already meeting and
greeting at the bottom of the flight, having arrived from
opposite directions on foot. Two gentlemen of mature
age, in top hats and pelerines — in one Charlotte recognized Dr. Riemer — were shaking hands with a younger,
seemingly having come from close by, as he wore full
dress with no cloak, only an umbrella in his hand.
This was Herr Stephan Schütze, "our excellent belletrist
and editor of albums," Charlotte learned, as the pedes-
trians turned towards the family group and the custom-
ary introductions took place, amid much cordiality and
swinging of top hats. Riemer jocosely declined the presentation, expressing his confidence that the Frau Councillor would not have forgotten an old friend of as much
as three days' standing. He gave young Lotte's hand a
fatherly little pat; and was copied therein by his com-

panion, a man of fifty, rather stooped, with a mild cast of features and long hair bleached in strands, hanging down below his tall hat. This was no less a person than Herr Hofrat Meyer, the art professor. He and Riemer had each arrived direct from their occupations; their ladies would find the way hither of themselves.

"Let us hope," Meyer said as they entered, in the discreet staccato of his native land, wherein a homely old-German something seemed to mingle with foreign, French-sounding traits, "let us hope we have the luck to find the master in a good and lively key, not taciturn and *marode*, giving us to feel we are a burden upon him. That is always distressing."

He had turned to Charlotte to say this, expressly and seriously, plainly oblivious of how such words from an intimate of the house might unnerve a new-comer. She could not forbear replying:

"I know the master of this house for even longer than yourself, Herr Professor; I am not unversed in the variable moods of his genius."

"The later acquaintance is after all the more authentic," said he unperturbed, equably doing justice to each syllable of the last word.

Charlotte was not heeding. She was looking at the impressive stateliness of the entrance hall and staircase: the wide marble balustrade, the broad steps of the splendid leisurely ascent, the classic ornament dispensed with such exquisite measured taste. On the first landing white niches displayed classic bronze figures and in front of them on a marble pedestal the bronze figure of a greyhound turned towards them in a pose strikingly faithful and well observed. On this landing August von Goethe, attended by a footman, awaited the guests. He looked very well, despite some puffiness of face and figure; in a silk neck-cloth and damask waistcoat, his hair parted and waved, decorations on his chest. He led them some way up the steps to the reception-room, but had then to return to greet other arrivals.

It fell to the servant to attend them further: a young man with a dignity and poise in keeping with the aristocratic picture, in blue livery with gilt buttons and a yellow striped waistcoat. He guided the Ridels and Kestners and the three friends of the house for the rest of the way and helped them to lay off their wraps. Here at the top too the scene was most splendid, elegant, and artistic. From the light surface of the side wall there stood out darkly gleaming a group known to Charlotte as *Sleep and Death:* two youths, the arm of one laid along the other's shoulder. Above the door a white relief served as lintel; on the threshold a blue enamel *Salve!* was let into the floor. "There!" thought Charlotte, taking heart; "then we *are* welcome, despite this talk of taciturn and *marode*! But the lad has certainly a fine berth here! He lived more modestly in the Corn Market at Wetzlar. There he had my silhouette on the wall, that we gave him out of pity and friendship; morning and evening he greeted it with eyes and lips — he wrote that down himself. Have I a special right, or no, to take this *Salve!* to myself? "

At her sister's side she passed the open portals of the salon — somewhat startled at the unfamiliar practice of the servant, who formally called out the name of each guest in turn, her own among them: "Frau Councillor Kestner!" The reception-room, with its grand piano, was elegant enough, yet rather disappointing by its moderate proportions compared with the spaciousness of the staircase. Open double doors revealed a perspective of other rooms beyond. Two gentlemen and a lady were already present, standing together near a colossal bust of Juno; they interrupted their chat to turn their attention towards the guests just announced — one guest in particular, as well she knew — and to make ready for the ensuing introductions. But in the same instant the liveried servant announced fresh comers, Herr Chamberlain Kirms and spouse, who entered with the son of the house, the ladies Meyer and Riemer following on their heels. As usual in small communities of short distances, the complement of invited guests was suddenly filled up. The introductions became general; Charlotte, the centre of a little cluster, made acquaintance through the offices of Dr. Riemer and young Goethe of all those still strange to her, the Kirms', Chief Architect Coudray and wife, Superintendent of Mines Herr Werner from Freiburg, who lodged at the Erbprinz, and the ladies Riemer and Meyer.

She knew to what curiosity — in the ladies probably tinged with malice — she was exposing herself; and met it with a dignity in any case forced upon her by the necessity to check the nodding tendency of her head, now much aggravated by all the circumstances. Her weakness was remarked with a variety of sentiments by all those present, contrasting oddly, as it did, with the maidenliness of her appearance as she stood there, a quaint and dainty little figure, in her ankle-length flowing white frock, caught up into folds at the bosom with an agraffe and garnished with pink bows; perching on tight little black button boots with heels. The ash-grey hair stood up above a fair unwrinkled brow; the face was irretrievably elderly, with sunken cheeks on either side a well-formed, rather roguishly smiling mouth; the small nose had a naïve red tinge, the forget-me-not blue eyes looked out with gentle and weary distinction. . . . Just as she was she received the greetings of those presented, their assurances of their enchantment at her sojourn in their midst, and their sense of the honour vouchsafed them in being present at so memorable and meaningful a reunion.

Beside her stood her critic and conscience, young Lotte — if we may venture to call her so — and sank in a curtsy from time to time. She was far and away the youngest of the company, consisting as it did of people of ripe years — even Schütze, the writer, being a man in the middle forties. Brother Carl's nurse and housekeeper looked positively austere, with smoothly parted hair drawn back over her ears, and a heliotrope frock with an almost clerical starched round collar. She smiled ungraciously, and drew down her brows at the polite nothings said to her and even more to her mother, regarding them as offences wilfully provoked. And she suffered — not without effect upon Charlotte, who defended herself stoutly against the stealing influence — from her mother's juvenile appearance: the white frock might just pass, as a caprice and affectation; but certainly not the flagrant pink bows. Her heart was torn by conflicting feelings: the wish that people might understand the meaning of the unseemly

garniture and not find it scandalous, and the dread lest
for God's sake they might misunderstand it!

In short, young Lotte's humourless annoyance at the
whole affair bordered on desperation; Charlotte was sensitive and intuitive enough to share her feelings, and had
no small difficulty in clinging to her belief in the excellence of the little jest. Yet no woman could have had
much ground for worry over her costume in such a circle,
or for fearing the reproach of eccentricity. A tendency to artistic licence, even to theatricality, was visible
throughout the female part of the gathering, by contrast
with the official exterior of the gentlemen, who, Schütze
excepted, all wore in their buttonholes this or that order
of merit, medal, ribbon, or cross. Madame Chamberlain
Kirms, indeed, might be counted an exception: as the
wife of a high official she evidently held with strictness
of convention; yet even she, in the exaggerated size of
her silken cap-wings, detracted from her own principles,
for they verged on the fantastic. And Madame Riemer
—that orphan whom the scholar had married from this
very house—as well as Frau Councillor Meyer, née von
Koppenfeld, struck in their garb a strong note of the artistic and individual, not to say extravagant. Frau Riemer's taste was for the sombre intellectual, with a collar
of yellowed lace on her black velvet gown, a hawklike
profile, and ivory-tinted, darkly glooming face and brow,
shadowed by curled locks of midnight black shot through
with white. Frau Meyer, a more than mature Iphigenie,
affected a lemon-coloured robe in classic style, with a
half-moon on the girdle directly beneath the full bodice,
and an antique border at the hem. A dark-coloured veil

flowed down from her head; and as a modern touch she had added long gloves to the short sleeves of her gown.

Madame Coudray, the architect's wife, was distinguished not only by her voluminous frock but by a great broad-brimmed Corona Schröter hat with a veil round the crown; the brim bent down and rested upon the ringlets of hair at the back. Even Amalie Ridel, with her ducklike profile, had made essays in the direction of the picturesque by a complicated arrangement of frills to her sleeves and a shoulder-throw of white swansdown. Among all these Charlotte's figure was actually the least pretentious — and yet in her elderly girlishness, the dignity of her bearing constantly threatened by the nodding of her head, she was the oddest, the most striking and appealing of all, a sight to make one ponder if not to make one mock — to mock, that was it, the tortured Lottchen thought. She was bitterly convinced that the ladies of Weimar came to a spiteful little understanding together as soon as the introductions were over and the company broke up into groups dispersed through the room.

The son of the house displayed to the Kestners, mother and daughter, the painting hanging above the sofa, showing them how to draw aside the green silk curtain that shrouded it. It was a copy of the so-called *Aldobrandini Marriage*, most kindly made by Professor Meyer. The professor himself came up to them, and August went to mingle with other guests. Meyer had arrived in a top hat, but had now replaced it by a velvet cap. It looked so domestic by contrast with the dress clothes that Charlotte involuntarily looked down at his feet, to see whether perhaps he wore felt slippers. He did not, although his shuffling gait, even in his boots, suggested them. He had his hands clasped comfortably across his back, and his head inclined demurely on one side; all together the professor seemed to wish to appear in the character of an old family friend, reassuring by his own tranquillity the nervousness of new-comers to the house.

"We all seem to be here," he said, in the slow even staccato he had brought with him from Stäfa on the Lake of Zürich and never lost throughout all the years in Rome and Weimar. He talked entirely without the aid of gesture. "We seem to be our full count, and let us hope our host will present himself without delay. It is comprehensible that new-comers should feel a certain nervousness in these last long minutes, though they should rejoice to be able to accustom themselves beforehand to the surroundings and atmosphere. I always make it my affair to give such people the benefit of a little advice which should make the *expérience* easier and pleasanter — though it always remains difficult enough."

He accented the French word on the first syllable, and went on with unmoved countenance:

"What I mean is that it is always best" (he said "besht") "to conceal as much as possible the tension one is unavoidably in; and to greet him with the utmost possible unaffectedness, with no sign of stress. That sensibly lightens the strain on both sides, for him as well as for oneself. For he is sensitive to the guests' nervousness and shares it with him; he gets the contagion, so to speak, from afar; so that he too is subjected to a compulsion working with the embarrassment of the other side to become mutually intolerable. It is distinctly the sensible thing to be entirely natural — for instance, not to think one must enter on high intellectual themes, as for example his own works. Nothing is more ill-judged. Much better talk about simple and concrete matters within one's own experience; for he never tires of the human and actual, becomes animated at once and is able to give free rein to his responsive kindliness. I need not say that I have in mind no familiarity leaving out of consideration the distance between him and us; he would know how to put a stop to such a thing at once, as we have seen in more than one instance."

Charlotte listened blinking to the instruction of this faithful satellite and knew not what to say in reply. Involuntarily she was perceiving — and finding herself thoroughly ripe for the perception — how hard it is for people overtaken by stage fright to draw comfort or profit from advice to be calm. The quite opposite effect was far more likely. Personally she felt offended at the man laying down the law, for mixing into her affairs.

"Thank you very much, Herr Hofrat," said she at last, "for your suggestions. Many people must have already been grateful for them. But we must not forget that in this case we are dealing with the renewal of a friendship of four-and-forty years' standing."

He responded dryly: "A man who is a different person from day to day and from hour to hour will certainly have become a different person in four-and-forty years. — Well, Carl," said he to the servant, who passed them on the way through the suite of rooms, "what sort of mood are we in today?"

"Pretty jolly, on the whole, Herr Hofrat," the young man replied. A moment later, standing at the double door, whose two wings, as Charlotte only then perceived, could slide into the wall on either side, he announced, without much formality, rather in an easy, sociable key:

"His Excellence."

Meyer crossed over to the other guests, who had broken off their conversation to collect in a group standing at some distance from the ladies Kestner. Goethe entered with a quick, firm, rather abrupt tread, his shoulders back and abdomen somewhat forward. He wore dress clothes: a dress coat with a double row of buttons, and a finely worked glittering silver star rather high up on his chest; silk stockings, a white batiste neck-cloth crossed over and fastened with an amethyst pin. His hair, curling on the temples, but above the high arched brow already thin, was evenly powdered. Charlotte knew and did not know him — and both facts disturbed her. She knew again at first glance the peculiar wide-openness of the actually not very large, darkly lustrous eyes in the brunet skin of the face; the right eye sat distinctly lower than the left. That naïve, wide-open gaze — just now accentuated by the lifting of the finely arched brows running down to the somewhat depressed outer corners of the eyes — it seemed to be saying: "Who are all these people?" Dear God, how she knew those youthful eyes, after all this lifetime of years! Their actual colour was brown, they were rather close-lying; but they passed for black, because at every change of mood — and when did his mood not change? — the pupils so expanded that they impinged on the iris and gave the impression of blackness. It was he — and it was not. Certainly he had not had that towering brow — of course, its height was due to the retreating hair, though hair there still was in abundance; it was simply the effect of stealing time — one tried to reassure oneself with that, but without success. For time in this sense was life, was work, that through the decades had chiselled at the marble brow and so profoundly and movingly reshaped and graven the once smooth features. Time, age — here they were more than a loss, a liability, a natural decline, touching and even melancholy to reflect on; they were full of meaning, they were intellect, achievement, history; their effects, far from giving rise to pity, made the contemplative heart beat high with joyful amaze.

Goethe was now seven-and-sixty years old. Charlotte might count herself lucky that the reunion was taking place now instead of fifteen years earlier, at the beginning of the century, when the heaviness of body that began in his Italian period had been at its height. He had got rid of it again some time before. Despite the stiff gait — though even that was characteristic of his youthful period — his legs looked slender and young below the exceedingly fine and glossy cloth of his black suit; in the last decade his figure had approached again to that of his youth. Our good Charlotte had missed seeing some things, especially in the face; it was more altered from that of the friend of Wetzlar days, since it had gone through phases she knew not of. At one time it had had a fat and morose look, with sagging cheeks; she would have found it far harder to recognize her youthful friend than at his present stage. His features wore just now a rather disingenuous look, and one asked oneself why; it showed especially in the look of innocent surprise at sight of the after all expected guests. But added to that there was an excessive mobility of the mouth, generously cut and altogether beautiful though it was, neither too thin nor too full, with deep corners buried in the grooves carven by age in the cheeks. There was a nervous excess of swiftly contradictory possibilities of expression; his hesitation amongst them seemed to cast doubts on his sincerity. There was unmistakable conflict between the statuesque dignity and significance of these features and the childlike vacillation, a sort of coquettish ambiguity, that sat upon them.

As he entered, the master of the house was clutching his left arm, the rheumatic one, with his right hand. After a few steps he let it go, stood still, and made an affable ceremonial bow to the company in general; then advanced towards the ladies standing nearest him.

The voice — yes, it was altogether the old voice, the resonant baritone, the very tones of the slender youth as he spoke or read aloud. Perhaps a thought more slow and measured, but even of yore there had been a shade of solemnity in them — how strange it was to hear their very accents proceeding from the settled man!

"My dear ladies," said he, putting out a hand to each, to Charlotte the right and to Lotte the left, then bringing them together and holding them in his own, "at last I can welcome you with my own lips to Weimar! You behold a man to whom the time has seemed long until this moment. I call this a capital surprise — it does my heart good. How it must rejoice the heart of our good Finance

Councillor, this dearly desired visit! We need not say how much we treasure it that once within these walls you have not passed us by! ''

He had said: "dearly desired"—and his smiling mouth wore an expression half embarrassed, half relishing, that gave the little improvisation an added charm. It was only too clear to Charlotte that there was diplomacy in the charm: a purposeful vagueness calculated to regulate the situation from the first word on—the discretion and deliberation of his words betrayed it. And in pursuance of his design he made capital of the fact that not she alone but her daughter with her stood before him; he put all four hands together, he spoke to them in the plural; he even referred to himself as "we," withdrawing, as it were, behind the shelter of his house and suggesting the possibility that she might have "passed it by." Even the delightful little improvisation had reference to the Ridels.

His gaze wavered between mother and daughter, and also passed beyond them in the direction of the window. Charlotte had the impression that he did not really see her; but what his fleeting glance did take in, she perceived, was the now ungovernable trembling of her head; for a brief second he shut his eyes against the sight with a look of avoidance and gravity that was almost deathly. But he returned in a breath from this cloudy retreat and to the conventional present, as though nothing had happened.

"And youth," he went on, turning to face young Lotte, "comes like a ray of golden sunshine into the shadowed house—"

Charlotte, up to now, had merely indicated by a gesture that it went without saying she would not pass by his house. She now broke in at this point with the obvious and indicated introduction he was evidently expecting. It had been her chiefest wish, she said, to bring to his notice this daughter, Charlotte, her second youngest, now on a visit of some duration from her home in Alsace. She addressed him as Excellence, if rather hurriedly and slurringly, and he did not demur or ask for another title, perhaps because he was busy looking at the person presented.

"Pretty, pretty, pretty!" he said. "These eyes have probably done some damage in the masculine world."

The compliment was so conventional, so unsuited to Brother Carl's companion and helper, that it cried to heaven. Young Lotte gave a tortured and contemptuous smile and set her teeth cornerwise in her lip. Her look may have moved him to begin his next sentence with an "In any case" that dismissed the subject.

"In any case," said he, "it is very charming that I am vouchsafed to behold *in natura* at least one member of the little group whose silhouettes our dear departed Hofrat sent me. Time brings one all, if one will but wait."

That sounded like a concession; the mention of Hans Christian and the silhouettes was something of a departure from the rules. Charlotte felt it to be so; but it was probably mistaken of her to recall to his mind that he had already made the acquaintance of two of their children, August and Theodor, they having taken the liberty of visiting him at the Gerbermühle. Probably she should not have even mentioned the name of the estate, for he looked at her a moment, as it fell from her lips, with a sort of vacancy of spirit too intense to have been caused by any thought of the meeting.

"Oh, yes, of course! " he cried. "How could I forget it? Forgive this old brain! " But instead of indicating the forgetful brain he rubbed his left arm with his right hand as he had on entering the room, evidently wishing to attract notice to its ailing state. "How are those fine young men? Good, I thought so. Success lies in their excellent natures, it is inborn in them—and no wonder, with such parents.—And the ladies had a pleasant journey? " he proceeded. "I feel sure of it; the stretch from Hildesheim, Nordhausen, and Erfurt is a much used and favoured one: good horses for the most part, several good inns on the way—and moderately expensive, you will hardly have paid more than fifty thaler *netto*."

As he spoke he was breaking up this separate conversation and moving to manœuvre the Kestners over towards the rest of the gathering.

"I assume," he said, "that our invaluable young man here"—he meant August—"has made you acquainted with the small company present. These equally lovely women are your friends, these good gentlemen your admirers. . . ." He greeted in turn Madame Kirms in her cap, the architect's lady in her enormous hat, the intellectual Frau Riemer, the classical Frau Meyer, and Amalie Ridel, on whom he had already cast a speaking glance from afar, as he mentioned the dearly desired visit. Then he shook the gentlemen by the hand, with especial cordiality that of the stranger, Superintendent of Mines Werner, a stocky, friendly figure in the fifties, with small

lively eyes, a bald crown, and curly white hair at the
back, his smooth cheeks nestled comfortably into the
white shirt-collar held up by a white neck-cloth and
leaving his chin free. Him the master looked at with a
very slight sidewise and backwards movement of the
head as though he were weary of formal phrases and
abandoned them with a "There, at last we can cut the
cackle and get to the horses." The gesture called forth
on Meyer's and Riemer's faces a look of patronizing approval, the real source of which was jealousy. The master, after doing his duty by the rest, took occasion to
return to the geologist, while the ladies pressed round
Charlotte; whispering behind their fans, they wanted to
know if she found Goethe very much changed.

They stood about for a while in the reception-room,
presided over by the colossal bust and adorned with
bands of embroidery, aquarelles, oil paintings, and
copperplate engravings. The simply designed chairs
were arranged symmetrically along the walls between
the white door-frames, interspersed with white-lacquered
display-cabinets. There were bowls of carven chalce-
dony on the marble tables; a winged Nike adorned the
covered sofa-table beneath the *Aldobrandini Marriage*;
figures of gods and fauns and antique masks stood under
glass bells on the bureau; and all these art objects gave
the room the look of a museum. But Charlotte kept her
eyes fixed on their host, standing there with his feet
apart, his elbows stretched out and hands laid together
on his back, in his satin-soft dress coat with the star on his
breast glittering at each motion, making conversation
with one and other of the masculine guests, Werner,

Kirms, Coudray, by turns — for the present no more with her. It was good and pleasant to look at him thus, privately, without having to talk to him — but that did not prevent her being filled with a compelling urge to go on talking; she felt it as an imperative need, though even so, watching his intercourse with her fellow guests, she was equally put off the idea and convinced that the person just then enjoying the privilege of his attention was not particularly to be envied.

The friend of her youth made an entirely elegant impression, no doubt of that. His apparel, once so dashingly eccentric, was now very choice, deliberately a little in the rear of the fashion; something a little old-style about it harmonized with the stiffness of his bearing as he walked or stood, and made for dignity. He held his fine head high, his manner was confident and reserved; yet even so the dignity seemed not to be quite firm on its legs. Whoever stood before him, his bearing had about it something hesitating, uncomfortable, embarrassed; the absurdity of it upset the observer as much as it did the person at the moment suffering under the constraint of the dialogue. Everyone feels and knows that objectivity of mind lies at the bottom of a free and unembarrassed manner. Forced behaviour is enough in itself to lay a man open to the charge of lacking sympathy for men and things; it is likely to make any and every subject repugnant to the helpless partner in the dialogue. The master's eyes habitually rested upon the speaker, as long as the speaker did not look at him; so soon as that happened, the eyes glanced aside and began to move about his head into space.

Charlotte's sharp feminine eye saw all this, and we can only repeat that it made her dread to talk again with her one-time friend, and at the same time ardently crave to do that very thing. In any case, much of his manner might be laid to that unease of the minutes before the meal, which were lasting too long. Several times he looked with lifted brows at his son, on whom seemed to rest the responsibility of a major-domo.

At last the servant approached the host with the desired announcement, and he quickly communicated it to the guests as they broke up their groups.

"Dear friends, we are invited to take our places," he said. He went up to Lotte and Lottchen, took them by the hands with a certain country-dance elegance, and led the procession with them into the adjacent room, called the yellow salon; the meal had been laid there, as the "small dining-room" farther on was not adequate for sixteen people.

The word "salon" was rather too large for the room in which the guests were now received, though it was larger than the one they had just left. It too was dominated by colossal busts, two of them: the Antinous in its melancholy beauty, and a majestic Jupiter. The walls were adorned by a set of coloured plates of mythological subjects, and a copy of Titian's *Heavenly Love*. Here too there were glimpses, through open doors, into other rooms; particularly charming was the vista through a door on the narrow side of the room along a hall of busts and an ivy-clad gallery to the stair leading to the garden. The table was laid with more than middle-class elegance: fine damask, flowers, silver candelabra, gilded porce-

lain, and three glasses at each cover. The young liveried
servant waited, assisted by a rosy-cheeked young country girl, in cap and stays, white puffed sleeves, and home-
made stuff frock.

Goethe sat in the middle of the long side of the table,
between Charlotte and her sister; on their right and left
Kammerrat Kirms and Professor Meyer; beyond, on
either side, the ladies Meyer and Riemer. August had
not been able, because there were too many men, to keep
to the principle of alternating the sexes. He had put
the Bergrat opposite his father, with Dr. Riemer as his
neighbour, sharing the society of Lotte the younger.
Madame Coudray was placed at Werner's left, on the
other side, that being filled out by Dr. Ridel and Madame
Kirms. Herr Stephen Schütze and chief architect Coudray shared the narrow end of the table.

The soup, a rich consommé with marrow-balls, stood
already at the places. The host broke his bread with a
ritualistic air over his soup-plate. He looked much better and freer seated than standing or walking; one would
have taken him for a taller man than when he was on his
legs. But it was probably the situation itself, the position as host, as father of the family and giver of the feast,
that lent him more ease and freedom. He seemed to feel
in his element. With a roguish twinkle in his eyes he
looked around the still silent circle; as he opened the meal
with the ceremony of breaking bread, so he seemed to
wish to set the key of the conversation too. For he addressed the whole circle, in his deliberate, clearly articulated, well-modulated tones, in the accents of a south
German brought up in north Germany.

"Let us give thanks to the heavenly powers, dear friends, for vouchsafing so happy an occasion for this joyous meeting. Let us be glad of the modest, yet well and truly prepared meal!"

Therewith he began to ply his spoon and the company all followed suit, not without exchanging glances, nods, and enthusiastic smiles at the excellence of the little speech — as much as to say: What can one do? He always puts it in a way not to be improved on.

Charlotte sat enveloped in the aroma of eau-de-cologne emanating from the person of her neighbour on the left. Involuntarily she was reminded of the sweet odour that according to Riemer betrayed the presence of the godhead. She half mused, half thought that the eau-de-cologne, fresh though it was, represented the prosaic reality of the so-called divine ozone. At the same time her housewifely perceptions told her that the marrowballs were certainly well and truly prepared, they were fine and light as feathers. And all the while her whole being hung in suspense, in an expectancy that defied the regulations and had not given up the idea of brushing them aside. The vague hope, difficult of clear definition, was strengthened by her neighbour's relaxed and more comfortable air as head of the table. A pity, she thought, that she was, of necessity, sitting beside and not opposite to him. How much more favourable to her inward hopes it would have been if they were face to face; how much it would have improved the chance of his seeing the symbolism of her attire, the vehicle of her hopes! Waiting in suspense for the address of her neighbour, she was jealous of the lively-eyed Werner and felt how much better it would be to confront it face to face. But the host did not address her separately, he spoke in general to all his neighbours, after taking a few mouthfuls of soup. He held up one after the other the two bottles of wine standing before him in silver holders (a similar pair stood at either end of the table) and tipped them sideways to read the labels.

"I see," he said, "my son has come down handsomely, he has given us two admirable elixirs, and the domestic cordial can vie with the imported. We hold with the patriarchal custom of pouring out for ourselves—it is superior to being served by ministering spirits and the finicking round with glasses; that I cannot endure. By our method a man has a free hand and can see how it is going with his bottle. What do you think, ladies, and you, my dear Bergrat? Red or white? I say first the native wine and then the French with the roast—or would you rather lay a good heart-warming base with this one to start off? I can vouch for it: this vintage Lafite of the year '08 works gently upon the spirits, I would not swear not to come on to it later—though the '11 Piesporter Goldtropfen is likely to make you a monogamist, once you begin with it. Our dear Germans are a crack-brained lot, and have always worked their prophets as hard as the Jews theirs; but their wines are the noblest gift of God."

Werner, surprised, simply laughed straight out. But Kirms, a narrow-headed man with a crop of curly grey hair on his crown, and heavy eyelids, replied:

"His Excellence forgets to reckon to the credit of these worthless Germans that they produced you."

The applause, led by Meyer on the left and Riemer diagonally opposite him, betrayed that they had been listening to their host's conversation and not to their neighbours'.

Goethe laughed too, but without opening his lips — perhaps in order not to show his teeth.

"We will let that pass, as a passable trait," said he. Then he inquired of Charlotte what she would like to drink.

"I am not used to wine," she replied. "It goes too easily to my head — I only sip a little for friendship's sake. And what I would rather sip from is the fountain there" — she motioned with her head towards the bottles of water. "What may they be?"

"Oh, that is my Eger water," answered Goethe. "Your inclination counsels you well; I am never without this mineral water, of all the temperance drinks in the world I have had the best experience with it. I will pour you out some, on condition that you will take a little of the golden spirit as well — and the further condition that you do not mingle the two elements, that you put no water in your wine. That is a very bad custom indeed."

He superintended the pouring from where he sat, while farther down the table his son and Dr. Riemer performed the same office. Meanwhile the plates were changed, and they were served with a ragout of fish and mushrooms au gratin, in shells. Charlotte felt no appetite; but she had to admit the excellence of the dish. Intent upon every detail and full of silent zeal of research, she found the excellence of the cuisine very interesting indeed, and ascribed it to the requirements of the master of the house; particularly when she saw, both now and later, that August's eyes, the father-eyes save for their melancholy sweetness and infinitely weaker penetration, went almost anxiously to the parent's face to see if he found the dish a success. Goethe was the only person to take two of the shells; but he left the second almost untouched. With the next course too he showed that, as the saying is, his eyes were larger than his appetite; it was a capital filet, served on long platters and plentifully garnished with vegetables. He heaped his plate so full that he left half of it uneaten. He took great draughts, both of the Rhine wine and the Bordeaux; the pouring out, like the bread-breaking, was a little ceremony, but he ministered largely to himself. The Piesporter in particular had soon to be replaced. The always dark teint of his face showed as the meal progressed an ever greater contrast to the whiteness of his hair.

As he poured out, Charlotte watched his hand with the same compelling, almost paralysing intensity that held her throughout. That hand, with its frilled cuff and short, well-kept finger-nails, had with all its breadth and strength something cultured and spiritualized, as it grasped the neck of the bottle. He repeatedly poured out the Eger water for her, and went on talking, as he did so, in his slow, clearly articulated voice, deep without monotony, and only now and again yielding to the local practice of his home and leaving off the end-consonants. He was expatiating upon his first acquaintance with this excellent mineral spring. Every year, he said, he had it sent to Weimar by the so-called Franzensdorf carriers and still did so, for since he had stopped going to the

Bohemian baths, he practised a systematic cure with the Eger water at home. It was probably his unusually precise and clear delivery, from those mobile, half-smiling lips, and the something involuntarily penetrating and dominating about it, that made the table generally listen when he spoke; the converse *à deux* remained thin and fitful throughout the meal; as soon as he began to speak, the attention of the whole table was diverted to him. He could scarcely help this, or at most by pointedly addressing his next-door neighbour and lowering his voice; but even so the others kept their ears open.

In this way it was, after the good word Hofkammerrat Kirms put in for the German people, that the host began to speak to Charlotte as it were alone, and to enlarge on the person and advantages of her partner on the right: what a capital economist he was, how deserving of the rewards of the State; the mind of a lord Chamberlain, yet a friend of the muses and sensitive amateur of the drama; invaluable as a member of the newly established board of management at the Hoftheater. It would almost have appeared that he wanted to put her off on Kirms, if he had not gone on to inquire of her own attitude towards the theatre, and conjecture that she would take advantage of her sojourn to form an opinion of the powers of the Weimar company. He would put his box at her disposition, whenever she felt the wish to use it. She thanked him cordially and said that for her part she had always greatly enjoyed the theatre, but in her circle there was no great interest, and the Hannover theatre was not calculated to arouse it. Thus, being always occupied with her many duties, she was somewhat a stranger to this form of enjoyment. She would find it both delightful and instructive to make the acquaintance of the famous Weimar company he had himself trained.

She so expressed herself, in a rather low voice, and he listened with his head bent towards her place, nodding his understanding. And, to her chagrin, as he listened he delicately pushed with his ring-finger the small balls and crumbs she had absently made with her bread, and assembled them in a tidy little pile. He repeated his offer of the loge, and hoped that circumstances might permit him to show her a performance of *Wallenstein*, with Wolf in the title rôle, an offering well worth seeing that had much impressed visiting strangers. After that, he said it was amusing that a double connecting link, the Schiller play and the table water, had brought him to the old castle in Bohemia, where the noblest of Wallenstein's followers had been slain; as architecture it greatly interested him. He went on to describe it, turning slightly away as he did so from Charlotte's place and abandoning his more intimate tones; straightway he had the ear of the whole circle round the table. The so-called black tower, he said, as seen from the former drawbridge, was a magnificent piece of work, the stone had probably come from the Kammerberg. This he said to the Superintendent of Mines, nodding at him in professional understanding. The stones, so he said, were cut with extraordinary skill and so placed as to offer the best resistance to the weather, so that they had almost the form of certain loose field-crystals at Elbogen. His eyes sparkled, his animation increased as he arrived, by association with this resemblance, at a find he had once made

when on a driving-tour in Bohemia, on the way between
Eger and Liebenstein, whither he had been drawn not
only by the Knights' castle but also by the geologically
instructive and really sublime Plattenberg opposite the
Kammerberg.

The road thither, as he described it, with mounting
temperament and liveliness of style, had been a break-
neck one, strewn with pot-holes full of water, some of
them very deep. His companion, a local official, had
been in lively fear, ostensibly for the narrator's person,
but actually and obviously for his own, so that Goethe
had repeatedly had to calm him and point out the skill
of the driver, who knew his business so well that Napoleon, had he seen the man, would certainly have made
him his personal coachman. He carefully drove through
the middle of the big holes—much the best way to avoid
an upset. "And then," he continued, "as we bumped
along at a slow pace up the still ascending road, I see
something by the side that makes me get out, cautiously,
from the wagon to look at it. Well, how did *you* get
here? I asked, for what was it shining up at me out of
the mud? A feldspar twin crystal! "

" The deuce—you don't say! " said Werner. He was
probably the only person present—Charlotte suspected,
she almost hoped—who knew what a feldspar twin crystal was; but everybody showed the greatest delight at
this encounter of the narrator with the freak of nature—
and indeed quite spontaneously, for he had given it such
enlivening dramatic form, especially the joyful surprise
and the address to the discovery, that it was truly charming; it had such a fresh and appealing and fairy-story

effect, that a man — and what a man! — had spoken so humanly to a stone; it was by no means the Mines Superintendent alone who was beholden to him. Charlotte, looking with equal intensity at speaker and audience, saw love and pleasure on every face; for instance on Riemer's, where they mingled strangely with his habitual peevish expression; on August's too, yes, she saw them even on Lottchen's, and notably on Meyer's otherwise dry and immobile features as he leaned over past Amalie Ridel to hang on the narrator's lips; such warmth of affection was mirrored there that tears, she knew not why, came into her own eyes.

She felt by no means pleased that the friend of her youth, after the brief private colloquy, had shifted his attention to the whole circle — partly because they wanted it, no doubt, but also, she did not conceal from herself, on account of the "regulations." And yet she could not help sympathizing with their characteristic pleasure; their characteristic, one might almost say mythically conditioned pleasure in this patriarchal monologue by the presiding father of the house. An old verbal association and vague memory came into her mind and obstinately persisted. "Luther's Table-Talk," thought she, and defended the impression against all the dissimilarity of the actual features.

Eating, drinking, pouring out, at times leaning back with his hands folded over his serviette, he went on talking; for the most part slowly, in a low key, and searching conscientiously after the words; but also more lightly and rapidly, the hands freeing themselves to make gestures of great ease and charm. They reminded Charlotte that he was in the habit of discussing with artists problems of delivery and dramatic effects. As he talked, his eyes, with the peculiar depression at their corners, embraced the whole table with their warm and brilliant glance; his lips moved freely, not invariably making a pleasant impression, for they seemed at times to be drawn down by some unlovely compulsion that was torturing and puzzling to behold, turning the pleasure at his words into uneasy pity. But as a rule the pressure lifted speedily, and then the motions of the finely formed mouth were so full of satisfying charm that one felt how precise and unexaggerated a description was the Homeric epithet "ambrosial," even though one had never before applied it to a concrete instance.

He went on talking about Bohemia, about Franzensbrunn and Eger and the cultivated beauty of its valley; described a harvest feast of the Church he had once attended, the beflagged procession through the market square of guilds and militia and peasants, led by clergy in heavily embroidered vestments, carrying relics. Then, lowering his voice and sticking out his lips, with a portentous expression that had something epically humorous about it, as when one tells frightening stories to children, he talked about a night of blood that remarkable town had experienced in the late Middle Ages, an uprising against the Jews, a sudden and violent attack like a paroxysm; there was an account of it in the old chronicles. A good many of the children of Israel dwelt in Eger, in the streets assigned to them, where they had also a very famous synagogue and a Jewish school of higher learning, the only such school in Germany. One

day a barefoot friar, who clearly possessed the fatal gift
of eloquence, had preached from the pulpit on the sufferings of Christ, to most piteous effect; he painted the
Jews as the source of all evil, so revoltingly that a soldier,
quite beside himself as the result of the sermon and ready
for any deed, sprang to the high altar, seized the crucifix,
and with a yell: "He who is a Christian, let him follow
me!" set the spark to the highly inflammable congrega-
tion. They followed him; outside the church they were
joined by a great rabble, and an outrageous slaughtering
and plundering began in the ghetto. The unhappy dwel-
lers were dragged to a narrow alley between two of their
main streets and there butchered — in such wise that the
blood ran down like a stream and to this day it was
called the Murder Street. A single Jew escaped alive
from this massacre, by crawling up the chimney and remaining hidden there. When order had been restored,
the penitent community, having been punished with
severity by the then reigning Charles IV, solemnly made
the Jewish survivor a citizen of Eger.

"Citizen of Eger!" cried the narrator. "So then he
amounted to something and had been splendidly recom-
pensed. He had lost his wife and children, his friends and
relatives, all his property and possessions, his whole society, not to speak of the suffocating effect of the dreadful hours he spent up the chimney. He stood there naked
as he was born, but he was a citizen of Eger, and after
all he was proud of it. Human beings! That is the way
they are. Give way with gusto to the impulse to commit
the cruellest deeds, and after their heads are cool again,
enjoy quite as much the large gesture of repentance with

which they think to pay for the crime. It is laughable—
and touching. For in the mass you cannot speak of a
deed, but only of a happening; it is better to regard such
events as incalculable natural phenomena rising from the
temper of the age. In this light the corrective intervention of a humane power is beneficial; even though too
late, even though it could have acted before and did not;
in this case it was the majesty of Rome that saved as far
as possible the honour of humanity, instituting an investigation into the grave *casus* and formally levying a
a fine on the existing magistracy."

The horrid episode could not have been narrated with
more objectively disarming and soothing comment; thus,
Charlotte felt, it should probably be treated, if such
a thing was to be told at table at all. Goethe lingered yet
a while on the subject of the Jewish character and destiny, listening to and as it were digesting the remarks
thrown in by one or other of the guests—Kirms, Coudray, or the adroit Meyer. He expressed himself with
objectivity and faintly humorous respect on the peculiarities of this remarkable people. The Jews, he said,
were pathetic without being heroic; the age and blood
experience of their race made them wise and sceptical,
and that was the precise opposite of the heroic. There
was definitely a certain wisdom and irony in the very
accents of even the simplest Jew—alongside a definite
inclination to pathos. But that word must be understood
in its most precise sense, in the sense of suffering, and the
Jewish pathos was an emphasis on suffering that often
made a grotesque, really offensive impression on the rest
of us—a man of finer feelings has always to suppress in

himself stirrings of disgust and even a natural hatred before the behaviour and gestures of a man smitten by
God. It was very hard to define the feelings, singularly
mixed of laughter and unexpressed respect, of one of us
when he hears a Jewish pedlar turned roughly away by
a servant on account of his obstinate persistency; hears
him, with arms outstretched to heaven, cry out: "The
villain has scourged and tortured me!" Such strong
words, coming from our older and more high-flown
vocabulary, are not at the disposal of every average native; whereas the child of the old bond has direct relations with that sphere of the pathetic and does not scruple
to apply its syllables grandiloquently to his own lowly
fortunes.

That was all most engaging; the company were no
little diverted — for Charlotte's taste rather too loudly —
by the wailing pedlar and his picturesque Mediterranean
gesturing and posturing, imitated, or rather indicated, by
the speaker in a swift play of mimicry. It was inimitable
— Charlotte herself had to join in the mirth — but she was
too little attentive to the subject-matter, and too many
thoughts were criss-crossing in her head, for her to go
further than a rather laboured smile. She felt an impatient contempt for the obsequious note in the laughing
applause, because it referred to the friend of her youth —
but just for that reason she felt personally flattered by it
as well. Naturally she could not but be touched at seeing
from the expression of his mouth that the friendliness so
freely expended from his rich store cost him not a little.
Back of the social contribution lay his great life-work,
giving his voice such resonance that it was easy to under-

stand an immoderately grateful response, if not to sympathize with it. And the strange thing was that reverence for his intellectual powers was mixed with respect for his social and official position in such a way that you could no longer make a distinction between them. A great poet was, by chance — and yet again not by chance — a great gentleman as well; and this second quality was considered not as something different from his genius but as its representative expression in the world. The cumbersome title of Excellence, that made him seem so unapproachable, had originally as little to do with his genius as had the star on his chest; they were both attributes of the minister and court favourite. But these distinctions had taken on such added meaning from his intellectual stature that, on a yet more profound level, they seemed to be one and the same thing. Quite possibly, Charlotte thought, they were so in his own consciousness too.

She mused thus, uncertain whether it were worth the trouble to linger upon such thoughts. Certainly the ready laughter of her fellow guests expressed their pleasure in this peculiar combination of the spiritual and the secular, their pride in it, their willing subjection to it; and in one way she did not find that right and good, but rather revolting. Should further observation prove that the pride and enthusiasm were really adulation and slavishness, then she was clearly justified of her scruples and the pain bound up with them. It seemed as though it was made too easy for people to bow down before the spiritual when it took the form of an elegant and sparkling-eyed elderly man, who was laden with orders and titles, who lived in a house like a museum, with a splendid state staircase; whose fine hair grew like that of the Jupiter on his pedestal, and who spoke with ambrosial lips. The spiritual, she felt, needed to be poor, ugly, and bare of earthly honour, in order to test aright the capacity of men to honour it. She looked across at Riemer, because something he had said found an echo in her and still lingered in her ear. "In all that there is no Christianity." Well, then, not; then no Christianity. She would not judge, she had no desire to assent to any of the complaints that chronically injured man had mingled in the hymns of praise for his lord and master. But she looked at him, and saw that as he vied with the others in laughter, a little ridge of caution, opposition, dislike, in short of peevishness, stood out between his troubled ox-eyes. And then her mild but persistently inquiring gaze travelled on two places, past Lottchen to August, the erring, overshadowed son, who bore the stain on his character of having shirked the service, and who meant to marry the little person. She looked at him, not for the first time during the dinner. When his father told how the clever driver had saved them from upsetting on the bad road, she had fixed her eyes upon him, remembering the odd incident of his telling her what had befallen the friend of her youth, and how conscious greatness had been spilt into the ditch. Her eyes roved between August and the famulus, and a sudden distrust not only of them but of the whole company came into her mind and made her start: it seemed to her for one dreadful moment that the loud and general laughter of these devotees was meant to cover up and drown out something else, something the more uncanny in that it was like a personal threat to her very self, while at the same time it concealed an invitation to share it and be one of them.

It was, thank God, an anomalous, senseless temptation. Love, nothing but love, was voiced in the laughter round the table, spoke from the eyes hanging on the deliberate yet lively enunciation of her friend. They wanted more — and they got it. Luther's patriarchal table-talk went on and on — a sonorous, witty discourse, enlarging on the subject of the Jews, with a lofty moderation of itself carrying conviction in the matter of the fine it would have levied on the magistracy of Eger. Goethe praised the rare and special aptitudes of this extraordinary stock, its understanding of music and its medical learning. Throughout the Middle Ages the Jewish and the Arabian physician had enjoyed the confidence of the world. Then there was literature: the Jews, like the French, had special affinity for it, and even an indifferently gifted Jew usually wrote a purer and more precise style than the average German, who, by contrast with the peoples of the south, lacked respect for language and enjoyment and precision in its use. The Jews, indeed, were the people of the Book, and from that one deduced that their qualities as human beings and their moral convictions should be regarded as secularized forms of the religious. But the religiosity of the Jews was characteristically directed towards the things of this world and bound up with them; and it was just this capacity and tendency of theirs to give to earthly affairs the dynamism of religion that made one conclude that they were called to play a significant rôle in the shaping of the future on earth. Most remarkable, and hard to fathom in view of the considerable contribution they have made to civilization in general, was the ancient antipathy for ever smouldering in the other peoples of the world against the figure of the Jew, for ever threatening to blaze up into active hatred, as was amply instanced in the tale of the disorders at Eger. This antipathy, this aversion, only heightened by the feeling of respect inseparable from it, could be compared with that felt in the case of only one other people: the Germans. And the destined rôle of the Germans and their inward as well as outward situation among the other peoples showed the most extraordinary likeness to that of the Jews. He would not venture to enlarge upon the point, that would be foolish; but he confessed that sometimes he was conscious of a fear that almost took away his breath lest one day the concentrated world hatred against that other salt of the earth, the German stock, would be released in a historic uprising of which that mediæval night of butchery was but a rehearsal in miniature. . . . But it was best they should let such apprehensions take care of themselves and be of good cheer — and forgive him for making such extravagant comparisons and parallels among the nations. Others might be made, even more striking. In the ducal library there was an old globe of the earth, whereon were short inscriptions describing the characters of various peoples. About Germany it said: "The Germans are a people displaying great likeness to the Chinese." Was that not amusing? — and yet with something apt about it too, when one thought of the German pleasure in titles and their bred-in-the-bone respect for scholarship. Of course such *aperçus* upon folk-psy-chology always had something arbitrary about them — the comparison fitted the French just as well or even better; their cultural self-satisfaction and the rigorous officialism of their examination system resembled that of the mandarin caste. They were democrats too, like the Chinese, though their democratic convictions were not nearly so radical. Confucius' countrymen, indeed, had a saying that "the great man is a national misfortune."

Here came another outburst of laughter, even more boisterous than before. That word, from those lips, caused a perfect storm of merriment. They threw them-selves back in their chairs, they bowed over the table, they struck it with the flat of their hands — shocked into self-abandonment by this nonsensical dogma and pos-sessed by the wish to show their host they could appre-ciate his quoting it and at the same time to convince him what a monstrous and blasphemous absurdity they con-sidered it. Charlotte alone sat on the defensive, stiffly upright, her forget-me-not eyes wide with alarm. She felt cold. She had actually lost colour, and a painful twitching at the corners of her mouth was her only con-tribution to the general merriment. She seemed to see a spectral vision: a scene with many roofs, towers with little bells, and in the street beneath, a train of people, repulsively sly and senile, in pigtails and sugar-loaf hats and coloured jackets; they hopped first on one foot and then on the other, then lifted a shrunken long-nailed fin-ger and in chirping voices pronounced words that were, utterly, fatally, and direfully, the truth. This nightmare vision was accompanied by the same dread as before,

running cold down her back, lest the too loud laughter
round the board might be hiding an evil something that
threatened in a reckless moment to burst forth: somebody might spring up, overturn the table, and scream
out: "The Chinese are right!"

She was certainly very nervous. But nervousness like
that is always in the air, and a sort of tension and apprehension, when humanity divides itself into the one and
the many, and a single individual confronts — in whatever sense or connection — the masses. Charlotte's old
friend sat in a row with them at the table; but even so
the situation — uncanny and yet just for that reason fascinating — had arisen, chiefly because he led the conversation and the rest were the audience. He looked with
large dark shining eyes along the table at the storm of
mirth his words had evoked; and his face, his manner,
had that same disingenuous naïveté and pretended surprise as when he entered the salon. The ambrosial lips
were already moving in preparation for further speech.
When it was quieter he said:

"Such a saying is certainly poor evidence for the wisdom that reigns on this earth. It betrays an out-and-out
anti-individualism that is enough to end all talk of similarity between the Chinese and the Germans. The individual is dear to us Germans — and rightly, for only in
him are we great. But that being true, far more explicitly
than with other nations, the relation between the individual and the general, considering all the scope it gives
to the former, has its melancholy and dangerous side.
Beyond a doubt, it was more than chance that the natural *tædium vitæ* of Frederick the Great's old age ex-

pressed itself in the remark: "I am tired of ruling over
slaves."

Charlotte did not venture to look up. If she had she
would only have seen thoughtful nods, and here and
there more expressly approving smiles; but her excited
fancy pictured malicious glances cast at the speaker from
under lowered eyelids, and she shrank in horror from
seeing them. She felt sunk in gloomy abstraction; it kept
her for some time from following the thread of the talk
and she could not have said what led to the subject under
discussion when from time to time she became aware
of it. She almost failed to hear when her neighbour once
more turned to her and addressed her personally. He
was begging her to take "a minimum" — so he expressed
himself — of the compote he handed her, and half absently she did so. Then she heard talk of the theory of
colour, coming up in connection with certain beakers of
Karlsbad glass he promised to display after dinner; the
painting on them showed the most wonderful transformation of colour according to the way the light fell upon
them. He added some adverse, even offensive comment
on Newton's theory, jesting about the ray of sunlight
coming through a hole in the blind and falling on a glass
prism, and spoke of a sheet of paper preserved by him as
a memento of his first studies in this field, and his earliest
notes on it. They were spattered with rain that had fallen
on them through a leaking tent during the siege of Mainz.
He cherished piously all such little relics and souvenirs
of the past and preserved them carefully, too carefully,
for in the course of a long life far too many such deposits
accumulated. The words set up a violent throbbing of

Charlotte's heart beneath the white frock with the lacking ribbon; scarcely could she resist inquiring after other such items deposited at some time during his life. But she saw the impossibility — once more she lost the thread of his discourse.

As the plates were changed for the sweet, she found herself in the middle of a narrative with no idea how it had come up: their host was entering with great warmth into his tale concerning the strange career of a certain Italian singer. On its moral side, he said, it was charmingly edifying: she had made public her extraordinary gifts with the sole desire of assisting her father, a collector for the *monte di pietà* in Rome, who had fallen on evil days owing to his weakness of character. The young woman's extraordinary talent had been discovered at an amateur concert; she was snapped up on the spot by a theatrical manager and aroused such lively enthusiasm that on her first appearance in Florence a music-lover gave, instead of a single scudo, a hundred zecchini for his ticket. She did not fail to give generously to her parents from this first gift; and her ascent to fame was very swift. She became the brightest star in the musical firmament, money flowed into her hands in streams, and her first care was to surround with every comfort her old parents at home. The narrator invited them to imagine the mingled chagrin and satisfaction of the father when his brilliant child made up by her loyalty and energy for his own lacks. But the vicissitudes of her career did not end here. A rich Viennese banker fell in love with her and offered her his hand. She bade farewell to fame to be his wife; her ship seemed to have come to haven in the safest, most splendid way. But the banker failed, he died a beggar; and after several years of luxurious security she returned, no longer young, to the stage, to experience the greatest triumph of her life. The public hailed her reappearance and new achievements with an homage that first taught her what she had given up and of what deprived humanity when she thought to see in the wooing of her Crœsus the crown and conclusion of her career. This triumphant return after the episode of a brilliant private social interlude was the happiest day of her life; it made her for the first time body and soul an artist. She lived but a few years after that.

The narrator made comments upon his tale, referring to the peculiar lack of seriousness, the indifference and unawareness shown by this extraordinary woman towards her individual calling. With easy and sovereign gesture he seemed to try to animate the company with satisfaction in this kind of detachment. A strange sort of idealist! Obviously, despite her great gift, she had never taken very seriously either her own art or art in general. Only to lift her fallen parent to his feet had she made up her mind to practise the talent till then unsuspected by everyone, even herself. And she had used it always in the service of filial affection. Her readiness to abandon fame and retire to private life at the first and not very romantic opportunity, no doubt to the despair of the impresarios, was most striking. There was every indication that she had not, in her palatial Vienna home, shed any tears for her art or found it a hardship to give up the footlights, the theatre sights and smells, or the bouquets that rewarded her roulades and trills. True, when harsh necessity again made demands upon her, she had without more ado gone back to public life; and now there was forced upon her by the demonstrations of her audiences the realization that her art, never regarded by her with great seriousness, but always as more or less a means to an end, was her true and genuine calling. And then how striking it was that a brief time after her triumphal return her life came to an end, she passed away! Obviously it had not answered; this late discovery, this definite decision that her life was bound up and identical with art, her existence as its priestess, had not been suitable or possible for her. He, the narrator, had always been fascinated by this theme of the relation of the artist to his art; it was a tragicomedy wherein the rôles of modesty and superiority were inextricably mingled. He would very much like to have made the acquaintance of the lady.

His hearers indicated that they would have enjoyed it too. Poor Charlotte laid less stress on the idea. There was something painful and disquieting in the story or rather in the accompanying comment. She had been hoping — for her own gratification but also for the speaker's sake as well — that some moral edification would be the issue of this instance of filial piety. But he had given a disappointing turn to the gratifying sentiment, it was at best psychologically "interesting"; it showed an approbation of this example of the artist's contempt for his art — and that chilled and frightened Charlotte, again for his sake as well as for her own.

The sweet was a raspberry crème, mixed with whipped cream, with a delicious bouquet, and served with sponge fingers. Champagne was handed, the servant poured it out, after all, from a bottle wrapped in a serviette. Goethe had partaken copiously of the earlier wines, but he now drank two beakers of champagne in quick succession, as though he were thirsty, holding the emptied glass over his shoulder to the servant for the second filling. He seemed for a brief moment to be contemplating another diverting reminiscence, gazing diagonally upwards into space with his close-lying eyes. They watched him with smiling expectation, Meyer with a look of speechless affection; then he addressed himself across the table to Herr Bergrat Werner and said he had something for him: "Oh, I must tell you somethin'!" he expressed it. The slip, or whatever it was — sounded very odd after the precise and deliberate eloquence their ears had been attuned to. He added that most of the resident guests would certainly remember the amusing old anecdote, but it would be new to the strangers present and it was so good that surely everybody would like hearing it again.

He went on, with an expression that revealed his own inward enjoyment of the subject, to talk about an art exhibition of thirteen years earlier. It had been got up by the Weimar Friends of Art and supported from outside from many other collections. One of the finest things had been the copy — an extraordinarily able copy — of Leonardo da Vinci's head of Charitas: "the one from Cassel, you know, and you know the copyist too, it was Herr Riepenhausen, a man with a most pleasing talent, who in this case had done an exceptionally sensitive and praiseworthy piece of work. The head was in aquarelle, giving most faithfully the subdued tones of the original, and reproducing the languishing expression of the eyes, the gentle pleading bend of the head, and in particular the sweet melancholy of the mouth, with the greatest fidelity.

"The exhibition was later than usual in the year, and the public interest in it kept it open longer too. The rooms got colder and for economy's sake they were heated only at the hours when they were open to the public. Visitors were charged a small entrance fee; for Weimarians there was a subscription, allowing them to enter outside the regular hours.

"Now here is the story: the authorities, themselves highly diverted, sent for us one day to the place where the Charitas was hung, to confirm by the evidence of our own eyes the most demure and delightful phenomenon: on the mouth of the picture, I mean on the glass at that spot, there was an unmistakable imprint, a well-formed impression of a pair of pretty lips; in other words, a kiss bestowed upon the lovely semblance.

"You may imagine our amusement, and the criminological zest we applied to our secret investigation into the identity of the criminal. He was young — one might take that for granted — even if the imprint on the glass had not proved it. He must have been alone, for else no one would venture on such an act. In other words, a resident of Weimar, with a subscription permitting him to commit his tender folly when the rooms were unheated. He had breathed upon the cold glass and imprinted his kiss on his own breath, which then congealed. Only a few of us were acquainted with the circumstance, but

it was not hard to find out who had been alone in the
unheated rooms. Our suspicions, amounting to certainty,
came to rest on a certain young man — I will neither name
nor further designate him — and he never knew how we
found out about his romantic little venture; but we in
the know had occasion afterwards to observe those really
very kissable lips when we greeted that young man in the
street."

Such the story, begun with the slip in pronunciation,
and greeted not only by the Bergrat but by all the rest
with exclamations. Charlotte had got very red. She
blushed as deeply, up to the roots of her crown of grey
hair, as her delicate colouring would allow, and the blue
of her eyes looked by contrast pallid and harsh. She sat
turned away from the narrator towards her neighbour
Hofkammerrat Kirms, and almost looked as though she
wanted to fly for refuge to his bosom; but, being highly
entertained by the story, he did not mark it. The poor
woman was in terror lest their host might expand further upon the physics of this kiss into vacancy. He commented indeed upon his story, but confined himself to
æsthetic considerations. He spoke of the sparrows that
picked at the cherries in Apelles' painting; and of the
deceptive effect of art, the most singular and precisely
therefore the most fascinating of all phenomena, upon
the reason. Not alone in the sense of illusion, for it was
by no means a deliberate deception; but in a profounder
way, through art's relation with the earthly and the
heavenly sphere at once, because its effect was both spiritual and sensuous, or, to speak in platonic language, it
was divine and visible both, and through the senses

worked on the spirit. Hence the peculiar inwardness of the yearning aroused by the beautiful — expressed, in the present case, by the youthful art-lover's act, through the medium of the laws of heat and cold. The joke, of course, lay in the muddle-headed inadequacy of the poor youth's act. You could not help being sorry, even while you smiled, for the deluded young wretch's feelings as his lips touched the cold smooth glass. Could one conceive a more telling or touching allegory than this of hot-blooded emotion embodying itself by chance upon icily unresponsive matter? It was a sort of cosmic jest. And so on.

Coffee was served at table. Goethe took none. He drank a glass of southern wine called *tinto rosso* with the dessert, to which he addressed himself at once after the fruit; it consisted of all sorts of confections, rings of gum tragacanth, sweet lozenges, and raisins. After that he gave the signal by rising and the company went back to the Juno-room, and into the adjoining side-cabinet, called by the familiars of the house the Urbino-room, after the Renaissance portrait of the Duke of Urbino hanging there. The ensuing hour — actually it was only rather more than three quarters — was thoroughly tedious; but in a way to leave Charlotte in doubt whether she preferred it to the excitements and embarrassments of the dinner itself. She would gladly have dispensed her old friend from the diligent provision of amusement he thought it right to make. He had in mind mostly the guests for the first time in his house, namely Charlotte and her family, and Bergrat Werner. He was concerned to "show them somethin' worth seein'," as he expressed it. With his own hands, with assistance from August and the servant, he lifted the great portfolios of plates from the shelves, opened their heavy covers before the ladies as they sat, to display the layers of curiosities therein — that being the word he used to describe the baroque pictures. He paused so long at the top one that there was not much time for the rest. A *Battle of Constantine* in large sheets gave occasion for long-winded explanations; he pointed here and there, called attention to the grouping of the figures, the correct drawing of human beings and horses, and sought to impress on his audience how much talent and originality it took to draft and complete such a scene. Then the cabinet of coins, brought in drawers out of the portrait-room, must needs be examined; it was, if the guests had presence of mind to observe, astonishingly rich and full; containing a complete set of papal coins from the fifteenth century up to the present time. He emphasized with great justice that such a collection afforded a most happy insight into the history of art. He seemed to know the names of all the engravers and the circumstances under which the various medals were struck, with anecdotes about the lives of the people they commemorated.

The glass beakers from Karlsbad were not forgotten. Their host had them fetched, and by turning them to and fro in the light produced the very charming variations of colour they did indeed display, from yellow to blue, and red to green. Goethe explained the phenomenon in detail by means of a small apparatus devised, if Charlotte understood him aright, by himself; he had August fetch it. It was a wooden frame with small tinted glass plates to be moved to and fro across a black or white ground, thus reproducing the phenomena of the beakers.

At intervals, when he had done his duty and thought he had provided his guests with enough occupation for a while, he walked up and down in the room with his hands behind his back and from time to time drew a long, deep breath, expelling it with a little sound not unlike a groan. Or he stopped and talked with various unoccupied groups familiar with his collections, as they stood round the room and in the passage to the cabinet. The strange sight of him talking thus with Herr Stephan Schütze, the writer, made an abiding impression on Charlotte as she bent with her sister over the optical apparatus, shoving the coloured plates to and fro, quite near to where the older and the younger man stood. She divided her attention between them and the colour effects. Schütze had taken off the glasses he habitually wore and held them as it were concealed as he looked with his protruding eyes, dulled and half blinded from lack of the accustomed support, into the browned and muscular features before him. They wore, these features, a conflict of expressions. The two were talking about an *Album of Love and Friendship* compiled by Schütze a few years earlier. Goethe had brought up the subject; standing there, with his legs apart and chin stuck out, he praised it highly and said that the compilation was both varied and suggestive and declared that he had regularly drawn much entertainment and instruction from it. He suggested that Schütze's own humorous contributions should

some time be published in a separate collection. The
other, blushing and goggling still more, confessed that
he had played sometimes with the idea himself and only
doubted whether such a collection were worth while.
Goethe, vigorously shaking his head, protested against
the doubt; basing his view, however, not on the tales
themselves, but on purely human, so to speak statutory,
grounds. Things must be, he said, collected when the
time came, the autumn of life; the harvest must be
gathered and stored, the grain got under roof; otherwise
one would not depart in peace, not having lived a right
or pattern life. The only thing was to find a good title.
His close-lying eyes roved about the ceiling — without
much prospect of success, so Charlotte feared, for she had
the clearest intuition that he was not acquainted with the
tales. But now Herr Schütze betrayed how far his hesitating thoughts had carried him, for he had a name ready
at hand: he had thought — just in case — to call the proposed book *Happy Hours*. Goethe found that capital.
He could not have thought of a better title himself. It
was most pleasing, and not without dignity and elegance. It would appeal to the publisher, attract readers;
and most important of all, it fitted the contents. That
was as it should be. A good book has its title born with
it; and that it was clear and unequivocal was precisely
the evidence of its soundness and justification. "Excuse
me," said he, as Architect Coudray came towards him.
But Riemer hurried up, as Schütze put on his spectacles
again, obviously to hear what Goethe had said.

    Almost at the end of the party the host happened to
think of showing Charlotte the counterfeits of her chil-

dren, sent to him long ago by that active, worthy pair. The Kestner ladies had finished with the coins and copperplates and the colour apparatus, and he was leading them about the room to display various of his curiosities; the statuettes of the gods under glass, an ancient lock with a key hanging on the wall by the window, a little gilt Napoleon with hat and dagger enclosed in the bell-shaped end of the tube of a barometer. And then he thought of it: "Now I know," he cried, slipping into more familiar address, "what I must show you, children: the old birthday present, the silhouettes of yourselves and your splendid progeny! You shall see how faithfully I have cherished and honoured it all these years! August, be so good, fetch me the por'feuille with the drawin's, the silhouettes, I mean," he called, dropping again into Frankfurtese. As they were looking at the quaintly incarcerated little Napoleon, August brought the fascicle from somewhere and laid it on the Streicher piano, beckoning them thither as there was no more space on the round table.

Goethe himself untied the covers and opened the volume. Inside was a time-yellowed and mildewed confusion of emblematic souvenirs and relics, silhouettes, occasional poems in faded wreaths of flowers, drawings of rocks and roofs, river-banks and flocks and shepherds, such as their owner might have sketched in hastily as aids to his memory, on journeys in years gone by. The old gentleman did not very well remember the contents and could not come on what he sought. "Devil take it, where is the thing?" said he with mounting vexation, tossing the sheets about faster and faster with nervous hands.

The circle deplored his trouble and kept repeating their readiness to give up the idea of seeing the portraits. It did not need looking at the actual picture again to have it clearly before their eyes. In the end Charlotte herself found it among the chaos and drew it out. "I have it, Excellence," she said, " here it is." He looked at the sheet with the profiles stuck on it, rather taken aback and even incredulous, and answered with a trace of anger in his voice: "It certainly is, it was reserved to you to find it out. There you are, my good friend, neatly cut, and the departed archivist and your five eldest hopefuls. Our lovely Fräulein is not there. Which are the ones I know? These? Yes, yes, children grow up."

Meyer and Riemer approached. They made a cautious signal, each shutting his eyes with drawn brows and slightly nodding. They felt, it seemed, that the epi-sode brought the sitting to an end, and everyone agreed they were right in sparing the master fatigue. And the guests chatting in the Urbino-room felt the same.

"So you will leave me, children, all of you at once? " said their host. "Well, no one can blame you for return-ing to your own duties and pleasures. Adieu, adieu. Our Bergrat must stop awhile with me, yes, my dear Werner, you agree? I have something interesting for you back in my study, something from abroad, we old augurs must have a little after-celebration: fossil fresh-water snails from Libnitz in the Elbogen region. "My dear friend," said he to Charlotte, "farewell! I am convinced that Weimar and your dear ones will keep you here for some weeks longer. Life has held us sundered far too long a time for me not to ask of it that we may meet often during your sojourn. No, no, thanks! Until, then, dearest madame! Adieu, ladies! Adieu, gentlemen!"

August conveyed the Ridels and Kestners back down the splendid staircase to the house door, where stood their hired coach as well as other two for the Kirms and Coudray couples. It was raining hard now. The guests from whom they had taken leave above bowed again as they passed.

"Father was exceptionally animated by your presence," said August. "He seemed entirely to have forgotten his bad arm."

"He was charming," responded the Landkammerrat's lady, and her husband gave emphatic assent. Charlotte said:

"If he was in pain, then his spirits and liveliness are the more to be admired. I hate to think it, and blush to recall that I did not ask him about his trouble. I should have offered him some of my opodeldoc. After a separation, especially a long one, there are always many omissions to regret."

"Whatever they are," replied August, "you will have occasion to make them good, even though not at once. For I think my father must rest now and not enter into more engagements. If he asks leave to absent himself from court, he cannot accept other invitations. I make the remark by way of precaution."

"Heavens, yes, of course!" they said. "That goes without saying. Our thanks and greetings once more."

Then the four sat again in their high calèche and rolled away through the narrow streets towards home. Lotte the younger, bolt upright on the rear seat, her nostrils fluttering in and out, stared into the well of the coach past the ear of her mother, whose pomp of ribbons was once more shrouded in her black mantle.

"He is a great and good man," said Amalie Ridel, and her husband confirmed her: "That he is."

Charlotte thought or dreamed: "He is great, and you are good. But I am good too, good deep down in my heart, and wish to be. For only good men can esteem the great. Those Chinamen, hopping and chirping under their pagodas, are both wicked and foolish."

Aloud she said to Dr. Ridel: "I feel so guilty, brother, that I must confess at once before you ask me. I spoke of omissions and knew but too well what I meant. I am returning home with disappointment and regret. For the truth is that neither at table nor afterwards did I come to speak of your hopes and wishes to Goethe and enlist him for them, as I certainly meant to do. I do not know how the omission could have occurred; but in the whole of the time there was no place that it fitted in. I am to blame—but yet only in a way. Forgive me!"

"No matter, dear Lotte," answered Ridel. "Do not distress yourself. It was not so necessary to speak of it; just by your presence, and the fact that we dined with His Excellence, you have been helpful enough to us, and it will all work out for the best."

CHAPTER NINE

CHARLOTTE remained in Weimar until nearly the middle of October, lodging all that time with Lottchen, her daughter, at the Elephant. Frau Elmenreich, the proprietress, met her half-way on the price of the lodging, partly out of calculation but also because Headwaiter Mager put in his word. We do not know too much about this sojourn of the famous lady in the equally famous city of Weimar. It seems — as befitted her years — to have borne the character of dignified retirement, though she was by no means inaccessible. Her time was largely devoted to her dear family; still, we hear of several small and even a few important gatherings graced by her presence in those weeks, in various social circles of the Residence. One of them, quite properly, was given by the Ridels themselves, and others by people in the Landkammerrat's official circle. Herr Hofrat Meyer and his lady, born von Koppenfeld, and Oberbaurat Coudray and his, each invited to their home on one occasion the friend of Goethe's youth. She was also seen in court society, in the house of Count Edling, member of the Board of the Weimar Theatre, and his lovely wife, Princess Sturdza from Moldavia. At the beginning of October they gave a soirée, embellished with music and recitations. It was probably on this evening that Charlotte made the acquaintance of Frau von Schiller; the latter wrote a letter to a friend with a shrewd and sympathetic description of her person and manner. This other Charlotte speaks of Amalie Ridel as well, by way of comment on the "transitoriness of earthly things": she remarks how very mature and settled the once "saucy blonde" looked as she sat among the ladies.

On all these occasions, of course, Charlotte was the object of homage. Her friendly and composed dignity in accepting all such attentions had at length the result that she received them no longer as the due of her literary renown, but as a tribute to her own person and qualities, not least attractive among them being a kind of gentle plaintiveness. Any noisy demonstrations she rejected mildly but firmly. We are told that an excitable female dashed up to her in an evening company, arms outstretched, crying out: "Lotte! Lotte!" Charlotte retreated, and recalled the foolish creature to reason with a quiet "Calm yourself, my love!" Thereafter, however, she conversed most affably with her about local and world affairs. Malice, gossip, and prying curiosity did not, of course, wholly spare her; but they were held in check by the decency of the better-minded. There leaked out and got abroad by degrees, probably through the indiscretion of Sister Amalie, a report that the old lady had gone to visit Goethe in a garb that made tasteless allusion to the Werther romance. But by that time her moral ascendancy was so secure that gossip could do little to harm her.

At none of these events did she encounter again her

friend of Wetzlar days. It was known that he was suffering from gout in his arm, and also busy with revision of two forthcoming volumes of the Collected Works. We have a letter written by Charlotte to her son August, the Legation Councillor; it describes the dinner at the Frauenplan; one can but say of it that it must have been written on the impulse of the moment, with small pains to give a fair-minded report — or even with a tendency in the other direction. She wrote:

> I have, indeed, said nothing as yet, even to you, about my meeting with the great man. Actually I have little to say: only this much, that I made a new acquaintance, with an old man who, if I had not known he was Goethe, and even knowing it, made on me no pleasant impression. You know how little I promised myself from this renewed, or rather this new acquaintance, and so it did not touch me. And in his stiff way he did all he could to show me courtesy. He remembered you and Theodor with interest.
>
> Your Mother, Charlotte Kestner, née Buff

Comparing these lines with the note addressed to Goethe, quoted early in our tale, we are driven to remark the much greater care and consideration expended on the latter.

But in actual fact the friend of her youth had written to her too, once in these weeks. Early on the morning of October 9th, to her surprise, she received at the Elephant a little note, brought up by Mager as she was dressing. She had a hard time getting him out of the room. Then she read:

Should you care, my dear friend, to use my box this evening, my carriage can fetch you. No ticket is needed, my servant will escort you through the parterre. Forgive me for not coming myself, and not showing myself in all this time — I have been often with you in my thoughts.

With heartiest good wishes,

Goethe

She tacitly granted the writer the absolution he sought for not coming himself and not seeking her out ere now — tacitly, in that she made use of his invitation. She went alone. Young Lotte had a Puritan distaste for the gifts of Thalia, and Sister Amalie and her husband were bespoken elsewhere. So she was driven alone, in the Goethe equipage, a comfortable landau upholstered in blue broadcloth, drawn by two glossy brown horses; and in the theatre the Hannover housewife spent the evening, the cynosure of many lorgnons and much envy, unperturbed by stares, in the place of honour lately occupied by a woman of very different appearance, Christiane, the Mamsell. Even during the long entr'acte she did not leave her proscenium box.

The play was Theodor Körner's historical tragedy *Rosamunde*. The performance was polished and well-rounded; Charlotte, in her usual white frock, this time trimmed with heliotrope bows, followed it with the greatest enjoyment from beginning to end. Refined diction, lofty delivery, shrieks of passion entrusted to practised and adequate organs, flattering to human ears, it all struck on hers, accompanied and enhanced by noble, measured gesture. Conscious command of technique sus-

tained the crises of the plot, the glorified death scenes
where the dying delivered their lines in verse, with the
ideal strength of their voices up to their very end; the
passages of violence and cruelty beloved of the tragic
muse; and the consolatory finale, where even the evil
principle itself was driven to confess that "hell is no
more." There was much weeping in the parterre, and
Charlotte's eyes were wet a few times, though she permitted herself some private criticism on the score of the
author's well-known youth. She did not like to hear the
heroine, Rosamunde, in a solo recitative, address herself
repeatedly as Rosa. And she knew too much about children to be convinced by the behaviour of these infant
Thespians. They had daggers put to their breasts, to con-
strain their mother to drink the poison; and they said to
her: "Mother, thou art so pale. Be blithe, as we also
would be!" And they pointed to the coffin, in full view
on the stage throughout the scene, and cried: "Lo, see
how joyously the candles gleam!" Sobs from the parterre at this point, but Charlotte's eyes were dry. So
silly as that, she thought in annoyance, children never
were; a man had to be a very young "fighter for freedom" indeed to conceive them thus.

And the sentiments to which these actors lent the authority of their trained organs and popular personalities
—they did not sound so inevitable or irreproachable
either, to her. With all that skill and warmth in presentation, she found they lacked profounder experience of life
—it was probably not easy to come by, in a cavalryman's
career in the open. There was a tirade in the play that she
could not get over, continuing to ponder and dwell on it

in her critical mind until she was in danger of losing the thread of what followed. Even after she left the theatre she was still unsatisfied, still mentally turning it over. One speaker had praised recklessness as a noble trait. Another, of riper judgment, deplored the all too great human temptation to consider sheer audacity a virtue in itself. Let a man dare lay reckless hands on all values, even sacred ones, and people make a hero of him straightway, name him great, and enroll him among the stars of the historical heavens. But it was not heroic, so the author made the actor say, for a man simply to be utterly abandoned. That confine of humanity which lies next to hell was easily overleaped, it was the kind of risk just ordinary wickedness could take. The other confine, bordering on heaven, could be crossed alone by the soul's highest, purest flight. All very fine, of course. But the solitary guest in the loge felt that the poet and volunteer rifle, with his two confines, had a feeble and immature idea of the topography of the moral sphere. The boundaries of humanity, she mused, might be not two lines but a single one; beyond that might lie neither heaven nor hell, or rather just as much hell as heaven; and the greatness that overstepped the border was quite possibly single too, good and evil mingling in it in a way this soldierly and immature poet understood as little as he did the enormous shrewdness and fine perceptions possessed by the childish mind. Possibly, of course, he did know these things and merely thought it was the province of poetry to make children out touching little idiots and assert that two confines existed to humanity. It was an accomplished performance; but its talent aimed at producing a theatre piece according to accepted standards, and the poet did not once overstep the confines of humanity on either side. Well, the young generation of writers, with all their skill, were certainly at rather a low ebb, all in all, and the great of an earlier time had little to fear from them.

Thus she mused and marshalled her objections, and the curtain went down for the last time to loud applause, the audience rose up, and the servant from the Frauenplan reappeared respectfully at her side to lay her mantle about her shoulders.

"Well, Carl," said she, for he had told her his name, "it was very fine. I enjoyed it very much."

"His Excellence will be pleased to hear it," replied he. And the commonplace prose of his voice, the voice of reality and everyday after her sojourn in loftier spheres, made her realize that her carping had been in a measure willful. It was meant to counteract the sense we often have, after contact with the beautiful, of rather fretful and condescending estrangement from ordinary life. We turn our backs with regret upon that sphere; the persistent applause down below was evidence of the fact. It was not so much enthusiasm for the actors as a means of clinging yet a little longer to the beautiful before one dropped one's hands and resigned oneself once more to the commonplace. Charlotte too, in hat and wrap, the servant waiting, stood some minutes at the front of the loge, applauding with her bemitted hands. Then she followed Carl and he put his rosetted hat back on his head and led her down the stairs. Her eyes blinked with staring from the dark into the light; yet they sparkled in-

tensely, and their gaze was not directed outwards, but
rather slantingly upwards, in sign how well she had enjoyed the play, despite her objections to the theory of
the two boundaries.

The landau stood before the door with its top up, and
a lantern either side the high box where the coachman
sat bracing his Hessians against the dash-board and saluting her as she came out. The servant helped Charlotte
to mount and solicitously spread the rug over her knees,
then closed the door and sprang lightly up to the coachman's side. The coachman chirrupped to his horses, they
pulled at their traces, the carriage moved off.

Its interior was snug and convenient, and no wonder,
for it had served on long journeys, likewise in the Bohemian forests and on the Main and the Rhine. The up-
holstery of tufted blue cloth was most comfortable, there
was a candle in a wind-glass in the corner, and also writ-
ing-materials: on Charlotte's side a leather pocket with
paper and pencil.

Quietly she sat in her corner, her hands crossed on her
nécessaire. Through the little screen dividing the interior from the box, flickering, uncertain light fell from
the lanterns; by it she perceived that she had done well
to sit down where she sat, for she was not so much alone
as she had been in the loge. Goethe sat beside her.

She did not start. One does not start at such things.
She only drew a little farther into her corner, a little more
to one side, looked at the shape of her neighbour there
in the fitful, flickering light, and hearkened.

He wore an ample cloak with a stand-up collar faced
and bordered with red. His hat he held in his lap. There

was the massive brow with its Olympian growth of hair, this time unpowdered and almost youthfully brown, if less youthfully abundant; beneath it his eyes, large, black, and bright, looked at her dancing.

"Good evening, my dear," said the voice that once had read Ossian and Klopstock to her, a girl and Kestner's bride. "I had to forgo my place at your side this evening, and I have been invisible all these days. I would not relinquish the pleasure of fetching you home from the play."

"That was most courteous of you, Excellence Goethe," she replied, "and chiefly pleases me because the thought, and the surprise you have given me, bespeak a certain harmony between our two minds—if one can talk of such a thing between a great man and a little woman. They show that you too would have found it unsatisfactory, or even almost sad, if our adieux after the last edifying meeting had been in truth the last; if there had not come another, one I am quite prepared to regard as in very truth the last for ever, if it can only give this story a tolerably redeeming close."

"A division," she heard him say from his corner, "parting is a division. Meeting again is a little chapter, a fragment."

"I do not know what you mean, Goethe," she responded—and the poor soul slipped unawares into the familiar "thou" of bygone days—"or scarcely even whether I heard aright; but I do not wonder, nor should you—once for all, I yield nothing to the little woman with whom you lately made poetry by the shining waters of the Rhine. Your poor son told me of her: it seems she simply entered into you and your song, and wrote as good poetry as you did yourself. Well, of course, she is a child of the stage, and probably has volatile blood in her veins. But women are women, and all of us, when needs must, enter into the man and his song. . . . So meeting again is a short chapter, a fragment? But you yourself felt it should not be so fragmentary that I must needs go back with a sense of utter failure to my lonely widowed state."

"Thy dearest sister," said he, "hast thou not embraced her, After long parting? Then canst thou lament Thy journey's failure?"

"Ah, do not mock me," she countered. "That is just it: I used my sister as a pretext to gratify a desire that had long robbed me of my peace, to journey to your home, to seek you out in your greatness, with whom fate involved my life, to find an end to the fragment and tranquillize the evening of my days. Tell me, did you find I did so ill? Was it a pathetic schoolgirl trick?"

"We will not call it that," he answered, "by no means that, though it is not good to feed the sentimental curiosity and malice of the crowd. But from your point of view, dear friend, I can well understand the impulse to this journey. I too, at least in a deeper sense, found your coming not ill done. Indeed, I would call it good, or even inspired, if it be true that spirit is the guiding force that lends significance in art and life and makes us see in things of the senses a mask for higher concerns. Any life that has significance has also unity; in it there is no such thing as chance. It was no chance put our book, the *Werther*, into my hands again in the spring of this year and plunged your friend back into old and early times. For he realized then that he was entering on a phase of renewal and recurrence. And he foresaw that the presiding powers might elect to dissolve the passions into spirit. But where the present so stimulatingly makes itself felt as a rejuvenescence of the past, it is not surprising that the unrejuvenated past comes too, borne back upon the welling tide, to visit us. Nor even that it brings with it faded allusions, and betrays its bondage to time by touchingly nodding its head."

"It is unhandsome of you, Goethe, to point out this little habit so expressly. You call it touching, but that does not mend matters, because you do not care about the touching, and where ordinary mortals might find it so, you simply find it 'interesting.' I saw you notice my little weakness. It has nothing to do with the state of my health; my constitution, thank God, is strong and unimpaired. The trouble is not bondage to time so much as the bondage of being involved in your overwhelming life; that, I can only say, makes me nervous. What I did not know was that you saw the faded allusion, as you called it, in my dress. But of course that roving eye of yours sees more than one would think. After all, you were meant to see it, that was why I did it, and I counted on your sense of humour to see the joke — though I see now myself it was not particularly funny. But to return to my bondage to time: let me tell you, Your Excellence, you have small reason to boast, for all your poetic renewal and rejuvenescence; for you are so stiff, standing and walking, that it is pathetic, and your rigid politeness seems to me just as much in need of opodeldoc."

"I have made you angry, my dear," he said, in his gentle bass, "with my passing allusion. But bear in mind I made it in justifying your reappearance and explaining why I found it well done and wise for you too to float along in the spirit train."

"How strange! " she broke in. "August told me you always said 'thou' to his mother, the Mamsell, but she always said 'you' to you. I notice it is just the other way about, with us."

"The two forms," he replied, "were always in your time unsettled between us; what we say for the moment, moreover, probably depends on our two dispositions."

"Well and good. But you just said 'your time' instead of 'our time,' and, after all, it was your time too. But now it is your time again, renewed and rejuvenated as the stimulating present, and as that it was mine only once upon a time. Truly it should not wound me deeply to have you refer straight out to my insignificant little weakness; after all, it just means, alas, that it only *was* my time! "

"My friend," returned he, "how can your present time-form trouble you, or any reference to it wound you, when destiny has favoured you above millions and given you eternal youth in a work of art? What was of time, my work has preserved."

"A good hearing," said she; "I realize it gratefully, despite all the burden and distress bound up with it for me, poor soul! But I should like to add what your stately sense of politeness would probably not mention, that it was silly of me to drape my present form with emblems of the past that belong only to the timeless figure in your work. After all, you have not the poor taste to go about in the blue coat with the yellow waistcoat and trousers eccentric youngsters wore in our day! Your coat is of the finest black cloth, like silk, and I must say the silver star becomes you as well as the Golden Fleece did Egmont. Ah, Egmont!" she sighed. "You did well, Goethe, to perpetuate your own youthful form in a poem too. You can resign yourself with dignity now to being a stiff-legged Excellence, and saying grace for your sycophants!"

His voice, coming after a pause, was deep and emotional. "My friend," it said, "cherishes ill feeling. But not alone because I spoke of that mark of age. My words only seemed untender, they were meant in affection. Nay, the anger, or the pain that expresses itself as anger, has a better, has only too just a ground. And did I not wait upon thee with the carriage because I felt the need to face this angry pain, admit its justice and propriety — and perhaps soften it by a heart-felt plea for forgiveness?"

"Oh, my God!" exclaimed she, quite aghast. "How can Your Excellence condescend — ? That was not what I wished to hear, I am as red as I was at the story you told over the raspberry crème! Forgiveness! My pride, my great happiness — they are to forgive? Where is the man who may — even compare with my friend? As the world does now, so will posterity speak of him with reverence."

"Neither humility on the one hand nor innocence on the other," he responded, "can take away the sting of the refusal. To say: 'I have nothing to forgive' means you are still unforgiving; it seems it has always been my fate to involve myself innocently in guilt. And when the craving for forgiveness speaks, humility herself should not deny it. That only means it does not know the secret torment, the searing pain, that pierces a man's breast at a justified reproach. There he sits, in the darkness of his own confident self-esteem; suddenly his breast glows like those heaps of red-hot mussel-shells they use in some places to build with instead of lime."

"My friend," she said, "I should be horrified if the thought of me could even for one moment trouble your confident self-esteem — it means far too much for all the world. But I rather think this sudden burning glow had to do in the beginning with the first object you renounced and in so doing set up the pattern — I mean the daughter of the people, and your bidding her farewell leaning down from your horse. At least it comforts me when I read that you took leave of me with a less burning sense of guilt than of her, poor soul, lying there under her mound in Baden! But I confess I have no overwhelming sympathy with her: she did not behave very well, she let herself languish and pine — and surely it is our duty to be resolute, to make ourselves our own end, even though we be a means as well. There she lies, while others have lived a full life and now rejoice in honourable widowhood, despite a little trifle of nervous head-shaking that does not count in the least. And I am the successful one, the clear, unmistakable heroine of your little book, undoubted and unquestioned down to the smallest details, no matter for the little mix-up about the black eyes. Even that Chinaman, whatever outlandish views he may have, paints me with trembling hand, on glass, at Werther's side. Me;

and no other. I may boast of that—what if the other there under her mound did come in too, in the very first place, and perhaps laid open your heart for Werther's love? For no one knows it; it is my face and my circumstances that are in the public eye. My only worry is lest some day it might come out and be discovered that she is the real one, and belongs to you in the Elysian Fields, like Laura and Petrarch. That would depose me, and cast out my image from its niche in the temple of humanity. That is the thought that sometimes disturbs me until I am near to tears."

"Jealous?" he asked, with a smile. "Is Laura's then the only name that shall be sung? Jealous—of whom? Of your sister, nay, your reflection and other you? When the cloud forms and re-forms, is it not still the same cloud? The hundred names of God, do they not all name only the One? And you, beloved children? Life is but change of form, in many oneness, permanence in change. And you and she, you are all one in my love— and in my guilt. Did you make your journey to be consoled for this?"

"Nay, Goethe," said she. "I came to see the might-have-been, the possible. Its deficiencies compared to the actual and existing are plain to see. Yet there it is, beside the actual, in the world, whenever we say 'If only' or 'As once it was.' And it is worth our questioning. Do you not find it so, old friend, do not you too sometimes, in all the glory of your actual, question the might-have-been? For your actual, well I know, is the effect of renunciation, and in consequence of impairment and loss; for renunciation and loss lie close together. and all reality and achievement are nothing but the impaired possible. There is something frightful, let me tell you, about that impairment. We humbler folk must avoid it, we must brace ourselves against it with all our strength, till our heads quiver with the strain; for else there is nothing left for us, so to speak, but a mound in Baden. With you it was different. You had something to put to it. Your reality looks different; not like renunciation, or unfaithfulness; but like purer fulfilment and a higher faith. It is so imposing, no one dares even inquire after the might-have-been. I congratulate you! "

"Your feelings, dear child, are so involved, they embolden you to an ironic kind of congratulation."

"This much at least I insist upon: to have my say, and sing my praises with a difference, not in the same key as all the unfamiliar throng! Let me tell you, Goethe: so perfectly at ease I did not feel in your presence, in your circle and your museum of a house. I was oppressed and fearful, I admit. It smells too much of sacrifice where you are. I do not mean incense, that I like, and Iphigenie too consented to burn it before Diana of the Scythians. But human sacrifice she could not bear, she sought to soften the harsh decree. Alas, in your circle it looks too much the same; it is almost like a battlefield and the kingdom of a wicked emperor. These Riemers with their mutterings and grumblings and their manly honour floundering about in the bird-lime; and your poor son with his seventeen glasses of champagne, and this little person who will marry him at the New Year and fly into your upper rooms like a moth to the candle — to say nothing about Marie Beaumarchais, who did not know how to stand up as I did and so consumption took her off to lie under her mound — what are they all but sacrifices to your greatness? Ah, it is wonderful to make a sacrifice — but a bitter, bitter lot to be one! "

The unquiet lights flickered and whisked across the cloaked form at her side. He said:

"Dear soul, let me answer you from my heart, in expiation and farewell. You speak of sacrifice. But it is a mystery, indivisible, like all else in the world and one's person, one's life, and one's work. Conversion, transformation, is all. They sacrificed to the god, and in the end the sacrifice was God. You used a figure dear and familiar to me; long since, it took possession of my soul. I mean the parable of the moth and the fatal, luring flame. Say, if you will, that I am the flame, and into me the poor moth flings itself. Yet in the chance and change of things I am the candle too, giving my body that the light may burn. And finally, I am the drunken butterfly that falls to the flame — figure of the eternal sacrifice, body transmuted into soul, and life to spirit. Dear soul, dear child, dear childlike old soul, I, first and last, am the sacrifice, and he that offers it. Once I burned you, ever I burn you, into spirit and light. Know that metamorphosis is the dearest and most inward of thy friend, his great hope, his deepest craving: the play of transformation, changing face, greybeard to youth, to youth the boy, yet ever the human countenance with traits of its proper stage, youth like a miracle shining out in age, age out of youth. Thus mayst thou rest content, beloved, as I am, with having thought it out and come to me, decking thine ancient form with signs of youth. Unity in change and flux, conversion constant out of and into oneself, transmutation of all things, life showing now its natural, now its cultural face, past turning to present, present pointing back to past, both preluding future and with her dim foreshadowings already full. Past feeling, future feeling — feeling is all. Let us open wide eyes upon the unity of the world — eyes wide, serene, and wise. Wouldst thou ask of me repentance? Only wait. I see her ride towards me, in a mantle grey. Then once more the hour of Werther and Tasso will strike, as at midnight already midday strikes, and God give me to say what I suffer — only this first and last will then remain to me. Then forsaking will be only leave-taking, leave-taking for ever, death-struggle of feeling and the hour full of frightful pangs, pangs such as probably for some time precede the hour of death, pangs which are dying if not yet death. Death, final flight into the flame — the All-in-One — why should it too be aught but transformation? In my quiet heart, dear visions, may you rest — and what a pleasant moment that will be, when we anon awake together! "

The long-familiar accents died away. "Peace to your old age! " was all she whispered. The carriage stopped. Its lights fell together with that from the lanterns on either side the entrance to the Elephant. Mager stood there between them, hands on back, nose in air to sniff the misty, starry autumn night. Now in his soft-soled waiter's shoes he ran across the pavement, to be beforehand with the servant at the carriage door. He did not actually run, of course; but moved as one to whom running is somewhat foreign, with a mincing dignity, his hands raised to his shoulders, the fingers elegantly curled.

"Frau Councillor," he said, "welcome, as always! I hope Frau Councillor spent an elevating evening in our temple of the Muses? May I offer this arm for your support? Good heavens, Frau Councillor, I cannot refrain —I really must say: to help Werther's Lotte out of Goethe's carriage, that is an experience that -- what shall I call it? It ought to be put down."

A NOTE ABOUT THE AUTHOR

THOMAS MANN, born in 1875 into one of Lübeck's prominent merchant families, was only twenty-five when *Buddenbrooks* was published. His second great work of fiction, *The Magic Mountain*, was issued in 1924. Five years later he was awarded the Nobel Prize for Literature.

The chance request of an artist for an introduction to a portfolio of Joseph drawings was the genesis of his tetralogy, *Joseph and His Brothers*, the first volume of which was published in 1933. In that same year Mann left Munich—where he had made his home— and Germany, to settle for a time in Switzerland.

In 1941 Mann moved to Pacific Palisades, California. It was there that he wrote *Dr. Faustus* and *The Holy Sinner*. Three years later he became a citizen of the United States. In 1952 he moved to Kilchberg, a suburb of Zurich. There he wrote *Confessions of Felix Krull, Confidence Man*, the continuation of a fragmentary story that had been published more than thirty years earlier. He died in 1955, not long after a memorable three-day celebration of his eightieth birthday.